THE SUBMISSION

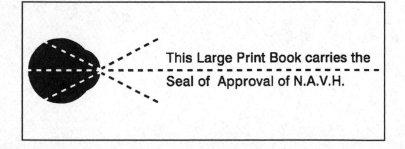

This Large Print Book carries the
Seal of Approval of N.A.V.H.

THE SUBMISSION

AMY WALDMAN

THORNDIKE PRESS
A part of Gale, Cengage Learning

GALE
CENGAGE Learning™

Detroit • New York • San Francisco • New Haven, Conn • Waterville, Maine • London

LIBRARY OF CONGRESS CATALOGING-IN-PUBLICATION DATA

Waldman, Amy, 1969–
  The submission / by Amy Waldman.
    p. cm. — (Thorndike Press large print basic)
  ISBN-13: 978-1-4104-4349-6 (hardcover)
  ISBN-10: 1-4104-4349-3 (hardcover)
  1. September 11 Terrorist Attacks, 2001—Social aspects—Fiction.
2. Memorials—Designs and plans—Fiction. 3. Large type books. I. Title.
PS3623.A35675S83 2011b
813'.6—dc23   2011033858

Published in 2011 by arrangement with Farrar, Straus and Giroux, LLC.

Printed in the United States of America
1 2 3 4 5 6 7 15 14 13 12 11

To my parents,
Don and Marilyn Waldman

Like the cypress tree, which holds its head high and is free within the confines of a garden, I, too, feel free in this world, and I am not bound by its attachments.

— an unidentified Pashto poet

1

"The names," Claire said. "What about the names?"

"They're a record, not a gesture," the sculptor replied. Ariana's words brought nods from the other artists, the critic, and the two purveyors of public art arrayed along the dining table, united beneath her sway. She was the jury's most famous figure, its dominant personality, Claire's biggest problem.

Ariana had seated herself at the head of the table, as if she were presiding. For the previous four months they had deliberated at a table that had no head, being round. It was in an office suite high above the gouged earth, and there the other jurors had deferred to the widow's desire to sit with her back to the window, so that the charnel ground below was only a gray blur when Claire walked to her chair. But tonight the jury was gathered, for its last arguments, at

Gracie Mansion's long table. Ariana, without consultation or, it appeared, compunction, had taken pride of place, giving notice of her intent to prevail.

"The names of the dead are expected; required, in fact, by the competition rules," she continued. For such a scouring woman, her voice was honeyed. "In the right memorial, the names won't be the source of the emotion."

"They will for me," Claire said tightly, taking some satisfaction in the downcast eyes and guilty looks along the table. They'd all lost, of course — lost the sense that their nation was invulnerable; lost their city's most recognizable icons; maybe lost friends or acquaintances. But only she had lost her husband.

She wasn't above reminding them of that tonight, when they would at last settle on the memorial. They had winnowed five thousand entries, all anonymous, down to two. The final pruning should have been easy. But after three hours of talk, two rounds of voting, and too much wine from the mayor's private reserve, the conversation had turned ragged, snappish, repetitive. The Garden was too beautiful, Ariana and the other artists kept saying of Claire's choice. They saw for a living, yet when it came to the Garden they wouldn't see what she saw.

The concept was simple: a walled, rectangular garden guided by rigorous geometry. At the center would be a raised pavilion meant for contemplation. Two broad, perpendicular canals quartered the six-acre space. Pathways within each quadrant imposed a grid on the trees, both living and steel, that were studded in orchard-like rows. A white perimeter wall, twenty-seven feet high, enclosed the entire space. The victims would be listed on the wall's interior, their names patterned to mimic the geometric cladding of the destroyed buildings. The steel trees reincarnated the buildings even more literally: they would be made from their salvaged scraps.

Four drawings showed the Garden across the seasons. Claire's favorite was the chiaroscuro of winter. A snow shroud over the ground; leafless living trees gone to pewter; cast-steel trees glinting with the rose light of late afternoon; the onyx surfaces of the canals shining like crossed swords. Black letters scored on the white wall. Beauty wasn't a crime, but there was more than beauty here. Even Ariana conceded that the spartan steel trees were an unexpected touch — reminders that a garden, for all its

13

reliance on nature, was man-made, perfect for a city in which plastic bags wafted along with birds and air-conditioner runoff mixed in with rain. Their forms would look organic, but they would resist a garden's seasonal ebb and flow.

"The Void is too dark for us," Claire said now, as she had before. Us: the families of the dead. Only she, on the jury, stood for Us. She loathed the Void, the other finalist, Ariana's favorite, and Claire was sure the other families would, too. There was nothing void-like about it. A towering black granite rectangle, some twelve stories high, centered in a huge oval pool, it came off in the drawings as a great gash against the sky. The names of the dead were to be carved onto its surface, which would reflect into the water below. It mimicked the Vietnam Veterans Memorial but, to Claire, missed the point. Such abstraction worked when humans could lay their hands on it, draw near enough to alter the scale. But the names on the Void couldn't be reached or even seen properly. The only advantage the design had was height. Claire worried that some of the families — so jingoistic, so literal-minded — might see the Garden as conceding territory to America's enemies, even if that territory was air.

14

"Gardens are fetishes of the European bourgeoisie," Ariana said, pointing to the dining-room walls, which were papered with a panorama of lush trees through which tiny, formally dressed men and women strolled. Ariana herself was, as usual, dressed entirely in a shade of gruel that she had patented in homage to and ridicule of Yves Klein's brilliant blue. The mockery of pretension, Claire decided, could also be pretentious.

"Aristocratic fetishes," the jury's lone historian corrected. "The bourgeoisie aping the aristocracy."

"It's French, the wallpaper," the mayor's aide, his woman on the jury, piped up.

"My point being," Ariana went on, "that gardens aren't our vernacular. We have parks. Formal gardens aren't our lineage."

"Experiences matter more than lineages," Claire said.

"No, lineages are experiences. We're coded to have certain emotions in certain kinds of places."

"Graveyards," Claire said, an old tenacity rising within her. "Why are they often the loveliest places in cities? There's a poem — George Herbert — with the lines: 'Who would have thought my shrivel'd heart / Could have recover'd greennesse?' " A col-

15

lege friend had written the scrap of poetry in a condolence card. "The Garden," she continued, "will be a place where we — where the widows, their children, anyone — can stumble on joy. My husband . . ." she said, and everyone leaned in to listen. She changed her mind and stopped speaking, but the words hung in the air like a trail of smoke.

Which Ariana blew away. "I'm sorry, but a memorial isn't a graveyard. It's a national symbol, an historic signifier, a way to make sure anyone who visits — no matter how attenuated their link in time or geography to the attack — understands how it felt, what it meant. The Void is visceral, angry, dark, raw, because there was no joy on that day. You can't tell if that slab is rising or falling, which is honest — it speaks exactly to this moment in history. It's created destruction, which robs the real destruction of its power, dialectically speaking. The Garden speaks to a longing we have for healing. It's a very natural impulse, but maybe not our most sophisticated one."

"You have something against healing?" Claire asked.

"We disagree on the best way to bring it about," Ariana answered. "I think you have to confront the pain, face it, even wallow in

16

it, before you can move on."

"I'll take that under consideration," Claire retorted. Her hand clamped over her wineglass before the waiter could fill it.

Paul could barely track who was saying what. His jurors had devoured the comfort food he had requested — fried chicken, mashed potatoes, brussels sprouts with bacon — but the comfort was scant. He prided himself on getting along with formidable women — was, after all, married to one — but Claire Burwell and Ariana Montagu together strained him, their opposing sureties clashing like electric fields, the room crackling with their animus. In her critique of the Garden's beauty, of beauty itself, Paul sensed Ariana implying something about Claire.

His mind wandered to the coming days, weeks, months. They would announce the winning design. Then he and Edith would visit the Zabar's at their home in Menerbes, a respite for Paul between the months of deliberation and the fund-raising for the memorial that would begin on his return. It would be a major challenge, with the construction of each of the two finalists estimated at $100 million, minimum, but Paul enjoyed parting his friends from serious money. Countless ordinary Americans were sure to open their wallets, too.

Then this chairmanship would lead to others, or so Edith assured him. Unlike many of her friends, his wife did not collect Chanel suits or Harry Winston baubles, although she had quantities of both. Her eye was for prestigious positions, and so she imagined Paul as chairman of the public library, where he already sat on the board. It had more money than the Met, and Edith had pronounced Paul "literary," although Paul himself wasn't sure he'd read a novel since *The Bonfire of the Vanities.*

"Perhaps we should talk more about the local context," said Madeline, a community power broker from the neighborhood ringing the site. As if on cue, Ariana extracted from her bag a drawing she had made of the Void to show how well it would play against the cityscape. The Void's "vertical properties," she said, echoed Manhattan's. Claire arched her eyebrows at Paul. Ariana's "sketch," as she called it, was better than the drawings accompanying the submission. Claire had complained to Paul more than once that she suspected Ariana knew the Void's designer — a student, a protégé? — because she seemed so eager to help it along. Maybe, although he didn't think

18

Ariana had done any more for her favorite than Claire had for hers. For all her poise, Claire couldn't seem to handle not getting her way. Nor could Ariana, who was used to dominating juries without this one's slippery quota of sentiment.

The group retreated to the parlor, with its warm yellow walls, for dessert. Jorge, the chef at Gracie Mansion, wheeled in a cart laden with cakes and cookies. Then he unveiled, with little fanfare, a three-foot-high gingerbread reconstruction of the vanished towers. The shapes were unmistakable. The silence was profound.

"It's not meant to be eaten," Jorge said, suddenly shy. "It's a tribute."

"Of course," said Claire, then added, with more warmth, "It's like a fairy tale." Chandelier light glinted off the poured-sugar windows.

Paul had piled his plate with everything but the gingerbread when Ariana planted herself in front of him like a tiny spear. In concert they drifted toward a secluded corner behind the piano.

"I'm concerned, Paul," Ariana said. "I don't want our decision based too much on" — the last word almost lowed — "emotion."

"We're selecting a memorial, Ariana. I'm

19

not sure emotion can be left out of it entirely."

"You know what I mean. I worry that Claire's feelings are having disproportionate impact."

"Ariana, some might argue that you have disproportionate impact. Your opinions command enormous respect."

"Not compared to a family member. Sorrow can be a bully."

"So can taste."

"As it should be, but we're talking about something more profound than taste here. Judgment. Having a family member in the room — it's like we're letting the patient, not the doctor, decide on the best course of treatment. A little clinical distance is healthy."

Out of the corner of his eye, Paul saw Claire deep in conversation with the city's preeminent critic of public art. She had seven inches on him, with her heels, but she made no effort to slouch. Dressed tonight in a fitted black sheath — the color, Paul suspected, no incidental choice — she was a woman who knew how to outfit herself for maximum advantage. Paul respected this, although respect was perhaps the wrong word for how she figured in his imaginings. Not for the first time, he rued his age (twenty-five years her senior), his hair loss, and his loyalty — more institutional than personal, perhaps — to his marriage. He watched her detach herself from the critic to follow yet another juror from the room.

"I know she's affecting," he heard; his eyeing of Claire had been unsubtle. He turned sharply toward Ariana, who continued: "But the Garden's too soft. Designed to please the same Americans who love impressionism."

"I happen to like impressionism," Paul said, not sure whether to pretend he was joking. "I can't muzzle Claire, and you know the family members are more likely to support our design if they feel part of the process. We need the emotional information she provides."

"Paul, you know there's a whole critique out there. If we pick the wrong memorial, if we yield to sentimentalism, it only confirms —"

"I know the concerns," he said gruffly: that it was too soon for a memorial, the ground barely cleared; that the country hadn't yet won or lost the war, couldn't even agree, exactly, on who or what it was fighting. But everything happened faster these days — the building up and tearing down of idols; the spread of disease and rumor and trends; the cycling of news; the development of new monetary instruments, which in turn had speeded Paul's own retirement from the chairmanship of the investment bank. So why not the memorial, too? Commercial exigencies were at work, it was true: the developer who controlled the site wanted to re-monetize it and needed a memorial to do so, since Americans seemed unlikely to accept the maximization of office space as the most eloquent rejoinder to terrorism. But there were patriotic exigencies, too. The longer that space stayed clear, the more it became a symbol of defeat, of surrender, something for "them," whoever they were, to mock. A memorial only to America's diminished greatness, its new vulnerability to attack by a fanatic band, mediocrities in all but murder. Paul would never put it so crudely, but the blank space was embarrassing. Filling in that blank, as much as Edith's ambitions, was why he had wanted to chair the jury. Its work would mark not only his beloved city but history, too.

Ariana was waiting for more from Paul. "You're wasting your time on me," he said brusquely. The winner needed ten of thirteen votes; Paul had made clear he would abandon neutrality only if a finalist was one short. "If I were you, I'd go rescue Maria from Claire."

Claire had seen Maria heading outside, cigarette in hand, and hurried after her. She had been pleading — no other word for it — with the critic, telling him, "Just because we're memorializing the dead doesn't mean we need to create a dead place," watching him roll his head as if his neck hurt from looking up at her. But she also had been scavenging her memory for tidbits from law school: the science of juries. The Asch experiments, what did Asch show? How easily people were influenced by other people's perceptions. Conformity. Group polarization. Normative pressures. Reputational cascades: how the desire for social approval influences the way people think and act. Which meant Claire's best chance was to get jurors alone. Maria was a public art curator who had made her mark placing large-scale artworks, including one of Ariana's, around Manhattan. This made her an unlikely defector, but Claire had to try.

"Got an extra?" she asked.

Maria handed her a cigarette. "I wouldn't have pegged you as a smoker."

"Only occasionally," Claire lied. As in never.

They were standing on the veranda, the lawn spread before them, its majestic trees mere smudges in the dark, the lights of the bridges and boroughs like proximate constellations. Maria ashed complacently over the railing onto the lawn, and although it struck Claire as somehow disrespectful, she did the same.

"A ruined garden within the walls — that I could get behind," Maria said.

"Excuse me?"

"It would be so powerful as a work of art, would answer any worries about erasing the hard memories. We have to think of history here, the long view, a symbolism that will speak to people a hundred years from now. Great art transcends its time."

"A ruined garden has no hope and that's unacceptable," Claire said, unable to help her sharpness. "You all keep talking about the long view, but the long view includes us. My children, my grandchildren, people with a direct connection to this attack are going to be around for the next hundred years, and maybe that's a blip when you look back at the Venus of Willendorf, but it certainly seems a long time now. So I don't see why our interests should count any less.

You know, the other night I dreamed about that black pool around the Void, that my husband's hand was reaching up from the water to pull me down into it. That's the effect the Void has. So you can go there and congratulate yourself on what a brilliant artistic statement you made, but I don't think family members will be lining up to visit."

Her anger was no less genuine for her having learned, months back, its power. On a wintry afternoon, as she and the other widows left a meeting with the director of the government's compensation fund, a reporter in the waiting press pack had shouted, "How do you answer Americans who say they're tired of your sense of entitlement, that you're being greedy?" Claire had gripped her purse to keep her hands from shaking, but she didn't bother to mute the tremble in her voice. "Entitlement? Was that the word you used?" The reporter shrank back. "Was I entitled to lose my husband? Was I entitled to have to explain to my children why they will never know their father, to have to raise them alone? Am I entitled to live knowing the suffering my husband endured? This isn't about greed. Do your homework: I don't need a penny of this compensation and

25

don't plan to keep it. This isn't about money. It's about justice, accountability. And yes, I am entitled to that."

She claimed, later, to have been unaware the television cameras were rolling, but they captured every word. The clip of the death-pale blonde in the black coat was replayed so often that for days she couldn't turn on the television without seeing herself. Letters of support poured in, and Claire found herself a star widow. She hadn't meant to make a political statement, in truth had been offended by the notion that she was grubbing for money and was seeking to set herself apart from those who were. Instead she emerged as their champion, the Secretary of Sorrow Services. Her leadership, she knew, was the reason the governor had picked her for the jury.

On the veranda Maria was eyeing her quizzically. Claire met her stare and took a drag so dizzying she had to grip the railing for support. She felt only a little guilty. Everything she said had been true except her certainty that the hand reaching up was Cal's.

Maria switched first. "The Garden," she said bravely. Claire started to mouth "Thank you," then thought better of it. The critic came next. "The Garden." This gave slightly less pleasure: Claire, studying his basset-hound face and poodle hair, had the disappointed sense that he had changed his vote because he was tired. Still, the Garden had eight votes now, which meant victory was in sight. But instead of celebrating, Claire began to sink inside. Tomorrow, absent the memorial competition, her life would lose its last bit of temporary form. She had no need of income, given her inheritance from Cal, and no commanding new cause. Her future was gilded blankness.

Aftermath had filled the two years since Cal's death, the surge of grief yielding to the slow leak of mourning, the tedium of recovery, bathetic new routines that felt old from the get-go. Forms and more forms. Bulletins from the medical examiner: another fragment of her husband had been found. The cancellation of credit cards, driver's license, club memberships, magazine subscriptions, contracts to buy works of art; the selling of cars and a sailboat; the scrubbing of his name from trusts and bank accounts and the boards of companies and nonprofits — all of it done with a ruthless efficiency that implicated her in his effacement. Offering her children memories of their father, only to load the past with so much value it strained beneath the weight.

But aftermath had to end. She sensed herself concluding a passage that had begun fourteen years ago, when a blue-eyed man notable less for good looks than for sheer vitality and humor and confidence had stopped her as she came off the tennis court he was taking over and said, "I'm going to marry you."

The comment, she would come to learn, was typical of Calder Burwell, a man with a temperament so sunny that Claire nick-named him California, even though it was she, having grown up there, who knew the state's true fickle weather: the frost and drought that had kept her grandfather, a citrus farmer, perched near ruin for years before her father plunged straight into it. Of all her anguished, unanswerable wonderings about Cal's death — where, how, how much pain — the worst, somehow, was the fear that his last moments had buckled his abiding optimism. She wanted him to have died believing that he would live. The Garden was an allegory. Like Cal, it insisted that change was not just possible, but certain.

"It's eleven o'clock," Paul said. "I think someone may need to reconsider his or her vote. How can we ask this country to come together in healing if this jury can't?"

Guilty looks. A long silence. And finally, from the historian, an almost speculative "Well . . ." All bleary eyes turned to him, but he said nothing more, as if he had realized he held the fate of a six-acre chunk of Manhattan in his hands.

"Ian?" Paul prodded.

Even if inebriated, Ian wasn't going without a lecture. He noted the beginnings of public gardens in suburban cemeteries in eighteenth-century Europe, segued into the garden-based reforms of Daniel Schreber in Germany ("We're interested in his social reforms, not the 'reforms' he carried out on his poor sons"), jumped to the horror conveyed by Lutyens's Memorial to the Missing of the Somme at Thiepval, in which seventy-three thousand names — "Seventy-three thousand!" Ian exclaimed — were inscribed on its interior walls, pondered the difference between "national memory" and "veteran's memory" at Verdun, and concluded, some fifteen minutes later, with: "And so, the Garden."

Paul, then, would be the tenth and final vote, and this didn't displease him. He had insisted, for himself, on not just public neutrality but internal neutrality as well, so that no design had been allowed to catch his fancy. But over the course of the evening he had begun rooting for the Garden. "Stumble on joy" — the phrase had knocked something loose in him. Joy: What did it feel like? Trying to remember, he was overcome by longing. He knew satisfaction, the exhilaration of success, contentment, and happiness to the extent he could identify it. But joy? He must have felt it when his sons were born — that kind of event would surely occasion it — but he couldn't remember. Joy: it was like a handle with no cupboard, a secret he didn't know. He wondered if Claire did.

"The Garden," he said, and the room broke loose, less with pleasure than relief.

"Thank you, Paul. Thank you, everyone," Claire whispered.

Paul slumped in his chair and allowed himself some sentimental chauvinism. The dark horse had won — he hadn't thought Claire could trump Ariana — and this seemed appropriately American. Champagne appeared, corks popped, a euphonious clamor filled the room. Paul clinked his flute to command their attention for a moment of silence in the victims' honor. As heads bowed, he glimpsed the part in Claire's hair, the line as sharp and white as a jet's contrail, the intimacy as unexpected

30

as a flash of thigh. Then he remembered to think of the dead.

He thought, too, of the day, as he hadn't for a long time. He had been stuck in uptown traffic when his secretary called to say there had been an accident or attack and it might affect the markets. He was still going into the office in those days, not having learned yet that in an investment bank, "emeritus" translated to "no longer one of us." When the traffic stopped completely, Paul got out of the car. Others were standing outside looking south, some shielding their eyes with their hands, all exchanging useless information. Edith called, sobbing "It's falling down, it's falling down," the nursery-rhyme words, then the mobile network went dead. "Hello? Hello? Honey?" all around, then a silence of Pompeian density so disturbing that Paul was grateful when Sami, his driver, broke it to say, "Oh sir, I hope it's not the Arabs," which of course it would turn out to be.

Oh sir, I hope it's not the Arabs. Sami wasn't Arab, but he was Muslim. (Eighty percent of Muslims were not Arab: this was one of those facts many learned and earnestly repeated in the wake of the attack, without knowing exactly what they were trying to say, or rather knowing that they were

31

trying to say that not all Muslims were as problematic as the Arab ones, but not wanting to say exactly that.) Paul had known his driver was Muslim but never dwelt on it. Now, despite all efforts otherwise, he felt uncomfortable, and three months later, when a sorrowful Sami — was he ever any other way? — begged leave to return to Pakistan because his father was dying, Paul was relieved, although he hated to admit it. He promised Sami an excellent recommendation if he returned, politely declined to take on his cousin, and hired a Russian.

The trauma, for Paul, had come later, when he watched the replay, pledged allegiance to the devastation. You couldn't call yourself an American if you hadn't, in solidarity, watched your fellow Americans being pulverized, yet what kind of American did watching create? A traumatized victim? A charged-up avenger? A queasy voyeur? Paul, and he suspected many Americans, harbored all of these protagonists. The memorial was meant to tame them.

Not just any memorial now but the Garden. Paul began his remarks by encouraging the jurors to "go out there and sell it, sell it hard," then, rethinking his word choice, urged them to "advocate" for it instead. The soft patter of the minute-taker's typing filled the interstices of his speech, and the specter of the historical record spurred him to unsteady rhetorical heights. He drew all eyes to a gilded round mirror topped with an eagle shedding its ball and chain.

"Now, as at America's founding, there are forces opposed to the values we stand for, who are threatened by our devotion to freedom." The governor's man alone nodded at Paul's words. "But we have not been bowed, will not be. 'Despotism can only exist in darkness,' James Madison said, and all of you, in working so hard to memorialize the dead, have kept the lights burning in the firmament. You handled a sacred trust with grace and dignity, and your country will feel the benefit."

Time to put a face on the design, a name with it. Another unfamiliar feeling for Paul: avid, almost childlike curiosity — glee, even — at that rarity, a genuine surprise. Best if the designer was a complete unknown or a famous artist; either would make for a compelling story to sell the design. He clumsily punched away at a cell phone that sat on the table before him. "Please bring the file for submission number 4879," he said into the phone, enunciating the numbers slowly to avoid misunderstanding.

33

"Four eight seven nine," he repeated, then waited for the digits to be repeated back to him.

The jury's chief assistant entered a few minutes later, aglow with his own importance. His long fingers clasped a slim envelope, eight and a half by eleven inches, sealed as protocol demanded. "I am dying with anticipation," Lanny breathed as he handed the envelope to Paul, who made no reply. The envelope's numbers and bar code matched those of the Garden; the envelope's seal was unbroken. Paul made sure both the jurors and the minute-taker noted this and waited for the reluctant assistant to take his leave.

Once the door shut, Paul picked up the silver letter opener the young man had left behind — he did have a flair for detail — and slit the flap, taking care (again, the specter of history) not to tear the envelope. His caution somehow recalled Jacob, his eldest son, at a childhood birthday party, obsessively trying not to rip the wrapping paper, even then misunderstanding where value lay. An impatient Paul had told him to hurry it along.

Hurry it along: the same message from the room's quiet, in which the jurors seemed to breathe as one. He pulled out the paper, sensing thirteen pairs of eyes upon him. To know the winner's identity before the jury, not to mention the mayor or governor or president, should have been a small but satisfying token of his stature. What better measure of how high Paul Joseph Rubin, grandson of a Russian Jewish peasant, had climbed? And yet reading the name brought no pleasure, only a painful tightening in his jaw.

A dark horse indeed.

2

The piece of paper containing the winner's name was passed from palm to palm like a fragile folio. There were a few gasps and "hmmms," an "interesting," an "oh my." Then: "Jesus fucking Christ! It's a goddamn Muslim!" The paper had reached the governor's man.

Paul sighed. It wasn't Bob Wilner's fault they were in this situation, if indeed they were in a situation, but Paul resented him for forcing them to confront that they were, possibly, in a situation. Until Wilner spoke, no one had voiced what was written, as if to do so would bring the problem, even the person, to life before them.

"Ms. Costello." Paul addressed the minute-taker in an almost musing tone, without meeting her eyes. "That will be expunged, naturally. We'd like to keep the record free of — of profanity." He knew this sounded ridiculous: What New York City

36

body cared about profanity? What minute-taker bothered to transcribe it? "Perhaps you could step out for a few minutes. Go help yourself to some more dessert."

"Oh, Ms. Costello," Paul called as she walked toward the door, his tone as light as her back was stiff. "If you could, please make sure no one's hanging around outside the door. And let's remember our confidentiality agreements, shall we?"

The door shut. He waited a few seconds before saying, "Let's stay calm here."

"What the fuck are we supposed to do?"

"We know nothing about him, Bob."

"Is he even American?"

"Yes, it says right here under nationality, American."

"That actually makes it harder."

"What's that supposed to mean?"

"How did this happen?"

"What are the odds?"

"I can't believe it."

"It's Maya Lin all over again. But worse."

"What are the odds?" the mayor's aide kept repeating. "What are the odds?"

"One in five thousand!" Wilner barked at her. "Those are the odds."

"Maybe more," the historian mused, "if more than one Muslim entered."

"We don't know. Maybe it's just his

37

name," Maria said. "He could be a Jew, for all we know."

"Don't be an idiot." Wilner again. "How many Jews do you know named Mohammad?"

"It's true though," the art critic said; "maybe he converted to another religion. I became a Buddhist three years ago. Or a Jew-Bu, I guess."

"Well maybe he's a woman!" Wilner said sarcastically. "Maybe he had a sex change! Wake up; it's on the page in black and white."

"I think we need to assume the worst — I mean, that he's a Muslim," the mayor's aide said. "Not that that's the worst" — she was flustered now — "I don't mean to say that at all, just that in this case it is." Her name was Violet, and she was a compulsive pessimist, always looking for the soft brown spot in the fruit, pressing so hard she created it. But even she hadn't seen this coming.

"It could be a healing gesture," observed Leo. He was a retired university president, of sonorous voice and Pavarottian girth.

"That's not the gesture that comes to mind," Wilner said. "The families will feel very offended. This is no time for multicultural pandering."

"Please don't forget you have a family member right here," Claire said.

"Fine, Claire, I apologize. Many of them will feel offended."

"I ran three universities, and in none of them was I known for pandering to multi-culturalists," Leo said.

"There's a lot of confusion," Maria said. "We still don't know what most Muslims think —"

"About?"

"I don't know — us, or holy war, or —"

"We don't know if he's really the practic-ing kind —"

"It doesn't matter," Wilner said. "You can't opt out of the religion. They don't let you."

"I didn't know you had a degree in theol-ogy," said Leo. "Whatever kind he is, he had the right to enter the competition."

"But we have no obligation to pick him!" Wilner exclaimed. "Look, it's not his fault, whoever he is, but we have to consider the associations people will bring to him. And what if he is one of the problematic ones? Would you still say he has every right to design the memorial?"

Violet sighed. "I . . . I need to talk to the mayor."

"There's nothing to talk about," Claire

said. Her words were tougher than her voice, which wavered. "The vote's been taken. It's over."

"Nothing's over unless we say it is, Claire."

"Bob, you're the lawyer. You're supposed to be preventing that kind of stuff, not encouraging it. Our votes are on the record."

"The record of our proceedings is a fungible thing, Claire, and you know it. Paul's had the lady — what's her name? — Costello do minutes only when there would be nothing spicy in them."

"Bob, you voted for the Garden. That was the design you wanted."

"Well, I'll be honest here. I'll be honest." The governor's man glared around the table, as if defying anyone to tell him not to be. "I'm not sure I want it with the name Mohammad attached to it. It doesn't matter who he is. They'll feel like they've won. All over the Muslim world they'll be jumping up and down at our stupidity, our stupid tolerance."

"Tolerance isn't stupid," Claire said in a schoolmarmish tone. "Prejudice is."

Her color was high. She had to be recoiling. Paul's own head throbbed: the aftereffects of the wine, the prelude to a storm.

"Look, I'm not pretending this isn't a surprise," she continued. "But, but . . . it

40

will send a message, a good message, that in America, it doesn't matter what your name is — and we don't have much more here than a name — that your name is no bar to entering a competition like this, or to winning it." She twisted her napkin as if trying to squeeze water from it.

"Yes, of course," said Maria. "And every American has the right to create — it's our birthright. We all understand that. We're New Yorkers! But will the heartland? They're much more narrow-minded. Trust me, I'm from there."

"Perhaps we're missing the point." Ariana's voice unfurled into the fray. There were a few nods, even though no one knew what the artist had to say. "It's absolutely unconscionable to say he should be denied if he won. Imagine if Maya had been stripped of her commission." Claire looked relieved — Ariana had pronounced — but Ariana wasn't done. "I will say, however, that the circumstances are dramatically different this time. To somehow make a connection between Maya being Chinese American and Vietnam being an Asian war — it was absurd, a red herring raised by philistines who didn't like her memorial. But this time, if this guy is a Muslim, it's going to be much, much more sensitive, and

41

rightly so, perhaps, until we know more about him, and — well, I'm just not sure the design's strong enough to withstand that kind of resistance. Maya's could. I wonder if we should reconsider our decision."

"Now hold on —" Claire said.

"It's true," Violet interrupted. "This — this Mohammad hasn't technically won the competition yet. I mean, there are safeguards built in, right, against criminals. Or terrorists."

"Are you saying he's a terrorist?"

"No, no, I'm not saying anything. Nothing at all. I'm just saying if he were, we wouldn't let him build the memorial, would we?"

"Any more than if, say, Charles Manson submitted a design from prison, we would let him build it," the critic said.

"This is hardly comparable to Charles Manson."

"To some it might be," said the historian. "Not to me, of course. But to some."

"The bylaws say that if the designer selected is deemed 'unsuitable,' the jury has the right to select another finalist," Paul said. This proviso he had insisted on himself, as a safety valve: he considered the memorial too important to risk an anonymous competition, especially one open to all. He would have preferred to solicit designs from noted artists and architects. History's great monuments and memorials — from the Sistine Chapel to the St. Louis Arch — had been elite commissions, not left to, in Edmund Burke's apt phrase, "warm and inexperienced enthusiasts." Only in America did those enthusiasts reign, enthroned by politicians who feared nothing more than appearing undemocratic. Over Paul's protests the decision had been made to provide a channel for the citizenry's sluicing feelings, and the families of the dead had cheered this, eager for the outpouring of interest, of caring. Caring there was, to judge by the number of submissions, but Paul wondered what the families would have to say about their precious democratic process now.

"I thought someone was supposed to vet the finalists for suitability —"

"They did," Paul said. "The security consultants. I didn't see the report, obviously, but they concluded there were no problems, nothing to flag."

"How is that possible?" Wilner asked.

"They looked for criminal records, custody battles, arrest warrants, bankruptcy filings. Links to any organization on the government's terrorist watch list. Both finalists came back clean. Suitable, if you will."

"He's unsuitable by definition!" Wilner said.

"I can't believe the lawyer, of all people, is making that argument," Claire said.

"Of course he's not unsuitable by definition," Ariana said almost soothingly. "Claire, let's figure out the sensible thing to do by looking at this clearly. Objectively. When I do crits I always encourage my students to step back and look at their work as if it were someone else's — you see much more clearly that way. So try to step back and forget which design you backed."

"Ariana, my backing the Garden has nothing to do with this. If your pick had won and the designer was Muslim, I would still say we should go ahead with it."

"Well he isn't Muslim!" Ariana snapped. There was silence as the import of what she had revealed sunk in. She tried to back-pedal; it was the first time Paul had seen her off-balance. "I mean, what are the odds that he would be . . ." Her voice trailed away as she plundered her purse for some phantom item.

Leo spoke up in his luxe baritone. Paul spotted three specks of white — cake crumbs? — in his jet-black beard. "Claire, I absolutely agree with you — it's unconscionable to even think of stripping this man of his victory. But people are afraid. Two years on we still don't know whether we're up against a handful of zealots who got lucky, or a global conspiracy of a billion Muslims who hate the West, even if they live in it. We're rarely rational in the face of threats to our personal safety, let alone our national security. We must be practical — our job is to get the memorial built. If we fight for this I will lead that fight —"

At this perceived usurpation, Paul's ego rose in protest. Was Leo implying, somehow, that Paul wasn't up to the job? Maybe Paul's silence implied as much, but he had been preoccupied by the question of whether to wake the mayor and governor, who might expect to be told immediately of this development, though the very fact of a midnight awakening would suggest something wrong, and Paul had yet to decide whether they should proceed as if something was wrong.

Leo continued: "But let's first make sure it's a fight we want to take on. We must consider the public reaction, the possibility of an uproar. You know better than anyone the sense of ownership the victims' families feel — rightly, of course — toward this site. Fund-raising will be more difficult, possibly much more so. The memorial could be ensnared in years of controversy, even litigation. Is that cost worth the point we want to make?"

"Although if this designer ever finds out we took it away from him, he could litigate, too," Violet interjected, worried.

"Leave the lawyering to me, Violet," Wilner said. "He's not going to find out anything."

Claire broke in, her voice strong, almost abrasive now. "So that's what you propose? That we quash it, when the majority of us believed it to be the best design? That's a total betrayal of what this country means, what it stands for. My husband must be turning —" She pulled up short. "He would be appalled if he were alive," she resumed, with a new quietness.

"But your husband's not alive, Claire, and that's why we're here." The historian spoke as gently as he could, which wasn't very gently. "History makes its own truths, new truths. It cannot be unwritten, we must acknowledge —"

"Nonsense," she interrupted, in a tone that sounded more like "Shut up." "Things — ideals — change only if we allow them to. And if we do, they've won."

Elliott, the critic, interjected, "Look, my

sympathies here are with the Muslims — I know you'll take that in the right spirit, Bob — in that things are just beginning to normalize for them. The backlash to this could deal a real setback to their quest for acceptance. So while it may be in this particular Muslim's interest to win, it may not be in the interest of all the other Muslims. We can't privilege the desires of the one over the good of the many. We don't want to turn up the heat on them all over again."

"Yes," the mayor's aide said. "For their own good it might be better to . . . to . . . not change the outcome, but, well, just think if there's perhaps a different way to arrive at an outcome that could be different — or the same, of course! — for their own good. As I said, just something to think about. What is the best outcome for everybody? Then we can figure out how to get there."

"She's right," Wilner said. "Claire, you know I respect you and your loss. But you are out of your mind if you think we can pretend this is just any winner."

Claire's mouth was tight, a cinched purse; Paul could see she wouldn't be budged tonight. He proposed that they adjourn for a few days so he could further assess Khan's suitability. "As I would do for any designer," he was quick to add. They would meet again at the end of the week. "No talking to the press. Or anyone. Not even your families."

"I told you, Paul, but you wouldn't listen," Wilner launched in before he left. He sounded almost triumphant. "I told you we should bring the finalists in for interviews, instead of keeping them anonymous until the end. It would have solved everything. He could have been a finalist, but he wouldn't have had to *win.* We would have looked liberal, but we wouldn't be stuck. You've really put us in a pickle, Paul. You really have."

Paul had always counseled his juniors at the bank to consider remote contingencies. Their improbability did not make them impossible; their unlikelihood would not reduce their expense. And here was the most remote of all contingencies. Or was it? Why had something like this never occurred to him? His imagined contingencies included fights over the cost of maintaining the Garden, or the ordering of the victims, or whether to differentiate the rescue workers' names from the others, but never this.

"If you'll remember, Bob, I was against an open competition, and it was my idea to vet the finalists."

"Lot of good that did," Wilner said. With glum faces and defeated postures, the jurors gathered their possessions and departed, leaving Paul to preside over a congress of crumpled napkins and smeared glassware. Did Muslims ruin whatever they touched? The question, so unfair, startled him, as if someone else had asked it.

At last he heaved himself from the table and made his way outside, to his black Lincoln Town Car ("Satan's limousine," his son Samuel called it). Vladimir glided past the mansion gate into the dead quiet of East End Avenue. A block west, where a thin stream of traffic still flowed, Paul saw some of his jurors standing on different corners, angling for taxis, pretending not to see the others doing the same. He couldn't offer one a lift without offering all; he wanted the company of none. Vladimir drove on. But the image of his jurors scattering like loose petals came to Paul over the next hours almost as often as Mohammad Khan's name.

3

His name was what got him pulled from a security line at LAX as he prepared to fly home to New York. The attack was a week past, the Los Angeles airport all but empty except for the National Guardsmen patrolling. Mo's bag was taken for a fine-tooth combing while he was quarantined for questioning in a windowless room. The agents' expressions remained pleasant, free of insinuation that he had done anything wrong. An "informational interview," they called it.

"So you say you're an architect?"

"An architect, yes."

"Do you have any proof?"

"Proof?"

"Proof."

Mo fished out a business card, ruing that the Gotham font screamed his full name, MOHAMMAD KHAN, although of course the agents, four of them now, already knew it.

On the metal school-issue desk between them he unrolled a slim stack of construction plans and began to leaf through them. "These are of the new theater I — we are building in Santa Monica. It's been written about in the *Los Angeles Times, The Architect's Newspaper, Metropolis . . .*" In the corner of the blueprints he pointed out the firm's name, ROI — recognizable enough, he was sure, to elicit some deference. The agents shrugged and examined the designs with suspicion, as if he were planning to bomb a building that existed only in his imagination.

"Where were you during the attack?"

"Here. Los Angeles." Naked beneath the sheets in his hotel room, the attack a collage of sound — panicky sirens, fissuring broadcasters' voices, rescue helicopters pureeing the air, the muffle and crush of implosion — from his hotel clock radio. Only when the buildings were gone did he think to turn on the television.

"Here," he said again. "Working on the theater." Working and longing for New York. Southern California was the white dress at the funeral, ill-suited to national tragedy. Its sun and BriteSmiles still gleamed; its deprived bodies and contrived breasts strutted. Even the sunset's glorious mottle

51

seemed a cinematic mock-up of the fires burning back home.

Each day brought more proof that the attackers were Muslims, seeking the martyr's straight shot to paradise — and so Mo braced for suspicion as he returned to the theater under construction. A few days later, as he heard himself say to the contractor, "Would you mind if I suggested an alternate location for that wall chase? Only if it would help," he realized that the difference wasn't in how he was being treated but in how he was behaving. Customarily brusque on work sites, he had become gingerly, polite, careful to give no cause for alarm or criticism. He didn't like this new, more cautious avatar, whose efforts at accommodation hinted at some feeling of guilt, yet he couldn't quite shake him.

Cloistered at the airport, he struggled to maintain his self-respect even as the avatar encouraged obsequiousness. The agents' questions were broad, trifling, and insinuating; his replies laconic. When they asked where he lived, he told them; when they asked his business in Los Angeles, for the second time, he told them that, too. He regretted, as soon as he made it, his suggestion that they call the client, the chair of the theater's board of directors. But they didn't seem interested anyway.

"There are probably a lot of people we could call about you," said the agent Mo had labeled Pinball for the way his hands jittered at his thighs. He smiled as he said it, as if to suggest, but not definitively, that he might be joking.

They asked about his travels in the past few months; asked where he was born.

"Virginia. Which is in America. Which means I'm a citizen."

"Didn't say you weren't." Pinball popped his gum.

"Do you love this country, Mohammad?"

"As much as you do." The answer appeared to displease them.

"What are your thoughts on jihad?"

"I don't have any."

"Well, perhaps you could tell us what it means. My colleague here isn't good with the foreign languages."

"I don't know what it means. I've never had cause to use the word."

"Aren't you a practicing Muslim?"

"Practicing? No."

"No?"

"Yes."

"Yes? Yes or no? You're confusing me."

Abbott and Costello in suits. "No. I said no."

"Know any Muslims who want to do harm to America?"

"None. I don't know any Communists, either."

"We didn't ask about Communists. Do you believe you'd go to your heaven if you blew yourself up?"

"I would never blow myself up."

"But if you did . . ."

Mo didn't answer.

"Been to Afghanistan?"

"Why would I go there?"

They exchanged glances, as if a question as answer was evasion.

"Coffee?" Pinball asked.

"Please," Mo said crisply. "One sugar and a little milk." The agent standing by the door vanished through it.

Mo checked his watch: only half an hour until his flight.

"I do have a plane to catch," he told the room, which didn't answer.

The coffee came black; it was unsweetened. Mo drank it anyway, pausing his answers to take careful sips. He hid his disdain for the bland cuts of their jackets; the openness of their faces, so unquestioning despite all their questions. The artlessness of their interrogation. But when Pinball asked point-blank "Do you know any Islamic terrorists?" Mo couldn't help but snort in derision.

"Is that a yes or a no?" Pinball said.

"What do you think?" Mo snapped, his anger crowning.

"If I had thoughts I wouldn't have asked the question," Pinball said neutrally, and tipped so far back in his chair that only his fingertips, anchored lightly to the desk, saved him from falling. Then, without warning, he rocked forward. The legs of the chair slammed the floor, his hands the desk. His face — the pale fuzz between his eyebrows, the dot of dark blood afloat in his iris — was close enough for Mo to smell the faint cinnamon on his breath. The move, so carefully calibrated, so casually executed, must have been practiced. Here was the art, and Mo could have done without it. *Pop pop pop* went the gum. Mo's legs quivered as if he had dodged three bullets.

"No," he said with forced politeness. "No, I don't."

"Try harder, Mohammad."

"I've done nothing," he told himself. "I've done nothing."

"Excuse me?"

Had he murmured aloud? "Nothing," he said. "I said nothing."

No one spoke. They waited. In architecture, space was a material to be shaped, even created. For these men, the material was silence. Silence like water in which you could drown, the absence of talk as constricting as the absence of air. Silence that sucked at your will until you came spluttering to the surface confessing your sins or inventing them. There were no accidents here. For Pinball to hold out a pack of Big Red was an act as deliberate as Mo's decision to bend the walkway at the theater to conceal the lobby for a visitor's approach. The agents, who now seemed to think it strategic to demonstrate their friendliness, were asking him if he "minded" spending a little more time with them while they retrieved another colleague. When they left the room he surveyed it. They had used a partition with the texture of a gray, moldy bulletin board to shrink the room's dimensions and maximize its oppressiveness. The room wasn't windowless after all: the partition blocked the natural light to create the ambience of a cell. Someone among them understood the manipulation of space.

Removing the gum, he spotted a trash can in the far corner, but as he rose he imagined them watching him and sat back down. He didn't want to provide grounds for suspicion. Perhaps the gum was a trick to get his

DNA; he'd read about that happening in criminal or paternity cases, or maybe seen it on a *Law & Order* episode. He put the gum back in his mouth, gave it a final roll, and swallowed it while swatting away the irrational fear that he had just destroyed evidence. Down went the rubbery nub to join the knot of nerves in his stomach.

His effort to avoid being seen as a criminal was making him act like one, feel like one. And yet he had been, with a few merited exceptions, a good kid and was a good man, legally speaking. Being an occasional asshole — shedding girlfriends, firing contractors — didn't count. The law itself he had rarely broken. He ignored speed limits and perhaps over-deducted on his taxes, but that was as much his accountant's fault as his own. As a teenager, he had shoplifted a Three Musketeers bar simply to see if he could. That was the sum total of his crimes, and he was prepared to confess them all to show the absurdity of accusing him of anything grander. Really, he wanted to say, this is absurd! You have not just the wrong man but the wrong kind of man. The wrong kind of Muslim: he'd barely been to a mosque in his life.

His parents, immigrants to America in the 1960s, made modernity their religion, became almost puritanical in their secularism. As a boy he had no religious education. He ate pork, although he hadn't grown up doing so. He dated Jews, not to mention Catholics and atheists. He was, if not an atheist himself, certainly agnostic, which perhaps made him not a Muslim at all. When the agents came back in the room he would tell them this.

But when they returned, dragging their heels and cracking their jokes, he told them nothing. His boast of irreligion stayed on his tongue, for what reasons he couldn't say, any more than he could say why words long unuttered floated unbidden into his mind: *La ilaha illa Allah, Muhammad rasulullah.* The Kalima, the Word of Purity, the declaration of faith. It almost made him laugh: at the moment he planned to disavow his Muslim identity, his subconscious had unearthed its kernel.

The "interview" ended as capriciously as it had begun. Without explanation, they asked to photograph and fingerprint him. Instead of refusing, as he believed was his right, he allowed them to press down his fingers as if he were a paralytic, an acquiescence that marked off the man who left the room from the one who had entered. At the agent's physical touch — the hand lifting his — there was a brief flare of fury, an impulse toward violence, then the almost instantaneous checking of it. Returning home, he found that they had pillaged his suitcase: crumpled his precisely folded shirts, unpaired his socks, uncapped his shampoo and toothpaste so that a nebulous ooze coated his toiletries. He upended the suitcase on the bed, dumped the toiletry kit in the trash, kicked the wastebasket to the wall.

But his bitterness was overwhelmed by the magnitude of mourning around him. The city reeled — the air ashy, the people ashen, the attack site a suppurating wound you felt even when you didn't see it. One night, soon after his return, Mo walked toward the zone of destruction. The moonlight picked out a strange fine dust clinging to leaves and branches; his toe rested on a paper scrap with charred edges. The eternal lights were off in the nearby office towers, as if the city's animal appetites had been quelled. A quilt of the missing — bright portraits of tuxedoed men and lipsticked women — had been pasted on fences and construction plywood, but the streets were empty, and for the first time in memory, he heard his own footsteps in New York City.

He imagined, couldn't avoid it, the shaking hands that must have placed each of these photos on a photocopy machine, that roll of blue light, cold, mechanical hope. False hope. The centers of hundreds upon hundreds of webs of family, friends, work had been torn out. It staggered Mo, shamed him. These men who had given vent to their homicidal sanctimony had nothing to do with him, yet weren't entirely apart. They represented Islam no more than his own extended family did, but did they represent it less? He didn't know enough about his own religion to say. He was the middle-class Muslim son of an engineer, a profile not all that different from some of the terrorists. Raised in another society, raised religious, could he have become one of them? The question shuddered through him and left an uneasy residue.

Behind a police saw horse an Indian man in a bedraggled white jacket and black bow tie held a sign: WE ARE OPEN. The man motioned to a tiny restaurant down the block, and although Mo wasn't hungry, he followed and ordered a sympathy chola. The waiter left him to the cook, who also served, and alone, Mo picked at his chickpeas and naan. Here he could hear himself chew.

What was it he was trying to see? He had been indifferent to the buildings when they stood, preferring more fluid forms to their stark brutality, their self-conscious monumentalism. But he had never felt violent toward them, as he sometimes had toward that awful Verizon building on Pearl Street. Now he wanted to fix their image, their worth, their place. They were living rebukes to nostalgia, these Goliaths that had crushed small businesses, vibrant streetscapes, generational continuities, and other romantic notions beneath their giant feet. Yet it was nostalgia he felt for them. A skyline was a collaboration, if an inadvertent one, between generations, seeming no less natural than a mountain range that had shuddered up from the earth. This new gap in space reversed time.

4

Claire jackknifed into the water, pinned her arms to her sides, and kicked until she rose to the surface and began wheeling her arms. Her eyes opened behind her goggles, and her senses opened to cobalt tiles, the light lurking on the pool floor, the chlorine smell, her own gasps for air. Her solitude. Cal at work, William at preschool, Penelope down for a nap. After every two laps she pulled up to listen to the monitor she had set at the edge of the pool and, hearing only even breaths, plunged back in.

An aquarium sea lion that no one bothered to watch: that's what she was. She had assumed she would keep working once she had children; Cal had assumed she wouldn't. It astonished her, in retrospect, that they had never discussed it before they married, but maybe they *couldn't* have discussed it. In theory, no one ever liked to give in, but in practice — in marriage, if it were to last — someone had to.

"I just can't imagine finding a nanny as smart as you," Cal had said with a smile, when, five months into her pregnancy with William, she raised the issue.

"I didn't go to Dartmouth and Harvard Law to be a nanny."

"And I didn't marry you so our kids would have a good lawyer, although it could come in handy if they punch anyone at school." He turned serious: "I'm not saying I'm right on the merits, I'm saying maybe I'm more traditional than I realized."

Telling him that she needed the independence her lawyer's income guaranteed would have implied some lack of faith in the marriage, which wasn't the case. There was only the fear of having to depend on anyone at all. At sixteen she had seen her father die and her mother inherit his previously hidden mountain of debt. In response Claire had driven herself harder than ever, becoming class valedictorian, tennis team captain, debating champion. She put away every dollar, schemed for every scholarship and loan, and made it to Dartmouth. Marrying Cal, the scion of a family whose wealth dated to the Industrial Revolution and had multiplied through every turn of the American economy since, ought to have eased her worries about failing to climb as high as she believed she deserved. But the money was his, not theirs. The unspoken power this gave him kept her from asking: Why don't *you* stay home?

They agreed to interview nannies. Cal was right: they weren't as smart as she was, or so she rationalized her decision to stay home. She was only a week shy of her due date on the first day he went into the city without her. She dropped him at the Chappaqua train station, turtling through the line with the other wives, and when she turned the car to face home couldn't shake the sense she was facing backward.

Four years had passed since then, passed at toddlers' soccer practice and at ladies' lunches; passed in music groups and on playdates, shopping trips, and philanthropic committees. Claire pretended this was the life she wanted. But when Cal, dressing for work, had asked for the second time whether she had found a tennis coach for William, she snapped at him, "Why don't *you* try being social secretary for a four-year-old?"

With calm, infuriating sympathy he said, "Would you like me to call? I'm happy to," which only made her feel worse. Calling would take two minutes, far less than it would take to convey her feelings about her life narrowing to phoning pro shops. It was easier to apologize for her mood, to cite Penelope's poor sleeping habits, and when she dropped him at the train station they made a kissing peace, but perhaps a false peace, for she had come to the pool to splash out the lingering anger that, as much as the exercise, warmed her against the air's faint chill.

After forty-five minutes she emerged calmed and stretched out to sun herself and let her pounding heart slow. There was no sound beyond her daughter's waking bab-blings through the monitor, the dog's tags clinking as he scratched himself, the water's faint lapping, a relentless woodpecker somewhere within the shirred line of spruces and maples at the edge of the lawn. Walking back to the house, she broke into a barefoot jog as she heard the phone ringing, an ordinary ring.

"Mommy, you smell like the pool," William sniffled a day — or was it two? — later. She had not thought to shower since the news. She would think often about having been submerged in water while her husband was consumed by fire. What did this say? It was like a myth, a dark poem whose mean-ing just eluded her.

It was Cal's hand she had reached for when she read Mohammad Khan's name at Gracie Mansion last night, Cal's indignation she channeled, but also Cal's specificity she sought. It had been two years. He appeared in her dreams but vanished on waking, and she spoke of him in qualities — positive, ebullient, smart, principled — that had no texture.

So on this morning, instead of swimming she went to his study. Small, oak-paneled, a nook in a house of grand spaces, it had been a sanctuary for Cal and, in the months after his death, for Claire. On bad days, when the loneliness howled or the children shrieked, she would come to the study and leave fortified by this fiction of his enduring. Better a dollhouse than no house. The study was largely as he had left it, intact, a museum of sorts. When the children were old enough, she would let them touch and read his books, dip into his papers and files. She often had done the same in those first months. Now she couldn't recall the last time she had sat at his desk.

Settling herself there, she stared down the painting opposite. It was a liverish red that

66

clotted to blackness at the center. "It makes me think of childbirth," she had told Cal, distaste in her voice, the night they spotted it in a Chelsea gallery. "You're wrong," he replied, his tone, as always when he over-ruled her, as respectful as it was certain. The next day he bought it, Claire pretend-ing indifference to the price. Wrong how? That it was like childbirth? Of this he had no better idea than she: they were, then, still childless. Or wrong in her dislike? Lose someone prematurely, and you had endless time to pore over finite conversations. Over fossils.

In the cabinets next to his desk Cal had kept neat files: Art, Politics, Philanthropy, Travel. A Claire file, the sight of which always made her smile. She rifled through them, not sure what she was looking for. In the Art files — mostly detailed dossiers on the art Cal had collected, or wanted to, or on artists he admired — she found, to her semi-amusement, an article on Ariana Mon-tagu's *Tectonics,* a huge piece, gargantuan slabs of granite tilting into one another, as if they had fallen that way, installed some years back in Central Park.

Other files held information about causes he had backed, generously, sometimes astonishingly so: environmental groups; human rights organizations; Democrats trying to reform the party; a program in Bridgeport to help teen mothers continue their schooling, which Claire now financed, although she didn't visit as often as Cal had. All of this suggested a decent man, an earnest liberal, a citizen trying to leave his country better than he found it. The clearest view into his principles was a letter he had written, at the age of twenty, resigning from his parents' and grandparents' golf club. It had the endearing, aggravating righteousness of a college student who has just noticed the world around him and believes it will heel to his newfound idealism.

"It has come to my attention," the letter began — Claire had ribbed him about this: had the club's homogeneity really just then come to his attention? — "that the club does not have a single black or Jewish member. Whether or not this indicates a deliberate policy of exclusion, I am unable to associate myself with an institution that does not place a greater value on diversity."

The country club, from what Claire knew, was as lily-WASP as it had always been, which was just one reason she considered these files a chronicle of defeat. Cal had wanted to be a sculptor, had even set himself up in a studio after college. By the time Claire met him, he was in business school. Conceding that he would never be a great, or even good, artist, he had turned to collecting, to owning what he couldn't create. Creating wealth was the Burwell family talent, but Cal feared being known for that alone. The political engagement, the philanthropy: that was him casting about for a mark to make. He hadn't yet found his medium. Discovering this unformed spot in a man who seemed so complete at first disturbed Claire, still busy papier-machéing her own unfinished self. But if she had fallen for Cal's strengths, his charms, she came to love him most generously, she believed, where he was weakest. Just as he loved her where she was hardest — her seriousness provided both ballast and challenge, one he met with a constant effort to make her laugh. Let go.

Marrying Claire had been, for him, a small rebellion. She was presentable, highly so. But his family didn't know hers, and she plainly had no money of her own. She was in the Claire file now — photos (some nude, dating to their honeymoon; she scrutinized them for changes), scraps of middling poetry about her, ideas for her birthday presents. The documents recording Cal's unexpected payoff of her college and law school loans, some $100,000 of debt. He'd wiped it out in a single day without asking her if he could. It had seemed monumental at the time, less so once she learned the staggering scale of his fortune. She wished that knowledge hadn't diminished the gesture.

These documents narrated their history as much as their marriage certificate did. When they made love the night he told her about the loans, she sensed him expecting some new trick or abandon, some evidence of gratitude. This had made her tense because she wasn't entirely grateful: in giving her freedom from worry he had stolen a hard-won self-sufficiency. But the next morning she had decided she was overreacting. He wanted only the surrender of her anxiety.

"I want to draw the Garden," William said, clutching his coloring pad. He was at her elbow; she hurriedly shoved the nude portraits into the file and made space for him on the desk. He handed her crayons in wordless command.

They had been enacting this ritual for weeks, ever since she told him about the Garden, figuring that breaking her juror confidentiality pledge with a six-year-old didn't count. As she devoted increasing time to the memorial selection, William had become ever more difficult. Each tantrum sent sadness and guilt, anger at his manipulations, irritation at his whining squalling through her. Suffocation. The children needed her more, needed more of her, than ever: one less parent and more parenting required. Do more with less; an emotional recession. Every so often, she would grasp that her pain at William's pain was so unbearable that somehow she held it against him. His sadness, too big for his tiny frame, was like a shadow stunting a plant's growth.

The Garden, she told him, was a special place where his father could be found, even though William wouldn't be able to see him there. This was all too true: shards, less than shards, of Cal likely lay in the ground where the memorial would go, although William didn't know that. The idea of the Garden seemed to console him, and ever since, together they had drawn the trees and flowers, the pathways and canals. William always drew in two little figures: himself and his father. In his drawings, the sun always shone.

"Sometimes it will rain in the Garden," Claire said today, coloring a gray cloud. A small, inexplicable resistance quavered in her. William drew an umbrella over the figures.

71

The time for lunch was nearing. They left the study together, their sheaf of drawings in her hand. Glancing at them, she saw that she had mixed in the documents recording Cal's payoff of her loans. Her first instinct was to return them to the file. Instead she continued down the hall with her son.

Paul slept poorly and awoke achy. The sunlight bounded in and punched him in the eyes when he opened the curtains. He pulled them shut, showered too long, dressed too slow. "Paul!" Edith began calling once she heard him astir. "Your eggs are ready."

To the cook's chagrin, the eggs were cold by the time he made his way to the dining table. Like a child he pushed them in a circle, trying to ignore the rat-a-tat of Edith's questions: "Who won? What's the design like?"

His silence goaded her. "Paul, you're not answering me," she said, standing just to the right of his ear. "Do I need to make another appointment with the hearing doctor?"

"My hearing's fine, Edith," he said, staring down at the eggs, which brought to mind a leaking sun.

He went to his study, where his eye fell

first on a photograph of himself with the governor, displayed in a black leather frame propped against the decorously aged set of Gibbon. Paul and Governor Bitman were beaming and clasping hands, a shake that had sealed Paul's chairmanship of the memorial jury.

His cell phone rang as soon as he'd seated himself at his desk.

"Mr. Rubin, hello, it's Alyssa Spier. You remember — from the *Daily News.*"

He did remember, made it his business to know the beat reporters covering the memorial process. She was no worse than the rest of them, maybe a bit better — she truncated his quotes but didn't butcher them. He brought her features into focus: the short one, glasses, on the heavy side, tired hair, lips always twitching like she had something to ask. The kind who dreamed in questions.

"How can I help you?"

"I have a source who says a Muslim has won the competition. Could you confirm that?"

Paul gripped the desk as if it were a cliff's edge. Who was the Judas? Someone had leaked. "I can't confirm anything," he said. "We don't have a winner yet." Was this technically true? The last thing Paul needed was to be caught in a lie.

"That's not what I hear. It's, you know, Mr. uh, Mr. uh . . . hold on, I'm just checking my notes."

Her bluff could be sensed through the phone: she didn't have the name. He said nothing.

"Oh, I'll have to find it later. Look, I won't be quoting you on the confirmation — that's off the record, although I may then want to get an on-the-record reaction from you. I just need to make sure my source is right."

"And your source is . . . ?" He had to know: Was it one of his jurors? He tried to think who would want to make this public. Not the minute-taker, with that posture of fear when he reminded her of the confidentiality pledge. Claire: Would she think she could box them in?

"You know I can't give away my sources, just like I won't give you away," Alyssa cooed.

Paul deployed his "stern-father tone," which required sadly little effort. "Alyssa, on the record, off the record, I have nothing to say. I would help you if I could, and of course we'll have a winner shortly, but today I have nothing for you."

He ended the call. Think, Paul, think. Strange, but this crisis within the crisis provided a certain relief, for he knew how to handle this. You figured out whom to pressure, which levers to pull. You called in favors, dangled others. Feeling his old mastery returning, he found the number he needed and dialed.

"Fred, Paul Rubin. A drink later?"

Paul had told the *Daily News* editor to meet him at the Four Seasons. He wanted a setting that conveyed gravitas, and twenty-dollar martinis always helped.

"I think I know why I'm here," Fred said with a smile as they took seats in a discreet corner. The bar had the amber light of poured whiskey.

"What can I get you?" Paul asked.

"Jameson," Fred said.

"You sure?" Paul asked. "Why not try this GlenDronach Grandeur? Make it two," he told the waiter. "Neat."

Once they were alone, he turned toward Fred. "I'm sure I don't need to tell you how delicate this situation is."

"So Alyssa's right?"

"I didn't say that. Whether it's fact or rumor is really irrelevant."

"That's not how we see it in the newspaper business."

"But you haven't confirmed it?"

"You just did."

Paul started.

"I'm kidding, Paul, I wouldn't do that to you. But Alyssa's a bulldog — she'll confirm it eventually. Look, I see your position, but please see mine: it's an explosive exclusive."

"Explosive is right, Fred. This country can't handle this right now. I know you have a newspaper to run, and that you feel a . . . uh . . . duty to report the news, but there are more important principles at stake. It's as close to being a national security issue as it can be without being a national security issue. All I'm asking for is time, the chance to manage this in private a bit longer."

Fred was quiet for a few moments. Out of the corner of his eye, Paul saw Barry Diller peacock into the bar at Diane von Furstenberg's side. She looked pretty good for her age, those cheekbones protruding like tangerines. Paul crooked a finger, and the waiter refreshed their drinks and the salted almonds, a bowl of which Paul had emptied.

"So how do you rate Bitman's chances?" Fred asked, and Paul knew, for the time being, he was safe.

5

A year after the attack, news about Muslims arrested or suspected, the constant parsing of Islam's "true" nature, had become background noise for Mo. Foreground was work, behind which geopolitics, serious romance, even a second chair and a bed frame for his echoing loft receded. All of it could wait until he "made it," although he was well aware that such success, if it came at all for an architect, came late. "You can't keep deferring your life," his mother said. She worried that, as he neared forty, he was no closer to getting married or having children than he had been at twenty. At least now he could tell her that his sacrifices were about to pay off.

The rumor, repeated often enough that it had become an apparent inevitability, was that today Mo would be made one of the firm's project directors. At four, Emmanuel Roi, the firm's founder, swept into the office like a leaf blower, scattering everything, everyone in his path. He paused by the desk of an architect working on a model and said, "You know what this looks like? Merde. It looks like a doggy climbed on this desk and took a shit." He liked to make an impression early in his visits.

An hour later, he summoned Mo to his glassed-in office, meant to "hide nothing, show everything," in Roi's famous dictum. See everything, too. Mo had spent the previous half hour rehearsing how he would accept the promotion, so he took a few moments to grasp Roi's news: not Mo but Percy Storm — the manorexic whom Mo and Thomas Kroll, his best friend at the firm, called Storm Trooper behind his back — was being promoted.

"Storm — ?" Mo started to gasp, then stopped himself. He could barely breathe.

Roi's hands caressed his silver-stubbled head; his eyes were black cloaks. Mo pressed for reasons, without success. Had Roi, he wondered, gotten wind that Mo and Thomas planned, in time, to defect and start their own practice? Thomas, in fact, had already registered its name, K/K Architects. Mo couldn't ask, for to ask would be to reveal, and so he phrased generic questions about whether Roi was dissatisfied with him, to which Roi offered oleaginous reassurance: "Your turn will come."

"Any issue with . . . me? My conduct?"

"Of course not, Mo. I have no problems with you." This was a lie, of course, since Emmanuel was threatened by anyone with talent and ego, any younger version of himself. But that characteristic had never stopped Emmanuel from giving Mo prime work. As Roi became bigger — an icon, a blimp — he needed better talent around him to cover how thinly his own was spread. He was overseeing sixty-three projects in eleven countries: anyone could do the math — although no one beyond his employees did — and see that his true involvement in any of them must be minimal. Maybe grousing about this had been Mo's undoing. He couldn't ask: it was one of those conversations in which words brick over the cons and deceptions taking place.

Emmanuel was droning on about Mo's bright future and, aggravatingly, Percy's managerial capabilities, when Mo broke in: "Does this have anything to do with . . . with me being, you know?"

"No, I do not know," Emmanuel said, affronted by the interruption, not the insinuation.

"Muslim."

"To even suggest —" Having judged that fragment of a denial sufficient, Emmanuel sent his ursine hands ranging over the desk in search of distraction. Finding none — the vast glass surface was denuded of papers to shuffle or even a stray paper clip — he began to peck at the computer with his index fingers. Everyone knew he dictated his e-mails, not to mention his designs — he molded paper, or cardboard, or tin from which his young architects generated computer images — so this finger play was a farce. The meeting was over.

"Of course," Mo muttered. "Sorry."

Without saying goodbye he walked out. The envious eyes of his colleagues, sure he had been promoted, tracked him as he headed for the office exit. Their misperception, so soon to be corrected, tightened the clammy grip of humiliation around his throat. Outside his body shivered out of proportion to the temperature, and there was no plane above to account for the roar in his ears.

The memory of the airport interrogation was unpacked, shaken out, stuffed full of straw to make it lifelike once again. There was no evidence Roi hadn't elevated Mo because he was a Muslim but none against it, either. If he had been singled out once, why not again? Paranoia, no less than plasticine, could be molded.

Crushed into the corner of a subway car one rush hour soon after his non-promotion, Mo watched four black teenagers enter the car and begin tossing unfurled, though thankfully unused, condoms onto the heads of sardined commuters. They withstood their torment with bowed heads until a short African American man in a suit delivered a sharp reprimand — "Stop it, stop it now!" — earning for his trouble only an extra round of rubbers. He left the train soon after but lingered in Mo's mind. The man had intervened, a sympathetic Mo was convinced, because he felt tainted by the behavior of other blacks.

"But how do you know that's why he got involved?" Yuki, his girlfriend of the past two months, asked when he told her the story that evening. She was shaving limpid slices of pear with a mandoline. "Maybe he was just being a good citizen." Mo clutched his foul temper to his chest as if Yuki, with her prettiness and sober wisdom, was trying to take it away.

She had long hair and precision-cut bangs, and favored, in all seasons, miniskirts and expensive trench coats. An architect who

81

had branched into designing architectonic, extremely high-end baby clothes, she confessed on their first date that she didn't particularly like children. They ate, drank, made love, argued about buildings, and watched television, which was what they were doing later that night when Yuki, in possession of the remote, paused on Fox News.

A studio audience was watching a debate on, as the caption put it, "Should Muslims be singled out for searches at airports?"

"How could anyone defend that?" she asked.

Mo, still peeved, declined to engage. The debate was between Issam Malik, the executive director of the Muslim American Coordinating Council, and Lou Sarge, New York's most popular right-wing radio host. In the months after the attack he had added the tagline "I Slam Islam" to his show.

"Profiling is illegal, immoral, and in effective," said Malik. He resembled George Clooney with darker skin and a neatly trimmed beard.

"Ridiculous!" shouted Sarge. His hair had a black Cadillac's sheen, his face a stark, powdered pallor. "We should have separate security lines for Muslims to be searched at the airport."

"The police used to stop African Americans solely for 'driving while black.' Now it's acceptable to single us out for 'flying while Muslim'?" Malik asked. "And how will you identify the Muslims? Are you going to tattoo us? I am a peaceful, law-abiding American. Why should I get singled out when I have done absolutely nothing wrong?"

"You want us to search little old ladies waiting to board their planes just so Muslims won't feel bad?" Sarge asked. "Ridiculous!"

"You're ridiculous," Yuki said to the screen.

"He's right," Mo said.

"What?" Her posy of a mouth parted a little.

"He's right. We can't pretend that everyone's equally dangerous."

"I can't believe you're saying that!" Yuki sputtered. "That means you'd be one of those singled out."

"So be it — I have nothing to hide. I'm not going to pretend that all Muslims can be trusted. If Muslims are the reason they're doing searches in the first place, why shouldn't Muslims be searched?"

"We know who the enemy is!" Sarge was saying, or rather exclaiming. "Let's stop walking around like the emperor has clothes! He's naked! Radical Islam — naked radical Islam — is the enemy."

Mo got up from the sofa, switched off the television — knowing that, in the sedate precincts he and Yuki inhabited, this amounted to declaring war — and went into the kitchen for a beer. A Muslim drinking to cope with the stress of being a Muslim: he wasn't sure who would get the joke.

"I think we're on the same side," Yuki said when he returned from the kitchen.

"And what side is that?"

"The right side. What's the problem here, Mo?" What was the problem? He knew he was being deliberately contrarian, but something in the easy comfort of her outrage made him bristle.

"You're a hypocrite, to start," he said. "After accusing me of presuming to know how the black man on the train felt, you're presuming that because I'm Muslim I'll feel a certain way about how Muslims should be treated."

"I'm not presuming anything except that you don't want some security agent's hand down your pants because your name's Mohammad. Am I wrong?"

She wasn't, which made him argue all the harder. "It's patronizing, that attitude. You can't pretend Islam isn't a threat."

"If I thought Islam was a threat, I wouldn't be dating you," she said.

"What's that supposed to mean?"

"It means what it sounds like it means."

"What — that your dating me is conditional on your approval of my religion?"

"That's not what I said, but for the record I happen to think Islam is a very cool religion."

"Oh, so dating a Muslim turns you on?"

"Mo! What's gotten into you?"

They fought on, or rather Mo threw verbal punches and Yuki put up her hands until her arms tired.

"I don't care that you're Muslim, Mo, but I do care that you're an asshole," she said, and he knew they had reached their end.

The animated characters beetled around a plaza outside an office building until the camera zoomed in on a dark-skinned cartoon man with a beard and backpack, and —

BOOM! The sound of the bomb blast was so loud and sudden that a few people jerked in their seats. The screen went black and when it came back up, the figures were animated no longer because they were dead. The lights came on, revealing the banner

DESIGN AGAINST TERRORISM along one wall and a roomful of architects, Mo among them.

"So how do you think we could reduce the risk?" asked the British counterterrorism expert leading the seminar. His name was Henry Moore, which had evoked sad, wry smiles from some of his pupils. His skin was the texture of a shepherd's-pie crust, his teeth surprisingly excellent.

"Stop invading other countries," one man muttered.

"Search everyone — that's what they do in Israel."

"Ban backpacks."

"But those aren't really . . . architectural solutions," Henry said.

"Shatterproof glass," said a brownnoser. "And truck barriers, obviously."

"Great. Anything a little more . . . creative?"

Silence. Henry began with history — Crusader castles, high atop plateaus; moated cities — then moved to modern times: mammoth planters and giant benches artfully arrayed; a Richard Serra sculpture ("defensive art"); serpentining access roads with subtle security checkpoints; schools whose baffled windows made them look like prisons; false windows. Beauty and safety were not incompatible, he lectured, although he showed few examples to prove it. Which only goaded Mo to prove it himself. He worked best with design constraints. ROI had won multiple awards for a museum for the disabled, showing the history of their experience in America, that Mo had largely designed. As with many architects, his empathy was selective. Put him behind a man navigating a Manhattan sidewalk in a wheelchair, and Mo would curse the obstruction. But pose a paraplegic's plight as a design problem, and Mo would climb into his wheelchair, feel the deadweight of his limbs. For the museum, he had taken inspiration from mountain switchbacks, their giddy sense of ascension, to create a series of ramps that crisscrossed up the building's interior, offering unexpected vistas inside and out.

Now he played with the problem of urban security: Would you want buildings that advertised how safe they were or that made you forget your fear? It was easy to laugh off Crusader crenellations or moats; harder to see if they possessed anything adaptable. A barrier of water would make for a more pleasing setback than a concrete plaza. A zigzag approach, with views framed within walls, could make arriving a visual adventure. These thoughts he kept to himself.

"Don't you think if you create more hard targets, they'll just move on to softer ones?" one of the few women in the room asked. "Are we going to armor everything?"

"It's not armor," Henry said. "It's smart building."

He flashed a slide of a row of conifers that formed a verdant border between a sterile plaza and a generic office building.

"Cypress trees," Henry said. "They're very good at absorbing the kinetic energy of a blast. Strong trunks, leaves like scales — they hold tight. And they don't look . . . sinister. Think of them as a line of defense."

"Is our government going to pay for all this?" The architect spoke aggressively. "I mean, if we have to add barriers and shatterproof glass and cypresses? Unless you can prove there's going to be a terrorist attack next week, no developer's going to put money into it."

"This is about *preventive* architecture," Henry said.

"Yes, preventing creativity." There were chuckles.

"When I think of all the money I pissed away learning how to make buildings inviting . . ."

"There're bloody cameras everywhere

now — isn't that enough?"

"Maybe we should just get rid of public spaces," said the man who had suggested banning backpacks.

"Or get rid of Muslims, for that matter."

"Now, now," Henry chided.

Mo stared out the window. The sun, in the gray sky, looked like it had been sunk in dirty water.

From London, Mo was to go on to Kabul, where ROI was competing to design a new American embassy. Over beers, Mo and Thomas had dissected Roi's decision to dispatch Mo, but they arrived at no conclusion, only a drunkenness harmful to Thomas's marital harmony. Their theories included the following: Roi was compensating for not promoting Mo by sending him on an international junket that included a free trip to London, where the counterterrorism seminar was meant to buff the firm's credentials; Roi was punishing Mo by sending him to Kabul; Roi was trying to enhance the firm's odds of getting to design an embassy in a Muslim country by sending a Muslim, or trying to ensure they wouldn't get the commission by sending a Muslim.

"He wants to prove he doesn't consider you a liability," Thomas said. "Or, more cynically, maybe in this case he thinks you're an asset."

"What, with my special insight into the terrorist mind?"

After wondering whether he should tell Roi to fuck himself, Mo decided to take the assignment, mostly to escape smug Storm Trooper. But also because he wanted to see, up close, the kind of Muslim he had been treated as at LAX: the pious, primitive, violent kind. In asking, "Been to Afghanistan?" those agents had foretold his future.

Mo dozed off on the flight between Dubai and Kabul. He awoke to see a white woman across the aisle wriggling a long tunic over her fitted T-shirt and draping a scarf over her head. The massive brown drapes and folds of the Hindu Kush were below.

Kabul sat in a valley girdled by mountains, so the plane bounced down onto the runway like a basketball onto a court. Snow dusted the peaks; dust choked the city. As Mo disembarked, the particles and dry air entered his lungs. Shielding his eyes from the sun, he saw American helicopters, American planes, and American soldiers bestriding the runway.

After the disarray of immigration protocols and baggage claim, where grizzled men demanded a few dollars "baksheesh" for his own bags, a car from his hotel collected him. They entered the viscous traffic. Kabul was a minotaur of a city — a vigorous, erect young man above, where billboards advertised Internet cafés and hideous office buildings of blue-and-green glass sprouted; old, flaccid, depleted below, where raw meat hung exposed in sagging wooden stalls and bent, haggard grandfathers lugged hand-carts.

In the city center workers toiled on the construction of a giant mosque, the scaffolding around its dome a spiky bird's nest. A wooden walkway extended from the dome into the air and then wrapped, in the form of a staircase, around the minaret. Tiny workers made their way up and down the stairs, and in the absence of a crane, of any visible mechanical equipment at all, it was like watching a mosque being built four hundred years in the past.

The Hotel Inter Continental seemed of more recent epoch: it struck Mo, who was checking in, as drably Soviet. The drafty lobby bustled with a mélange of turbans and ties, Westerners and Afghans, all bathed in natural light since, not for the first time that day, the power had gone.

On a hard bed, Mo fell into a deep sleep. He was awakened before dawn by the call to prayer. The plume of the muezzin's voice drifted into his room and swelled within him. *Allah-hu akbar,* God is the greatest: the celebratory words, the strangely mournful tone. The call dipped into valleys before climbing mountains and higher than mountains. It trellised up some unseen lattice, twined over Mo, pinned him in place although it was meant to rouse him. Sinuous, cavernous, the voice scaled to the edge of breaking, then firmed. It was lonely. It was masterful. In the darkness men rose, washed, bent to prayer. Mo trailed them in his imagination before slipping back into sleep.

To get to the American embassy, Mo endured three pat-downs, four checks of his identification, and a long wait before he received clearance. Across the street from the main building, rows of white trailers — housing for the embassy staff — gleamed like bathroom tiles in the sun. The official who was briefing the architects from the twelve firms competing for the bid explained that the new embassy would dwarf the current structure. It would squat along both sides of the road, which would be forever closed to "outsiders," as the Afghans were defined.

Before Mo left New York, Roi, on speakerphone from Paris, had bloviated about the glory days of embassy architecture, when great modernists — Saarinen, Gropius, Breuer (all immigrants, Mo had noted to himself) — were sought out to design buildings that embodied American values like democracy and openness. But those days were long gone, despite the pretense of inviting top architects to compete. The only design value that mattered now was security: making sure the embassy didn't get blown up. Public diplomacy would be conducted from behind nine-foot blast walls. Architecture, once an ambassador, was now a DynCorp guard menacing anyone who came too close.

In place of glass walls or sculptural buildings — the gestures, or follies, of a more innocent time — there was Standard Embassy Design: a build-by-numbers box that came in small, medium, and large. Fortresses on the cheap. Hardly how ROI had earned its reputation, yet Mo knew he wasn't here for the artistic challenge. More than a hundred embassies and consulates around the globe were to be replaced, mostly for security reasons. Even a small piece of that work would be lucrative for ROI.

But the firm, Mo quickly concluded, had

no chance of winning the embassy commission. ROI specialized in highly insecure buildings known for their transparency ("hide nothing, show everything"). Its rivals for the commission specialized in the quick and generic. So he daydreamed through monotonous talk of "defensive perimeters" and "pre-engineered design solutions" and imagined defying the guidelines to submit an embassy design copied from a Crusader castle. The location lacked height, but he could suggest building a hill, a promontory — a true "Design Against Terrorism" right in the middle of the city . . .

At the day's end the architects were piled into a caravan of SUVs for a tour of Kabul, their "local context." Along the way the driver pointed out the Russian Cultural Center, a decaying, pockmarked wreck that now sheltered refugees and drug addicts.

"The way of all empires," Mo murmured. "That's how our embassy's going to end up."

"How about a little team spirit?" asked the plump, middle-aged architect seated next to Mo. He looked like he'd been on a few too many of these driving tours.

"We're not on the same team, remember?" Mo said.

After a while they entered a roundabout

lined with the jagged dun-colored crusts of bombed-out buildings, visual rhymes to the seismograph of the mountains behind. The barren craters were the work of shells lobbed during the civil war in the 1990s, the driver was saying. To Mo the ruins had a timeless quality.

"The way of all fucked-up third world countries," his seatmate said.

They were dropped off for dinner at a French restaurant hidden behind high earthen walls. There was a garden draped with grapevines, a small apple orchard, and a swimming pool full of Europeans and Americans dive-bombing one another. Chlorine and marjoram and marijuana and frying butter mingled in an unfamiliar, heady mix.

"Wonder what the Afghans think of this," one of the architects said, waving his hand to take in the bikinied women and beery men.

"They're not allowed in," said Mo's seatmate from the van. "Why do you think they checked our passports? It's better if they don't know what they're missing."

"Hot chicks and fruit trees: they're missing their own paradise," said someone else at the table — Mo hadn't bothered to remember most of their names. "I'm surprised they're not blowing themselves up to get in here."

"Some of them don't have to," his seat-mate from the van said, his eyes on Mo.

6

At Paul's request, the security consultants had expanded their initial report on Mohammad Khan to include more detail about what Paul called his "identity." A messenger delivered the revised report well after dark. Paul clutched the envelope and hurried from the foyer's marble and mirrors into his voluptuously tweedy study, seated himself at his Louis XV desk, and began to read. Khan's résumé, first: stellar, and thus unremarkable. He was thirty-seven years old, educated at the University of Virginia and the Yale School of Art and Architecture. Four years at Skidmore, Owings and Merrill; six at ROI. Khan had been the project architect for a museum in Cleveland, a residential tower in Dallas, and a library in San Francisco that had won enough acclaim for Paul to have read about it. He had been featured, along with Emmanuel Roi, in some of the press clippings. Khan was on the ascent, and this made Paul remember the time in his own life when his appetite and ability to climb had seemed limitless. In retrospect the anticipation, that hunger, was almost as rewarding as the success it brought.

Khan, the report said, had been raised in Alexandria, Virginia. His parents had emigrated from India in 1966, which, Paul reckoned, would have been soon after the United States had lifted its quotas on Asian immigrants, a policy decision that, nearly four decades later, had translated into an Indian American, albeit a Hindu one, running his old investment bank. Khan's father, according to the report, was a senior engineer at Verizon, his mother an artist who taught at a local community college. They had bought their house in 1973 and owed $60,000 on their mortgage. Khan himself owned no property; he lived in Chinatown, which struck Paul, the uptowner, as an odd place for an Indian American. He had no criminal record, no lawsuits pending against him, no tax liens.

The website of a mosque in Arlington, Virginia, recorded two donations from Khan's father, Salman, both made after the attack; this, along with inquiries to the mosque as well as the family's neighbors and colleagues, had confirmed that the family was, indeed, Muslim.

The mosque, which had opened in 1970 and moved to its current building in 1995, had "no known radical ties," although the cousin of the son of one former board member had gone to school with some Virginia youths recently accused of training for terror through paintball games ("I used to see them hanging out in the parking lot," this cousin had told *The Washington Post*). Sixteen, not six, degrees of separation.

On ROI's behalf, Khan had made a trip to Afghanistan earlier in the year, but he had no known or identifiable link to any organization on the terrorist watch list. He had made no political contributions to fringe candidates or, for that matter, to mainstream ones. His only membership appeared to be in the American Institute of Architects. There was nothing to suggest he was an extremist. Anything but: he seemed all-American, even in his ambition.

Paul took out a yellow legal pad, his favorite reasoning tool, and set it on the desk before him. He drew a line down the middle and titled the columns "For Khan" and "Against Khan." There were in life rarely, if ever, "right" decisions, never perfect ones, only the best to be made under

the circumstances. It came down to weighing the predictable consequences of each
choice, and trying to foresee the unpredictable — those remote contingencies.

In Khan's favor he wrote:

principle — he won!
statement of tolerance
appeal of design
jurors — resistance: <u>Claire</u>
reporter has — story out?

From that last entry, he drew a line to the
"Against" column and wrote "Fred," who
served to neutralize the reporter. Paul was
grateful for the hierarchy of newspapers,
even as he knew it was giving way to the
democracy, or rather, anarchy, of blogs and
the Internet. For now, at least, reporters still
answered to editors who controlled their
jobs.

But though he had dammed the leak,
another could open, a threat that called for
swift and decisive action. No gain in too
much reflection. In the "Against" column,
his pen scratched vigorously:

backlash
Distraction
families divided

raising $$$ harder
governor/politics

It was unlikely that the governor, whose national ambitions dangled like a watch chain, would take a stand for a Muslim now.

He kept on. Opposite "statement of tolerance," he wrote:

statement of appeasement/weakness

Under both columns, with the heading "Unpredictable," he wrote:

VIOLENCE

From the legal pad, he took a visual tally. The arguments for Khan looked paltry, not just in number, as if the "For" column had been written in paler ink. Perhaps "principle — he won!" should have ended the argument before it began, but Paul's job was to get a memorial built, and he wouldn't sacrifice that goal for a man named Mohammad.

So the decision was clear, the mechanism for killing Khan's design less so. Their only choice was to pronounce Khan unsuitable, but on what grounds? Paul looked up "unsuitable" in the dictionary: "Not appropriate." He looked up "appropriate": "Suitable for a particular person, condition, occasion, or place; fitting." He looked up "fitting": "Being in keeping with a situation; appropriate." This was why he was a banker, not a wordsmith. Could they say Khan was not "fitting"? As a jury behind closed doors they could say whatever they wanted, so the answer was to eliminate Khan as unsuitable before his name became public. There was the Claire problem, of course, but Paul suspected that she could be brought around by considering the outraged sentiments of the families she was meant to represent. Not that he shared those sentiments. For him, Khan was a problem to solve.

As required, the architect had provided a photograph with his entry. He appeared a handsome young man, his skin pale brown, his hair black, curly, and short, his brows dark and paintbrush thick over a wide, strong nose. His eyes, pale, greenish, were masked somewhat by the reflection in his glasses, which, unobtrusive and rimless, raised his estimation by Paul, who couldn't stand the primary-colored rectangles so many prominent architects favored. Khan wasn't smiling, but he didn't look unhappy. Seeing the face made it plain how much Khan was about to lose, what Paul was about to take. He turned the page over on his desk.

"The *Post,* have you seen it?"

It was 6:00 a.m., and Paul had seen nothing beyond the blinking light of his cell phone. He struggled to place the voice. Lanny, the jury's chief assistant.

"The *Post*?" Paul warbled.

"Yes, the *New York Post.* They're saying a Muslim has won the memorial competition. You told me —"

"The *Post*?"

"You told me there wasn't a winner yet, Paul." He sounded wounded. "I told the whole press corps that. I look completely out of the loop."

"How you look is fairly low on my list of priorities right now, Lanny. Let me call you back."

How had the *Post* gotten it? he wondered as he threw an overcoat over his pajamas. Didn't that reporter — Spier — work for the *News*? Someone else must have leaked, or the original leaker had gone to another paper . . . he was trying to piece together a jigsaw puzzle on its back. Edith replied only with a drowsy grunt when asked if she had seen his glasses, his misplacing and her recovering of them a forty-year routine she was disinclined to enact at this hour. He gave up, pulled on his shoes, and speed-walked to the nearest newsstand, seeing Khan's face before him. Halfway there it occurred to him he could have just switched on the computer. Old habits die hard, hardly die, but more than that: he needed to hold his calamity in his hands.

He reached the newsstand. There it was and going fast — the paper the *Post,* the author Alyssa Spier, and the photo of an unidentifiable man in a balaclava, scary as a terrorist. The headline: MYSTERY MUSLIM MEMORIAL MESS.

As usual, the Pakistani news vendor at Mo's corner was framed by the plush bosoms of a dozen white women and the buttocks of a few black women, all of them blooming from the fronts of glossy magazines. Today the vendor had his feather duster out and was sweeping the city grit from his candy rows. As Mo smiled, half in appreciation, half in amusement, his glance chanced on the stack of *New York Post*s below. His heart began hammering so audibly, or so he imagined, that he put his hand on his chest to muffle it. The vendor, thinking it a greeting, put his hand on his chest in return and said, *"Asalamu alaikum."*

"Alaikum asalam," Mo replied, the words foreign and rubbery on his lips. He snatched up the paper. Inside, the words ADDING IS-LAM TO INJURY? blared over a picture of the rubbled attack site. His trembling hand ransacked his pocket for change, then foisted a five-dollar bill on the vendor. Mo read as he walked, heedless of the sidewalk's jostle and cuss. An outsider might have wondered what news of the day could be so smiting to render him blind, deaf, mute, and stupid enough to wander into a New York crosswalk, then pause to read, letting the crowd flow around him like water around a boulder.

A Muslim had won. But no one knew who —

A taxi's blaring horn pitched him from crosswalk to sidewalk. He stood shaking with exhilaration. There were five thousand submissions. Other than a confirmation months back that his entry had been re-ceived, he hadn't heard a word. But a Muslim had won. It had to be him.

He taped the *Post* cover to his bathroom mirror that night, only to find the man in the balaclava looking back at him with cold, hard eyes. Executioner's eyes. Mo couldn't find himself in that picture, which was the point. The next day he enlarged his submission photo and pasted it on top of the *Post* picture. With the ugliness covered, he could pretend it was gone.

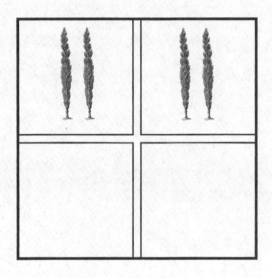

7

There were no buildings, no roads, only burning dunes of debris. His brother, Patrick, was somewhere here and Sean was conscious of wanting, a little too much, to be the one to find him, and of fearing he might not recognize him if he did. They hadn't seen each other in months, and Sean kept trying to call up Patrick's face, only to realize, as they came upon damaged bodies, that the faces of memory and death might not match.

Hours passed. Days. He couldn't breathe well, couldn't hear well — some new kind of underwater, this. Movie-set lights glared overhead, but the only true light came from the other searchers. Often, obscured by smoke, hidden by piles of rubble, the rescuers were only voices, but that was enough. Every time he put out a hand to take or to give, another was there, waiting. With time came a mappable order: the remains here, the personal effects there, the demolished cars beyond, the red sifters and the yellow ones, the tents and roster areas and messes and medics, the assembly line, a world more real to Sean than the city outside. Returning to Brooklyn each night was like coming home from war, except that it no longer felt like home. It amazed him what people talked about and what they didn't, how clean their fingernails were, how pristine their routines. His wife told him he smelled like death, and he couldn't believe this repulsed her. The dust he brought home was holy — he shook out his shoes and his shirt over newspapers to save it.

Nearly two years later, the attack site was a clean-swept plain. Across the river in Brooklyn, the Gallagher house hummed like a campaign headquarters. Ten members of Sean's family and as many of his Memorial Support Committee were crammed around the table, all its Thanksgiving leaves in use. Copies of the *Post* splayed under legal pads and two laptop computers. The poster board had been hauled out, the Marks-A-Lot marshaled for duty. Sean's mother, Eileen, and his three sisters cleared empty plates and refilled coffee cups with grim efficiency.

Frank, Sean's father, was on the phone with a reporter: "Yes, we plan to fight this until our last breath. What? No, sir, this is not Islamophobia. Because phobia means fear and I'm not afraid of them. You can print my address in your newspaper so they can come find me." A pause. "They killed my son. Is that reason enough for you? And I don't want one of their names over his grave." Another pause. "Yes, we found his body. Yes, we buried him in a graveyard. Jeez, you're really splitting hairs here. It's the spot where he died, okay? It's supposed to be his memorial, not theirs. Is there anything else? I've got a long line of calls to take . . ."

A voice from below: "You heard anything, Sean?" Mike Crandall was stretched out on the floor, his back having given out again. Retired from the fire department, he never missed a meeting, although sometimes Sean wished he would. His committee was a motley crew of former firefighters, along with the fathers of dead ones.

"Nothing," Sean said. He hated to say it. He was supposed to be the one with the lines into the governor's office, to Claire Burwell. That those lines had gone dead convinced him, suspicious of power by nature, that the story was true, and to his shame this relieved him. A Muslim gaining control of the memorial was the worst possible thing that could happen — and exactly the rudder Sean, lately lacking one, needed. Catastrophe, he had learned, summoned his best self. In its absence he faltered.

The decade prior to the attack had been a herky-jerky improvisation, a man lurching wildly through the white space of adult life. Each bad choice fed off the last. He cut up in school, dropped out of junior college. Absent other options, he started a handyman business. He drank because he hated bending beneath the sinks of people he'd grown up with. And because he liked to drink. He married because he was too tanked to think straight, then fell out with his parents over his marriage.

Five months before the attack, Sean got a little sloppy, a little loud, over dinner at Patrick's, or maybe he was lit when he arrived. He roared about their parents' dislike of his wife, Irina; he cursed profusely, creatively, when he dropped a bowl of soup. A stony Patrick pocketed his car keys and drove him home, and when Sean went to retrieve his beat-up Grand Am the next day, Patrick intercepted him outside and told him not to come around for a while. "You can't just expect people's respect," Patrick said, by way of saying Sean had lost his. To this day Patrick's three children treated him with the politeness of fear.

On that insultingly beautiful morning, though, Sean's first thought was of Patrick, whose engine company wasn't far from the site. Sean raced to his parents' house, trying not to be hurt that they seemed surprised to see him, then went with his father to look for Patrick. Someone else found him, which was probably just as well, but Sean didn't leave. Not that day, not for the next seven months. When he was kicked off the actual recovery crews because he wasn't police or fire or construction, he worked around the edges, helping organize a protest to keep the firefighters working in the hole; forming a committee to agitate for more space for the memorial. He got the acreage doubled. His "trouble with authority," as parents and teachers had always termed it, had become an official advantage. Soon he was giving speeches all over the country — most often in the small towns no one else wanted to visit — to Rotary Clubs and Kiwanis Clubs and police and firefighter and veterans' organizations, all of them eager for a first-hand account of the rescue and recovery. In his head as in his speeches, even his derelictions became proof of devotion. "For seven months, every single day, I went to the hole," he told the crowds who gathered to hear him. "I lost my marriage" — always murmurs at this point — "I lost my career, I lost my home, but that's nothing." A pause. "My brother — my only brother — lost his life." Sometimes people would break into inadvertent applause at this, which was awkward. Sean learned to lower his eyes until it stopped.

Even returning home to live with his parents after he and Irina split seemed right. Their modest Brooklyn Victorian had always been carefully tended — Eileen knew how to husband scarce resources — but by the time Sean moved in, the paint was peeling, the doors squeaking, a mouse leaving brazen shit. Sean, without asking, fixed, cleaned, cleared, painted, sanded, oiled, caulked, trapped. Put his hands to good use. Took down all the family pictures in the hall and replaced them with pictures of Patrick. Eileen, who'd always given Sean, the youngest of six, a threadbare mothering, warmed.

But then he was left off the memorial jury. The requests for him to speak tapered off, as if the country was moving on without him. In the movies Sean watched, redemption was a possession never lost once obtained. In life, redemption was walking up the down escalator: stop to congratulate yourself, and back you slid. The old him kept popping up, often in his mother's eyes. In recent months she'd reverted to her brusque self, telling him to make his bed, which grated doubly because it was the twin of his childhood. His father kept calling him by Patrick's name, and Sean didn't have the heart to correct him, though Eileen, acidly, did. And Sean's "contracting" business, which he'd tried of late to restart, felt like a suit he'd outgrown without money for a new one. Two days earlier, he had stalked off a job installing IKEA shelves after the housewife who hired him asked if he would carry her garbage down to the street at the end of the day. "Do you know who I am?" he had wanted to scream at her, but the true answer burned. He was a handyman living with his parents.

Alyssa Spier watched, transfixed, as her Mystery Muslim scoop entered the news cycle and rolled forward, crushing every other minor story before it. By noon she was booked on three television news programs and had done four radio interviews.

She sat in a chair, waiting to be made up, next to a local anchorman who was complaining that the foundation color being applied diluted his tan. As the makeup artist turned her attentions to Alyssa, who had no tan to dilute, the anchor began to practice saying "Muslim" — "the *New York Post* is reporting that a Muslim has been selected" — with just the right note of ironic surprise on the first syllable. "The jury's not talking, but stay tuned," he continued in a confiding tone that masked that he had nothing to confide. The TV lights glinted off the gel in his tight curls like sunlight on a river.

Every politician was talking about her news, or avoiding talking about it. "I'm not going to comment on unconfirmed reports," the mayor said on NY1. He'd been a brawler of a politician in his youth but had mellowed into a civic paterfamilias. "Right now I'm more concerned about unauthorized leaks — which may not even be true — from what's supposed to be a closed process. The last thing we need is the press anointing itself a juror."

Even as he insisted he wouldn't comment on hypotheticals, he couldn't help adding: "There's nothing inherently wrong with being a Muslim. It all depends what kind of Muslim we're talking about. Islam is a religion of peace, as I've said many times. The problem is that some people haven't gotten that message . . ." It wasn't clear whether "some people" referred to the violent Muslims or to people who slandered the peaceful ones.

Alyssa returned to the newsroom between interviews and found herself mobbed by happy editors and ignored by dour reporters. "This story has more legs than the Rockettes!" Chaz, her new editor, crowed, flipping channels and announcing drinks in her honor. She couldn't quite believe her change in fortune. Two days earlier she had been a *Daily News* reporter with a radioactive scoop her boss didn't want to run. Now she was a *New York Post* reporter whose reporting was the talk of the town, maybe even the country.

Fred, her editor at the *News,* had blocked the story. She needed a second source, he said, then before she could find one he deployed her to investigate cost overruns on repairs to the George Washington Bridge. His newfound editorial probity irked her — he never asked for a second source, which was why the paper's reputation had declined during his tenure. Her whiny first source kept calling to ask when the story was coming out. She kept stalling, fearful he would give it to someone else, unsure how to hold him off. She'd already bought him dinner at Balthazar, complete with the seafood

117

tower. That alone was enough to get her expenses flagged. "They'll pick someone else and then it will be too late," he kept warning. "You won't have a story."

She cajoled, she flattered, all the while thinking, What's his agenda? She needed motives to test for untruths, vulnerabilities to extract the next nugget. Had he gotten a kickback from another applicant? Did he have a thing against Muslims? Did the chairman shit on him, and he wanted revenge? Or did he relish the drama he would cause? Everyone liked to give history a little twist when they could.

"I'm going to lose the story," she told Fred. "We're going to lose it. My source is getting impatient."

"Manage him," Fred said. He swallowed his words with the banana he was eating. It sounded like he had said "Massage him." He went on: "Handling sources is an art." He made her feel it was her own failure.

When she called her source to stall yet again, he said, "This is ridiculous. I'm going to the *Post* with it." No, she thought, I am. She asked Sarah Lubella, an old acquaintance there, to broker a meeting with the paper's editor.

"I've got a great story — I promise," Alyssa said.

"So why won't your paper run it?" Sarah asked, miffed at not knowing the story she didn't have and not having the story she didn't know.

"They're scared," Alyssa said. "Under pressure."

"But if you do this you can't go back to the *News.* Can you handle coming to work for the lowly *Post*?" Her cracked-leather voice testified to thirty years of overflowing ashtrays in the overcrowded press rooms of a pre-smoke-free New York.

Alyssa had always looked down on the *Post,* just as she knew the *Times* reporters looked down on her. But this wasn't the first time that Fred had screwed her. His new-found caution wasn't an asset for a tabloid editor, but it was his clubbishness that she couldn't stand. He and Paul Rubin were friends, she knew. Alyssa had made her way from a depressed river town upstate. She didn't have those kinds of friends.

It had taken her a long time to get to New York City, which was where she had always imagined herself. During her exile in the wilderness of nowhere America — Brattle-boro, Duluth, Syracuse, backwaters too much like her birthplace — she had the strange, horrible sense that things were not going as planned, even though she told

119

everyone they were exactly what she had planned. By the time she got to the *Daily News,* eleven years and eight rungs later, she had her own measure. She wasn't a good enough writer for the blue-blood papers, nor was she interested in their stodgy, mincing version of news. A tabby all the way — that's what she was. She had no ideology, believed only in information, which she obtained, traded, peddled, packaged, and published, and she opposed any effort to doctor her product. The thrill every time she unearthed a scrap of news and held it up for the public's inspection was as fresh as the first time, when she'd confronted her high-school principal with the rumor — she played it like fact — that a teacher was being investigated for pocketing bake-sale money. Shock, fear, appeasement moved like clouds across his face, and she saw that she could make the weather. She also could get larcenous geometry teachers transferred to other school districts.

The editor, the chairman, their whole titled, entitled tribe were different, faithful to the truth only until it inconvenienced their clique. So she had defected, and the consequences of that defection were raining down upon the city. Relatives' Rumination, a journalistic genre that had evolved over the preceding two years, was in full gear. Every reporter had a digital Rolodex of widows and widowers, parents and siblings of the dead, who could be called for a quote on the issue of the day: the state of the site, the capture of an attack suspect, the torture of said suspect, compensation, conspiracy theories, the anniversaries of the attack (first one month, then six months, then yearly), the selling of offensive knickknacks depicting the destruction. Somehow the relatives always found something to say.

The governor, mysteriously absent at the onset of the controversy — awaiting the instant polls, Alyssa was sure — emerged to express "grave concern" about the possibility of a Muslim memorial-builder, not bothering with any of the mayor's palliative liberal sentiments. Governor Bitman had the glow of a woman in love, or one who has just found an issue that could catapult her to national prominence. Alyssa, her ambitions rhyming with the governor's, began to imagine trailing a presidential campaign from state to state.

Paul Rubin scanned the restaurant, an Upper East Side bistro he had chosen because no one he knew patronized it. All but empty, as he had hoped, except for a few matrons pickling at the dark-wood bar. Disoriented by the light-spangled mirrors on the mustard walls, he didn't see Mohammad Khan in the long, narrow room. Then he spotted a dark-bearded man watching him from a table at the back. Paul recalled the photo that had accompanied the Garden's submission. This couldn't possibly be Khan. He was — Paul scrambled for the words as he approached the table — "funked up," his wavy black hair grown longer and swept back, his jawline blurred by a neatly trimmed beard, his eyes by lightly tinted amber rectangles.

Khan stood. He had a good three inches on Paul. He had taken the seat with the view of the restaurant and the door, which was Paul's preferred seat; sitting with his back to a room unsettled him. Once they sat, Paul sipped water, hoping to imbibe a sense of equilibrium. He noted that Khan was drinking creamed coffee the shade of his skin, then disavowed the comparison for fear it was racist.

"You look different," he began. "From your picture."

Khan shrugged. "It was an old picture." He wore an uncreased white shirt of a fine fabric, the cuffs turned up, a tasteful tuft of dark hair visible at the neck. He looked like

Paul's idea of a Bollywood star. In his bow tie, Paul felt like he had overdressed for the school dance.

A moment of silence. Then another. Even in the restaurant's dimness, even through the glasses, Khan's eyes were — and Paul had never said this, even thought this, about a man — beautiful. Beautiful in the way marbles had been to him as a child. Beautiful in a way that women must fall hard for.

"Thank you for coming on such short notice," Paul began.

"Of course, but I'm curious why I learned this from the *Post,*" Khan said. There was sketch paper in front of him, a few lines scratched on it.

Paul hesitated. "Nothing is final yet. We're doing the due diligence required for any selection."

"So this is part of that?"

"Yes, yes, this meeting is part of that," Paul said. Khan's question gave him room to maneuver.

"But I won." He picked up his pen and began doodling. No, doodling was what Paul did. Khan was drawing. With great discomfort, Paul saw the bare outlines of the Garden materialize before him; even upside down, there was no mistaking it, the

123

four quadrants, the canals, the walls, the trees —

"There's no winner until the end of the process. Until the governor signs off."

Coolly, Khan studied Paul's face. "But the jury picked my design. It picked the Garden."

Paul folded. He had to. "It did."

That shimmer in Khan's eyes: joy. It vanished behind steel gates. "So what do you need to finalize it?" he asked.

"Well, once the due diligence is complete, the public will weigh in. In fact, as you may have noticed, it already is weighing in."

Khan didn't take the bait. "The public," Paul said again. "Look, we are living in difficult times, strange times —" He broke off. "Why did you enter?" he asked, surprised to be genuinely curious.

Khan looked at him as if he were a feeble old woman. "Because I could."

"The public," Paul said, newly fond of this vague, insistent entity, "will want a little more eloquence."

"Of course," Mo said, struggling — Paul could see it — to bring accommodation into his face. "My idea felt like it had the right balance between remembering and recovering. I wanted to contribute," he added, stiffly.

Paul nodded. "As I was saying, the public is already expressing a certain amount of . . . agitation. Which suggests that I may have a very difficult time raising the funds to get the Garden built. Which would leave you with only a titular victory, and me with no memorial to speak of. Hardly a desirable outcome for either of us. So I'm wondering if we should come at this a little more indirectly. You work for Emmanuel Roi, correct?"

"Yes."

"Perhaps this could proceed under his name. Which would mean you would still be working on it. You would be instrumental. Isn't that how these practices work anyway?"

Astonishment crossed Khan's face; anger followed, and stayed. He set down his pen, the gesture all the more unsettling for its deliberateness, and said quietly, "That's exactly how they work, which is why I entered the fucking competition on my own."

"So this is about your career," Paul said.

"I must have missed the question about motives on the competition's entry form. I want the same credit for my design as any other winner."

"As I said, there's no 'winner,' per se,"

Paul said. "Not until after the public has weighed in. For now there is only the jury's selection."

"Fine. The same credit as any selection would get."

"If what we've seen so far is a foretaste of the reaction to come, I'm not sure you'll want credit. You may come to wish you were still anonymous."

Khan put his long, tapered fingers to his temples and seemed to swell with irritation. "That's my problem, isn't it? Or is that some kind of threat?"

Paul didn't answer. Instead he tried to summon the list of questions Lanny, after an all-night crash course in Islam, had put together for him: Sunni or Shia? Self-described moderate? Jewish girlfriend? If they had to present a Muslim as the designer, it was critical to probe what kind of Muslim he was.

"Your background . . . it seems fairly secular," Paul said. "Is that correct?"

"Why does it matter?"

"Just exploring things. If not secular, I'm sure you would describe yourself as moderate?" The fan overhead twirled in miniature in the bowl of Paul's spoon.

"I don't traffic in labels," Mo said.

"Moderate's not really a label," Paul said.

"More of an outlook. I'm a moderate myself."

"Congratulations," Mo said. His tone had soured. Then he seemed to reconsider. "I'm a Shia Wahhabi, if you must know," he said.

"I see," Paul said, taking out a pen. "Do you mind if I write that —"

Khan pushed over a blank piece of paper, waited for Paul to finish writing, then said, "I wouldn't run to the press with that. Shias and Wahhabis are trying to kill each other, from what I know. Which isn't much."

Paul's face burned as it hadn't in a very long time. With his age, his stature, he had thought himself beyond such humiliation. He was taken back to an incident he had once revisited almost daily. He was twenty-four, a summer associate at a law firm. He had gotten there on brains and determination: always the best student in the class, awkward and shy without a book, fearful of failure or missteps. A senior partner had taken him to lunch. At the stiff, elegant restaurant, where the waiters draped white napkins over their arms, Paul toppled his glass of cranberry juice, a poor order to begin with. The partner did not ignore it, or make a kindly joke. Instead he watched the stain's migration across the tablecloth as if menstrual blood were on the move. Then he looked straight into Paul's eyes. To his great surprise — to this day it still surprised him — Paul looked back at the man without squirming or blushing or bothering to blot the stain. He made no eye contact with the waiter who soon rushed over to change the tablecloth in what struck Paul as an unnecessarily billowing flurry. That endless, wordless moment taught Paul what nearly two decades of school, college, and law school had not. Brains were only half of success, maybe less; the other half was a nameless game whose coin was psychological. To win, you had to intimidate or bluff. Over the next few years, this revelation slowly freed him from himself and from a life buried in law books. He never practiced, went straight to an investment bank as a junior associate, making baby deals. He liked the game of risk. Learning that disaster could be survived, even manipulated, freed him. Khan appeared to have learned this, too. Or maybe Paul was teaching him. He wasn't sure, today, if Paul's humiliation of Khan or Khan's of Paul had evoked the memory.

"You seem to think this is a game, Mr. Khan."

"It is a game. One for which you made

the rules. And now you're trying to change them."

"I'm changing nothing," Paul said. "I'm doing due diligence, as I told you. The public may wonder, for example, what their memorial designer was doing in Afghanistan." Paul hadn't planned to bring this up, but he decided not to regret it. It would be useful to see how Khan behaved when put off-balance.

He responded with the aplomb of a well-coached judicial nominee. "I went to Afghanistan six months ago on ROI's behalf," he said. "We were competing to build the new American embassy there. We didn't get it — not much of a surprise if you know ROI's work at all. But I was glad to have the chance to see a country that's become so important to America," he finished smoothly.

"Then you'll care about how important this memorial is to America," Paul said, and with more urgency: "You won't want to tear your country apart."

"Of course I don't want to tear it apart."

"Then — it's hard to see how this plays out any other way. If you persist."

"Are you saying what I think you're saying?"

"I'm not saying anything but what I said.

129

I'm not saying anything except that I don't know why anyone who loves America, wants it to heal, would subject it to the kind of battle the selection of a Muslim would cause. Think of Solomon's baby."

"Shouldn't you be making that point to the people gearing up for battle? I've done nothing but design a garden."

"And they've done nothing but lose husbands, wives, children, parents."

"So that gives them the moral high ground?"

"Some might say so, yes." Paul gave a wintry smile and turned to summon the waiter.

"I could change my name," Khan said, when Paul had finished ordering coffee.

"Many architects have," Paul said. "Mostly Jewish ones."

"It was a joke."

"My great-grandfather — he was Rubinsky, then my grandfather comes to America and suddenly he's Rubin. What's in a name? Nothing, everything. We all self-improve, change with the times."

"It's a little more complicated than that, picking a name that hides your roots, your origins, your ethnicity."

"Rubin hardly hides anything."

"It reveals less than Rubinsky. Not everyone is prepared to remake themselves to rise in America."

Was Khan implying something about the Jews, their assimilations and aspirations? Edith's comment from the morning came to Paul. "A Muslim country would never let a Jew build its memorial," she said. "Why should we act differently?" Edith had a habit of voicing all the sentiments Paul never would, as if his more illiberal self had taken up residence in his apartment with him.

"This isn't a Muslim country, Edith. We're better than that. We can't deny him just for being Muslim," he had said, even though that was his plan.

"Daniel Pearl paid a much higher price for being a Jew," she replied with airy un-assailability.

Khan raised his arm. Paul flinched, then realized Khan was merely calling for the check. Paul had the disquieting sense that he had set something new in motion without meaning to. Whatever kind of Muslim Khan was, he would leave as an angry one.

Paul arrived home ill-disposed toward his next appointment, a long-scheduled meeting with his eldest son, Jacob. He had tried to postpone. Edith wouldn't hear of it.

These meetings were ostensibly planned

131

for father and son to "catch up," but really so Jacob, a mendicant with baby-soft palms, could ask for more money. Paul timed these interchanges so they wouldn't overlap with meals. He hated the pretense of familial affection when dollars were being discussed.

Jacob called himself a filmmaker, but his films — three shorts, one feature-length that had made a few marginal festivals, then gone straight to DVD — were not ones Paul, or Paul's friends, had heard of. Calling yourself an artist did not make you one. He was tired of financing Jacob, but Edith was always pestering him, relentless, and Paul knew they must conspire in back-channel conversations to keep the checks coming. Edith was stiff-spined, except when it came to her son.

Paul's dispersals to Jacob left mere pockmarks in his fortune, but the presumption that there would always be more silted the flow of his generosity. To make matters worse, Jacob wore a tetchy air of mild resentment that Paul couldn't begin to understand. He was forty and his father was bankrolling him; what could he possibly feel aggrieved about? He pushed unrealized potential before him like a baby carriage. Before investing in his son Paul had studied the economics of the film business. It was rare for independent films to make real money, and Jacob, in his black leather jacket (always the same well-cut fit and always replaced whenever it began to wear), prided himself on his anticommercialism. That meant, barring some stroke of success that his talent, so far, did not seem to herald, he would be on Paul's dole for life. Fatherhood gave less, not more, pleasure through the years, which perhaps explained why his friends mooned over their grandchildren: the chance to start over. Having, as yet, no grandchildren of his own, he was left with his sons, grown, along with all the usual ways, in their capacity to disappoint.

Paul's younger son, Samuel, was a go-getter, at least. He ran a prominent gay rights organization and had been featured on the cover of *New York* magazine as one of 40 Under 40 New Yorkers to Watch. Paul did not object to his sexual preference; he had read up enough, when Samuel came out, to convince himself both that homosexuality was immutable and that he as the father was not to blame. But he hated having it flaunted, hated the endless stream of interchangeable young men brought to Passover and Thanksgiving. "You want me to live like I'm straight," Samuel had accused him once. This was exactly right. Paul couldn't quite surmount his perplexity that it was Jacob who was the washout.

When Paul entered his office, seeing the back of Jacob's curly head brought on a familiar, unwilled coldness. They shook hands. Jacob had a tan, or, more accurately, a salmon glow in his usually pale face. "Been traveling?" Paul asked, pretending to study some mail.

"Just a brief vacation," Jacob said, his shoulders hunching slightly.

"Vacation," Paul repeated. "Must be nice."

Jacob made no reply, so Paul asked after his wife, an unsettlingly gorgeous Taiwanese American.

"Bea's great. So what are you going to do, Dad?"

"About — ?" Paul said curtly, although he knew. He was touched, since Jacob rarely inquired about Paul's own stresses, then sour: it took something this sensational to make him inquire.

"The memorial, of course."

"What would you do in my shoes, Jacob? If it's true?"

"Give it to him. Or her: I told Bea I think it's Zaha Hadid." No response. "Whoever it is, if they won, they won."

Like the simple son at the Passover seder, Paul thought. "So what are we here for today?" he asked. Jacob began to talk about his new film — something about a woman who takes her nine-year-old son on a journey to Laos. Laos sounded expensive.

"You know, Dad, the woman who was a minor character in *Exiled*? And she got pregnant? This is her child!" The content of his speech could not bear the weight of his excited tone, and this, Paul concluded, was what made Jacob a poor salesman: he had no sense of when to modulate, no care for how his audience received him. This judgment, Paul knew, was also a dodge for his own guilt: he had missed the screening of *Exiled* for a dinner at Gracie Mansion in honor of the governor, when he was trying to secure his jury chairmanship. Later he had dozed, bored and confused, through the film at home, waking only for the credits, where he saw his name as executive producer, an acknowledgment of the money lost to this folly. He had sent Jacob a note dictated by Edith commending the "originality and passion" of *Exiled,* but today he was distracted, his caution frayed. "I think I slept through that part," he said, unthinking, gruff — even, he realized in retrospect, snide.

Two spots of deep red glowed in Jacob's cheeks, and Paul saw him as a stricken boy seeking comfort after being wounded by some insult at school. But his own father had done the wounding. Perhaps, Paul thought, parenting meant protecting children until they were strong enough to sustain the hurt their parents inflicted.

"I'm —" No, he wouldn't apologize. "I'm tired," he said. "I have a lot going on." Jacob opened and closed his mouth but said nothing. This silence, this failure to speak, only diminished Paul's respect.

"How much do you need?" he asked, wanting the business done.

"Four hundred," Jacob mumbled, the thousands not needing spelling out. The amount was high, and Paul half hoped that Jacob had been quick enough in hurt to raise it. He couldn't help comparing his son, and not favorably, to Mohammad Khan.

8

How could you be dead if you did not exist? Of the forty Bangladeshis reported missing to their consulate in the days after the attack, only twenty-six were legal, and Asma Anwar's husband was not among them. The undocumented also had to be uncounted, officials insisted. The consulate could not abet illegals, even posthumously. They were very sorry about Inam, "if indeed he had existed" rolling off their tongues as often as *Insh'Allah,* but they could do nothing about repatriating the body, if it were found, or helping with funds for the widow.

The subcontractor who had employed Inam as a janitor argued similarly: there was no Inam Haque, since he had taken the job using a fake name and Social Security number. The subcontractor had insisted on this pretense of legality, but now used it as an excuse to deny Asma help. "He paid real taxes," she kept telling Nasruddin, the

137

"mayor" of Little Dhaka, as their Brooklyn neighborhood was called, even though its people mostly came from Sandwip. "Doesn't that count for something?"

Nasruddin just shook his head. He had lived in Brooklyn for longer than Asma, who was only twenty-one, had been alive. In that time, people said, his face had barely aged — though his stomach had swelled, like a very slow-gestating pregnancy. He made his living overseeing a crew of Bangladeshis who remodeled and maintained the dozen Brooklyn brownstones owned by an Irish American butcher. But his real energy went to tending his community, smoothing its way through green card applications and business licenses, public schools and hospitals, real estate negotiations, marriages and divorces, arrests and fines for trash on the sidewalk and double-parking. His English was excellent, his fairness unquestioned. Inam had worked for him and had been safe under his wing. Nasruddin had counseled him against taking the job in Manhattan — it was like another country. But Asma had insisted, believing that to work in the towers, so much taller than the brownstones of Brooklyn, suggested Inam and she were moving higher, too. With what vanity she had imagined this news crossing the sea.

Nasruddin never spoke of her misjudgment; he didn't need to.

He had brought her the news; perhaps this was why he became her protector. Eight months pregnant, she was dozing in her room when she heard frantic knocking on the door of their landlords, the Mahmouds. Mrs. Mahmoud, who had been on the phone all morning, put the receiver down, waddled to the door, and opened it to a panting Nasruddin. He was wearing his work overalls.

By now Asma had lumbered out.

"Has Inam called?" Nasruddin asked.

Mrs. Mahmoud was the owner not just of the viewless room they rented but of the phone they relied on. "No," she said. She looked back over her shoulder at the cupboards, as if Inam might be hiding inside.

Nasruddin looked at Asma and said, too formally, "Please sit." He waited until she was arranged on the couch, her swollen feet propped on a plush footstool by Mrs. Mahmoud.

"The buildings have fallen," he said, and she knew.

In the haze that followed, Asma gave statements about Inam's work, his schedule, his habits, his history, to consular officials, investigators hired by Inam's employer, the police, the FBI, and the American Red Cross. She received all of these visitors and promptly forgot them, attuned only to an inner world of fragile and unpredictable rhythms. She caressed her distended belly compulsively, measuring her own life from kick to kick. Never had she prayed so deeply, never had she felt the contrast between the tranquillity within prayer and the disturbance outside so strongly. Her belly was far too big for her to bend, but she trusted God to sense her prostration.

Like Inam, Asma was in America illegally. All of this official attention, she was sure, would end with her deportation. Resigned to this, she held only two hopes: that she give birth first, so that her child would be an American citizen, and that Inam's body be found, so the three of them could fly home together. In the meantime she subsisted on money from the mosque's Widows and Orphans Fund, to which Inam had always contributed, and on the generosity of the Mahmouds. "Stay for as long as you need to, for free," Mrs. Mahmoud said, knowing that Asma would soon return to Bangladesh.

When the baby came, Asma studied him, looking for Inam. Everyone said he was there, in the boy, "a perfect copy," in Mrs. Mahmoud's words, as though he had been made in a garment factory. But Inam's face, though gentle, had been long and sallow. This baby had the vitality of Asma's own father: the big eyes, the dark brows, the round face, the warm-hued skin. Even his reflexively gesticulating arms brought her father's storytelling to mind. She looked harder for Inam, feeling it important to find him there. A perfect copy.

She named him Abdul Karim, Servant of the Most Generous. She hoped God would safeguard him. At night she huddled with him beneath thin blankets in an under-heated apartment and whispered stories. She told him how she had suggested Inam as a groom to her parents, after her bad habit of opening her mouth at every meeting with prospective in-laws had doomed three other matches. Inam was six years older, his family poorer, but she couldn't be picky. She remembered, vaguely, from childhood, his face being kind. He lived in America, and she wanted to live there, too. Her father she informed that she wouldn't, like most wives, stay in Sandwip, pregnant, under her in-laws' thumbs, waiting for her husband to return once a year. She would go, too. To her surprise Inam agreed.

When they spoke by phone — Inam in Brooklyn, she still in Sandwip — he was so quiet that she had to fill the silences herself. Their marriage had been much the same. But she missed his stillness. She hadn't realized how much it soothed her.

Gold seal, black letters: the death certificate arrived. The Bangladesh consulate acknowledged Inam as one of theirs and provided Asma with a small stipend. With the help of a Jewish lawyer who had made the undocumented relatives his cause, Nasruddin got the subcontractor who had employed Inam to fork over a small amount, too. Three months passed, then six, without a body or even a piece of one. Abdul learned to turn over, and the unspoken question grew louder: When would Asma go home? "They are saying some of the bodies may never be found," Mrs. Mahmoud said bluntly one day. "They were cremated."

Were her words meant to sting? Cremation was anathema to Muslims. God had forbidden the use of fire on His Creation, or so Asma had been taught. Then why had God allowed these men to cremate her husband — and claim to have cremated him in God's name, no less? Where would Inam's soul go? Would this leave him outside paradise? The next morning, when she heard the Mahmouds leave, she crept to their phone and called the local imam. It was easier to frame her questions without having to face him. She could picture his eyes blinking behind his glasses, the sparse beard that always made her think of a fire struggling to light.

Why did my husband suffer so? she asked.

"It was written," he said, as she knew he would. The burning Inam might have suffered was nothing next to the torment of the hellfire, which was forever, the cleric continued. If Inam was a believer, she could rest easy — he was in the garden now. His pain here had been momentary; his bliss would be everlasting.

She had no doubt that Inam had been taken into the gardens of paradise. He gave zakat. He always fasted during Ramadan. He prayed, if not five times a day, as often as he could. The morning of his death, lying in bed with her eyes closed, pretending to sleep, too lazy and heavy with child to get up and cook him breakfast, leaving him to the cold dal she had prepared the night before, she had heard the rustling as he prostrated himself. He believed.

And yet the knowledge that he would gain paradise failed to give her the peace or joy that signaled submission to God's will. Fearful of what the scratching in her chest signaled instead, she prayed to feel peace.

Why did Inam have to die? she asked the imam, knowing this question was not hers to ask. She had the urge to keep him on the phone, string out the conversation. The imam quoted a sura: "No soul may die except with God's permission at a predestined time." God was all-pervading, all-knowing, he said, "the creator, owner, and master of the universe. We cannot question His destruction; we are His Creation to deal with as He chooses."

His words — words she had heard, in one form or another, her whole life — now made God sound like a rich man free to reward or punish His servants as He chose. These thoughts made her ashamed, even apologetic toward God. Yet she persisted in her questions. The men who killed Inam believed it was an act of devotion, one that would get them to paradise, she told the imam. Everyone said so. They believed they were fighting for God, and the Quran promised those who did so a great reward. How could the same paradise make room for both them and her husband?

"God knows best," he said. But I want to know, too, she thought. Faith for her had always been something like an indestructible building. Now she had spotted a loose brick whose removal could topple the whole structure, and her hand hovered near it, tempted, afraid.

And yet it was God, the greatest of plotters, whom she believed would decide her fate. Or maybe He already had. She expected to be deported; she hadn't been. She planned to leave when Inam's body was found; it hadn't been. One day she realized the wait had become a pretext. Clinging to the thin thread of hope for his body's recovery also let her hold on to the entire imaginary American future Inam had woven for their unborn son. Even after spending six years earning a degree from Chittagong University, Inam couldn't get a job in Bangladesh unless he was willing to buy one. With hundreds vying for every opening in the civil service or a private company, the positions went to the highest bidder. He wasn't willing, but even if he were, how could he earn the money to buy a job when he didn't have a job to begin with? It would be different for their son, Inam always said. She determined to make it so. Kensington had such a high concentration of Bangladeshis that she could meet all of her needs for food, clean-

145

ing supplies, medicine, and clothing without uttering a word of English (and could make no move that was not fully vetted in Bengali). But she couldn't stay without money, and the amounts doled out to her wouldn't keep her and Abdul for long.

God is the greatest of plotters. One day Nasruddin took her to see a lawyer who wanted to help Asma receive compensation from the government for Inam's death. All the legal relatives of the dead were getting compensation, so there was no reason Asma shouldn't as well. And if she truly wanted to stay in America and raise her son, Nasruddin told her, she needed to do this.

The lawyer, he said, was an Iranian American. A Muslim, but unlike any Muslim Asma knew. Her dark hair, unlike Asma's, was uncovered. The skirt of her snug-fitting turquoise suit struck just above the knee. Her pale legs were bare; her heels, which matched her suit, high. Her lips were painted the color of a plum. Asma would have liked to ask her questions all day, most of them having nothing to do with the attack, but Laila Fathi had no time. Her words came fast; her phones rang often; her calendar, which sat open at her elbow, was full.

Asma herself had never kept a calendar,

never needed to: even after the attack, she relied on Nasruddin to call the day before — or even that morning — and tell her they had an appointment. In Sandwip the passage of time was calendared by events, not dates, and so were her memories: the harvesting of summer paddy, autumn paddy, winter paddy; the arrival of the first mangoes; school holidays and religious ones — the sighting of the crescent moon at Ramadan's beginning and end. The two Eids. Election time, a season of violence. Schedules, back home, were provisional. Appointments made were often not kept. People were delayed by poor roads, flat rickshaw tires, gasoline shortages, or simply conversations that stretched on. In America time was gold; in Bangladesh, corrugated tin.

Laila was like a baffling dream, which made it hard to concentrate on what she, in Nasruddin's translation, was saying. The politicians had agreed, after some months of arguing, to compensate illegal aliens who had lost relatives in the attack. Nasruddin and Laila wanted her to meet the man from the government who was distributing the funds. It would be a way to assure Abdul the future her husband had wanted.

Walk right into the government's arms? Were they crazy? She did not believe any country could be that generous.

"It must be a trick," Asma said, "a way to find illegals and deport us."

Laila said that the government had promised that no information obtained through this process would be shared with immigration officials. "Believe me, I would never expose you to any kind of danger," she said. "But that doesn't mean that if you come to the government's attention some other way — getting arrested, for example — they can't deport you, so I'd avoid contact with the police."

"Will they put in writing that this is not a trick?" Asma asked, impressed by her own shrewdness. Laila's smile suggested that she was impressed, too.

In the end Asma was persuaded by her faith in Nasruddin. The three of them worked on her claim, trying to estimate what Inam's income over time would have been. Asma walked into the meeting with the government man shaking with fear, scrutinized his face for deceit, and walked out with $1.05 million for the lifetime loss of her husband's earnings. She knew it could not have been simple, but for her it was. Just like that, she was a millionaire, although once Nasruddin did the math for her, showing how that money would have to sustain Abdul until his adulthood, and her for perhaps her whole life, she saw how careful with her dollars she would have to be.

And how careful with herself, for she wasn't just a millionaire but a secret one. Government largesse had made her rich; government fiat kept her illegal. She had the money to fly to Bangladesh and back a hundred times, but she couldn't leave America because she might not be allowed back in. There were other relatives of the dead like her, Laila said — relatively well-off, illegal — but Asma did not know how many or who they were. Maybe they passed on the street every day, each of them hiding alone in the dark, fearful that the glimmer from their piles of gold would give them away. God wove a spiderweb to hide Mohammad, sheltering in a cave, from his pursuers. If He wanted to protect her, He would.

There was another reason Nasruddin counseled discretion: he didn't want the community catching on to her newfound wealth or sending word of it back to Bangladesh. Someone could turn her in to the immigration authorities. Relatives back home could be kidnapped and held for ransom. The money had to stay hidden like a new roll of fat beneath her clothes. So even as financial advisers picked by Laila Fathi invested Asma's million, she still lived like she was poor.

The most incremental increase in her spending attracted Mrs. Mahmoud's notice. "You bought brinjal?" she sniffed when eggplants had gone up nine cents a pound. Or "Celebrating, are we?" when Asma, trying to return Mrs. Mahmoud's all-too-frequent hospitality, offered her some chocolates wrapped in purple foil. They had cost $2.20. Asma told the Mahmouds that the subcontractor had given her a little more money and she planned to stay in America. Their evident displeasure soon yielded to pity. Asma needed to make her money last as long as possible, they said. She would stay with them and pay only fifty dollars a month for her room. To accept felt dishonest, when she could pay more, but Asma saw no choice. Maybe listening to Mrs. Mahmoud talk could be a form of payment.

The status of her dead husband remained as provisional as her own. Nasruddin told her there was to be a memorial to the victims, but that an anti-immigrant group wanted Inam and other illegal immigrants left off it. To include them, the group claimed, would condone their "law-breaking" and make them equivalent to citizens. The prospect of her husband's exclusion gnawed at Asma. It would be the final repudiation of his existence — as if he had lived only in her imagination. He had to be named, for in that name was a life.

When the anti-immigrant group held a small protest near city hall, she and the Mahmouds watched it on the local news. Mr. Mahmoud translated. The angry man being cheered by the crowd, he explained, was a popular radio talk-show host, Lou Sarge, who had become ever more popular by assailing Islam. He frightened Asma, with his skin too white and hair too black.

"Respect for the law is what makes America, America," Sarge roared. "If we put illegals on the memorial, we will be spitting in the face of the law-abiding Americans, including legal immigrants, who died. The illegal immigrants who died came here seeking opportunity, but if they had stayed home they would still be alive. Isn't that the greatest opportunity of all?"

Asma ground her fists into the sofa cushions, furious that there was no one to speak for her husband, for the army of workers who cleaned and cooked and bowed and scraped and when the day came died as if it were just another way to please. But the next day, the mayor said he thought all of the dead, illegal or not, should be listed, and soon the governor and the chairman of the memorial jury agreed. Inam would take his place as a permanent resident on whatever memorial came to be. But she couldn't shake the sense, like the shudder after a near-accident in a Chittagong bus, that history had only narrowly made room for him.

9

Mo stood in the lobby of the God Box, a name that reflected both the building's shape and the dizzying array of religious organizations it housed. The Muslim American Coordinating Council — MACC — was one of three Islamic groups listed on the directory, along with five Jewish committees and a dozen Christian ones that ranged from mainline Protestants to evangelical missionaries. It reminded him of a ribbon shredded into narrower and narrower strands.

He had never heard of MACC and its executive director, Issam Malik, until he had watched that televised debate on Fox with Yuki. At the time, Malik had struck Mo as the slick front man for a special interest, even if that interest happened to be Mo's own. But in the wake of his meeting with Paul, Mo reconsidered. Perhaps Malik was the man to make the case that Mo had the same right as any other American to win. He had decided, in that French fun house of a restaurant where he'd met Rubin, that he would not give in to pressure to withdraw, nor would he reassure anyone that he was "moderate" or "safe" or Sufi, whatever adjective would allow Americans to sleep without worrying that he had placed a bomb under their pillow. It was exactly because they had nothing to worry about from him that he wanted to let them worry.

The walls of MACC's third-floor suite were covered with framed posters from the ad campaign that the council had launched in subways and newspapers right after the attack. "Safeguard us and we'll safeguard you" had been the motto, its image two giant hands clasping. At the time Mo had considered it misguided — threatening in a way he was sure they hadn't intended; naïve in proposing to strike a bargain when Americans were in anything but a bargaining mood. As he wandered down the hall, the clasped hands brought to mind Issam Malik, who in photo after photo was shown gripping the hands of governors, mayors, movie stars, even the president, as if locking them all into agreement.

Mo found Malik on the phone behind the prow of a huge V-shaped desk afloat in a vast office. *"Asalamu alaikum,"* he said, hanging up the phone. Three televisions flickered — CNN, MSNBC, Fox News — but all were on mute. Three remotes were lined up neatly on the desk.

"How's it going," Mo muttered.

Malik rose and came around the desk to shake hands. His grip was firm. He was as well groomed and well built as he had appeared on television. But shorter.

Mo had cold-called him, feeling like a fugitive wanting to turn himself in. "I'm the Muslim," he'd said when he finally got Malik on the phone. And, when Malik didn't get it: "The Mystery Muslim. The memorial."

"Ohhh," Malik had said. "Wow."

The gleam that had been in Malik's voice then was in his eyes now. He led Mo into a room where MACC's executive committee had assembled. The council was an umbrella organization for assorted Muslim groups, some political, some theological, others legal. The group was striking in its diversity: South Asians, African Americans, Arabs; bearded men and clean-shaven, in suits and in djellabas; two women in headscarves and one — striking and black-haired in an aubergine suit — without. Mo's eyes lingered on her dark eyes, full lips, and prominent

155

but appealing nose, and registered a nod that suggested conditional approval.

At Malik's request, Mo recounted his story. "I sympathize," an older man, who had introduced himself as Imam Rashid, responded immediately. "You tried to do the right thing — make a gesture of reconciliation. After the attack, I went to the site. I volunteered. I got other imams to do the same. Then the FBI put an informant in my mosque."

"Allah will reward you," said another. "You've done something good for the *ummah,* to show that Muslims want to live in peace in America."

"But does America want to live in peace with Muslims?" a man named Ansar, who ran a foreign-policy lobby, asked in a more challenging tone. "Since we're talking about memorials, where is the memorial to the half-million Iraqi children killed by U.S. sanctions? To the thousands of innocent Afghans killed in response to this attack, or the Iraqis killed on the pretext of responding to this attack? Or to all the Muslims slaughtered in Chechnya, or Kashmir, or Palestine, while the U.S. stood by? We keep hearing that it takes three hours to read the names of the dead from this attack. Do you know how long it would take to read the names of half a million dead Iraqi children? Twenty-one *days*."

"We're far afield," Malik murmured.

"No, this is the field," Ansar said. "The attack here becomes no less tragic if we acknowledge these other tragedies and demand equal time, equal care for them. They say that when you watch the movies, you root for the cowboys, but when you read the history, you root for the Indians. Americans are locked in a movie theater watching Westerns right now, and we've got to break down the walls."

"I'm an architect, not a politician," Mo said, hoping to redirect the conversation. "And I'm an American, so it was the attack on America I was moved to commemorate. The Afghans, the Iraqis, the others you mentioned — they are free to design their own memorials."

"It's hard to think about memorials when you're under occupation or bombardment," Ansar said.

"We can't ask Mohammad to carry water for every Muslim cause, or country," Laila Fathi, the bareheaded woman, said. Her voice had a lilting quality that Mo suspected made people underestimate her. "Right now, he is the cause. If they take away his victory, which is clearly what they want to do, or if his opponents pressure them into taking it away, the message is that we're lesser Americans."

"We are lesser Americans," a man in a djellaba said. "Eid is not a school holiday."

Malik turned on him. "Do you have to bring that up at every meeting?"

"As a matter of fact I do, until it changes. I'm guessing Mohammad doesn't want to speak out on that issue, either."

"I'm basically secular," Mo said.

A woman in a tightly wrapped beige head-scarf looked at him curiously, then raised her hand. This was Jamilah Maqboul, MACC's vice president. "I just wonder if we have considered whether Mr. Khan's battle is productive — or constructive — for the Muslim community. He's shown no interest, here at least, in taking on issues that matter to Muslims. All he's done is remind us that he's not particularly inter-ested in Islam — that he's not political, that he's secular."

"Exactly," Ansar said. "Do we use our limited capital to fight for his right to design a memorial that, by ignoring the far greater death toll in the Muslim world from Ameri-can actions, obscures America's complicity in its own tragedy?"

"All the while picking an unnecessary fight

158

with the families of victims, a constituency we gain nothing from offending," Jamilah added.

"This is about amassing capital, not squandering it," Malik said. "We're just starting to see the polarization from this, and to be blunt that's when you need to rally your base, do fund-raising, make the apolitical majority of our brothers and sisters realize that their rights are at stake, that they need to organize, and that they need us to defend them. The media attention allows us to talk about other issues that impact Muslims. And how can we ignore the Islamophobia this has touched off?"

"He won," Laila Fathi said. "And if this organization is just going to sit back and leave him twisting in the wind like some . . . some piñata for people to take whacks at, then this isn't the organization for me."

Mo saw looks pass among some of the men.

"This is how history works," Malik picked up. "Cases — battles — emerge from unexpected places. Rosa Parks was tired. Mohammad Khan was inspired." He paused. "Tired, inspired. Not a bad slogan."

"But that story's not true, about her just being tired. She was chosen to be the face of a movement," said Aisha, an African

159

American woman, also in a headscarf.

"You all can work out the historical verities," Malik said. Having checked his watch and his BlackBerry, he was all business now. "As you can see, Mohammad, we favor healthy debate here. All in favor of taking on Mohammad's case, please raise your hand."

Seven of the twelve hands went up. Jamilah hesitated, then raised hers.

"Excellent," Malik said. "We have a two-thirds majority. Now we need a strategy. Laila, can you walk us through the options on the legal front?"

She was brief and to the point. Their best bet, she said, was to create the fear of a lawsuit without actually filing one. Mo, she said, should publicly identify himself as the winner, which would force the jury's hand. "You have a press conference, introduce me to imply the legal threat, or maybe have me take the questions —"

"I don't think that's the right approach," Ansar said.

"We should have the committee leadership — Issam, Jamilah — up there, or people will mistake Ms. Fathi for the face of MACC," Imam Rashid said.

An awkward, even unpleasant, mood had taken hold in the room. Mo looked at Laila.

She was studying, too intently, her notes.

"I think it's an excellent idea," he said. "Ms. Fathi will answer all the questions for me." She compressed her lips. Mo couldn't tell if she was pleased.

"The committee should be up there," Imam Rashid said. "Issam?"

The meeting broke up soon after, and Mo managed to walk out with Laila. "What was going on in there between you and them?" His much longer legs had to work to keep pace with hers.

"Which of these things is not like the other."

"I don't get it."

"You didn't notice I was the only uncovered woman in there? It's a big deal for me to even be in that room. Those other women fought for seats on the council, and they couldn't have won if they weren't wearing the hijab. I'm new. Malik got me in there because I've been getting high-profile cases involving Muslims. Because I'm good. But it's tense, as you noticed."

"So why bother with them? They don't seem focused — that guy droning on about the Iraqis."

"I'm a solo practitioner. They can send cases my way. They publicize what I do. They lobby for my issues. The law is politi-

161

cal, especially right now. If the government wants to find a way to forget the Constitution and detain people without charges, it will. Just as they will deny your memorial if they want."

"Not with you on my side."

She ignored this. "As for Ansar, he's annoying but he's not wrong. Not about the history of our foreign policy, not about how many Muslim civilians we've killed since the attack because of what was done to us or what *might* be done to us. We barely even pretend anymore that we're trying to spread good in the world; it's only about protecting us because we *are* good."

"I guess I've stumbled into something bigger than I realized."

"You don't strike me as a stumbler," Laila said.

Maybe it was a coincidence, but the week the jury learned Mohammad Khan's name, Claire's son, William, dreamed that his father couldn't find his way home. The nightmare came night after night, in black harmony with Claire's tension over the memorial. After soothing William to sleep yet again, she poured a glass of wine and tried to think how Cal would have comforted him.

The air was sharp, the grass dew-beaded, when she took the children outside early the next morning. Collect the stones, she told them, pointing to the dozens that bordered the flower beds, spiraled in the close-cropped grass, edged the paths to the pool and tennis court. She and Cal had scavenged them on trips to beaches, woods, mountains. Lavender, pale mint, coal black, veined, smooth, striated, glitter-traced, dull as mud. River-polished, sandpaper-rough, dagger-sharp.

"Do you remember what Daddy showed you when you went hiking?" she asked William. "About how to find your way home when you were lost?"

William shook his head no, and she nearly screamed at the speed of his forgetting. But he hadn't even been four when Cal took him to the Catskills. She crouched and stacked some stones into a little pile. "You put a pile on the trail so you remember which way you came. Then, a little farther on, you put another one, then another. Just like the bread crumbs in Hansel and Gretel, but no animals will eat them."

William nodded and repeated the explanation to Penelope. "Animals don't like stones," he said. "They don't taste good."

Penelope put one in her mouth.

163

"No school today!" Claire announced. "We're going to make a trail for Daddy."

The idea was pure Cal — impulsive, creative. Before they set out, the word for the piles came to her, and she double-checked the dictionary. "Cairn: a heap of stones piled up as a memorial or as a landmark." The memorial part she didn't tell William. Let him pretend he was bringing his father home, just as she was pretending the whole city wasn't consumed with another, more consequential memorial.

She checked the news briefly before they left. On NY1 a reporter was interviewing, yet again, Sean Gallagher, founder of the Memorial Support Committee. His chin jutted out like an Indian arrowhead. "It's like being stabbed in the heart to hear that a Muslim could build this, stabbed in the heart," he said. "We want that message to go out to the jury loud and clear."

He thought he should have been on that jury, Claire knew — he had argued so to the governor herself. But he was volatile, even aggressive, and so it had been constituted without him. The families stood behind him because he promised to yell on their behalf. Yet for the same reason he would never reach the precincts of real power, whose denizens knew to whisper.

164

They hadn't spoken since the news of the Muslim winning. This made her nervous, but Paul had told her to hold off calling family members, Sean or others, until he came up with a plan.

She and the children drove into the city and had the nanny wait nearby with the car. Their first stop was near the attack site but not within sight of it. The children she took there only on the anniversary, when people and pomp camouflaged the barrenness. Now, especially, William's vividly imagined garden needed safeguarding.

They placed three stones at the base of a lamppost and stepped back. William began to cry. Without knowing why, Penelope joined him.

"What's wrong? What's wrong?" Claire stooped to their level.

"It's too small," William wept. "He won't see it."

The hapless pile did look meager — disappointing — against the city's vertical thrust. So did the three of them, for that matter.

"Well then, we'll make the pile bigger," she said, balancing three more stones on top.

She hustled them north: SoHo, Fourteenth Street and Sixth Avenue, Madison Square Park, Times Square (William inexplicably insisted on the military recruiting station), Central Park (the Turtle Pond, the Sheep Meadow, Strawberry Fields). There was something enjoyably illicit in making these tiny, easily missed interventions in the city. The few people who slowed enough to notice them smiled at the children, thinking it a game. When William and Penelope began squabbling over which stones to use where, Claire started to say "It won't work if you fight," then caught herself.

At lunch, William and Penelope giggled as they stacked their fries into cairns. Claire was, to her shame, bored of the game, and anxious. The nonstop calls on her phone had gone to voice mail like ballots into a box. The tally, she knew from checking her messages, was almost unanimous: the families were opposed to the Muslim, as they called him. When the phone rang again, on impulse she answered.

"Claire, I just want to tell you, it's like a stab to the heart," a man's voice said. They were all using Gallagher's language; it was tiresome. She couldn't quite place the caller's name, but it didn't matter. "Are you hearing us, Claire? Tell me you're hearing us."

"I hear you," she murmured; the children were in earshot. "I hear you."

Eager to get home, Claire spaced their stops farther apart to hurry the end. They arrived back in Chappaqua amid the long shadows and leaf glow of late afternoon, and began, with improvised ceremony, to place the last pile of stones beneath the gnarled copper beech by the house. At William's dark look, Claire turned off her phone and knelt to bear witness. The children rearranged the stones as if they were perfecting a haiku.

Sean was listing all of the relatives' and first responders' associations represented in the high-school auditorium when the families before him broke into outsize applause. Governor Bitman was striding across the stage toward him, her hair burnished by the theatrical lights. "This is a surprise" was all he had time to say before she had one manicured hand on his back and the other easing the microphone from his grip.

"I'm here today so you know you have my support," she said, speaking with practiced empathy. Her arm casually slid off of Sean so she could clutch the microphone with both hands. A tiny American flag pin glinted from the lapel of her forest-green pantsuit. "My goal is — has always been — a memorial the families, especially, can embrace.

It's all you have."

Sean knew that most of those present hadn't voted for Bitman, who was a Democrat. But their applause now promised they would. Having taken office less than a year before the attack, she'd been publicly stalwart in its wake, donning a mask to visit the site, air-kissing her way through hundreds of firefighters' funerals. And now she was here, with them.

"We can't take this away from the jury," she continued. "We have to respect the process. But the process includes public input, and that allows us to expand the jury to include all of you — to include all Americans, if necessary. We're going to have a public hearing on this design, so if you don't like it, go to the hearing and say so."

"What if we don't like the designer?" Sean said. "I'm sorry to interrupt, Governor, but that's why we're all here today."

"Not liking the designer is not a legitimate objection, I'm afraid." When he started to speak again she held up a "let me finish" hand. "But I think it's safe to say that if you don't like the designer, you're probably not going to like his design." She smiled. The crowd roared.

"Before I go I just want to thank Sean Gallagher for leading the fight for this memorial," the governor said. "He's showing the same bravery as those who gave their lives that fateful day."

Sean reddened. He didn't need to see his parents' faces to read their scorn. He couldn't even pretend that he would have been as brave as Patrick if given the chance: faced with a building pouring fire and smoke, he would have run away as fast as he could. Nor was he sure this would have been wrong. Patrick had charged into a building that pancaked almost immediately on top of him, and he'd left three sad-eyed children behind.

The governor took Sean's hand and raised it high and from somewhere a rock 'n' roll version of "America the Beautiful" began to play. Then, with the air seeming to slosh like water in her wake, she was gone.

With his microphone back, Sean tried to reclaim his audience's attention. He began to pace. "You know, the night they picked the memorial, the jurors were up at Gracie Mansion, drinking Dom Pérignon. And they find out they picked a Muslim, and they say, 'Wow, that's terrific, what a message that will send to Muslims, that we're their friend, that we have nothing against Islam, because what did Islam ever do to us?' " Knowing, bitter laughter rose from the

169

seats. "And the families? They need to just get over it. Even our supposed family member on the jury — Claire Burwell — hasn't reached out to us."

That this was particularly bitter for him, he didn't say. Knowing that Sean's support would be crucial for whatever memorial they picked, Claire had cultivated him. His awareness of this only partly diminished its effect. After one of the meetings between the jury and various family members, she invited Sean, who had been outspoken as usual, for a beer. When he said he didn't drink, she seemed slightly thrown, as if she had counted on booze to bond them. She ordered a beer anyway, sipped it as if it was wine, and plied Sean with questions. He was awed by her beauty, her wealth, her intelligence; he'd never met a woman with so many advantages. At the end of the night — two beers for her, three jittery-making Cokes for him — he leaned and planted a kiss on her just to prove he could. She didn't resist, simply withstood it, taut, even then wanting to keep his goodwill. His self-respect would have done better with being shoved. She had a decade on him, she said; his youth was better spent elsewhere. He'd spend it where he wanted, he told her.

That had been the end of any actual physical contact, but only the beginning of the pretend kind. Over the succeeding months he projected Claire like a movie onto the ceiling of his bedroom, where he'd once tacked posters of Victoria's Secret models on the fifty-fifty bet his mother wouldn't look up. He undressed her like his nieces' paper dolls, took her every way he could think of. Her flirting when she did see him couldn't keep up with this fantasy life and so always read like a rebuff. This history — real, imagined — rumbled beneath her failure to call.

"I'm here." A voice sailed from the back of the room. "It's me, Claire Burwell." He located her at the entrance to the auditorium. Another woman stealing his thunder. Claire, clearly maneuvering for the advantage of surprise, hadn't replied to the message he left about the meeting. With resentment he watched her move down the aisle at a deliberate pace.

"Tell us it's not true!" caromed a voice from the dark. Then dozens, shrapnel shredding her: "Is it true? Is it true? Tell us!"

"What happened, Claire?"

"Tell us you'll stop it!"

Half of what she heard had nothing to do with the memorial, as if two years of frustration and grief and anger had found their proper vent.

"Three weeks, the Red Cross said —"

"What they did to us —"

"A Muslim —"

"Protect the airlines who didn't protect us —"

"Counseling every goddamn Friday —"

"They hate us —"

"A big phony —"

"A violent religion —"

Claire, trying to speak, kept getting shouted down and so stopped trying. Her underarms prickled, but she worked at projecting serenity. Sean was prowling the stage with the bounding walk that always made her think of a young man trying to look older, a short one trying to look taller, maybe a poor one trying to look richer. From a distance his eyes looked sleepy, as if they had bedded down on the pillowy pouches beneath, but up close they were quick. Quick to suspect. Which was why, ever since she was picked for the jury, she had tried to be kind to him, if only to appease him. The solicitous phone updates. The regretfully flirtatious smiles (too flirtatious, per that uninvited kiss), suggesting that, if things had been different, if they hadn't met under these circumstances, if, if,

172

if . . . It had been a mistake not to call him once the news broke. She saw that now. She shot him a baiting look as she ascended the stage, suggesting he couldn't control the crowd. As she had hoped, it provoked him into proving he could.

"All right, all right," he said, holding up a hand until he heard silence. "Claire's here, we need to let her talk."

"Thank you, Sean; I'm sorry to be late — I didn't have much notice," she said. I'd just returned home from laying a trail for my dead husband; I had to leave my children, get into decent clothes, drive like a madwoman all the way back down through the city, only to be screamed at by all of you: this she didn't say. "Thank you all for coming today. Your concern for this memorial is very powerful and reinforces what a sacred trust we, as the jury, have. I can't go into much detail, but let me ask: How many of you like gardens?"

Perplexed looks skittered across the audience. "Don't worry, it's not a trick question. Raise your hand if you like gardens. And yes, men, too. My husband wasn't afraid to admit that he loved them."

Slowly hands rose, from the women first, then a good number of the men. When Claire was satisfied by the show of hands, she said, "That's what the memorial is going to be. A garden. It's perfect. A garden."

"What about the Muslim?" Sean said belligerently.

"I can't discuss rumors, and to be honest, I know almost nothing about the designer, since this competition was anonymous. What I do know is the beauty, the power of this design, the way it evokes all of our loved ones, and the buildings, too, so I hope you'll keep an open mind."

"My mind closed toward Muslims the day they killed my brother," Sean said.

"I understand," said Claire. "We've all struggled with that. But if you let them change you, they've won."

"The restrooms — do you know where . . . ?" Claire asked the first person she saw when she got backstage, a woman with short, severe gray hair who seemed to be awaiting her. Her mood was slightly giddy, thanks to the applause when she left the stage. She had made them love the idea of a garden memorial as much as she did.

"I hope you're not trying to fool us," the woman said. A chill ran through Claire.

She mustered a neutral look and said, "Of course not. I want you to know about the memorial. I assume you lost —"

"My son," the woman said. "My first-born."

"I'm so sorry," Claire said, as if she hadn't lost her own husband.

"I don't want your sympathy" — Claire blanched — "I want your vigilance. We don't want a Muslim's memorial, but I think you know that."

"If he won fairly, we can't take it away," Claire said, then instantly regretted it. She had just confirmed Khan's selection when Paul had told her not to. There was something about the woman — a moral astringency — that begged both confession and challenge.

"So he did win."

"The Garden won," Claire said. "That's what matters. What the memorial will be. That's what matters."

A muscle memory of a smile moved the woman's lips. "Sometimes I wish Patrick had died in a regular fire. No firefighter dies a private death, not if he dies on the job. But to have all these politics mixed in — I don't like it, all . . . the noise. Grief should be quiet. A memorial should have the silence of the convent. Maybe it's different losing a husband —"

"I loved my husband," Claire said, with deliberate hauteur.

175

"I didn't say otherwise." That mirthless, mechanical smile again.

Before Claire could respond, Sean came backstage. The meeting had ended.

"Ma," he said, to the woman with Claire.

"It's fine," Mrs. Gallagher said. Her eyes didn't leave Claire, who hadn't thought, in her moment of candor, that she might be speaking to Sean's mother. This magnified, considerably, the import of her mistake. She hadn't lied onstage, exactly, but Mrs. Gallagher would likely hold her to account, just as she must hold Sean. Pleasing his implacable mother, filling the too-big shoes of his dead brother: these were dangerous, impossible goals. The fearsome pressure on him made him more worthy of fear. Her dread built, crows landing one by one in a field.

"I was looking for the restroom," she said, grasping for graceful egress.

"The Muslim's name — can you tell it to me?" she heard. The party had been joined by a reporter — Alyssa Spier. She covered all the memorial events, never seemed especially taken with the hagiography of Claire.

"The jury's deliberations are confidential," Claire said.

"But you talked about the design up there," Sean said.

"Only because of the frenzy around this. What I said up there is true: I know almost nothing about the designer."

"Almost nothing," Alyssa said. "So you know his name."

"Perhaps I wasn't clear. The jury will speak to the press when we're ready to reveal the design," Claire said, feeling Mrs. Gallagher's stare bore into her. Squirming inside, Claire tried to wrest free. "I've got to get home," she said. "My children. Sean, I'll be in touch. Mrs. Gallagher, it was a pleasure to meet you." About to hold out her hand, she stopped herself. It might be refused, which would be awkward. "An open mind," she said. "We can't let them take that from us."

As she picked her way toward the exit, steering clear of theater equipment and set pieces, she realized Alyssa Spier was with her. Claire quickened her pace, only to be followed down halls, around corners, out of the building and into the parking lot. She could hear the footsteps behind her, the panting — the reporter's legs were short — the endless questions: "Mrs. Burwell, what's his name? Is it a him? What's the jury going to do? What's your response to the anger in that auditorium? Mrs. Burwell! Mrs. Burwell!"

Near her car Claire increased her pace, tucked her hand in her purse to locate her keys, pressed the unlock button, twisted into the driver's seat, and slammed the door, praying it didn't catch the reporter's fingers. Spier shouted questions through the window, and when Claire pulled away, Spier was in the rearview mirror, still shouting, although by then she could no longer be heard.

Claire drove up Manhattan in the dark. The wind roughed facets into the black river, its foreboding look coloring Claire's thoughts.

The radio was replaying Governor Bitman's remarks. Now Claire understood why the crowd had been so riled up. But what was Bitman, whose campaigns Cal, then Claire, had donated to, suggesting? She was supposed to rubber-stamp whatever the jury did, or so the jury had been told. Claire saw that, inside and outside the jury, she was fighting alone.

It was after ten when she made it back to Chappaqua. As she walked to the front door from her car, she spotted what looked like a homeless man's encampment beneath the copper beech. Moving closer, she saw, in the milky light cast by house and moon, a box of Raisin Bran ("Daddy's favorite," she had told the children, although she was no longer sure that Cal had loved Raisin Bran, only that saying so got William and Penelope to eat it); a pile of books pillaged from Cal's study; a stray tennis racket; his $2,000 wedding tuxedo — all of it arranged around the cairn. A child's necromancy: William believing he could coax the stones to life, or his father home.

"For all we know some one-eyed, bearded killer wearing pajamas came up with this — that's what's scary," Alyssa had told Lou Sarge on his radio program that morning.

Said killer was now before her, about to reveal his identity to waiting reporters, and he didn't look the part. He had a beard, but it was tastefully trimmed. His suit looked expensive, and his bearing, unlike the grasping, too-eager-to-please Indians in her neighborhood, was haughty. Next to him sat a dark-haired, foreign-looking woman in a cardinal-red suit that suggested she was not only comfortable with attention but craved it. Men, some of them in Islamic costumes, and a few women in headscarves, stood stiffly against the wall behind them, looking like a police lineup of terrorism suspects. Alyssa gnawed her cuticles until she tasted metal. Blood.

She was in the offices of the Muslim American Coordinating Council, an organization she had never heard of until that morning. The entire New York press corps seemed to be crammed in with her. Together, the reporters endured the introduction of all twelve members of the council, who then took their seats.

The main attraction waited for the rustling to die down before holding up the *Post* with the picture of the ski-mask-clad face. "My name is Mohammad Khan, and I believe this is meant to be me." Flashbulbs popped, cameras clicked — for a moment, the only sounds in the room.

"I am an architect and an American," he said. "I also happen to be a Muslim. I was born in Virginia and have lived most of my adult life in New York. In Manhattan. I entered the memorial competition because I believed my idea would provide a way for the families, the nation to mourn and to remember all that was lost that day, and also to heal. Apparently the jury agreed: everyone knows by now they chose my design." He gestured at illustrations of a garden, placed on an easel to his right. "It seems they just have a problem with the designer."

Alyssa scribbled fast, not wanting to miss a word, although her tape recorder was running and she knew his words would be replayed dozens of times on television. It was an exercise in redundancy: there had to be fifty reporters and cameras in here, all itching to report the same news, the same words.

After a pause, Khan continued: "I have been asked to withdraw from the competition, or to remain anonymous rather than have my name associated with the design, or to partner with someone else who could submit under their name. But I will not withdraw, and I will not make any of these accommodations. To do so would be to betray not only myself but this country's credo that merit matters, not name or religion or origins. The jury wanted this design; the designer comes with it. And if now you don't want the design —"

His voice had risen — the tone of impending harangue. "He's looking for a fight," someone near Alyssa whispered. But the woman next to Khan leaned into the microphone with a look at him and said, "The process needs to move forward as it is supposed to, as is spelled out in the guidelines for the memorial selection."

"Who are you?" someone called out.

"My attorney, Laila Fathi," Khan said, calm now. He spent some time discussing his design — some sort of garden, with the names of the dead scrolled on the surrounding walls. The note-taking slowed, the room deflated, the reporters pranced in place. No one cared about the design, Alyssa thought. Didn't he get that?

"Any additional questions can be directed to Ms. Fathi," he said, gesturing at her before rising and heading toward a side door. The order in the room collapsed. A thud in her back jolted Alyssa forward; a fat cameraman shoved by. "Move!" he shouted. Before she could reply she was hit again and again by waves of men gunning for Khan, trampling anyone in the way.

"Fuck!"

"He's over there!"

"Get him!"

"You're in my shot!"

"Motherfucker! That's my bad leg! Motherfucker!"

He was gone. In the stampede the easel had been knocked over, sending the illustrations to the floor. One of them bore the brown imprint of a pixilated rubber sole. "Get a shot of that," Alyssa ordered her photographer. More dramatic than the drawings on the easel — his dream trod upon. Serves him right, she thought, except she wasn't sure if it was her thought at all or her imagination of what her readers thought.

Her hands full with notebook and tape recorder, Alyssa wiped her forearm across her face, trying to stanch the sweat stinging her eyes. It was always the same in these media mosh pits — the close, hot air; the chafing bodies.

"Guess you got scooped by your own subject," Jeannie Sciorfello, a *Daily News* reporter, said, and it was all Alyssa could do not to punch her.

Back at the office, she filled a bag with ice and tried to drape it across her bruised back. She wished she could ice her ego. Nameless, Khan had been hers. Now he was everyone's. Clearly he thought he could seize the initiative by unveiling himself. Alyssa chuckled at the phrase, then realized it would make great cover type: "Muslim Unveiled." They could run the ski-mask photo and Khan's side by side. She sent a quick e-mail to her editor, hoping the cleverness would hide her lack of an exclusive.

After filing her story, she began investigating Khan. The paper had already dispatched reporters to the architecture firm where he worked and to his home, so she turned to the computer, Googled his name, and got

134,000 hits. "Mohammad Khan": the "John Smith" of the Muslim world. The glowing mentions of the correct Mohammad Khan's architecture would make for mealy copy at best. The rest of the entries referred to rulers and doctors named Mohammad Khan, businessmen and villagers, heroes and war criminals, a global community in name only. She skimmed past intriguing tales ("Taxi driver Mohammad Khan listened to his conscience when he decided to return a bag containing gold ornaments to its owner") and seductive scraps ("Mohammad Khan, a son of Firoz, devoted all his time to pleasures"). There was an order to the order, a hidden hierarchy, but only Google or its algorithms knew it.

She began a public records search. Criminal databases yielded nothing, but business records turned up a K/K Architects, registered by a Mohammad Khan and a Thomas Kroll. Kroll, she found through a quick Web search, worked at ROI, too, which meant this must be her Khan. Relief surged through her — it was something — then panic that other reporters were on the same trail. Unable to reach Kroll at ROI, she found his home listing: a Brooklyn address that matched the one given for K/K Architects. She picked up the phone to dial, then thought better of it. If he hung up, she was out of luck. Heart thumping hard, she took the subway out, praying that no one would get there before her.

Thomas Kroll lived in a dowager of a building, stately at birth, shabby with age, on Eastern Parkway. The lobby was dim; the doorman, Indian or something, was resolute: "No, no, madam, you cannot go up without announcement."

"He's expecting me," she said, then, "It's a surprise." She considered slipping him a twenty but worried it could backfire. As he picked up the phone to call Kroll, she read the doorman's ledger upside down and saw the apartment, 8D. She headed for the elevator at a fast walk; as she had hoped, he put the phone down to follow her. "Madam, excuse me, you cannot just go, madam, ex—" The elevator doors clipped his words.

By the time she reached the apartment, a woman — the wife, she guessed — was waiting in the doorway, arms folded.

"Who are you?" The voice was angry, the look distraught. No, disputatious. Her hair teetered in a lopsided bun, and her right hand gripped a red toy car like a weapon.

"Alyssa Spier, *New York Post.*" Uttered with the authority of the Internal Revenue

Service, as if they had no right to refuse her.

"Great, Thomas, it's already started," the woman called back into the apartment. "The tabloids are here. At our house." She turned back to Alyssa with a venomous stare.

A man with brown hair flopping in defeated eyes came to the door. "You'd better go," he said. "We've got no part in this."

"I found a business listing with your name on it, and Mohammad Khan's," she said, flipping through her note pad: "K/K Architects."

His milky skin paled further. "You're not going to print that, are you?"

"Why?" she asked, innocently. "Boss doesn't know?"

"Shit," Thomas said to his wife, and they made way for her.

The living room, down a long, claustrophobic hall, was strewn with toys: trains, blocks, Legos. Children, three of them, seemed to be break dancing off the crayoned walls. Alyssa had assumed that architects, being professionals like doctors and lawyers, made a lot of money; the cramped, careworn feel of the place surprised her. Did Khan live like this, too? Probably not, since, her research showed, he was unmarried, as was she. But with his style, he probably didn't live like her, either.

The little girl grinned at her, revealing a row of missing front teeth. Alyssa fake-smiled while looking for a clear space to sit.

"Alice," Thomas said, "maybe you could take the children in the back?"

A baleful look, then the posse was rounded up.

"She's upset," Thomas said quietly, and unnecessarily, once they were gone. "Worried it could put the kids in danger."

Alyssa fumbled for soothing words. She wasn't going to help matters by putting him in the paper, which reminded her that she needed a photographer. After sending a quick text, she accepted the water he offered in a smudged glass.

"About the business registration," Thomas began. "I'd rather you not mention it."

"No need," she said, noting his immediate gratitude, "if I have better stuff for my story."

He nodded. But when she tried to ask about Khan's decision to enter, or whether Thomas had helped with the design, words abandoned him. He just kept looking at her, his eyes like blue snaps. And suddenly she knew. "He didn't tell you anything, did he?" she said. "He didn't warn you this was coming."

Bull's-eye. Kroll looked down. The bald spot lurking within the full hair reminded her of the blank spot in Manhattan, its aerial view, and a fleeting urge to reach out and touch his head came over her.

"This must be difficult," she said, with a compassion that surprised her.

"He's my friend," he said finally, his voice hoarse. "Not just my partner. My best friend."

Alyssa couldn't tell whether he said this to emphasize the depth of the betrayal or to warn her that he would remain loyal despite it. She did a mental dog paddle, trying to think how to proceed. It wouldn't count as news to her editor that Khan had screwed his partner, but it told her quite a bit about Khan. He was selfish, a pronouncement she made not in judgment but in recognition. He was as ambitious, as competitive as she was.

"Well," she said, "why don't you tell me a little about that friendship." He looked warily at her. "Help us understand who this man is."

"Right now I don't entirely understand that myself," he said, and she reached for her notebook. Could she use that? She would.

"Mo's got a strong personality," he said.

"Mo?"

"That's what everyone calls him."

Everyone but her. Mo didn't have the ring — theological, historical, hysterical — of Mohammad.

"Look, I'm not pleased he didn't bother to fill me in on this whole thing." A good sound bite. "But as far as I can see, he won the competition fair and square." Not so good. "There's no argument for taking it away from him."

"Is he religious?"

"Mo? Hardly." Thomas chuckled at the thought. "He's way more decadent than I am." She underlined "decadent."

"Decadent in what way?" she asked, as if they were sharing a joke.

"Normal," he said, cocking his head to examine her from a different angle. "That's the better word. Normal."

"Like with girls? Drugs? Alcohol?"

"My point was, he isn't religious," Thomas said, the eyes now mistrustful slits. "He isn't some crazy Muslim. And he's fucking talented — make sure you print that."

Somehow she was prompting Kroll to rally to Khan's defense. She wanted his disappointment, Khan's backstabbing, his compromising of a friendship and this all-

189

American family. She wanted the wife, who she guessed would be happy to plumb those depths with her.

"So he never told you he was entering? Isn't that a little odd — I mean, you're planning to start a firm together, such good friends, right?" There was shrieking from the bedroom; she let it play out. "I would guess you collaborate on everything."

Thomas reddened a bit and began to slide his wedding ring on and off. The masculine ego — one had to handle it with tongs. She couldn't go too far in the interview with the humiliating aspect of this, the best friend who was duped by his buddy. "I mean, I'm sure he had his reasons," she said, "but what do you think they were?"

"I don't know," he said, wearily. "I'd like to ask him that myself."

The phone had begun ringing during their talk. Alice ignored it, and Thomas finally rose to answer. "How many?" Alyssa heard him say. "I see. No, no — don't let them up."

The competition had arrived. The interview was over. Alyssa coached Thomas on how to fend off the other reporters, suggesting he talk to their co-op board about hiring temporary extra security and training the doorman to be more vigilant, as if her presence were his fault. "The two words 'No comment' are your best friends," she instructed. "You have every right to use them, and nothing to gain from talking. To anyone else, I mean."

She said goodbye, patting the head of the little boy, the eldest, who had come out from the back. He twisted away and looked at her with suspicion. Those clear blue eyes, their seraphic reproach. She never had been good with children.

In the lobby reporters were pestering the doorman, who had grown so flustered he was mixing up his "sirs" and "madams" and threatening to call the police. They recognized her and hurried over. "What apartment? What apartment?" She shrugged as if she didn't know, then said, "Don't bother, there's nothing, it's a dry sponge." She emerged from the dark lobby. The sunlight made her blink. Across the street she saw green — Prospect Park, Brooklyn's lungs. She breathed air into her own.

10

At Mr. Chowdhury's fish-and-grocery store, Asma loaded up on wheat flour, rice, tomatoes, milk, cooking oil, four kinds of vegetables, and the Bengali-language papers. There seemed to be a new paper for Bangladeshis every week, which made her proud of how literate her people were, unless she was in a dark mood, in which case it only reflected their divisiveness. She paid for her papers along with her groceries, pleased not to be one of those cheapies who stood at the checkout counter reading the papers for free like it was a library, although she had to confess that until her windfall, she had done just that.

Much of the news the papers carried was about Bangladesh, and most of it was worrying: the political fights, this one and that one accused of corruption or jailed, the violence, the two lady leaders and rivals poking each other in the eye at every chance.

Floods washed over the land; people sought higher ground, saw their homes swept away, rebuilt. Ferries sank like stones. A strike crippled a city until it shook loose from whatever cause had grabbed its leg. Amazing how chaotic and impossible things could seem when they were concentrated into a few pages of black-and-white print, instead of diluted into long days of red chilies drying in the sun, light dancing on the water, tales of marriages arranged and awry, the tunes of Runa Laila, her niece's sweet laugh, her mother's spicy fish, her father's comic stories of waking the sleeping guards at his rice mill, the swaddled peace of daydreams. The worst things then had their balance, could be put in their place.

The papers' local news, like local life, tended to be blander. Changes in immigration rules. New Bangladeshi businesses or local associations in the New York area. Bangladeshis victimized by crimes or, in smaller type, arrested for them. Felicitations from local politicians for holidays and festivals. For a while after the attack, of course, the content had included stories about new immigration difficulties, threats to mosques, the detention of Muslims. But over the last year that sort of news had started to fall off, as if little by little everything might be returning to normal.

But now this Mohammad Khan had won the competition to design the memorial to Inam and the other dead. At Mr. Chowdhury's, she squeezed the bag of rice into the bottom of her handcart. The store owner was arguing with Dr. Chowdhury — no relation — over whether the effort to take away Khan's victory mimicked Bangladesh's history. They didn't include her in their discussion, so, as usual, she eavesdropped.

"It's just like 1970," Dr. Chowdhury said, smiling at Asma in greeting. "What Pakistan did to us, not wanting to recognize the election because it didn't like the result. Exactly the same. America should be better."

"This wasn't an election," Mr. Chowdhury said. He was an imperious man, undemocratic himself, Asma thought. "It was just a small group of people deciding. Because if it was an election, you think Americans would vote for a Muslim? So it's the opposite. They tried to give it to him without an election. Now Americans are saying they don't want him. We had the majority then; they have it now."

"We wanted freedom. They want to discriminate."

"Perhaps, but it's not a parliament. It's

194

just a memorial. I don't blame them for not wanting a Muslim name on it."

"There will be Muslim names on it regardless," Dr. Chowdhury said, jerking his head toward Asma, who was pretending to scrutinize the bitter melons.

"All I know is that in Dhaka, five thousand people would be living in the space they've set aside for it."

Asma bridled at this comment. Her husband had no grave. Only in this memorial would his name live on. Only there could his son see it, maybe touch it. A parliament of the dead deserved respect, too.

Pulling her handcart of groceries, she walked home, replaying their argument in her head. She knew well the history of which they spoke because her father had been a part of it. When the military overseers of Pakistan had refused to allow the winning party in Bangladesh — then East Pakistan — to form a government, her father had put down his textbooks, left the university, and joined the fight. Hundreds of thousands, millions of deaths later, Bangladesh had its independence. His stories had made a deep impact on Asma as a child. She had resolved to be as brave, only to learn that as a woman she wasn't expected to be.

At her building, Asma began the onerous task of carrying her bags of groceries up four flights, then coming down for the next batch. She left the bag of rice — twenty-five pounds — for last. It weighed less than her son but seemed harder to carry. As she heaved it from the cart, a few grains spilled onto the ground. Looking closely, she found a small hole in the bag's corner and a trail of slim white dashes leading back to the front door. Outside, more rice. The birds were already pecking at it. With a sigh she turned the bag upside down to make sure no more grains would escape, put it back in the cart, and followed her own trail back to the store.

Bravery, she thought as she walked, wasn't about strength alone. It required opportunity. Wars came rarely. She reminded herself of this whenever she had questioned whether Inam was as courageous as her father. Her husband had been born at a different, less momentous time. It was hard, in daily life, to find the right cause. She had learned this for herself.

Once she was married and settled in Kensington, Asma had decided she wanted to work. The request, unconventional, left Inam hesitant; even, in his mild way, apprehensive. It was also implausible: she had only a high-school education and spoke little English. But he approached a Bengali pharmacist on Church Avenue, a Hindu named Sanjeev, whose daughter-helper had just left for college, as he told everyone who came through the door. Sanjeev agreed to give Asma a try. He was safe: a respected man whose wife and sister-in-law also worked in the pharmacy. Asma would be his wife's assistant, helping to count out the pills for prescriptions. The work was dreary but relaxing, and she took great pride in her precision. Sanjeev's wife scoured her work for mistakes until she saw that Asma made none. Counting did not preclude absorbing the activity of the pharmacy. For a time, she knew more about the neighborhood's ailments than Mrs. Mahmoud did. Sanjeev was like a doctor, she would tell Inam at night. Everyone came to him for advice, not just Bangladeshis but the black people, the Spanish people.

Sanjeev's only fault, from what she saw, was his stinginess. He would almost never extend credit to anyone, except for a few Hindus he knew. People would need a prescription before their paycheck or government check came in, but Sanjeev demanded cash up front. One day she decided to say something. Her father had often loaned money to people for no interest. He would not have approved of Sanjeev, she was sure.

"Sanjeev-uncle," she said, trying to be very polite, "I don't understand why you won't give more credit. You know these people; I know these people. You know where they live."

He looked at her as if she were his daughter talking back to him, then said lightly, "If you think they're so worthy, why don't you extend them credit?" Sanjeev knew full well she had no money to lend. Her hands shook as she counted out pills for the rest of the day. That afternoon she thanked him for employing her and never returned. Inam, a little appalled at her impetuousness, went to make peace with Sanjeev. Asma could never be convinced to do the same.

Back at the store, she showed Mr. Chowdhury the hole in the rice bag.

"This is an old trick," he said gruffly. "You took out a cup, then you come say it leaked and want a whole new bag. It won't work. I know all the tricks."

Almost speechless with anger, she dragged him out to the street and showed him the rice, which feet and wind and fowl were already scattering. They walked together for half a block, until he asked, "This trail goes all the way to your building?"

She nodded vigorously, relieved he understood.

"You fool!" he said. "You dreamer. How did you not notice sooner?" He berated her at length, accusing her of reading newspapers while she walked instead of watching her rice.

"I didn't think it would run away," she said, which angered him more.

Mr. Chowdhury refused to give her a new bag, and she stewed all the way home, wishing Inam were alive to fight for her, although in truth she didn't know if he would have. "Maybe you tore the bag when you put it in the shopping cart," he might have said, not to suggest she was in the wrong but rather that anyone could have been. To him a cup of rice wasn't worth a fight. To her every grain was.

Yet she yielded to Mr. Chowdhury in the matter of the rice. As a woman, she had to.

"Paul," the governor said breathlessly.

Bitman was on her elliptical machine in a black velour sweat suit. It was seven-fifteen, an hour when Paul would have preferred to be contemplating the soft hillocks of a sleeping Edith's rear country. Summoned for breakfast at the governor's New York City

199

pied-à-terre, Paul had put on his suit and bow tie. An aide offered a glass of orange juice and pointed him to a chair.

The governor was watching herself on television. "Even if Mr. Khan is not a security threat — and there is no reason to think he is — his finding his way to victory in this anonymous competition reminds us that radical Islamists could use our democratic institutions and our openness to advance their own agenda," the governor on the screen was saying in a CNN interview from the previous day. The governor next to Paul nodded in time to her own words. The rise and fall of her legs suggested a riverboat churning. "As a woman, I can't stay quiet about that danger, given that if Islamists were to take power here, it is women who would bear the brunt of our lost freedoms. As you may know, Wolf, I joined a delegation of female politicians on a visit to Afghanistan last year . . ."

"Geraldine, I'm surprised at you," Paul said, unable to help himself. He had known the governor for more than twenty years, known her late husband for even longer. When Joseph Bitman died, bequeathing his wife his fortune and his unrealized political ambitions, Paul had been one of her early and ardent supporters. He had backed her from her first run for the legislature all the way to the helm of the state, and not only out of friendship. Her brio and clarity of mind impressed him, as did her cobbling from left and right her own unpredictable center. She was New York's first female governor, a first that led her to think of others. She wanted to be president.

"Read my senior thesis from Smith, Paul" — there was heavier breathing, more strenuous pumping: the machine had shifted to a sterner cycle — "it might alleviate your surprise. 'Hegemonic Hierarchies in the Women's Movement.' I was worried about women being oppressed by women. My concern about Islam is entirely consistent with that." Consistent, too, Paul thought for the first time, with her patronage of Bob Wilner: she hadn't appointed the lawyer, her former aide, to the jury knowing a Muslim would win, but his stridency on the issue couldn't have been a secret to her.

A pinkish glow; a seed pearl of sweat on her brow. Paul studied Geraldine from the side — her coiffed hair, a rich, lustrous artificial auburn from which her nickname, the Fox, was partly derived; a handsome aquiline profile that would suit a coin.

"To be honest, I'm surprised at you," she said.

"Meaning?"

"You don't have a grip on the process."

Her meaning was clear. Khan's assertion that he had been asked to withdraw from the competition had taken Paul aback because he had striven so hard not to ask Khan to withdraw but only to insinuate that it wouldn't be a bad idea if he did. So Paul had immediately issued a statement saying he had made no such request. This was Error Number One. Error Number Two was issuing a clarifying statement in which he said that he had not called Khan a liar, which was what reporters inferred from the first statement. The upshot of both statements was to confirm that Khan's design had, indeed, been selected by the jury, which meant Paul had to find a way to introduce Khan after Khan had already introduced himself. He was having to rebut accusations that the jury had attempted to thwart Khan's selection, even as the families shouted that the jury should have thwarted his selection.

"It's a tricky situation, Geraldine, which is why I don't think heightening the fear is helpful —"

"The fear is there, Paul. The fear is real. And the sense out there in Middle America, whose sentiments, I don't mind saying, happen to be of interest to me these days, is that the jury doesn't understand the fear. They should, given that they're mostly from Manhattan, and look what happened here, but they don't." Her pace was slowing, her ruddy color still deepening.

"My jury isn't at fault here. It was an anonymous competition — you know that."

"I do, but polling is showing that 70 percent of Americans don't. People need someone to blame at a time like this. They're not consoled by abstract notions of process."

Geraldine had not called him here for breakfast, Paul realized, since there was none on offer. She had called him, out of friendship, to warn him that she was going to target his jury — a bunch of Manhattan artists, elite as they come — as much as the Islamist threat. There were all kinds of protests he could make against this beyond the anonymity of the entries. Most of those artists hadn't even wanted the Garden. But the governor, with her man on the jury reporting back to her, likely knew that.

"And don't forget that I have the final say, Paul." He made no reply. When she'd asked him to chair the jury, she had urged him to make sure most of the jurors were artists, professionals. "We don't want a bunch of firefighters deciding to put a giant helmet in

Manhattan" had been her words. In private, of course. She had vetoed the campaign, led by Sean Gallagher, to have a jury of family members. They would bicker, she was sure; she would gain nothing by choosing among them. Claire Burwell, the only family member on the jury, was picked because her Ivy League credentials and art collection comported with the other jurors' sensibilities. The notion of public input — the hearing, the comment period, the governor signing off — had been written into the process to give the public the illusion they would be heard, when in fact they were being led. Token modifications to the winning design could be made, but the jury's selection would stand, blessed by the governor.

But now the bickering was here, on a scale unforeseen, and Bitman was clearly determined to profit from it. She wasn't rewriting the rules, Paul thought, so much as interpreting them with a new and cynical literalism.

Her cool-down period was over. She stepped off the elliptical, motioned for the towel draped on Paul's chair, and kissed him lightly on the cheek in farewell.

Staring down at her first column, Alyssa Spier had imagined herself as Carrie Bradshaw: golden hair tousled, cigarette in hand, petite, tank-top-clad frame perched on the bed, pithy comments filling the laptop screen. But Alyssa's one-bedroom smelled, as it always did, of the farted exhaust of the Indian restaurants around her building. Curry Hill, they called her neighborhood; she called it Curry Hell. More than the odor, a sideways glance at the mirror demolished the fantasy. She was in nubby sweatpants and an extra-large T-shirt from a 1992 Bruce Springsteen concert (could it really be that old? could she?). She had a few pounds — okay, more than a few — on Carrie, perhaps because she had substituted a bag of Mint Milanos for the cigarettes. Her hair was unstreaked, not to mention unwashed. And she was severely hungover. Drinks with Chaz, her new editor, had felt more like a hazing than a celebration. He drank four martinis, lining up the empty glasses, Rockette-like, before him. She surrendered after two, despite his ribbing, but that was two too many on an almost empty stomach, since Chaz apparently subsisted on gin alone. The handfuls of pretzels she wolfed down when he looked away proved a meager levee. She had puked three times during the night. Then there were their subjects, hers and Carrie's. Sexiness must come easily when your topic is sex and the single woman. Pondering terrorism — or "the Muslim problem," as Chaz called it — didn't exactly make for a seductive scribe. Nothing to do but press on. She was who she was, although these days, she wasn't exactly sure who that was.

Less than a week ago, she had been a mere reporter, scraping for scoops. She was dogged, which was how she got the Muslim tip-off, but she was one of a crowd — no illusions there. She hustled lawyers and aides to politicians and limo drivers and anyone else who might have a lead, using a wheedling voice and a knowing air to extract what she could. She called sources to joke and gossip even if there was no news to be had, making them feel like she was their friend, or maybe mistaking them for hers.

But now she was a Columnist — she always imagined it capitalized. Chaz had tossed out the idea amid the frenzy around her story. It was a way to hype the scoop, get as much play out of it and her as possible. Her ego warmed to the idea. They had already taken her picture, which thankfully flattered more than this morning's mirror image. Now she needed the words.

Chaz, last night, had given her some tips on how to proceed. The most important quality in a good columnist, he explained, was certainty: "No 'he said, she said,' just 'I say.' " She should seem to have answers. "People want to be told what to think," he said, swilling his martini. "Or they want to be told that what they already think is right."

But her habitual itch wasn't for telling people what to think but for finding out what they didn't know. Her mind kept straying to that meeting of the families at the high school, to her blowing it with Claire Burwell, turning her hard. Alyssa knew sometimes she got a little desperate without meaning to and that it scared people. She never felt it coming, only saw the wreckage afterward.

This line of thought took her, as it often did, to Oscar. He was the *News*'s — maybe the city's — best law enforcement reporter, surprisingly dapper for a short, squat man with square, black-rimmed glasses and mere tussocks of hair. He composed himself each day: an ironed shirt, a vest of subtle plaid or black, a natty tie. He wore well-cut cuffed pants and oxfords, always shined. He believed in the gym. He had a large nose and squinting eyes, and yet carried himself as if unaware of his own unattractiveness. They spoke the same language, a callous patois peculiar to reporters: a building collapse was a "great story," a fire that scattered families along with the ashes "the most fun they ever had." Outsiders hearing this might be shocked at the coarseness. But these stories were their quarries, not their tragedies. Alyssa had mistaken this tribal bond for something more, and for a brief period Oscar permitted such entertainments. Then the other shoe, the rejecting shoe, dropped, and it hurt like hell. A new newsroom, a fresh start: it would be easier not to see him.

Like a scratched record — it depressed her that she was old enough to scavenge similes from vinyl — her mind kept returning backstage at the high school. An energy secretive, charged, angry vibrated between Claire Burwell and Eileen Gallagher. Alyssa sensed it now as she hadn't then, when she'd taken off in pursuit of Claire. She'd never circled back to the mother. "Eileen," she wrote on an envelope close at hand, and drew a box around the name. She wondered where Mrs. Gallagher went to church.

Back to the column. "The problem," she typed, and stopped; "with Islam," she resumed, and stopped again, this time extracting a Mint Milano. The import of her mission, the magnitude of the challenge — her first first-person story! — were reason enough to break her "no sugar before noon" rule. It was also the only food she had in the house.

She chewed and swallowed. Her stomach heaved violently. Islam was violent. It believed killing innocent people was acceptable. It didn't like women. It didn't like other religions. It was as hateful as her nausea. She was going to puke again.

"The problem with Islam is Islam."

She had one sentence.

Trying to pretend nothing unusual had transpired, Mo went to work the day after his press conference. Before heading up to the firm, he lingered by the elevator, hoping to see Thomas, dreading seeing him. Thomas must be furious that Mo hadn't confided in him, warned him, or, perhaps worst of all, invited him to collaborate on the entry. Mo had acquitted himself dishonorably: he knew this. In the Kroll family, he was tantamount to the fourth child, adopted for every holiday, expected at every birthday party. Petey, the eldest, the five-year-old, especially revered Mo, who still remembered the first time Petey had called him by name — that feeling of being known by a child, as a thing apart from every other thing in his world, and thus valued. Truck. Helicopter. Mo. Traitor. His calls and e-mails of apology to Thomas had gone unanswered, and his guilt had been only mildly assuaged by the story in that morning's *Post:* "Muslim Winner 'Decadent,' Friend Says."

Thomas lit up by habit when he saw Mo, then remembered to glower. Mo was still arraying his excuses when Thomas shoved him against the wall, the gesture touchingly schoolboyish, as if Thomas's heart wasn't in the violence. It was how Mo himself would have lashed out. Unable to speak, he started laughing, mostly from relief that this moment was over.

"I deserved that," Mo said.

"If Alice were here you'd be bleeding."

"I don't doubt that."

"You are the world's biggest asshole. You drew up that design, what, four, five months ago and never thought to mention it?"

"I didn't think I would win, so it didn't seem worth bringing up."

"Bullshit!" Thomas said. "You're way too cocky to think you wouldn't win."

"I didn't even tell my parents. Does that make it any better?"

"I thought we were partners," Thomas said. "I thought that was the goal here."

"It was. It is. I still want to be. I just . . . this was about me, I admit that. But it was something I had to do on my own. And look

210

how well it's gone — serves me right."

"So I'm supposed to feel sorry for you? Reporters came to our house. Alice is scared. I'm scared. The kids — you asshole," he said again, with even more feeling.

"I didn't know they came to the house, Thomas. Shit, I'm sorry. Somehow it never occurred to me they would drag you into it."

"Of course it didn't occur to you because that would have required thinking about someone other than yourself."

Mo's patience for penance was starting to wane. How many ways could he say he was sorry? "Fine, I am the world's biggest asshole, but you did call me decadent. Decadent!"

Thomas started laughing. "I said you were more decadent than I am, which these days isn't hard. She trimmed the fat from my sentence. I was actually trying to help you, even in my pissed-off state, by making clear you're not some extremist. Her face lit up as soon as the word left my mouth."

"And I was trying to help you by winning this competition. Think how good it will be for our practice."

"There's not going to be a practice, Mo! K/K Architects is dead. You killed it. If nothing else, Alice will never allow it. Grudges

211

are her baby blanket."

"I'll work on her," Mo said, sensing, in the shift to Alice, a softening. Even this inspired guilt: he knew he had taken a chance on alienating Thomas because unlike his wife, or Mo himself, the man couldn't hold a grudge.

Roi could, apparently. He was in the office, but he didn't speak to Mo — not that day, not the next. Summoned at last, Mo braced for a dressing-down.

"It may amuse you to know I thought about entering that competition myself," Roi said, without preamble. "I had an idea — a good idea; one day I will show you some sketches I made. But I thought, once they learn a Frenchman has won? A Frenchman who, in his youth, was a devoted member of the Communist Party in Paris? They will never allow it. And so I didn't go forward. You were braver."

Mo was so surprised he couldn't speak. Better a French Communist than an American Muslim, he thought: Paul Rubin had suggested that Mo submit his design under Roi's name.

Roi went on. "No competition is ever pure, you know. Don't think otherwise: someone knows someone on the jury; one strong will dominates the deliberations.

They are all contaminated. I loathe them, actually. We do them only because that's how most of the work in Europe is given. But this is different, what people are saying about you. I am not fond of all Muslims, the ones who won't assimilate, I mean; France admitted too many. But that is separate. You won, and we must make sure you are allowed to go forward. I am talking to some of my friends" — he reeled off a list of the world's biggest names in architecture — "and we are going to do a statement of support for you."

"Thank you," Mo stuttered.

"But, Mo, you must also keep some perspective." An assistant scurried in, set Roi's macchiato precisely six inches and forty-five degrees from his right hand, and withdrew. "Your design — I am sure it will be a fine memorial, but do not let it distract you from your career. Remember that it is just a garden. What is the phrase? Parsley around the roast. You may make history with it, but you will not change the history of architecture."

With that Mo was dismissed. His gratitude was no less for wondering if Roi had entered the competition and was lying about it because he hadn't won.

■ ■ ■ ■

"U: NYPost 2mrw." The text from Lanny came as Claire was getting ready for bed. With reluctance she called him, wondering why this lupine soul had become her chief correspondent. "Paul wanted you to know: there's a column — it's online," he said, his studied neutrality indicating bad news. Chilled, she pulled her robe tight as she seated herself at the computer.

"The problem with Islam is Islam," Alyssa Spier's column began, before describing, in retread language, the religion's violent propensities, its oppression of women, its incompatibility with democracy and the American way of life. But halfway through, the screed took an abrupt, odd turn, as if a late-breaking bulletin had come in, or the columnist had jettisoned her Fouad Ajami pretensions to channel Cindy Adams: "Another family member tells me that the winsome widow on the jury has a soft spot for Mohammad Khan. If, metaphorically speaking, she's sleeping with the enemy, whose side is she on?" Claire's mouth opened in shock. Like a frenetic wing beat, her index finger delicately, compulsively tapped the screen, as if to blot the words away. Enemy.

She curled up in a chair in her bedroom, not wanting to be alone in her bed. It was a badge of honor to be targeted by the *Post,* she told herself. If she backed Khan, that meant backing him publicly. Her stand for him, as much as any physical place, would be Cal's memorial. Yet she would have preferred that her stance stay hidden. What was this cowardice, this fear, that kept her from owning her own beliefs? Knotted in questions, curled around herself, she fell asleep in the chair.

The phone woke her and the children; she didn't answer. It rang, rang again, again, again. "Who keeps calling?" William asked. He had, of late, begun to answer the phone himself.

"Don't pick up — it's broken, honey. The phone company's trying to fix it."

With the children packed off to school, she went to work unlisting their phone number. It was midmorning when she heard a car coming up the driveway. A dark-green Pontiac Grand Am pulled up next to the house, and Sean Gallagher and four other men emerged. Claire, with the maid, hid in her bedroom. The doorbell chimed, chimed again, went silent.

From behind a curtain, with a hammering heart, Claire watched Sean pace a ragged figure eight, occasionally looking up, watched as he bent and plucked one stone, then another, from the cairn beneath the copper beech. She turned her face away, braced for the sound of glass shattering. It didn't come. Down below, Sean was stalking around her Mercedes now. For a moment she thought he might actually urinate on it. One of the other men spoke to him; they seemed to argue. Then all five of them door-slammed themselves into the Pontiac and drove off. A safe interval later, Claire went outside to rebuild the cairn. The stones were gone.

11

Claire Burwell took Mo's hand. There was a brief but unmistakable pause. She flushed, then spoke. "Thank you for the Garden — it's lovely."

She was lovely, too, but obviously so, not unlike the neo-Georgian town house they were standing in. Perfect, even classical in proportion, refined in detail, but missing the unpredicted element that would stop his breath in envy or awe.

The pause was a beat of expectation, Mo was sure: she was waiting for his thanks for supporting him. He had read the *New York Post* column talking about her, seen the histrionic relatives berating her on the news. But to thank her would suggest, somehow, that she was doing something extraordinary. He wouldn't congratulate her for being decent. Her expectation made him want to refuse.

They were in Paul Rubin's living room, its

aspirational-aristocrat decor giving Mo hives, for the official announcement of his selection. The moment was anticlimactic, the location and setup peculiar, even hermetic. No press and, other than Claire, no relatives of the dead being memorialized. No sense of the historic weight, the monumentality of the commission. Just Mo meeting the jury for a group photograph, which would be handed out with a glossy press packet describing his design. Anyone else's submission, he was sure, would have been introduced with more fanfare. The jurors had each greeted and, mostly, congratulated him, then peeled off into small clusters, leaving him to Claire.

In one nearby group around Paul, an argument was unfolding. Mo tried to eavesdrop while also appearing responsive to Claire.

"The governor's talk is confusing, Paul," Leo, the retired university president, was saying.

"How did you know that a memorial that wasn't just bleak was exactly right for us, for who my husband was?" Claire asked Mo.

"Stressing the importance of the public hearing —" he heard.

"I felt like you got inside my head," Claire said. She seemed almost as uncomfortable

218

with this talk as he was, but she kept on.

"Dress parade or battleground —"

"I've told my son it's a place where his father will live," Claire said.

"Relax," Paul Rubin said, "it will be fine."

Mo nodded, blankly, before Claire's words latched on to him. The names on the Garden's walls had become, for him, just another design element, but they were the dead; they were the faces that had been plastered on every surface right after the attack, that first draft of a memorial. His architect's detachment wobbled at the image of a boy seeking his father in the Garden. Mo and Claire were almost the same height. He looked into her eyes and cleared his throat. "How old is he? I hope it will help him."

"If 90 percent of them come to the hearing and say they don't want a garden, she's not going to shove it down their throats," he heard the governor's man say.

"Six," Claire said, "and it will if we can make it come to —" She broke off, then moved away, at Ariana Montagu's approach.

Mo had met Ariana once, three years ago, at the elaborate bash Roi had thrown to celebrate his Pritzker, but she gave no sign of recollection. Most of the jurors had been neutrally pleasant. Ariana clearly saw neutral pleasantry as selling out.

"It wasn't my first choice," she began, as if to be sure she wouldn't be blamed. "You made some interesting choices, but a garden? So" — the word languorously extended — "precious. It doesn't seem to fit with your other work."

He wondered what her first choice had been, and who else hadn't wanted the Garden. It hadn't been designed with her in mind, but of all the jurors, he thought she would appreciate its Modernist influences and details like the steel trees, whose perpetual spareness would preserve the sightlines from the pavilion to the wall. He was about to impress these points on her when Rubin called them to assemble for the group picture.

"Smile," the photographer called out. From reflex Mo did.

He called Laila Fathi as soon as he left Paul Rubin's house. "Do you have time for a drink?" The question was posed as casually as it could be by a man holding his breath. Why, he couldn't say: she wasn't remotely his type. He tended to date architects or designers, thin of frame, delicate of feature, precise in dress, cool in style and affect. Laila was in no respect cool. She was small but curvy, and her features were bold, as were the lipsticks she favored. Her suits were vividly colored and her passions, he had already learned in a few working meetings, many: food of all kinds; Persian poetry and Iranian films; her large extended family. She was blasé about nothing, least of all her cases, which meant she found his determination to fight for his memorial noble. This, he insisted, was the cause of the weightlessness — the balloon just released by a child — he felt when he thought of her, and he had thought of her, since their first encounter at MACC, far more than was warranted.

He suggested a dark, intimate bar in the West Village. She countered with a restaurant, more convenient for her, near Madison Square Park. Waiting for her, he admired the art deco interior — ostentatiously high ceiling, clean lines. They sat in a banquette at a tiny round table, a candle flickering on top, their knees brushing beneath.

He repeated the scraps of overheard conversation that suggested the public hearing would be used to kill the design and shared his impression that Ariana would like nothing better. "It hadn't occurred to me" — he paused and licked his lips, embarrassed by his wounded pride — "that the vote for the Garden wasn't unanimous, and that maybe she or others would seize on me being Muslim as a way to push through another design."

"We'll deal with one step at a time," Laila said. "At least they've acknowledged you."

"But in such an odd way. It was like being at a cocktail party where nobody acknowledges a nuclear bomb just detonated. There's no way any other winner would have been handled that way."

"You're right, but you can't prove it, so legally it's irrelevant."

"I know that," he said. "It's not the legal —" He stopped. He didn't know how to explain.

"It's how it made you feel," she said. "I understand." Some connection formed with those words. There was no one he could talk to about his strain. His parents, in their twice, sometimes thrice, daily calls, were too worried. He couldn't complain to Thomas. He projected complete confidence, having long ago learned, as the sole brown boy in a white school, the power in appearing uninterested in the opinions of others. But he wasn't a robot.

"I've been having a lot of unfamiliar feelings," he told her. Most uncomfortably, bit-

222

terness toward those families who excoriated and caricatured him. "I did this for them and they don't appreciate it," he said.

"For them or for you?" Laila asked. She smiled at his look. "I'm sure you care about helping them heal. But my father's a political cartoonist. He wants to provoke and shape opinions, but he also loves to draw. Your design is really beautiful, by the way — moving, I should say. The pavilion is brilliant, as a way to encourage contemplation. It's a very Eastern, or at least Persian, concept, you know — that a garden isn't for walking, for action, but for sitting. Stopping. Which is exactly right in a memorial. I just keep imagining looking out over the water at all of those names."

Not ready to voice his most unfamiliar feelings, which were toward her, he offered to walk her home. They wandered up Third Avenue, the Empire State Building a lantern held aloft to light their way. Flushed with wine and night air, she seemed free in a way he wasn't, in a way that made his efforts to assert his individuality — to compose an identity — seem strenuous, even ridiculous by comparison. He had grown a beard on his return from Kabul merely to assert his right to wear a beard, to play with the assumptions about his religiosity it might cre-

223

ate. She would never adopt a headscarf for the same reason. He imagined himself as indifferent to the opinions of others. She really was.

His attraction to her was both sharply physical and strangely innocent, as if he wanted to take shelter in her. He took her hand. She took it back.

"No, Mo," she whispered. "Nothing in public. I would be kicked off the council. I tried to explain to you. Modesty matters to them."

"Then let them police their wives."

"It's not that simple. I have to respect their beliefs if I'm going to work with them."

It was late when they neared her building, but she invited him up for tea. "Should we enter separately?" he joked.

"Actually, yes," she said. "Ring 8D in five minutes."

Studying the group photograph of Khan with the jury in the following day's papers, Claire saw thirteen dour, even somber faces, and one smile. Khan's grin nettled her, suggesting deafness to the rancor and grief around him. It made her wonder if he saw the memorial as anything but a career milestone.

Until he failed to express gratitude toward

her, she hadn't realized she was expecting it. He must have seen the *Post* column, must have some inkling of the courage it took to stand up for him. So why not acknowledge it? She looked at the photograph again. A piece of history, but its meaning as yet unassigned. Before it hardened and came to seem as if it had never been otherwise, history was liquid, unfixed.

Claire reached for the *Times* Arts section, wondering if anyone had weighed in on the design itself. With so much else to report after Khan's press conference, the papers had made only generic references to his garden. But today she saw, stripped across the top of the Arts section, "A Lovely Garden — and an Islamic One?" A cavity opened within her. According to the paper's architecture critic, the elements of Khan's garden she loved — the geometry, the walls, the four quadrants, the water, even the pavilion — paralleled gardens that had been built across the Islamic world, from Spain to Iran to India to Afghanistan, over a dozen or more centuries. There were pictures of the Alhambra in Spain, Humayun's tomb in India, and a diagram of the typical chahar bagh, or foursquare garden, next to the diagram of Khan's design from the press packet. They were remarkably similar. The critic called the gardens one of many rich art forms produced by the Islamic world. He wrote: "One does not know, of course, if these parallels are exact, or even intentional — only Mr. Khan can answer that, and perhaps even he was unaware of the influences that acted upon him. But the possible allusions may be controversial. Some might say the designer is mocking us, or playing with his religious heritage. Yet could he be trying to say something larger about the relationship between Islam and the West? Would these questions, this possible influence, even be raised if he were not a Muslim?"

None of the jurors — not the artists, not the experts — had thought to raise it when Khan's identity was unknown, Claire thought, and his elegant, anodyne submission essay had given no hint.

He deserved the benefit of the doubt, she quickly decided. The benefit of a lack of doubt. The similarities could be coincidental. Or perhaps he had taken inspiration from these beautiful forms. He had every right to. Fearing a garden with Islamic elements — and she had to admit her first reaction had been, if not fear, anxiety — was no different from opposing a Muslim designer. She steeled herself to read on.

226

The gardens, the article said, had likely taken their characteristics from agricultural, not theological, imperatives, especially the need to water large tracts of land. In the first centuries of Islam, the gardens provided sensual pleasures — the scent of orange blossoms; the water burbling and cooling the baking air; shade — to rulers. Once the gardens became resting places for some of those rulers, their tombs began to transform the verdant settings into earthly representations of the paradise of the Quran — its "gardens beneath which rivers flow."

Claire turned on the television, wanting to know what the shouting classes would make of this. "In a potentially explosive development, the memorial design may actually be a martyrs' paradise," a Fox News anchor reported soberly, before turning to a panel of experts on radical Islam. One intoned: "As we all know by now, the terrorists who carried this out believed their act would get them to paradise, with the silks and wine, the pretty young boys and the dark-eyed virgins, and now it seems it has."

A second affirmed: "Their remains are in that ground, too. He's made a tomb, a graveyard, for them, not the victims. He would know that the Arabic word for tomb and garden are the same."

"He's trying to encourage new martyrs — see, here's a taste of where you'll get if you blow yourself up," a third chimed in.

Claire snapped off the television, not wanting to hear more. On edge all day, she slept poorly that night and came ragged to the next day's papers. "VICTORY GARDEN!" screamed the *Post.* A *Wall Street Journal* op-ed called Khan's design "an assault on America's Judeo-Christian heritage, an attempt to change its cultural landscape. It would appear to be a covert attempt at Islamization," the paper intoned. "Two decades of multicultural appeasement have led to this: we've invited the enemy into our home to decorate." The members of Save America from Islam dominated cable news with well-lathed lines — their leader, Debbie Dawson, saying, "Muslims believe it is okay to lie to convert people to their truth." And "Look at the history: Muslims build mosques wherever they've conquered. They could never get away with putting a mosque at this site, so they've come up with something sneakier: an Islamic garden, this martyrs' paradise, it's like a code to jihadis. And they've smuggled it in our memorial — it's the Trojan horse."

Bile burned up Claire's esophagus, rose in the back of her throat, and stayed there, corroding her ability to speak or swallow. Focus on the design, not the designer, she had insisted, even as the governor told the families, if you don't like the designer, you probably won't like the design. Khan had played right into Bitman's hands, or had the jury played into his by choosing, and in Claire's case defending, him?

If the reports were to be believed, Khan had given life and form to an idea so powerful Muslims were willing to die and kill for it. Islamic extremists would fatten their fantasies of eternity beneath the same trees, along the same paths, that she and other family members walked for consolation. The possibility that his garden was meant to eloquently, wordlessly bolster believers lapped with oceanic insistence at the edge of her thinking.

Then she regained her senses. Every news outlet stirring this already opposed Khan because he was Muslim. They would do anything to stop him. This was just the latest pretext, a more palatable one for reasonable Americans than his religion alone. Once Khan explained his garden, answered the accusations, the fearmongering would lose its power.

The radio host Lou Sarge had an occasional

229

sidekick, Otto Toner, whose role was to play the professional idiot. "I was just thinking," he said on-air. "Remember when the Russians bugged our embassy in Moscow? We built it, they bugged it, didn't the whole thing go to waste — never got used? Am I right?"

"Right off your rocker," Sarge said.

"Maybe this is like that — the same. Maybe they're planning to plant bugs."

"Of course they are, Otto," Sarge said. "It's a garden. You plant. And then come the bugs." The hammy sound of a ba-da-bing!

"But you know," Sarge said, shadows stealing into his voice, "even Otto's right twice a day. Maybe there's something sneaky, maybe they're planning tunnels underneath. Or planting — putting — something dangerous in that memorial. I mean, how do we know the danger's just symbolic here? Maybe this becomes some kind of base for them. I mean, has anyone really checked out this Mohammad Khan? Is he the Manchurian Candidate of Islam?"

The Gallagher clan was gathered in the living room, listening to the radio. Frank and Eileen. The daughters: Hannah, Miranda, and Lucy, the last two bouncing babies on their knees. The sons-in-law:

Brendan, Ellis, and Jim. Sean.

"Bloody hell," Jim said.

"What the fuck?" This was Brendan. "What the fuck?" Miranda put a hand on his knee, as if to physically tame his language.

Frank was watching Eileen. She was watching an invisible point on the wall opposite her. Her hand traced the same small circle on her thigh over and over, as if to burn through the fabric. Screams came from outside, where the youngest generation was playing touch football. The adults, on edge, froze. Sean, who'd been leaning against the wall, went to the window. A touchdown being celebrated. Tara, his four-year-old niece, had been given the ball to score. It always began this way, charitably, before the girls and the little ones were banished to the sidelines so the real play could begin. He, the youngest adult in the room, was momentarily wistful for the sweat and clarity of football in fall air. The rules were known to all.

He was batting away a sense that he had somehow screwed up, that by fighting to expand the memorial's size, all he'd won was more space for this Muslim to mock them. He'd failed to get on the jury, let alone gain control of it. By habit he raised and lowered the window, checking for stiffness and warp.

"Here's the governor." Jim turned off the radio and turned up the television. She was leaving the National Press Club, where she had given a speech on defense policy. "It's disturbing that a jury of so-called experts could miss that this is an Islamic garden," she said.

"You picked the jury!" Sean said. "Does she think we're stupid?"

"If it turns out to be true, it would be unconstitutional to allow the establishment of any religion on public land," the governor continued. "I'm going to seek legal advice. Even if the report isn't true, this may not turn out to be the best design. But I want the public to weigh in on that at the hearing."

"A hearing won't stop this," Ellis said, "not if they've let it come this far."

"It's too much," Eileen whispered, "too much." Frank half stood, leaned toward her slightly, sat back down. Miranda, next to her on the couch, took her left hand, and Lucy came and took her right. Eileen took it back so she could rub her leg again.

"It's not enough to kill us, they have to humiliate us, too," Brendan said. He'd led a brief protest at his local subway stop after the name Talib Islam was posted under the smiling face on the "Hello, I am your station manager" sign. "They expect us to look at that name every day?" he'd asked. The Transit Authority had posted cops in the station to protect Islam, which made Brendan apoplectic. Then, one day, the manager was gone. Brendan counted it a victory until he learned that Talib Islam had been promoted.

Now Khan's name, and his paradise, would torment them in a place far more sacred than a subway. Pity for his mother — stronger than his own anger, stronger than his love for her — overwhelmed Sean. Sometimes he thought she wished he, instead of Patrick, had died. And yet thinking that now only enlarged his compassion for her. To save the memorial was a chance to be vigilant as they hadn't been the first time. Eileen had been cleaning the attic when the planes flew overhead. Sean wanted to lock Khan in a room with his mother to see if he could withstand her pain.

"Please, Sean, don't let this come to be," she said. The look in her gray eyes — what was it? He'd never seen it, not from her. Pleading. His hard mother admitting her need. If, at that moment, she had asked him to strap on a bomb and blow up someone or something, he probably would have. But she hadn't asked. A plan was up to him.

A file clip of Claire Burwell in dark glasses flashed on the TV.

"Some other blood runs in those veins," his mother said. Maybe money made you feel less, Sean thought, picturing Claire in her mansion, which was bigger than he'd even imagined (and he'd spent a lot of time imagining it), bigger than any he'd seen. Different, too. So much glass. He hoped she'd been watching him, hoped she'd been scared, wished he'd thrown that rock into her house of light.

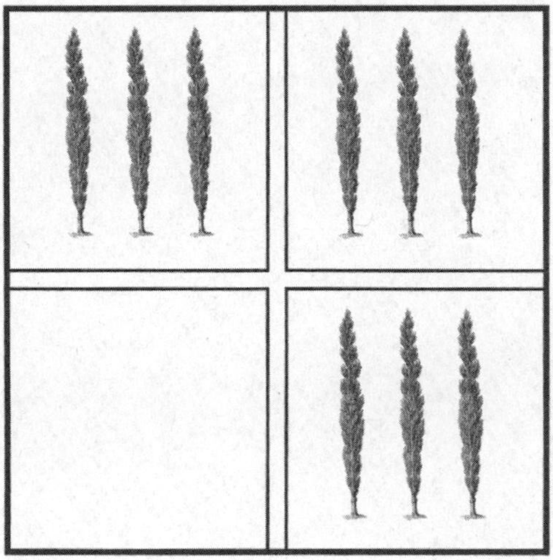

12

The threats began soon after Mo's official anointment. By phone, by letter, by e-mail, his countrymen promised to burn him as the terrorists had incinerated their victims, to stab him in the heart as he was stabbing America. The FBI placed him under watch. Agents much like his interrogators in Los Angeles posed, ineptly, as his assistants. In their presence, Emmanuel Roi wore the look of an ancient Brahman forced to host untouchables.

Next came the picketers. Two, or three, or ten of them, mostly women, foot-darned a circle in the park across from his house. They held signs with by-now familiar slogans — NO MECCA IN MANHATTAN or STOP JI-HIDING — and at the sight of Mo, they hooted, shouted, and shook rattles. A police officer soon joined to make sure they were targeting the whole neighborhood, as opposed to his residence, which would be illegal harassment. The distinction was lost on Mo. Photographers, drawn by the spectacle and the prospect of confrontation, showed up and drew onlookers, who drew more onlookers, and before long the park had become an encampment laying siege to Mo's peace.

He found refuge at Laila's. With Laila. Their relationship had deepened — tentatively, at first: she was his lawyer, she had protested, it was inappropriate; they would be discovered by the council — then in a rush of surrender, as if the pressure of controversy welded them together. Her Murray Hill studio had been inherited, along with its cheap rent, from a friend. Its lines suggested a hotel room or corporate apartment, but it had built-in bookcases and a long wall of windows. Laila had dressed the room in velvety Persian rugs and a rich red sofa, a small walnut table and two matching straight-backed chairs to eat on, her grandmother's elegant armoire to hold her serving pieces, and the family's old phonograph with its amplifier like a giant conch ear. All of it delivered the odd but enchanting effect of a live orchestra playing a Viennese waltz in a dentist's office. She had walled off her bed with a screen inlaid with mother-of-pearl, but in the morning, she would reach up to fold it aside, turning the cello of her back toward Mo. The first thing he saw out her window was the Chrysler Building, which he had loved as a child, and a circle he hadn't known to be incomplete closed.

On the single occasion that Laila stayed a night at Mo's loft, she had spent the entire next day trapped inside for fear that the photographers would expose their relationship. From now on, she told Mo once she had snuck out under cover of dark, he had to come to her place to see her. "And I'm not so sure your apartment is safe for you now, either," she said.

He took a suitcase full of clothes to her studio, where she gave him a corner of the closet and told him to keep to it. His stays without returning home stretched longer — three days, then five, until he stopped running the shrill gauntlet into his building at all. To his surprise, he was at Laila's studio more than she was. She had meetings, working dinners, cases, causes. Mo, out of sync with ROI's rhythms, was adrift between projects. Sometimes she let him know when she would be home, sometimes she forgot. By the time she returned, the apartment would be immaculate. It amused Mo that she didn't notice. She entered and warmed the room like a small sun, and in her absence both he and the furniture seemed to be waiting to be brought to life.

"Mohammad Khan has absolutely, unequivocally every right to proceed with his memorial," read *The New Yorker*'s weekly Comment, penned by its editor. "The question is whether he *should* proceed." Mo's stomach contracted. He had been taking comfort, to a degree, in the predictability of the opposition to him: hostile family members; conservative publications; opportunistic politicians like Governor Bitman, who had been speaking about "stealth jihad" in the early primary and caucus states. *The New Yorker* fit none of these categories.

Khan's opponents judge him by his fellow Muslims — not just those who brought down the towers but the significant numbers who believe that America brought the attack on itself, or that it was an inside job by the American government. This is unfair, even reprehensible. We should judge him only by his design. But this is where matters get tricky. In venturing into public space, the private imagination contracts to serve the nation and should necessarily abandon its own ideologies and beliefs. This memorial is not an exercise in self-expression, nor should it be a display of religious symbolism, however benign. The memorials lining the Mall in Washington reflect only our admiration of classical architecture and the reason and harmony that it, like our democracy, was meant to embody . . . Khan has refused to say, on the grounds that such a question would never be asked of a non-Muslim, whether he has created a martyrs' paradise. But to insist that any questions about his influences or motives are offensive is to answer the anguish of the victims' families with coyness.

His opponents claim, absurdly, that Muslims can't be trusted because they have religious sanction to lie. This is a bald misrepresentation of the concept of Taqiya, by which Shiites who live under Sunni rule are allowed to disguise their beliefs to protect themselves. But doesn't Mohammad Khan see that by refusing to discuss the possible meanings of his memorial, he fuels those stereotypes?

Mo set down the magazine and flipped through his stack of unread *New Yorker*s. To

241

be written about this way in its pages was like being called shifty by a roomful of people he had thought were his friends. The rhetorical switchbacks couldn't camouflage the demand that he address the suspicions he provoked. It barely consoled Mo when some of the editor's liberal peers denounced the piece's equivocation in their own publications, or when Susan Sarandon and Tim Robbins wore green ribbons — garden green, Islamic green — to a movie premiere to show solidarity with him. The Comment had made ambivalence respectable, and it began to pour forth.

Manhattanites who had always prided themselves on their liberalism confessed that they were talking to their therapists about their discomfort with Mohammad Khan as the memorial's designer. "It's awful," a thirty-two-year-old music executive who declined to give her name told *The New York Observer,* which accompanied the article with a color drawing showing an ominous-looking Mo looming over a shrunken Manhattan. "There's this primal feeling in my gut saying 'No' to it, even though my brain is saying 'Yes' — sort of like when you think you want to have sex with someone and your body won't cooperate; or you think you don't and your body cooperates *too much* — and I don't get where it's coming from. It's like I've been invaded. But what can I say? I don't have good reasons. It just makes me uncomfortable, and being uncomfortable makes me even more uncomfortable."

Mo began to put psychological distance between himself and the Mohammad Khan who was written and talked about, as if that were another man altogether. It often was. Facts were not found but made, and once made, alive, defying anyone to tell them from truth. Strangers analyzed, judged, and invented him. Mo read that he was Pakistani, Saudi, and Qatari; that he was not an American citizen; that he had donated to organizations backing terrorism; that he had dated half the female architects in New York; that as a Muslim he didn't date at all; that his father ran a shady Islamic charity; that his brother — how badly Mo, as an only child, had wanted a brother! — had started a radical Muslim students' association at his university. He was called, besides decadent, abstinent, deviant, violent, insolent, abhorrent, aberrant, and typical. Neutering his unhappiness allowed him to read, with the floaty interest he would feel toward a dental drill penetrating a numbed molar, that green ribbons were sprouting like seedlings from the lapels of those who supported his right to design the memorial, that in response a member of Save America from Islam had created an anti-Garden sticker — a green foursquare gouged by a red slash, which began appearing on car bumpers and hard hats and T-shirts; that both sides had begun wearing American flag pins to prove their patriotism, and that arguments were breaking out on subways and in the streets between the beribboned and the stickered, with at least one clash turning violent, leaving a stickered man with a bruised shin, although it turned out that a dispute over a parking space had also factored in. By training his face not to show feeling, he could receive the attention of the strangers who stopped him on the street to tell him to withdraw from the competition, or not to withdraw, or, most often, only that they recognized him, as if he were some B-movie actor they couldn't quite place.

"So," Paul Rubin said, "what can I do for you?"

It was eight-fifteen in a coffee shop on Madison Avenue. Sean had spent two weeks trying to get a meeting with Rubin; he wanted to impress on him his committee's, and his family's, opposition to the Garden.

In frustration — and perhaps in competition with the anti-Islam group picketing Khan's home, which was where Sean got the idea — he had his committee members set up their own picket on Rubin's block. SAVE THE MEMORIAL, their signs said. NO VICTORY GARDEN. Along with pressuring Rubin, the picket offered a useful outlet for Sean's growing and increasingly agitated membership. He now had nearly 250 family members and retired firefighters dropping by his parents' house or sitting around, all amped up and waiting for deployment. Making calls to elected officials wasn't exactly red meat. So he had the picket manned around the clock, other than a furlough between midnight and 6:00 a.m. Some of the guys told him it reminded them of working down at the site, although Sean didn't see how hoisting a sign on an Upper East Side sidewalk could compare.

At last Rubin's smarmy assistant called to say that the chairman would squeeze him in for breakfast, but Sean shouldn't be late. He arrived on time, settled into a booth, then waited fifteen minutes for Rubin, who peremptorily relocated them to a window table for more privacy.

The place looked ordinary to Sean, but the prices weren't: five bucks for half a grapefruit, twelve for a bagel and cream cheese. Lots of men in fancy tracksuits, women who appeared to subsist on grapefruit halves alone.

"Isn't that —"

"Yes," Rubin said. He was, even at this hour, in his bow tie. "Politicians love this place. So what can I do for you?"

"What you can do for me —"

"The usual," Rubin said. The waiter had come for their order.

"Uh, three eggs, bacon, coffee, juice," Sean said. "White toast. So, what you can do for me —"

A busboy, with water.

"What you can do for me —"

"Let me rephrase that," Rubin said, as their coffee was poured. "I'm always eager for the families' input, as you know, but there's a formal process in place now, and there will be a hearing for you to express your sentiments on the design. So what did you feel couldn't be conveyed —"

A silver-haired man stopped by the table to shake Paul's hand. "I have great confidence in the outcome because you're handling this, Paul. I wouldn't want anyone else in charge."

"Thanks, Bruce, I appreciate that." Sean was not introduced. He felt himself in the camp of the enemy — not Muslims but the people born with silver sticks up their asses, the people who had made Manhattan a woman too good to give Sean her phone number.

Bruce gone, Sean tilted across the table. "How the hell did this happen?"

"And you're referring to what, exactly?"

"Come on. Mohammad Khan. His Islamic garden."

"That's not how he refers to it."

"No, it's how I'm referring to it. Don't play games with me, with us."

"How did it happen? Was that what you asked? As I recall, people like you — you, the families — you wanted a competition, a democratic exercise everyone could partici- pate in. And so everyone did."

"That's not who we meant by everyone."

"It doesn't work that way."

"But it should. You think we'll stand for a Muslim memorial? I should have been on the jury. This never would have happened."

"We have a family member on the jury, as you well know, Sean, and we're not open to new members at this time." He made it sound like a country club.

"She's not representing us — Claire," Sean said.

"You mean she's not taking dictation from

you? That's not her role. Does your congressman do everything you want? She's on the jury to convey your desires — and those of many other relatives, who may or may not agree with you — to the jurors. Not as a puppet. She's her own woman."

"Yeah, well, the governor's ours."

"Then you should have nothing to worry about. But politics are rarely as simple as they look, Sean, and the bylaws written for this process are quite complicated as well: the governor can't simply decide she doesn't like a design. There have to be supportable grounds for her pronouncing it unsuitable. The whole idea was to respect the jury's work."

"The jury's fuck-up, is what you mean."

"The jury didn't know whose design it was picking, as you know, so you can't pin this on them. And please watch your language, Sean. There are children here." As if the whole coffee shop was in service of his reprimand, a young man carrying a strapping blond toddler approached. Rubin gave the boy a pro forma chuck on the cheek.

"Sounds like you've got a mess on your hands," the man said.

"Probably less of one than you've got, Phil," Rubin said; the boy had loosed a waterfall of chewed-up cracker from his mouth.

Phil smiled and said, "If anyone knows about cleaning up messes, it's you." He turned to Sean: "If you'd seen how Paul dealt with the Asian crisis . . ." He shook his head in admiration. "People were losing their . . . losing their cool all over, but Chairman Rubin here was so steady, never broke a sweat."

As he seamlessly interwove ass-kissing and financial-speak, Sean saw himself too clearly: A no-name worthy of addressing but not worthy of knowing. An audience, not a player, unshaven in his Windbreaker because he hadn't wanted to be late.

Rubin tapped his fingers with impatience, then dismissed the distraction. "Thanks, Phil, that's much appreciated, good to see you." Interloper and child gone, he lowered and toughened his voice at the same time. "There will be a public hearing. You can speak your mind there, Sean. But you might want to make your opposition a little less crude."

"Honest, you mean? We need to be more crude, not less. What's the point of a hearing if we can't speak our minds?"

"You can speak, but in a civilized manner, a manner befitting the fact that Khan is as

American as you are. He has rights, including the right not to be denigrated for his religion."

"What about my rights? The families' rights? The victims' rights? Don't they count for anything?" Sean raised his voice. Customers turned. Let there be witnesses. "My parents' rights. Do you know what this is doing to them?"

"Emotions are not legal rights."

"I tell you this is tearing up my parents and you lecture me about legal rights?" Sean exploded. In a code that could mean either "Call the cops" or "Check, please," Paul raised a single finger to the man at the cash register.

"What about right and wrong?" Sean barely tempered his volume. "Whatever happened to that? If you're going to police what we say at that hearing, then we'll find our own way to say what we want."

"Be my guest," Rubin said. His even tone made Sean's yelling ridiculous. His look whittled Sean to boy-size. "Go lie down on the site if it will make you feel better. But the hearing will stay within appropriate bounds."

Sean stood and tossed a twenty-dollar bill onto the table, and the small smile this triggered from Rubin, whose net worth exceeded Sean's by a factor of roughly four hundred thousand, sent him stumbling in unseeing rage out of the restaurant and down Madison Avenue. He stopped only to scowl at his image in a shop window, to confirm that every unkempt aspect of him called out for disrespect. His hair, smacked into order before he left the house, was now a melee; Sean had his father's habit of running his hands through it when stressed. If he tried to enter the shop, he suspected that the owlish, suited store clerk staring at him through the glass would refuse to buzz him in.

In the window, long white gloves were laid out like prone bodies, a display that brought to mind Rubin's mockery — "Go lie down on the site if it will make you feel better" — then, unexpectedly, an idea. Sean mustered his most lunatic smile, pressed the buzzer until he saw panic on the smug owl's face, and moved on.

The first joint meeting of Save America from Islam and the newly renamed Memorial Defense Committee came to order a few days later at a Brooklyn church borrowed for the occasion. The SAFIs, as they called themselves, like some lost Judaic tribe, were mostly from Staten Island,

Queens, and Long Island, and they were mostly women. As far as Sean knew, most of them hadn't lost anyone in the attack. Radical Islam was their freelance obsession. His mother's rage, most of the time, was so quiet you could forget it was there. Not so with the SAFIs. They were the professional wrestlers of activists.

Their leader, Debbie Dawson, looked like a poorly weathered Angelina Jolie. She had to be close to fifty, but her blog, *The American Way,* showed her in a see-through burka with only a bikini beneath. Today she was wearing a custom-stitched T-shirt that said "Infidel" and a rhinestone-encrusted PEACE around her neck.

It was Debbie who had called Sean to propose that their groups collaborate. "They're trying to colonize this hallowed ground," she said. "This is what they've done all over the world, all through history: they destroy something, then build an Islamic symbol of conquest in the same place. Babur tore down Ram's temple in India and put up a mosque. The Ottomans conquered Constantinople and made the Hagia Sophia — what else? — a mosque. Here, one set of Muslims destroys the buildings and now another comes along to put a paradise there for his dead brothers. For all

252

we know this was part of the plan all along."

Sean didn't get her and didn't want her — he was having enough trouble managing his own crew. But her membership was growing, too — there were now five hundred SAFIs, if you counted the satellite chapters in thirteen states — and given Sean's inspiration after his meeting with Paul, these numbers held new appeal. He agreed they should join forces.

Fifteen minutes into the meeting, though, he was deep in regret. He had imagined himself leading an even larger crusade against Khan's memorial, but nothing about these women — Christians, Jews; housewives, retirees, real estate agents — suggested that they would be easily led. They would barely shut up for one another. Their knowledge of the Islamist threat far outclassed his. They told anyone who would listen about how Quranic chapters from Mohammad's time in Mecca gave the illusion of tolerance by praising the "People of the Book," while the chapters set in Medina showed Islam's true, harsh nature: "Kill them wherever you find them." Some of them toted copies of the book marked up with orange highlighter. The best of them had memorized the offending parts. They tossed around terms like "dhimmitude" as if they'd learned them on the high-school cheerleading squad: "Hey, hey, ho, ho, dhimmitude has got to go!" three women were chanting in the pews.

When Sean asked what dhimmitude was, Debbie, dismayed, called out to a chanter: "Shirley, please educate Sean — all these boys — on dhimmitude."

Shirley's gray curls, glasses, and fuzzy cheeks invoked Sean's elementary-school librarian; he wondered if she also smelled of menthol and stale books. "It's the voluntary submission to being second-class citizens under Sharia law," she called out. This didn't exactly clear things up, but Sean kept quiet. "It's being stupid," she added. "Letting our own way of life be destroyed by liberal idiots as much as by Muslims."

Debbie and Sean were standing in front of the altar. Their members, together, filled most of the pews. Debbie's honk of a voice carried effortlessly down the nave. "What we have here, although it may not look that way, is a stroke of unimaginable luck," she said. "Two years after the attack, Americans were getting complacent. This attempt to claim our most sacred space — it's a wake-up call. This is what I've been trying to tell people: You think the violent Muslims are dangerous? Wait until you see what the nonviolent ones do! What's next? The crescent over the Capitol? They're trying to make this piece of land Dar al-Islam!"

"The House of Islam," she said, with exasperation, at Sean's blank look. "Make a cheat sheet, Sean. You can't fight this threat if you're not versed in the vocabulary."

"Words aren't the way to fight this," he shot back, to applause from his members, who also seemed to have tired of Debbie's schooling. "They want to police what we say about Khan at the public hearing. They call us un-American, then take away our free speech. So we're going to take back the site, literally — we'll lay our bodies down on it, and not leave until they agree to hold a new memorial competition. We'll turn Martin Luther King's techniques right back at them. Who's up for getting arrested?"

Hands shot in the air like they were doing the wave. There were cheers and whoops and cries of "Take it back! Take it back!" Sean passed around a sign-up sheet for the protest and scheduled a practice session.

"Don't forget to keep the pressure on Claire Burwell — she's the most important backer Khan's got," Debbie said when the church had emptied. Her hands were on her slim hips; PEACE glittered from her neck. She eyed the Virgin Mary as if sizing up a potential recruit.

"Asma!" Mrs. Mahmoud called, clapping her hands. "Come out for tea. I've bought gulab jamun."

Asma sat very still on her bed and wondered if she could get away with pretending she wasn't home. Ever since her pregnancy, she had hated gulab jamun — sticky, sweet, sickening. All she wanted was to curl up with the latest newspapers and read while Abdul played quietly. She was in the middle of a column translated from the English papers: "Islam means submission — it makes slaves of its followers, and demands that people of other religions submit to it, too. Their goal is to impose Sharia, Islamic law, wherever they can, including the United States. They will tell you this isn't true, but the problem is that Islam also sanctions lying — the Islamic term for this is taqiya — to help the faith spread or to wage jihad. The Muslim who entered this memorial competition practiced taqiya by concealing his identity . . ."

Asma paused to think about this. Because she didn't read or speak Arabic, her knowledge of the Quran came in pieces, through memorized prayers, through the sermons at

Friday prayers, through bits quoted and discussed by her grandfather, her father, the imams. None of those people had ever told her to wage war against non-Muslims or try to impose Sharia, although they probably wouldn't rely on the women to do that. Certainly no one had told her to lie. This didn't mean she never had. She lied to come to America, putting "honeymoon" as the purpose of her visit on the visa application, when she knew she was coming to America to live. But people from all over the world, from every religion, told that lie. She lied when she told Inam that it didn't hurt the first time they made love, but after that the pain had become pleasure, so deep she couldn't find words, so it wasn't a bad lie, and also she guessed that lie, too, wasn't told only by Muslim women. She lied, was lying still, to the Mahmouds by not telling them about her money . . .

"Gulab jamun!" Abdul sang out. Now there was no pretending.

"We'll be right out," Asma called, heaving a sigh that she hoped released all of her resistance.

She opened the door from her room and saw Mrs. Mahmoud inching her buttocks into her sofa, as if anchoring herself for a long chat. Setting Abdul loose to roam,

Asma took a seat next to her. Mrs. Mahmoud held out the plate of gulab jamun, and Asma managed a very small bite.

Tea with Mrs. Mahmoud was never just tea, rather it was a lubricant for the gossip that would be disseminated or collected, the measuring of everyone else's situation and the landlady's own.

"They say the rains in Sandwip are going to be terrible this year," she began, with authority. "But my husband's parents don't have to worry: they have a new roof because of the money he sent. They say it is the best roof for kilometers around . . ."

Mrs. Mahmoud slurped her tea and belched politely. She had twenty years, forty pounds, and several hundred gray hairs on Asma. Her talk was a solid object that filled the room, confining Asma to a tiny space.

"Salima Ahmed thinks she is special these days because she has found a match for her son," Mrs. Mahmoud said of her sworn enemy and sometime best friend. "She snuck into line in front of me at the butcher. She thought I didn't see, but I did. She took the cut of goat I wanted, not so much as an apology, barely even a Salaam."

Often these little dramas, revealing how Mrs. Mahmoud's feelings, her pride, were so easily hurt, almost as a child's might be,

258

brought Asma's affection for her to the surface. In her pushy way, Mrs. Mahmoud had been very kind to Asma, serving along with her husband as surrogate parents. But today Asma wasn't in the mood, and the boasting, the envy made her feel the prisoner of this petty woman who was as dishonest with herself as she so often was with others. Always at moments like this the little matter of the call-waiting returned to Asma, and the bitterness eddied inside her.

Sometime after Abdul's birth — two weeks? a month? — Mrs. Mahmoud came to see Asma with a confession. She had told Asma that Inam had not called the morning of the attack. The truth was that she didn't know. All that morning she had been on the phone, gossiping with her niece. Her call-waiting had clicked repeatedly but — now she looked down at her prematurely arthritic fingers — the truth was that for all her boasting about her call-waiting, she could never remember how to use it. It was entirely possible that it had been Nasruddin, calling to reach Asma. But it was also possible — this had troubled her ever since — that it was Inam. She hadn't wanted to upset Asma before the baby came. Now she could no longer keep such a torment to herself.

To share a secret, Asma understood then, was to shift a burden. She wished that day, as she often would after, that Mrs. Mahmoud had never told her, so unbearable was the thought of Inam calling and calling but never connecting, perhaps the last sound he heard the ringing of an unanswered phone. For a long time afterward Asma couldn't hear that sound herself without a sharp chill, as if she were watching his last moments through glass. Asma had pretended, that day, to forgive Mrs. Mahmoud. On days like today, she knew she never really had.

On the pretense of retrieving the remote control from Abdul, but really so she could breathe freer air, she went to him. In her own hands she took his, which were sticky with sugar syrup and softly scented with rose water. Looking into his wondering mischievous eyes, she tried to lose herself in the black dots of his pupils. He shrieked a laugh, threw his head back, nearly knocked her with his chin.

She tuned back in to Mrs. Mahmoud only when she heard Nasruddin's name. "And he promised to line up a job for my husband's nephew and he hasn't done a thing. I think he has forgotten about all the people who helped him become such a big shot"

— this term in English — "in Brooklyn."

"Helped him?" Asma snapped, incredulous, returning to the couch. "He is the one who has helped everyone else. He has no time for himself. You shouldn't say such things." Shut up, you fat water buffalo, rolling in the mud of other people's lives, is what she wanted to say. But she bit her tongue and reminded herself of how Mrs. Mahmoud had held her hand through Abdul's birth, which made her think that if she had found strength enough to push him out, she could hold her meanest comments in. At this moment it seemed harder.

Even restraining herself, she could tell her vehemence had surprised Mrs. Mahmoud. This, too, would probably get chewed and swallowed and regurgitated in other households. So be it. They sat unspeaking for a moment.

Then Mrs. Mahmoud said, "Well, none of us may be here to help anyone anyway."

"What are you talking about?" asked Asma, still curt.

"Now they — the English newspapers, the radio — they're saying Muslims don't belong here!" Mrs. Mahmoud was back on form, rolling slightly, like she was on casters, as she did when she got excited. "And then who, might I ask, would fix their build-

261

ings and drive their taxis? And who would give them halal meat?"

"No one will need halal meat if there are no Muslims," Asma said severely. Suddenly warm, she took off her cardigan sweater.

"What they say," Mrs. Mahmoud continued conspiratorially, "is that if we want to show we are loyal, we should tell this Mohammad Khan to stop trying to build his memorial. I think they are right," she said, as her tongue worked to extract a food particle from between her teeth. "I would tell him, if I knew him."

"No!" Asma said. Again the vehemence. This time it surprised her. Maybe she would have opposed Mrs. Mahmoud on any issue today. "He shouldn't stop doing anything! They can't just take this achievement away from him. It's like Pakistan taking away our election."

"You've been listening to the men talk again," Mrs. Mahmoud said, clucking in disapproval.

Her condescension infuriated Asma, who shifted a foot away from her on the couch. "Even if we say we don't support him they won't believe us, because they think we lie," Asma said.

"And if I do support him, what do I gain? What has he done for us, this Mohammad

Khan? Let them have their memorial."

Asma gritted her teeth. "It's my memorial, too, auntie."

"I know, I know." Mrs. Mahmoud patted her knee. "But it's not worth so much trouble."

"It is!" Asma said, but before she could find the words to say why, Mrs. Mahmoud rose, even she not immune to the demands of nature imposed by four cups of tea, and trundled off down the hall like an overloaded truck. "If we do have to leave," she said over her shoulder, "Salima Ahmed had better not try to get in front of me in the line."

Paul wanted Khan to drop out. This notion came to him, again, after yet another incensed call from a juror over the governor's attacks on their elitism. At every turn, Geraldine played up the importance of the public hearing and her right to veto the jury's choice. Paul, who saw himself as the patriarch of this oversized, cantankerous brood, didn't want his jurors quashed. But nor did he want to cross Geraldine, to whom he owed his position. The best outcome for the jury, for the country, for himself, for all, if not necessarily for Khan, was for him to withdraw.

He hit upon his strategy at a cocktail fund-raiser for his son Samuel's gay rights organization. Having already written the check, Paul didn't see why he needed to attend the party, but Edith had insisted, and two Scotches and three mini–lobster rolls in, he was starting to find it palatable. They were in one of those enormous downtown lofts whose style and art collection made Paul feel a century or two behind. The hosts, a pair of prominent gay philanthropists who sat on Samuel's board, were great champions of his and therefore took an interest in Paul. They escorted him into the bedroom to show off a Richard Prince painting for which they had paid a record price at a Sotheby's auction. Paul studied the painting — a cowboy riding a horse against the backdrop of a cloud-filled sky — for a long time, unsure whether the price made it seem more ordinary or extraordinary.

When he returned from his private tour, he joined a group that was standing around a windbag who was telling a long story about an incompetent employee. Not wanting to fire the laggard — "his old man was a major donor," words that made Paul, as Samuel's father, wince — the windbag had handed him ever more petty, mindless tasks: report collating, phone-list updating, and so on. "Place enough unreasonable demands on someone and eventually they'll throw their hands up and walk away," he said, to knowing laughter. Who hadn't tried the same type of thing with an incompetent underling or even just an irritating maid? Firing was messy, often costly. Offending pride came cheap.

Edith interpreted Paul's silence on the way home as a judgmental one. "Sometimes I wish you would be more open-minded," she said. "It would mean a lot to the boys. It was a lovely affair and they said such nice things about Samuel —"

"Edith, it was a very nice party," he said, putting his palms to her powdery-soft cheeks, not caring that Vladimir was watching in the rearview. "I mean it. I'm so glad we went."

The next day Paul informed Mo that he would have to partner with a landscape architect because he was too inexperienced to handle such a large project on his own. The partner would have to come from a short list that would be presented to him. Mo was suspicious — "Is this a tactic to get someone else's name on the project?" — then, once the list arrived, disdainful. "You — or whoever — picked the most conventional firms out there. We have no visual language in common."

"Find one," Paul said.

Next Paul requisitioned reports on the design from the jury's security consultants and summoned Khan to a meeting to go over them. They sat at the oval table where the jury had met for all those months. The consultants were advising against enclosing the garden entirely in walls because it would create too contained a target. Better to use very low perimeter walls, more like parapets. The canals were also a safety liability: "One child falls in and the whole memorial shuts down." They recommended scrapping them.

"You can't be serious," Mo said when the consultants had left. He and Paul were spaced several seats apart at the round table. Khan leaned elegantly back in his chair and crossed a thin leg. A certain comfort had been achieved between them, Paul thought, for all their arguing.

"If you read the bylaws, we are allowed to impose — request — changes."

"And I am allowed to refuse — decline — them."

"Yes, but if you agree to make them, it might increase your chances of securing the governor's approval."

A skeptical smile flitted over Mo's lips.

"Do you really believe that?"

"My job is to try to achieve a meeting of the minds," Paul said, choosing not to speak his own. "If there isn't one —"

"Then what? If you're making a threat, spell it out."

"No threats, just realities. We're meant to have a dialogue, which should lead to refinements. If the jury and the governor are not satisfied, then it becomes impossible to proceed. No winning entry is final. Any vision has to evolve. We're the client, after all. No one is immune to compromise. You think Maya Lin wanted that statue of the soldiers near her memorial?"

"But if you're worried about security, the walls actually provide an ideal way to screen who's coming in and out. They can be built with strong materials — fortified, blast-resistant, you name it. Your arguments seem . . . specious, for lack of a better word. For every one I could offer a counterargument that's as strong. Stronger."

"We have sound technical or financial reasoning for all our desired changes."

"Your changes would alter the essence of my design."

"An essence, as it so happens, now widely equated with a paradise for martyrs. Even if you didn't intend it that way, it's now read

267

that way — by your opponents, by America's opponents. You saw the Iranian president's statement, I'm sure. He's delighted — delighted! — to have an Islamic paradise in Manhattan."

"He's a buffoon."

"Anyway, there's nothing sacrosanct about your design. Ever read Edmund Burke?"

"Nope."

"His treatise *On the Sublime and Beautiful* — I was just rereading it. He argues for randomness over geometry: the number and disorder of the stars, the way their confusion constitutes a kind of infinity —"

"A grid subdividing endlessly can be a form of infinity, too."

"The point he makes is that man tried to teach nature its business with straight lines and mathematical shapes, but nature wouldn't be taught. He was writing around the time that English gardens came into being, Capability Brown and so on" — Paul's casual mention of this belying the hour he had spent researching the genesis and proliferation of English gardens, or, rather, perusing the research that he had asked Lanny to do — "and those gardens showed that mathematical ideas are not the true measures of beauty."

"I didn't know beauty was what we were

aiming for," Mo said.

"The importance of variation" — Paul decided to ignore him until he finished his piece — "to have parts not be angular but melted into one another, as he puts it. 'No work of art can be great, but as it deceives —'"

"That's affirming, since it's deception I'm being accused of."

"Yes, well, that's not the kind he means — he means tricking the eye."

"This is a memorial, not an English lord's estate. The Garden has order, which its geometry manifests, for a reason, which is that it's an answer to the disorder that was inflicted on us. It's not meant to look like nature. Or like confusion, which is what the attack left behind. If anything, it's meant to evoke the layout of the city it will sit in."

This obstinacy would be Khan's undoing, Paul hoped. Yet perversely, Mo's stubbornness was also increasing Paul's respect, even affection for him, and perhaps salving his conscience, too. Khan had drive, Paul's drive. If this contest didn't make Mohammed Khan, something else would. He carried his own path within him.

269

13

There was a Circle Line cruise around Manhattan for the victims' families. At all of these gatherings a small part of Claire rebelled: how false to pretend the relatives had anything other than loss in common, how morbid to have only that to share. Grief was not a country she had chosen to enter, but she could choose when to leave, even if joining the diaspora bore the taint of treason. Out there the dead were still remembered, but with less feeling. This had long been happening in Claire, in all of them. They believed they couldn't go on. They went on.

The word had gone out to the press beforehand — no questions on the memorial — and to the widows: no ribbons, no stickers, keep it civil for the children. Still, Claire braced for hostility and wondered if she would be strong enough to withstand it. The boat swanned out into the river. Soon swag-laden children were racing around mothers trying to hide their tipsiness from reporters cruising for angles beyond teary remembrance and admirable resilience.

Their interest in Claire was even more avid than usual, but she deflected them. "This is no place for politics," she scolded one puppy who approached.

Bolstered by a vodka tonic, she struck up a conversation with Nell Monroe, one of her favorite fellow widows, whose humor got drier the more she drank. "I'm glad it's you dealing with that whole business and not me," Nell said. "They can let a Martian design the memorial for all I care. It's not going to change my life. Unless, of course, the Martian's looking to get laid. Speaking of which, have you?"

"Have I what?"

"Gotten laid." Claire's sex life, or lack thereof, was a subject of continuing fascination for the other widows. She knew this because of the few, like Nell, who weren't afraid to tell her. She could date anyone, marry anyone, the rap went — half the men they knew had crushes on her. So why the nun act? No one's husband was irreplaceable, not even Saint Calder.

It wasn't entirely true that there had been no one; only that Claire had told no one.

271

The previous summer, at a neighbor's for a fund-raiser, a young man had come in from a run apologizing for being late. Claire had assayed the tall, hard physique beneath the black running shirt and shorts, the handsome bearded face, and thought simply: Him. Jesse, a cousin of the hosts, was staying in their pool house for a few months, helping out with the dogs and the children, until he started graduate school in photography in New York. He was twelve years younger than Claire. She had, by the end of the evening, found a way to invite him over to look at Cal's photography collection, and they had begun an affair — "playdating," they called it — that took place whenever her children were off on playdates of their own or on weekend visits to Cal's parents.

Jesse was as good-natured and open and hale as he had looked at first glance; the sex managed to be both depleting and energizing — people told Claire she hadn't looked so well, so *alive* (an unfortunate word choice, she thought) since the attack. A few times she allowed him to come over when the children were home. Watching him toss William around the pool or offer his suntanning body as a runway for Penelope's dolls, she had allowed herself to entertain the possibility of more than a summer fling.

272

But she was so straitjacketed by dignity — the widow's dignity, the almost-forty-year-old's dignity, the wealthy woman's dignity — that by the time he left in the fall she could barely wave goodbye.

That same straitjacket kept her from sharing the liaison — how would it look, a younger man, a nobody? — with Nell.

"Not lately," she said with a vague smile. "You?"

"I told you about the surgeon, right?"

"Only three times," Claire teased gently.

They were laughing when William showed up on the verge of tears. "Mommy, they won't let me play the fireman." Claire tousled his head. "William is obsessed with firemen," she told Nell. "His sheets. His pajamas. His Halloween costumes. I keep trying to propose new obsessions: no luck so far." Nell smiled at William with a sympathy Claire feared she herself had failed to demonstrate. Then Nell excused herself to go check on her own kids, saying, "They're probably the reason we need a fireman in the first place."

Claire knelt before William. "What happened? Don't you want to play something else? Why did they say you couldn't be the fireman?" He wouldn't meet her eyes, which was unlike him, and when she took him on her lap he began to cry. Around them the party for the "Heroes' Kids" was in full swing, and the microphones and cameras were roving — she saw one hesitate near her, then move on, sense enough at least to leave a crying child alone. "What's wrong, William?" she asked again. He still wouldn't meet her eyes.

"They said I couldn't be the fireman because of you."

"Who said?"

"Timmy and Jimmy."

The Hansen twins. Bulky, ruddy-faced redheads. Bullies, she considered them. At a birthday party she had seen them asking Bozo the Clown how much he earned as their mother pretended not to hear and the clown's runny mouth turned down farther in response. But they were also only eight years old. She knew children lived between the poles of invention and imitation. They had to have gotten this idea from their parents. At least they hadn't made William play a terrorist.

"And they said what, exactly?"

"That you like the bad guys. So I can't play the good guy. Do you? Do you like the bad guys?"

"Of course not," she said, kissing his head. "They're mixed up." She asked William to check on Penelope, who with a half dozen girls was keeping vigil by the uncut cake, and went to track down Jane Hansen. She lived in New Jersey and still looked like the sorority president she had once been. All of her features, even her up-do, looked chiseled.

"Your boys seem to be giving William a hard time because of some idea they have of me," Claire said, not bothering with hello. "Where would they possibly come up with something like that?"

"How should I know?" Jane said. "They have minds of their own, unfortunately."

"Come on," Claire said. "He's six. He lost his father."

"Didn't they all," Jane said evenly, looking not at Claire's eyes but at the roots of her hair, as if trying to ascertain its true color.

"Leave it," said the voice in Claire's head, but her actual voice said, "If you have something to say, say it to me. Your children need to learn how to behave."

"Did it ever occur to you that my boys behave the way they do because of what happened?" Jane asked. "I'm not going to pretend they were angels before, but they were a lot easier. They're different kids." Claire felt an unwelcome twinge of recognition. She often wondered what William would have been like if he hadn't lost his father. Less petulant, maybe; more carefree.

"Hundreds of hours of counseling," Jane was saying, "and now I need to feed them a bunch of crap about how America is such a great country that it let the very people who murdered their father design a memorial to him? An Islamic garden, no less."

"But it's not the same people — that's the point," Claire said. "And there's no proof the garden is Islamic. If it is, it could be benign. A gesture of peace, even."

"*You* try explaining that to an eight-year-old. Or have you? Have you given William your little civics lesson?"

William was suddenly behind her. Or maybe he had been there all along. What had he heard? "Where's your sister?" she asked.

"With-the-girls-at-the-cake," he said, running all the words together. And, although Claire hadn't asked: "She's fine." His feet were planted in place. His expression, as his eyes moved between her and Jane, reminded Claire of the deer in Chappaqua, the way they always paused with a look wistful and curious and fearful all at once before fleeing. But William wasn't going anywhere. He looked transfixed by the sight of his mother arguing.

"What's wrong with the Garden?" he asked.

"Nothing," Claire said.

"Tell him," Jane said.

"There's nothing to tell."

"Let him be the judge of that."

"You want to put this in the hands of a six-year-old?"

"He'd probably get it more than your jury did."

"Ladies," Nell said. She'd come up with a fresh vodka tonic for Claire. Her own speech was slightly blurred. "You may want to continue this another time."

Claire saw the Hansen twins standing with William, the three boys now united in wary confusion.

"You're right, Nell," she said. "Jane, I'm so sorry about . . . about everything. We'll talk another time. William, let's go check on your sister."

They walked off, hand in hand. Her knees were buckling. Maybe these events drew a certain kind, the conformists, the mainstream. Outliers knew better than to seek group consolation.

"What's wrong with the Garden?" William asked again.

"Some people want a different design," she said.

"Why?"

"Because they don't like the man who designed it."

"Why?"

"For no good reason, William. That's why we were arguing."

Cal's voice urged her to the margins, but if their positions were reversed, would he take their children there, exile himself for Mohammed Khan? Cal's own beliefs had cost little but money. A position to defend at a dinner party, a direction in which to channel donations, a box to check on the ballot. Pocket change. Noblesse oblige. These were the phrases Cal's mother had used to describe the Bridgeport teen-mothers program. His boldest move had been quitting the golf club. For all its merit, this was no great sacrifice. He wasn't good enough at golf to miss it.

They couldn't leave the cruise early, as Claire wanted, so she told a crew member she was feeling ill. He led her to a blanketed cot in an airless cabin, where, with the children baffled in their jackets, readied for departure, they sat and waited the long hour for their vessel to make land.

Flipping television channels one night, Asma came upon a news story about a boat trip for the families of the dead. The faces of the women — and it was mostly women — were familiar, and not just because she had seen some of them on the news before, giving interviews, holding press conferences, attending funerals. They had a look about them — blank and guarded, overprotective of their children yet not entirely present to them — that she sometimes caught on her own face.

The Circle Line she knew, too, because it was one of the few splurges she and Inam had made in their two years together. She could still remember the price per ticket — twenty-four dollars — which worked out to sixteen dollars an hour for the two of them, which was seven dollars more than Inam earned in an hour, and she could remember her doubt because she had heard from Mrs. Ahmed that the Staten Island Ferry was free, and you could see the same water, the same city, the same statue, but Inam had insisted and he rarely insisted on anything, and so she had agreed.

Six months after her arrival in America, on a Sunday, Inam's only day off, they had set out. The other passengers — Americans and Swedes, Japanese and Italians — were drinking, even at that morning hour; some leaned against the rails and kissed. She and

Inam had not drunk, had not kissed. They held hands and looked down at the water and studied the city, as if from this distance they could finally understand it. They walked over to look at the orange life vests and boats neatly lined up in case of disaster. Each thought about, and knew the other was thinking about, ferry travel back home: Bangladesh was a country of rivers perilously crossed on rickety, overcrowded boats that flipped or sank or collided, tossing bodies into the water the way these passengers tossed their plastic cups.

From the boat Manhattan had no sound, like a television turned to mute, but around them the wind whipped the water, which slapped the boat, and the tourists laughed and shrieked, and the cries of the white gulls dropped down like loose feathers. The impudent breeze had lifted the tail of her headscarf as if to unwrap her, and Inam had yanked it back down, pretending to battle the wind for her honor.

Inam took her picture with a disposable camera and asked a Swede to take their picture together, then a Japanese man asked Inam to take a picture of him and his wife, and so easily they became a part of everything, New Yorkers. They had no worries that day, money and jobs, language and family, all as insignificant at that moment as a bucket of water poured into the harbor.

On her television the widows were giving strained smiles to reporters who jabbed microphones at them like doctors probing for disease. There was the blond widow from the jury, her son crying on her lap. Mechanically, Asma spooned more rice pudding into Abdul's bowl, her attention on the television children, their faces and free T-shirts smeared with ketchup, their smiles, unlike their parents', bright and real. Abdul was watching her. He could always sense when grief or anger or envy took her elsewhere, and he always brought her back, those betel-brown eyes the deepest correction. He didn't know he was missing a father, hadn't come into the world expecting one, or expecting anything, including a free Circle Line cruise. Perhaps this was the secret to being at peace: want nothing but what is given to you.

She woke the next morning to the sound of her neighbors arguing. Asma thought American buildings would have been sturdier, their walls thicker, but this was like being back home: the ability to know, *having* to know, what was going on in lives not your own or your family's, so that sometimes it was hard to know where your own thoughts left off and others' began. The next-door neighbors, Hasina and Kabir, Bangladeshis who had arrived six months ago, were a married couple in their thirties with no children. This did not surprise Asma: she never heard sounds of love from next door, only anger. Quarrels, in her admittedly limited experience, did not make babies.

Hasina lived in strict purdah, never leaving the house without her husband. Sometimes she would ask Asma to bring her something from the market, an ingredient she needed for cooking, or sanitary napkins, or once even underwear, telling Asma her size. On occasion Asma and Mrs. Mahmoud would invite her for tea, but her husband disapproved of Asma living on her own in America with her son rather than returning home to family. Hasina had told her that, but Asma also knew it by the way Kabir avoided her eyes in the hallway, uttering only a gruff *"Asalamu alaikum"* to avoid being impolite. They were, of course, a favorite subject of Mrs. Mahmoud's, but Asma had grown as weary of talking about her neighbors as she had of listening to them. Twice she had heard Kabir hit Hasina, or at least she thought so from the sharp scream and muffled cries that followed. But everyone pretended they had heard nothing, that the fights did not exist. When she tried to check on Hasina, Kabir would say, through the door, that his wife was "busy."

Their fighting was like a radio Asma could not turn down, which gave her the idea of turning hers up. She switched on the BBC and turned up the volume, trying to drown their noise. The radio was so loud that until Mrs. Mahmoud shouted for her, she didn't hear the phone ringing to inform her of her father's death.

He had been sick for two weeks — "water in the lungs," the doctors said, as if he had taken the delta inside of him. His voice on the phone, on the days he could talk, was all rasp and rattle, faint and frail, nothing like the commanding music she remembered. Her mother kept insisting she should come home, and Asma packed and unpacked in her mind, sometimes even in her room. If she did not go, Abdul would never know his grandfather, as he had never known his father — wouldn't know that a father or grandfather could be anything other than the satiny surface of a picture to stroke. But once she left America, she might never be able to return. Why this mattered mystified her mother, for whom New York was as unreachable, as unimaginable, as unnecessary as the stars, which were proof of God's greatness but otherwise of negligible use.

Asma was also afraid to know her newly weakened father, since her stubborn strength was modeled on his. To hear him faded was to feel her own power ebb. So much of who she was came from him — and would keep her from him. Clinging to America, to the possibilities it dangled, was her own small war of liberation, if a lonelier one.

She harbored a secret fantasy that in America, she could remarry. Not now, not for a long time, not while her ache for Inam remained so deep. But someday she wanted her son to have more than a paper father. If she remarried in Bangladesh, she would have to leave Abdul with Inam's family. This she would never do. It wouldn't be easy to remarry in Brooklyn, but if she had gotten out of Sandwip, she imagined she could get out of Kensington, too. What would it be like to live in those neighborhoods she saw on TV, with white people and big houses and driveways with cars? And sprinklers? She wasn't saying she wanted to live that way. She just wondered.

"Will you come?" her uncle asked now.

Why, she wanted to say: her father would be wrapped and buried before she got home.

"Insh'Allah," she said.

She ended the call inconsolable and irascible. Abdul had put a pot over his head and was stumbling around, bumping into furniture, giggling hysterically. Her neighbors' argument continued, their voices rising and falling with no consideration for her loss. It was disrespectful, like bombing during Ramadan, not to pause for the news of her father's death, even if they didn't know of it. She resented them as much for having each other as for hating each other — for having each other to hate.

There was a moment of stillness; perhaps it was over. Then she heard Kabir's voice again, louder, angrier, then a shriek and a howl and sobs. She had had enough. She thought of her husband, the kindest man she knew, and of her father, the bravest; picked up Abdul, took the pot off his head, marched next door, and knocked loudly.

When Hasina's crying stopped, it left a vacuum — sharper than mere silence — in its wake, like the sudden, startling end of a monsoon. Even wriggling Abdul grew still, as if sensing something had changed. Asma banged again. There was a rustle; she sensed a presence behind the peephole. Then Kabir opened the door, and Asma pushed past him to Hasina, who was huddled on the couch, her face red and puffy, her right eye starting to swell.

"Come with me," Asma said, trying to grab Hasina's elbow without dropping Abdul. Hasina seemed to be making her body dead weight, hugging the couch with her thighs. Abdul, straining his own legs toward the floor, wasn't helping. "Come with me," Asma said louder, as if Hasina hadn't heard. "I'm going to find you a place to stay. You must leave this marriage." She had read about a shelter for abused Muslim women in one of the Bangladeshi papers. And now here was a perfect candidate, as if a character had walked out of a television serial.

"Leave?" Hasina hissed. "Where do you get such language, such thoughts?" Her venom took Asma aback. "I don't want to leave," she said. The skin of her socket was still puffing; soon the eye would disappear, like a rock in water. "Shame! Shame!" Her hysteria rose and she began screaming at Asma to mind her own affairs. Soon Kabir joined in. Asma clamped her hands over Abdul's ears, but he began to scream, too. Backing out of the apartment, she found the hallway full of neighbors, Mrs. Mahmoud among them, who had come to see

286

what was going on. Before they could investigate, opine, pronounce, she ran into her room, locked the door, and sobbed into Abdul's hair.

Two hours later came a knock on Mrs. Mahmoud's door. Three men known to Asma as residents of the building stood there announcing their concerns about her interference. Her response, as in any difficult situation now, was to call Nasruddin. He came quickly, in an elegant pajama, and she wondered, guiltily, if she had taken him from a family occasion. She told him the story, then sobbed to him about her father.

"Did I do the right thing not to go back to Bangladesh?" she wept. "Tell me I did the right thing."

"You did what I would have done," he said.

When she finished crying, she felt emptied of fight, tired enough to sleep for days. Nasruddin left her to go thread peace through the building. An hour later, he returned. To stay without worry, he warned, she must leave her neighbors alone.

"There is a right way to handle problems," he said. "You must learn it."

"But how am I supposed to live next door to such a man?"

"I will work on him," Nasruddin said, "but you must leave him to God's judgment."

"I am grateful," she muttered. Embarrassed and angry, too, but this she kept to herself. The sense that she had been outdone by malevolent forces nagged at her. Her father would have been braver.

"What did you say? How did you do it?" she asked.

"I told them the truth," Nasruddin said. Her father had died, and she had been mad with grief.

The Rally to Protect Sacred Ground kicked off on a balmy Saturday morning in a plaza opposite the site. The members of both the Memorial Defense Committee and Save America from Islam were there, gathered in a cordoned-off area in front of the stage. Behind them stretched a crowd of thousands: women holding signs that said NO TOLERANCE FOR THE INTOLERANT or ISLAM KILLS or NO VICTORY GARDEN or KHAN IS A CON; fathers hoisting small children on their shoulders; men in camouflage who may or may not have been veterans. There were hundreds of relatives of the attack victims there — Sean had called many of them personally to ask them to come. The crowd overflowed the small plaza, spilled along the sidewalk, out into the street, around and between the buses that had chauffeured protesters from across the country. News choppers huffed overhead.

Debbie Dawson was kitted out in tight black pants and yet another T-shirt she had designed, this one reading "Kaffir and Proud." Two buff men in Ray-Bans, blue blazers, and khaki pants trailed her through the crowd. When she stopped to give interviews or greet supporters, they positioned themselves on either side of her, facing out, feet planted in a wide stance, arms never fully relaxed. Bodyguards, Sean realized. She looked like she was having the time of her life.

Taking the stage for his speech, Sean surveyed the swelling crowd. Maybe all the nut jobs had gathered near the front; there seemed to be a lot of them. An obese man in suspenders held a poster that showed a pig eating a Quran. Three women hoisted a banner that said NUKE 'EM ALL AND LET ALLAH SORT 'EM OUT. A pimpled teenager dressed in black with Harry Potter glasses held a sign reading THEY CAN HAVE THE FIRST AMENDMENT BECAUSE WE HAVE THE SECOND, with a crude drawing of a gun aimed at the face of a turbaned man.

Human loose ends: an irregular army that Sean hadn't summoned and couldn't decommission.

His idea of whiting out Claire Burwell's face to paint in a question mark, which had seemed so creative, looked creepy when a hundred and fifty of the posters were being waved at him. The SAFI posters of Khan — a line drawn through his face or a target superimposed on it — didn't look much better. The police were encircling one man who, with the selective application of lighter fluid to his poster, had managed to ignite Khan's beard.

Every time Sean had given a speech since the attack — some ninety in all — he had been convinced that to lose a loved one in this way was a privilege as well as a curse. The overfed, overeager faces listening to him hungered for what couldn't be bought, and he pitied them for the desire to go somewhere deeper, be part of something larger. Horrible as the attack was, everyone wanted a little of its ash on their hands.

But this mass, the largest he had ever addressed, radiated neither reverence nor yearning. Patrick once had shown him how the back pressure from opening the nozzle on a fire hose too fast could knock a firefighter off a ladder. Sean didn't trust this crowd.

His game was off, his speech short. "It wasn't enough for Khan to demand his rights as a Muslim. Now his garden has rights, too . . ." The cheers were scattered, irregular, as if people couldn't hear well. The microphone's feedback was distracting. When he said, "We all know the Constitution matters, don't we?" there were uncertain roars, a few boos. "We just don't think it's the only thing that matters," he finished. Some applause, at least, but tepid.

When Debbie strode onstage, a SAFI volunteer moved in behind her to wave the flag. A battery-powered fan placed in front rippled back her long hair. "I want us to be clear that we are fighting for the soul of this country," she bellowed. The crowd, its hearing suddenly acute, roared. "For generations immigrants came to this country and assimilated, accepted American values. But Muslims want to change America — no, they want to conquer it. Our Constitution protects religious freedom, but Islam is not a religion! It's a political ideology, a totalitarian one." More roars. Sean rocked a little on his feet, unhappy that her broadside had revealed his to be utterly forgettable. She moved on to leading a cathartic, rousing cry of "Save America from Islam! Save America from Islam!"

At the chants, which were meant to cue the lie-in, Sean raised his right hand in the air and blew a whistle. He was important again. His committee members and the SAFIs bunched around him like excited schoolchildren, then smoothed into perfect marching-band rows as they moved into the street.

Sean's original vision had been constricted by a series of compromises. The governor claimed that she had no power to get them permission to protest on the site itself. "So the gates are open to Khan, but not to us," Debbie said, with satisfaction. She had a knack for turning any setback into proof of her worldview, any disagreement with her into evidence of dhimmitude. "Fine, we'll block the street," she said next, as if it had all been her idea, not Sean's. But even getting permission to do that in such a sensitive spot had required concession: the police wanted, in advance, the names of all those planning to be arrested. Now Sean, who had earlier been absorbed in watching the crowd, realized the police had already closed the street, which was as empty of cars as the weekday church parking lot where they had practiced. There was no blocking to be done.

With less gusto he blew again, and the marching band became a drill team: some five hundred well-spaced people kneeling as one, the move meant to mimic, then mock, Muslims praying: instead of touching their heads to the ground, they stretched out on their backs. "Giving Allah the Navel," Debbie called the move.

"Protect sacred ground!" his members chanted.

"Save America from Islam!" the SAFIs chanted.

Sean, after surveying the weave of bodies, lowered himself into a cloud of SAFI perfume and his own sweat. The ground beneath his back was hard, the sky above a piercing blue, smooth as newly made ice cream. A day as clear, as beautiful as the one that had brought the attack, a gift of a day, but irritation was stuck somewhere in him like a pebble in a shoe.

"You are blocking a public street," a police official said through a bullhorn. "I'm going to count to one hundred, and by the time I finish, you all need to disperse. If not we will begin making arrests."

The tight scripting struck Sean now as enfeebling (". . . forty-three, forty-four, forty-five . . ."), their defiance as nothing more than managed submission. His secret hope had been that maybe the police wouldn't arrest them at all, would refuse to follow orders, choose patriotism over duty (". . . sixty-nine, seventy, seventy-one . . ."). But listening for the sound of the blue wall cracking, all he heard were police boots scuffing. And then: "ninety-eight . . . ninety-nine . . . one hundred. Time is up, ladies and gentlemen," and, "Please stand, sir, let's not make this difficult, thank you, appreciate it, hands in front, these are plastic, don't actually hurt, thank you."

"Terrorist lover!" he heard a woman scream at a cop, who said, almost kindly, "Ma'am, I've got four kids; the only thing I love is my paycheck."

Their politeness was killing him, as was his back. Lifting his head to check on the police, he saw a silent group of counter-protesters standing on the sidewalk. Most, but not all, looked Muslim — headscarves on the women, beards on the men, dark skin. They held signs: WE ALSO ARE AMERICANS and ISLAM IS NOT A THREAT and MUSLIMS DIED THAT DAY, TOO and BIGOTS=IDIOTS. It was that last sign that flooded Sean's brain with red, which also happened to be the color of the headscarf on the woman holding it. Rubin wanted *him* to be less crude? He scrambled to his feet and stalked over to her. "Are you calling me an idiot?" His spittle flew; his voice cracked; he didn't care. "You're calling my parents bigots? A bunch of Muslims killed my brother. Why aren't you out protesting them? Have you ever held up a sign that said, 'Murder in the name of my religion is wrong'?"

"Of course it's wrong," the woman said steadily, "but discriminating on the basis of religion is wrong, too."

Her placidity, so provoking, made him want to provoke her in return, to get a rise, and the most provocative act he could think of was to tug back her headscarf, and he reached out, some small part of him also wanting to see what was so valuable it had to be covered, and caught the edge of the scarf as she stepped back in fear, so that the scarf came forward, a little roughly, maybe he blinded her for a moment, maybe his hand brushed against her head, then a police officer was separating them, or rather holding back then handcuffing Sean, and reading him his rights, bundling him in a van with his committee members and the SAFIs, who were still chanting "No Muslim memorial!" and flashing him wide smiles and thumbs-up, and at the station the others were taken and quickly processed and released, while he was held for arraignment on a misdemeanor assault charge along with a miscellany of shoplifters, public urinators, and trespassers before being released on his own recognizance.

Debbie called his pulling the headscarf "a stroke of genius." Outraged liberals called it a stunt. None of them would believe he hadn't planned it. His determination to escape the script served only to affirm it.

His chest housed a hard ache. At home, his mother greeted him with pursed lips and a silent shake of her head.

"It looked pretty bad," his wet-eyed sister Miranda whispered, to which Sean said, "Well, fuck that," and went up to shower. But he avoided his own eyes in the mirror. He'd out-Debbied Debbie, and it didn't feel all that great.

14

The Committee to Defend Mohammad
Khan, the Mohammad Khan Defense
Fund, the Mohammad Khan Protection
League — all of them lacked only one
ingredient, which was Mohammad Khan.
He didn't want to compromise his independence, didn't want to shoulder any donors'
associations, didn't want to be some radical-
chic pet, a Black Panther with a beard in
place of an Afro, but they organized on his
behalf even without him, staged press
conferences, plays, fund-raisers, and semi-
nars in his name. And parties, including one
that Roi asked, or rather ordered, Mo to attend. Its host was a film producer whose
Hamptons house Roi had designed. "People
want to be in the room with you," Roi said,
then sent his regrets as soon as Mo agreed
to go.

The party, in a vast, dimly lit, high-
ceilinged apartment at the Dakota, was

packed. Through enfiladed rooms currents of guests flowed onward without cease, carrying Mo and Laila — in a dress whose torn-petal layers made her look like a pink peony — with them. Strangers plucked Mo out of the processional to introduce him to other strangers, then returned him, like an unworthy pebble, to the stream. Champagne was passed for toasts no one could hear.

"You know Bobby, right?" De Niro nodded as if to say that yes, Mo did.

"I've been a great supporter of the Palestinian cause," a British baroness told Mo meaningfully.

"This isn't about the Palestinians," someone said, overhearing.

"Always, this attempt to disentangle," eye-rolled Mariam Said.

Rosie O'Donnell laughed behind him. Sean Penn was drunk.

I'm dreaming, Mo thought. Dreaming this is all happening to me. It was not unlike how he had imagined Frank Gehry's or Richard Meier's life to be, or his own if he reached their level. Except here was Meier now, waiting, like an acolyte, to have a word with him. The world was upside down. He was half god, half freak. He reached for Laila's hand, then remembered not to. Russell Simmons squeezed by and jostled him against her. She smiled without turning to look at him. He imagined them home, lacing fingers in bed.

Green ribbons curled vivaciously from dresses and lapels. Mo drank more champagne and struggled toward the windows overlooking the courtyard. Admirers checkmated him to offer inexact praise or overdone sympathy. A woman displaying biceps to rival Madonna's asked if anyone had bought the rights to his life.

"I didn't know they were for sale," he tried to banter. He was more than a little drunk.

"I know Shah Rukh Khan, a bit," her companion said. "Cousin — ?"

"Brother," Mo said.

"He's kidding," Laila interrupted. "Khan is a very common name in India. And elsewhere."

In the cab on the way home, Laila looked at him and said, "No jokes, Mo. Those people are on your side, even if you don't like them. And you can't complain about being misrepresented, then misrepresent yourself."

His buzz was fading. "I wasn't myself in there, in a good way," he said wearily. "I was actually having fun. Every day I'm different, Laila. I'm not the person you met three weeks ago. If this keeps up, in two weeks I won't be the person you know now. You can't misrepresent an object in motion."

Her gaze roamed from his mouth to his eyes. "You're underestimating your own solidity. I saw it in that first meeting. It's what drew me to you, and probably what will drive me crazy in the end. The edges of you may be changed by this. But Mohammad Khan is intact. You're like your steel trees."

Steel breaks, steel melts, he wanted to say — we all know that now. Instead he took her hand.

On the way to her newsroom cubicle, Alyssa decided to detour by her editor's desk. Chaz would be there by ten, sleeves rolled up, barking orders, berating reporters, mocking rival papers, downing black coffee, his immunity to hangovers as legendary as his benders.

He had been avoiding her lately, and in those eyes that wouldn't meet hers, she saw her demotion scheduled. The initial column had been provocative enough to land her two more, but they lacked exclusives, lacked bombs. The most recent had been so deadening that it had drawn a yawn, literally, from Chaz, who then killed it. Her currency was devaluing. That first column had earned her an appearance on Bill O'Reilly, a clip she replayed often enough to memorize.

"Are Muslims a fifth column, Alyssa?" O'Reilly had asked.

"I think that's too strong, Bill," she replied, his first name a lozenge on her tongue. "Maybe fourth and a half." He laughed hard and said afterward that he would invite her back to the show. But he hadn't.

Now Chaz ducked his head and picked up his phone when he saw her coming, then put it down when he thought she had passed. There it was, her dimmed luster confirmed. Like a junkie's, her addiction had progressed from reading the news, to reporting it, to breaking it, then — the crack cocaine of her business — to shaping it. Being it. The prospect of her supply being cut off triggered a cold sweat.

No one greeted her as she finished circumnavigating the newsroom, which was no surprise. She hadn't bonded with her new colleagues; they resented her, as she likely would resent them if the positions were reversed. Rare was the newsroom that celebrated anyone's ascent, especially a newcomer's. The energy instead went to spinning elaborate theories about why her success was undeserved, with any subsequent fall only proof of the notion. Never had she felt so friendless.

From her purse she extracted and fingered, as if it were fine silk, her one flimsy hope, Claire Burwell's cell-phone number, procured by another expensive dinner for that fey jury assistant. Lanny's power only seemed to be growing — he was overseeing press strategy for the memorial mess, and his strategy for some reason included passing her information. It amazed her no one had identified him as the leaker; instead he had convinced Paul Rubin to put him in charge of the leak investigation, then set about casting vague aspersions on various jurors and sundry employees.

She dialed Claire, nervous, and almost dropped the phone when she answered.

"Mrs. Burwell?"

"Yes."

"This is Alyssa Spier, from the *Post*." She hated, in that moment, her hissing name, her paper's name, all that sibilance.

Silence.

"How did you get my number?"

"From a friend. I'm —"

"No friend of mine would give you my number."

I didn't say *your* friend. Alyssa pressed on. "So sorry to bother you."

"What do you want?"

"I want to talk to you about the memorial, the hearing. Uh, I just want to get a sense of what you're thinking —"

"You wrote an appalling column about what I'm thinking, and now you want to talk?"

Alyssa held the phone slightly away from her ear and thought: Fuck you, you moral prig. You've had everything easy — okay, everything other than your husband dying — and you judge me?

"Maybe we could just meet and talk informally," she said. "You know, not for the record."

"Don't call me on this number again."

"Wait!" Alyssa hailed Mary. "Wait. I'm calling because I have information you'll want. On Khan."

There was a tantalizing hesitation on the other end of the line, then Claire said, coldly, "Why would your information be of interest to me?"

"Because," Alyssa said, "because — it could be explosive, for the families, and if I were you I'd want to be prepared for that."

"Fine," Claire said, after another pause.

For all her relief, Alyssa was surprised that Claire agreed to meet, and suspicious, as if by accident she'd stepped on a soft, rotting plank in an impeccable hardwood floor. There was some uncertainty, some vulnerability there. The only problem was that Alyssa had no tool to pry up that plank: she'd lied when she said she had ominous information on Khan. Under-promise, then surprise, Oscar had always told her. She'd promised "explosive," with only until tomorrow morning to find it.

She worked the phone and keyboard until the tendons in her forearms ached. There had to be something on Mohammad Khan she could use: there was something on everyone. She circled back to her contacts at the police department, the FBI. Was he on any terrorist watch list? Any no-fly list? Any general "suspicious Muslim" list? Nothing, at least nothing anyone would share. Plenty of dirt on the woman lawyer, but the blogs were already all over her maggoty client list — terrorist suspects, loud-mouthed Palestinian-defending imams, unidentified undocumented relatives of attack victims for whom she had secured windfalls. Anyway, guilt by such attenuated association probably wouldn't move Claire.

The newsroom began emptying out. When Alyssa looked outside, darkness had already dropped. She ate ramen noodles from the vending machine, their texture just a few molecular recombinations from the Styrofoam cup containing them. The janitor had begun pushing his supply cart and sadness across the cluttered room, and something deeper than panic pressed hard on her heart.

At ten, she left the building to walk across a city temperamentally indifferent to desperation. She rehearsed her words: "Oscar, I need help. Oscar, I need help." He had deeper law enforcement sources than anyone. Why he should share them with her, an ex-sort-of-paramour, now a reporter for a rival paper, she couldn't say. She could only hope.

By the time he answered his buzzer she was in tears, blubbering so that the words came out, "Monster, I weed kelp." He let her up anyway. It never occurred to her that he might not be alone.

"Alyssa, this is Desiree," he said, managing not to be awkward despite the fact that he was wearing a T-shirt and boxers, as was Desiree. "She's having a work issue," he told Desiree. "Give us a minute?" He wasn't wearing his glasses, and it took Alyssa back to her first time seeing his naked eyes, more meaningful to her, somehow, than his naked body had been. She would have given anything to be back in her newsroom now, but it was too late. With Desiree boudoir-bound, Alyssa confessed her predicament.

"What did I always tell you?" he said, his tone as reassuringly solid as a wall, and as impenetrable.

"I know, I know. But now I'm stuck. Please. Anything. I'll owe you. I don't even need anything to print. Just something to get her to talk."

"In that case you could make it up."

As Alyssa pondered this, Oscar put his glasses on and watched her through them. "That would be cheating," she said. "It's no fun, you know that. And once you start doing that, what's the point of doing this at all?"

His mouth turned up at one edge, like a wink. Good girl: she had passed the test. Ignoring the sound of the bedroom television and the woman watching it, she briefly let herself imagine a rekindled affair. That he then gave her a scrap to use only fed the dream. In their world, it qualified as a romantic gesture.

"Here's what I got," he said. "A buddy of mine at the bureau who was in Kabul for a while told me this, but it's Pluto" — their shorthand for "so far off the record it's on Pluto." His eyes commanded now: "And you'll see why I didn't run with it, and you won't, either. I have your word?"

My word, whatever else you want. She nodded.

She and Claire met near Arthur Avenue in the Bronx. It was neutral ground between Chappaqua and Manhattan. And who would spot them in an Albanian coffee shop? Its walls were mirrored, its tables marble, its espresso feral, its pastry stale. Wrinkled old men played dominoes at one table, the tiles clicking in place of talk. At another, three young men brooded, their eyes never leaving Alyssa and Claire. In posters on the walls, female fighters brandished AK-47s. Alyssa's glance lingered on them for a moment: Albanians were . . . Muslim. Maybe neutral ground wasn't so neutral after all.

Through bleary vision, she studied Claire's bone structure and sapphire eyes, until they narrowed in suspicion. "Why are we here?" Claire asked, cool.

"I have information, but I can't share it unless you give me an interview," Alyssa blurted. She was underrested, overcaffeinated, and jittery.

"I can't," Claire said. "It's against the rules. I told you that."

Something on background, Alyssa insisted, that would allow her to convey what Claire was thinking, even if it came from "knowledgeable sources" or "a friend of Claire Burwell."

"How do I know that what you're telling me is important?" Claire said.

"Trust me," Alyssa said, and they both looked embarrassed.

Claire unfolded and refolded her paper napkin. "This is a dirty business, isn't it," she said. A statement, not a question. Alyssa wasn't sure which business she was referring to. Journalism? The memorial selection? The Albanian coffee shop, which stank of being a cover for organized crime? For a minute she pitied Claire for having to soil her pristine values in the muck where everyone else lived.

"I like to think of it as practical," Alyssa said, in a way she hoped was soothing. She waited until Claire almost whispered "Oh, all right," and then pulled out her notebook.

"He was in Afghanistan," she told Claire now. "Kabul."

"So is that where —" Claire started to say.

"He made a threat against the embassy there."

"What?" Claire said, incredulous. "That can't be true." But she was white. Alyssa pushed a water glass closer to her. Claire

308

sipped. "There must be some explanation," she said, tremulous. "Why wouldn't everyone know about this? Why wouldn't they have arrested him?"

"I don't think it was an actionable threat," Alyssa said. "More threatening language. Supportive of threats, rather than making a threat himself. These cases are difficult — if they locked up every Muslim who said something anti-American, the prisons would be full. More full. Way more full. I'm just trying to give you a sense of how he thinks."

In the long silence that followed, Alyssa gobbled the meat pie she had ordered, hoping to absorb some of the acid in her stomach, even as she motioned to the surly waiter for another espresso. She was still chewing when Claire spoke.

"You really are despicable, trying to smear him," she said, curling her mouth in disapproval.

Alyssa shrugged. "I wasn't trying to smear him. I'm probably not even going to publish it," she said, not mentioning that, per Oscar's condition, she couldn't, or that the report had been dismissed because it came from an architect competing against ROI to design the new embassy and clearly trying to gain advantage. The "threat" was an offhand comment Mo had made. Alyssa didn't know what it was. Usually it was the Afghans narcing on each other to settle scores or win some personal gain, Oscar's friend had told him. This one lodged in memory because it was one American trying to shank another, using Mo's being Muslim to do it. Alyssa felt no guilt about sharing only part of this story with Claire. Fabricating reality was criminal; editing it, commonplace.

"I thought you would want to know, as you weigh things," she said. "And I wanted to talk to you, and it was a way to get through. So now how about it" — she paused to extract her tape recorder from her purse — "you going to keep your promise, or what?"

Claire glared at her. "If you're not going to quote me, why are you taping it?"

"For my own protection," Alyssa said with all the sincerity she could muster. "And yours."

The interview was a mess, as those conducted at gunpoint often are. Claire looked like she would have preferred to confide in the Albanian thugs. Her posture was so obdurate, her utterances so miserly, that Alyssa worried whether she could fill a story. She opted for provocation.

"Do you trust Mohammad Khan?"

"Why wouldn't I?" Claire snapped.

"Well, put another way, how much do you know about what he thinks? Putting aside whether this garden is or isn't a martyrs' paradise — and we all know he won't say, although I'm not clear on why he won't say — what's his position on jihad? On whether it's right for America to be in Afghanistan? On what brought the buildings down — does he subscribe to all the conspiracy theories saying it was an inside job? Does he think America got what it deserved?"

"None of that is relevant," Claire said.

"Really?" Alyssa said. "You really believe that? It's not relevant if he would be happy if the American embassy was blown up? Or if he believes Mossad or the CIA carried out the attack? You'd still want him to build your memorial?"

"Why don't you ask him these questions?" Claire snarled.

"He's not building a memorial to my husband," Alyssa said, wondering if this made it sound like she had a husband.

Tears filled Claire's eyes but, as if they knew their place, didn't leave. "We can't ask him," she said, in a subdued voice. "We're not allowed — it wouldn't be fair to him."

"Is it fair to you?" Some secular lust was burning in Alyssa, the desire to hack at this

311

glacier of a woman, to push her harder and harder until she confronted her own hypocrisies, the impossibility — the ridiculousness — of her position. Alyssa wanted to see Claire Burwell's principles collapse beneath her, and she was dimly aware that this desire told as much about her, Alyssa, as it did about Claire. Being a Columnist, trying to influence invisible masses, didn't suit her. But using information, insinuation, and the right line of questioning to rewire a woman in front of her eyes — that was a scary rush of a high.

"Can you live with never knowing the answers to those questions?" she asked.

"I have to," Claire whispered. Her hands were limp in her lap, her head slightly bowed. She was almost docile now, before Alyssa's onslaught, as if she was being justifiably berated.

"Or are you scared to know the answer? What if he does hate your husband, or everyone like your husband? What if he hates you, the infidel widow? Are there no conditions under which you would say he's not suitable?"

Claire's spine straightened. Clarity returned to her eyes. "Legally — no, morally, I can't, won't take this from him just because of what he *might* think."

"Then that's all the more reason to ask him what he *does* think!" Alyssa squawked. "Why don't you? He won't answer me, or other reporters, but you're a juror, a family member, I think he would have to answer you."

"Weren't you listening?" Claire spit the words. She clenched her jaw, balled her hands into fists on the table. Animus was turning her, if not ugly, something far from beautiful. "It's not fair to him to ask."

"That's his line, Mrs. Burwell, and I'm sure he's thrilled you've adopted it. But again, is that really what you think?"

Claire nodded, shook her head, nodded again, pressed her lips together like a child resisting food, and stared, as if just noticing them, at the AK-wielding women on the walls.

"Headscarf puller may have a history of violence against women: report at eleven."

The teaser, on a local news channel caught up in sweeps week, ran so often that the interview, aired as promised at eleven, was almost an anticlimax. Sean's ex-wife was claiming he had beaten her once: "He shoved me against the wall and I had to wear a sling for three days . . . No, I don't know why: he just lost his temper. He has a temper, everyone knows that now."

Her hair was different: short, punkish, dyed blond. She looked hot, if not entirely credible. The Body, Patrick had called her. She must have sold her story. Irina never did anything for free.

"She always was a liar," Eileen said. She and Sean were on the couch, Frank in his easy chair, where he had been dozing all night. Now he was fully alert.

Sean took a deep breath. "She's not lying." The signs of his mother's displeasure were so physically subtle that it was easy to miss them if you didn't know what you were looking for, but Sean did: the mouth thinning out, the ears shifting back and taking the hairline with them. "I mean, not entirely. She's exaggerating — she didn't have to wear a sling, she wore it just to make me feel bad and to get off work. But she's not lying."

Irina was a shadow that wouldn't vanish even at night, a mistake with an afterlife. They'd married a few months after they met — quick, drunk, Borough Hall. "No church?" was all that his mother had said when he told her. A judgment, but also an investigation, as if she was assessing, with her typical, irritating foresight, how hard it would be to end. They'd boozed their way through the next five months, until the attack. As he hunted for bodies, she gathered resentments, and when he came home she banished him to the couch because his new, persistent cough was keeping her up. She prattled on about the stupidity of her bar-owner boss, whether the fear was making people tip less or more, how much she hated her mother. Through the fog of his exhaustion he saw her clearly for the first time: a survivor of a rough childhood whose instincts toward self-preservation had become mere selfishness, and a drunk. No doubt his ability to grasp this came from his being, for the first time since they met, sober. The bottomless desire he had felt for the moons of her ass and the cream of her skin became a kind of revulsion. When she complained, one too many times, that there was a dead man in bed with them, his chest tightened and he shoved her into the wall. Cradling her afterward, he couldn't still the angry drumming of his heart, or hers. They divorced as soon as the state would let them. She stayed in their apartment, which used to be his.

"Well, that's done," his mother had said.

Now Sean tried to explain why he had manhandled her. "She was disrespecting Patrick," he said, hoping that defending his

315

brother's honor would outweigh the lousy deed, knowing, as soon as he saw the ears pull back, that it wouldn't.

"Patrick wouldn't have hit a woman," she said.

"Not even that one," said Frank.

The second headscarf pulling occurred less than a week after the rally. A man in a Queens shopping mall walked up to a Muslim woman pushing a baby stroller, tugged her headscarf back, and ran. The next took place in Boston. This perpetrator didn't flee — instead he waited for the police to arrest him so he could testify to the media: "I saw that guy do it on the news, and I thought, we all need to be that brave, take a stand." More men copied him, and copycats copied the copycats, so within a week there had been more than a dozen incidents around the country. Some non-Muslim women put on headscarves in solidarity, but no one preyed on them.

In an editorial, *The New York Times* called Sean representative of "a new, ominous strain of intolerance in the land." Reporters called him to ask how it felt to represent a new strain of intolerance. The atmosphere in his parents' house chilled. "It's Muslims that are supposed to mistreat women,"

Eileen said to him when he came into the kitchen before dinner one night. Her hands were full with a tray of roast chicken, but before he could get the swinging door to the dining room for her, she turned around and backed it open with her rear end.

When the FBI called to say they had tracked hostile references to Sean in jihadist chat rooms online, he brushed off the threat but welcomed the excuse to vacate his parents' house for a while. "I don't want to put my parents in danger," he told Debbie Dawson, knowing, somehow, that she would find him a place to stay. He didn't expect it to be in her apartment.

It was a sprawling aerie on the Upper East Side, two units her husband had conjoined before he split. She lived with her three daughters: Trisha, eighteen, flouncy, fond of flashing Sean the straps of her bra, when she wore one; Alison, sixteen and flitty; and Orly, at thirteen the baby, a pout. All three had signs saying NO ISLAM ZONE on their doors: Debbie wasn't allowed to talk about "the cause," as they disdainfully referred to it, in their rooms. When they didn't get their way, they threatened to marry Muslims.

Sean felt like he had come upon the Wizard of Oz in his bathrobe, since Debbie spent most of the day in hers. Once the girls went off to school, she entered her virtual world, obsessively updating her blog, rallying supporters and volunteers (two of whom acted, on occasion, as her bodyguards), flaming opponents across the Web. She made sure to shower and dress before the girls came home in the afternoon.

They were on the eighteenth floor, and at first the height elevated Sean's sense of his own worth. It was his first time living in Manhattan, and his days were his, since he had temporarily delegated Joe Mullaney, his lieutenant, to run the committee. He walked the blocks around Debbie's apartment trying to look like he belonged. But he didn't; he was the only man not in a hurry. Not even the children idled here. One afternoon he trailed a man who, with his slick affect and Middle Eastern complexion, reminded him of Mohammad Khan. The man went into a museum whose brutal gray concrete exterior put Sean off not just because he found it ugly but because he suspected it was meant to be beautiful in a way he didn't get — and he winced to realize that it was the architect Khan who would better fit here.

When he came back to the apartment, Debbie was out, and he glanced at her blog. Debbie's burka-bikinied body — the focus, he knew now, had been soft — had shrunk to make way for a new item. THE AMERICAN WAY IS CURRENTLY GIVING ASYLUM TO A REFUGEE FROM ISLAMIST POLITICAL VIOLENCE, it said in huge letters. DONATE NOW! This man has been threatened for being brave enough to speak up against the Islamist threat and against Mohammad Khan. Now he has had to flee his home. We are feeding and housing him. DONATE NOW!

"Is this me?" he asked when Debbie returned with the girls.

"I am housing you," she said. "And someone's got to put these girls through college."

"Daddy's going to put us through college," Trisha said.

Debbie cut her eyes at her eldest. "Women need to be financially independent."

"That blog," Trisha said, wrinkling her pert nose, "is not going to make you independent."

On a temperate fall day, Paul summoned Claire to Manhattan for lunch and a reprimand. The *Post* cover — WIDOW WAVERING — had caught him off guard. Alyssa Spier's story didn't quote her directly, of course, but the flimsy diversions ("Friends say Claire Burwell is concerned by Mohammad Khan's evasiveness") had the funk of

319

falsehood. He was peeved Claire appeared to have, against jury rules, talked to the press. He was shocked she had talked to the *Post*. And if she wasn't the source, she should have known better than to think out loud to her friends.

"I screwed up," she said, as the waiter pulled her chair out, then tucked her into the table. "I apologize, Paul."

"And I thought I was going to have to waterboard you to get the truth," he said drily. "Would that all of our country's information-gathering efforts went so smoothly."

"I'm not wavering, though. She mischaracterized me. She kept trying to provoke me into saying I thought Khan should come clean."

"So you, not just your friends, talked to her? Why the *Post,* of all places, Claire?"

"She told me she had information on Khan."

Paul raised his eyebrows in surprise. "And?"

"He was in Afghanistan, Paul, and —"

"Yes, I know," he said.

"You know? Why didn't you say something to us?"

"Because it has no bearing. He went for his architecture firm. It's perfectly legitimate, raised no flags."

"That's not what she — Alyssa Spier — said."

"Then perhaps we should hire her in place of our security consultants. What did she say, exactly?"

"It's — that he — there weren't really details," Claire said, and blushed, then seemed to blush at her blushing. She was now beautifully pink.

Paul, in vain, waited for more, then said, "Be careful, Claire. You're an important player in this — among the most important — and people are going to try to manipulate you. Even more so now with this story suggesting you're persuadable. It puts you in play."

"Well, I'm not in play; I haven't changed my position. I just needed to know if there was anything to know."

"You can't have it both ways."

A plate of melon and prosciutto landed between them. Claire paused while the waiter bowed off.

"What does that mean?" she asked.

"You can't say people shouldn't be suspicious of him just because he happens to be a Muslim, then have suspicions of your own."

"I don't have suspicions! I just want to

know what I'm defending. It hasn't been easy to have my position public. William has been picked on — it's very upsetting." Her agitation was evident; her pupils seemed to dilate.

"I'd still like to know how your support for Khan became public in the first place," Paul said. "It was also Alyssa Spier who reported that, wasn't it?"

"Paul, you don't think I would have —"

"It's hard to know what to think anymore."

"That didn't come from me. I'm fine with it being public but between us would have preferred that it wasn't. It limited my room to maneuver. I think you let Lanny off too easily on the leaks," she added provocatively.

He ignored this, took a bite of melon, and pushed the plate away.

"No appetite?" she asked, with a little too much surprise.

He tried to make light — "I'm too fat a target" — but he didn't feel light. The House minority leader, also a presidential aspirant, had labeled the jury Islamist sympathizers and vowed to sponsor legislation to block the construction of Khan's design. Geraldine Bitman's response to this was hardly reassuring: "The danger to America isn't just from jihadists," she said.

"It's from the naïve impulse to privilege tolerance over all other values, including national security. Mohammad Khan has brought us face-to-face with our own vulnerability." Paul was finding it ever harder to get his old friend on the phone.

The cacophony drowned out his repeated, and reasonable, attempts to point out that the jury had selected from anonymous entries. He prided himself on buffering his jurors from the onslaught, took the pressures on himself as evidence of his capacity to lead. But it was wearing. A flamboyant real estate mogul with a toupee and an inestimable fortune was vowing to sponsor his own memorial design competition, then underwrite construction of the winner, although no one was sure he had the liquidity to do it. Hearing this, a liberal hedge-fund billionaire of Paul's acquaintance had called to say he would underwrite a hefty chunk of the cost of the Garden.

"You think that will solve this problem?" Paul wanted to bark. He was angry. "You think it's fair to Americans to buy your way around a democratic process?" But all he said was, "Let's wait until the selection is finalized, then I'll hold you to that pledge."

As if the endless blare of news — a car alarm that wouldn't turn off — weren't enough, Paul couldn't turn on the television without confronting dark advertisements against the Garden. One showed frothing Iranians chanting "Death to America," stone-throwing Palestinians, burka-wearing women, RPG-toting Taliban, terrorist leaders in high-thread-count beards, nuclear bombs exploding, Muslims praying en masse, and of course Mohammad Khan, glowering beneath the words "Save the Memorial." No one knew who was paying for the ads — reporters could trace the group putatively behind them only as far as a post office box in Delaware.

"Have We Forgotten?" another began, the words white on black. Then came a montage of the attack's most harrowing sights and sounds: the jumpers swimming through air; the desperate messages on answering machines; the panicked voices of emergency dispatchers; the first fulminating collapse, and the second; the tsunami of smoke chasing terrified New Yorkers down narrow, rumbling streets; the aghast faces of witnesses, the distraught ones of orphans. Then, "The Jury Forgot" — and a faint, but unmistakable, image, almost a holograph, of Mohammad Khan — "But the Rest of Us Haven't."

But the worst for Paul, although he hated

to admit it, was being singled out for personal attack. *The Weekly Standard* had castigated "the heretofore respected chairman of the memorial selection jury" for failing to speak out against Khan's "martyrs' paradise."

"Does Rubin's acquiescence suggest a lack of commitment to fighting the Islamofascist threat; does it imply sympathy for that movement's goals? Is he, in short, with us or with them?" the magazine asked. "We would remind him what 1938 taught, that neutrality in the face of an existential threat is nothing more than appeasement. We would like to see from Mr. Rubin some indication of where he stands. The moment for Churchillian clarity is now." Reading this, Paul had slumped in his chair, his drooping head giving him only a Churchillian chin. Ever since, he had found it hard to eat.

"I'm sure that *Weekly Standard* column was unpleasant to read," Claire said now.

Surprised she had seen it — she was hardly the conservative magazine's standard reader — he gave her a curious glance.

"What else do I have to do at night but read up on this?" she asked with a self-mocking smile.

If she was seeking pity, she had won it.

Paul often thought of her alone — the children didn't count, not in the way he meant — in her house. It made him shudder. Like many long-married men, he couldn't abide even the thought of being alone, let alone the actual aloneness. His imagination occasionally tangoed him to a younger, more beautiful wife, almost identical to the woman sitting across from him, before he scurried back to the safe ground of Edith. But if Edith, God forbid, were to die before him, his bereavement, by necessity, would be brief. He would have to remarry. Yet here was Claire, two whole years on her own. He didn't know whether to admire or suspect her toughness.

"Not fun, is it, this whole thing," she said. "Sometimes I just wish it were over."

Again he was surprised. "But, Claire, if you get what you want — if the Garden is the memorial, it will never be over. Partly because someone or other may keep agitating against Khan, and the Garden, forever. But also: that will be the memorial. This isn't some hypothetical exercise where you pronounce a victory for tolerance and go home. The Garden, Khan's design — that's what we will build. That's what you have to want."

"I know that," she said irritably. "I want

326

the Garden as much as I ever did."

He didn't believe her, but he didn't push.

15

The self-defense squads began to appear sometime after the third or fourth headscarf pulling. Across the country, young Muslim men roamed the streets of their neighborhoods, baseball bats in hand, to menace and sometimes beat outsiders who came too near hijab-wearing women. Even the Orthodox Jews living adjacent to Kensington began detouring around it, although with their own women bewigged and well smocked, they were unlikely denuders.

One night Asma and the Mahmouds watched a special news report called "The Headscarf Crisis." Mr. Mahmoud, as always, translated for both women. Someone named Debbie from Save America from Islam ("I am starting to think it is we who need saving from America," Mr. Mahmoud said, with uncharacteristic wit) was criticizing the self-defense squads. "It's dhimmitude: non-Muslims aren't allowed in Muslim neighborhoods anymore. Whose country is this?" The headscarf pulling itself she defended: "In Iran, Saudi Arabia, they force women to wear headscarves, to submit. This is America. What these men pulling off the headscarves are doing — it's an act of liberation."

Mr. Mahmoud snorted at this. "Yes, our women feel so liberated they've stopped going outside."

Asma lay awake that night, thinking about what Mr. Mahmoud had said. He was only slightly exaggerating: most of the women in Kensington who covered their heads had stopped leaving the neighborhood, if not their homes. The fear of exposure, of violence was too strong. They were all becoming as invisible as Hasina, her next-door neighbor, which had to please the Kabirs of the world.

The next morning Asma put on her parrot-green salwar kameez and wrapped, more tightly than usual, a matching chunni around her head. She asked Mrs. Mahmoud to watch Abdul. Mrs. Mahmoud's mouth made a small involuntary smile as it always did when she saw news in the offing.

"I'm running to the pharmacy," Asma said. In truth her plan was to walk beyond Kensington to see what would happen. Or maybe ride the subway all the way to Manhattan and test the air there. She descended the four flights and made her way confidently down the street.

A block later she sensed someone behind her, too close. Her body clenched in apprehension. Then, seeing that it was only some young men from the neighborhood, she exhaled in relief. She paused to let them cross her path, then realized they were walking with her. Shadowing her.

"Asalamu alaikum," she said.

"Alaikum asalam," they all murmured politely.

They said nothing more to her, she nothing to them. They walked on together; together they traced a jagged shape around the neighborhood. The boys — there were six or seven — were trailing a foot behind her. She glimpsed them reflected in shop windows: their green headbands, the sticks two of them swung. They were good boys, some of them even students at the city's special schools, where you had to take a test to enter. Did their parents know they were absconding from school for this? She turned. They turned. Even if she walked all the way to Manhattan they would be glued to her. She no longer knew who was imprisoning her, only that the prison was well

330

sealed. At last she circled back to her apartment building. The boys gathered behind her, waiting for her to let herself in.

"Thank you," she whispered, without turning back to meet their eyes.

With an excessive flourish Issam Malik fanned mock-ups of the council's new ad campaign across the conference table in MACC's office suite. *"Et voilà!"* he said. "They've done a stellar job. We're putting a buy in sixteen papers and six magazines — or was it seven? And we're putting together a press release; possibly a press conference, too. They need to be news. If the ads get coverage, it's like getting ten dollars of free advertising for every one you pay for. Buzz, buzz, buzz."

"Can you get it in the *Post*?" asked Laila. "It's hardly fair we have to pay to answer their vitriol, but we want to reach those readers, not just liberals."

"No point in doing *da'wah* among the converted, you mean," Malik chuckled.

Their chatter faded to background as Mo stared at his own image. The full-page ads had been pasted onto newspaper, tabloid, and magazine-size poster boards, reminding him, for some reason, of his parents spreading his elementary-school photographs

331

(eight-by-ten, four-by-six, wallet size) across their dining-room table. In the ad, Mo was bent over a drafting table in a crisp white shirt with the sleeves rolled up. He looked faux-serious, as if he were advertising an expensive watch or a credit card, and he was drawing, or pretending to draw, on a blank page. Behind him loomed a model of an investment bank headquarters ROI had designed. To Mo, it looked like he was taking credit for collective work.

The shoot had taken place at ROI early on a weekend morning, when Mo was sure no one else would be there. The art director and photographer together demanded that Mo remove his glasses, insisting that the reflected light would make him look ominous. Against his better instincts, Mo complied, although he felt not just blind but naked without them. They seated Mo in front of the drafting table, even though he tried to explain how essential computer-aided design was to modern architecture, and that he didn't want to trigger a snide reaction from CAD aficionados, especially when he so often used CAD himself, albeit with reservations. But they were hearing none of it: they wanted the cliché or, as the art director put it, the "archetypal architect image."

The discomfort of that day paled next to what was roiling Mo now. The tagline on the ad read, in bold type meant to be eye-catching, "An Architect, Not a Terrorist." In smaller print beneath it said: "Muslims like Mohammad Khan are proud to be American. Let's earn their pride. Brought to you by the Muslim American Coordinating Council."

Without describing the campaign, Malik had made vague assurances that it would "humanize" Mo. Just the opposite: he felt like a new product being rolled out to market, a product he suspected had significant fund-raising potential for the council. But objectification wasn't his main concern. Didn't people skim over little words as they read — verbal joints like "an" or, more to the point, "not"? At a long-ago party hosted by a girlfriend's parents, an eccentric emeritus professor had given him a card stating FINISHED FILES ARE THE RESULT OF YEARS OF SCIENTIFIC STUDY COMBINED WITH THE EXPERIENCE OF YEARS and asked him to count the f's. He had missed three, all of them in the word "of." He hadn't liked being shown up — the professor seemed to take a little too much delight in Mo's blind spots, as if he had single-handedly shattered some stereotype of the smart Indian — and

Mo had kept the card for years, in part to have the satisfaction of watching his friends make the same mistake and in part to remind himself always to pay more careful attention.

The point being, if you stripped the little words — the articles, the negative — from the ad's tagline, only two nouns remained. Architect. Terrorist. Architect-Terrorist: he might as well print new business cards. And he had worried about other architects thinking him a Luddite.

Mo caught Laila's eye, tried to signal his unease. "What do you think?" he asked in an unhappy voice. She was leaning against the window ledge, her arms folded, watching him.

"I think it will get a lot of attention," she said reassuringly. "And I think it positions you exactly right — as an American, a proud American."

How much, at this moment, he regretted having gone to the council for help. Issam Malik had never seemed more of an unctuous phony. Mo faulted Laila for failing to see this, or for ignoring it if she did. And yet when he opened his mouth all that came out was, "I guess I'm still getting used to being a public figure."

Malik shrugged. "I didn't find there was

much to get used to."

Laila had a busy afternoon, then a working dinner, so she returned home only late that night. She was asleep before Mo could raise the ad with her.

He barely slept himself. Instead he memorized the fan of her dark hair, the fullness of her mouth, the voluptuousness of even her bones. He knew he couldn't go through with the ad, and he knew she wouldn't understand. And so as the morning light crept up outside, he cast a harsher light onto Laila. She became, with each hour, a little less miraculous in his eyes, a little more unyielding.

Her apartment was on the eighth floor, so the roofs of the neighboring buildings appeared to float above land. The street below sent up, at all times, the noise of sirens and horns and motors, but their sources were unseen, like a river that roars far beneath canyon walls. The roar grew louder; Laila's eyes opened; she smiled. He twisted his mouth, all he could manage, in return. In the shower he sponged her back and held her to him, cupping her breasts from behind. With the water raining down on them, blocking all sound but its own, they were safe. But she wrestled free.

"Mo, I'll be late for work."

Only when she had dressed and was sipping tea and reading a case file did he find his courage.

"Laila, can we talk about the ad campaign?"

"Mmmm?" she said, not putting her papers aside until he said bluntly: "I don't want to do it."

Now her attention was on him, intensely so.

"The language makes me uncomfortable — to say I'm 'not a terrorist' has the result of connecting me to terrorism."

"You're being connected to terrorism already, Mo — every time one of those commercials runs on TV. We can't even find out who's paying for them. We're powerless — the networks laugh off our threat of a boycott because they know we don't have the numbers. So you need to counter them. At least the MACC ad shows you as an architect, and that's a visual image that will stay with people."

"The damage from those commercials has been done," Mo said. "MACC putting me in a few newspapers isn't going to undo it. More than that, it's just not me. I have my way of doing things — there's a reason I entered the memorial competition instead of making big political statements. And — I know I should have thought of this before I agreed to the ad — but to be out there as part of a MACC campaign identifies me so thoroughly as a Muslim when I've been arguing I shouldn't be defined as one. It looks like I'm trying to have it both ways."

"Aren't you?" she said. She got up from the table, knelt beside him, and looked into his face. "Are you ashamed?"

Her grave gaze was hard to meet. "Of course not," he said, "although I'm not thrilled at becoming a prop in a propaganda war."

"What's that supposed to mean? The propaganda's coming from the people who want to make you a bogeyman. They are creating a climate where dangerous things can happen. The rhetoric is the first step; it coarsens attitudes. Look at the history of Nazi Germany. The Jews thought they were German, until they weren't. Here they're already talking about us as less American. Then they'll say we need containment, and next thing you know we'll be interned."

Mo's mind wandered off for a moment, to photographs he had seen of gardens at Manzanar, the Japanese American internment camp. Its internees had laid rocks, dug pools, even sculpted faux-wood limbs and logs from concrete. Would he have had the same tenacity of spirit? He pictured himself within the confines of a wire-fenced camp, marking off the borders of a small garden, digging its canals, planting its trees —

"Mo!" Laila could tell, even after their brief time together, when he had gone off into what she called his dream space.

"I think you're exaggerating the threat. I don't like what all these people are saying, but they have a right to say it. It's not fair to them to suggest that they're looking to put us in camps."

"Not fair to them?" She rose and began to walk a square within the studio. Her boot heels clacked on the floor, vanished into the carpet, then clacked again, as if she were disappearing into a tunnel, then reemerging. "Your mind operates like a kaleidoscope: just shift the view and suddenly everything looks completely different. You're so frustratingly rational, Mo. Where's your passion?"

"I have passion for you," he said haltingly. There was a net in his throat through which only small, inadequate words could pass.

She stared at him, then carried his French press and her teapot to the sink and began washing while she talked. Her back was to him, the water on. He strained to hear. "Not long after my family came here the American hostages were taken in Iran. My mother told us to lie about where we were from — not to tell anyone. And we still had to change schools because my brother got bullied. I had just turned eight, but I understood that people who didn't know me hated me just for where I came from, and the only way to avoid it was to make myself invisible to them. For a little while I stopped eating — I thought I really could make it so no one could see me. So they couldn't judge me, or punish me for something I couldn't control."

Mo had pictured Laila as the girl on the playground rushing in, fists balled up, to save the picked-on kid from the bully. Not as the picked-on girl herself, trying to disappear. "Stop cleaning," he said, in a low, urgent voice. "This is too important."

She dried her hands, stepped out of the tiny kitchenette, and began looking for a pair of small gold hoop earrings she had left on the table the night before. "So what's going on in this country isn't so new for me," she continued. "But I decided that this time I wasn't going to make myself invisible and let others define me. And I certainly wasn't going to let them detain or deport people just because they were Muslim. I was making a lot more money at the law firm, obviously. But career didn't matter as much as — those were my grandmother's, I hope I didn't lose them —"

He had put the earrings away in her jewelry box. He retrieved them and handed them to her. The way she tilted her head left, then right to put them on, shaking her hair away from her ear, reminded him of his mother. "But in a way your career has come out better," he said. "Before you were just an associate in a law firm. Now your profile — it's so much higher."

She shot him a disgusted look. "Yes, high enough for people to call me a traitor. You're missing my point, Mo." She began to put papers in her attaché case. "I was willing to give something up even though I thought it might hurt me. Maybe the ad won't help your career, but other things matter more. With this ad you're defining yourself. You're saying that you won't let other people caricature you or other Muslims, whether they're doctors, or taxi drivers, or accountants."

"A lawyer, not a terrorist." His joke earned only a scowl. "Sorry, but why not get one of those doctors or taxi drivers to do the ad?"

"You want someone else to do what you're afraid to do?"

"I'm not afraid," he said.

"Then do the ad. Do it as an American, because you don't like what's happening in your country." There was a mental translucence to Laila. Mo could read in her face, before she spoke, when her thoughts tracked in a new direction. "Let me ask you something," she said. "Your beard — you started growing it when you were overseas?"

"Yes . . ."

"And then worked on your design for, what, a few weeks when you came back?"

"Roughly, yes, but I don't see —"

"And so by the time you sent off your submission, your beard must have been pretty well grown in, like it is now."

He knew her next question before she asked it. "And the photograph you submitted with your entry — beard?"

A beat of silence. Of shame. Of considering actually lying to her.

"No beard." He could claim he'd had no more recent photo, but she was right — that wasn't the reason he had done it.

"It makes me sad" was all Laila said. Effortlessly she had nailed his effort to be a "safe" Muslim when it would help him; to be courageous or provocative only when he thought he could afford to, even if he sometimes misjudged. "Next you'll shave for them."

Her pressure was bruising and his mind rebelled, lashed out. Maybe she was sleeping with him only to secure his participation. Maybe she was conspiring with Issam Malik.

"Who did you have dinner with last night?" he asked.

"What?"

"Nothing, sorry." His suspicions collapsed; his heart somehow folded. Jealousy clings to love's underside like bats to a bridge. In pushing Laila away, he grasped what he felt for her.

She was putting on a navy quilted jacket, bandaging her neck with a white silk scarf.

"Maybe if I could shape the ad," he offered.

"To say what?"

"Could you stop getting ready?" he said instead of answering. "We need to finish this."

"I have an appointment with a woman whose husband has been detained without trial for seven months, Mo. Should I not show up so we can continue talking about how your principles keep you from doing anything that's actually principled?"

"Laila, that's unfair. If this — if what's between us is actually going to work out, you have to accept me as I am."

"How can I, when I'm not sure who that is?" She had paused before the window, as if seeing the view for the first time. When she wheeled around her eyes had an angry flash, not the lively spark of their first meeting. "You know, when you stood up for yourself in front of the whole country, I thought you were so brave, I had never seen that kind of confidence in a man. You put yourself on the line. But now I see that it was about you: *your* design, *your* reputation, *your* place in history. You will put yourself on the line for your own interests but no one else's."

"Laila, it's just an ad. Don't murder this, whatever is between us, because of it."

"This isn't about the ad! It's about whether the same things matter to us. I have to go. I need to think." She grabbed her attaché case and slammed the door behind her.

Sorrow swelled in him, seemed to press against his lungs. He knew he couldn't bend himself to fit her shape. But he didn't know how he would live with the hollow where hers had been.

Another headscarf pulling, the victim hospitalized for anxiety, her toddler son, who'd

343

been holding her hand, bawling on the news. The president of the United States, who had avoided taking a position on the memorial, went on television to ask for civility and respect, to say he was ashamed of what was happening in his country. He called what Sean had started "a plague."

"A plague of good sense!" Debbie snapped at the screen. She was reading, and marking up, Trisha's college application essay, which was entitled "My Mother the Firebrand." Trisha had told Sean that she feared liberal colleges would blackball her when they realized Debbie was her mother. So she had decided to write her essay about how she both respected her mother ("Two years ago she was a just a housewife who spent most of her time watching soap operas. The attack changed everything. She was called to fight for her country. She educated herself . . .") and disagreed with her ("Sometimes I think she tries too hard to be provocative. I believe in dialogue"). Debbie was totally on board with this strategy, but she had crossed out "watching soap operas" and replaced it with "taking care of my sisters and me."

The bawling son again: the cable channels couldn't get their fill of him. Sean kneaded his right fist into his left palm and eyed

Debbie's liquor cabinet, to which the girls, he knew, had copied the key. He'd been stone-dry since the attack, but for all the virtue in sobriety, it was harder to blame his mistakes on it. Pulling the woman's head-scarf had done nothing to derail the Muslim memorial, instead drawing attention from the huge crowd he had mustered to protest it.

"She called, you know," he told Debbie, who turned toward him, alert.

"The woman from the protest. Zahira Hussain. Well, she didn't call: Issam Malik did, from that Muslim council. They said that if I meet with her and apologize, she'll ask that the charges against me be dropped." He didn't say that Malik had talked about wanting to make this a "teachable moment." He knew how Debbie would take that.

"No apology," Debbie said. "Not to those people. Your ex — sure, by all means, apologize to her." Sean reddened. "But this has symbolic value," she went on. They're looking for a propaganda coup — a nice Christian boy, an American, submitting to them. Yet another example of Islam trium-phant over the West. I can hear it now: Jerusalem. Constantinople. Cordoba. Morn-ingside Heights — that's where their office is, right? This is legal jihad — using the

345

criminal justice system to persecute you. We'll raise money for a good lawyer."

"I was just thinking of talking to her," he said.

"Don't you dare apologize," she said.

"That's how she treats us," Trisha snickered.

"We're dhimmi," Alison sighed.

"No harm in talking," Sean said.

"No harm," said Debbie, with a musing, canny look.

The SAFIs were waiting for him when he arrived at the Muslim American Coordinating Council office the next morning. "No Apology! No Submission!" they screamed, with Debbie in the lead. A scrum of reporters and camera crews shouted questions at him. Feminists held signs that said NO AMNESTY FOR WIFE BEATERS.

His instinct was to flee. He clenched his fists and pushed through.

Alyssa Spier adhered to him. "Take me inside," she whispered. "You need a witness to make sure they don't spin it differently than it happens." But at the MACC office, Issam Malik gave Alyssa a look of recognition and said, "No, no, no. We're going to meet privately first. And when we open the doors to the press, she gets no access."

"Did you call the press?" Sean asked after Alyssa had sulked off. "I thought this was a private meeting."

"You can't teach to an empty classroom," Malik said. Sean disliked him instantly. They filed into a conference room. It was filled with men, mostly, along with a few women in headscarves. All shades of brown. He missed pasty Alyssa. For the first time in his life, he was the only Christian and, it appeared, the only white, in the room. Unsettled by this, he was scanning for danger when he heard, from an alarmed voice in the corner, "What's in the bag?" All eyes went to Sean's gym bag, which was over his shoulder. When he left Debbie's that morning, he had packed up all his things except for his suit, which he wore so it wouldn't crumple. He knew he wouldn't be welcomed back after going to the council.

"What?" Sean said.

"What. Is. In. The. Bag," Malik said slowly, as if Sean didn't speak English. Two men stood.

"Fuck!" Sean said. He ran his hands through his hair. He bent down, unzipped the bag, and began dumping its contents on the floor. Jeans, sneakers, T-shirts, sweat-shirt, shaving kit, *Sports Illustrated,* boxer shorts, and, mixed in with the dirty socks, a pair of pink cotton underwear — Trisha's. He'd lifted it. Excuses crossed his mind. It had gotten mixed up with his clothes in the dryer. She's legal. Nothing happened anyway. Forget it: they didn't know anything about where he'd been.

There was silence. The men were looking at one another. The women were looking down. No one wanted to look at Sean or his stuff.

He turned his gaze up to the ceiling. "I'm carrying my clothes because I had to leave where I've been staying," he said. His eyes stung. "I left because I was coming here today, and they thought I shouldn't. I am *homeless* because I came here today," he added, exaggerating a bit. "And you think I came in here with a bomb?"

"A gun," someone said in a low voice. "I thought you might have a gun."

"People — we — are on edge," Malik said. "The mood is very tense right now. There's violence in the air, and you bear some responsibility for that. We don't know you from Adam. You organized a rally where people were making death threats. You yanked a woman's headscarf. How are we to know what else you're capable of?"

I'm not capable, not capable of anything, Sean thought. He pulled his wallet from his pocket, sending a few stray receipts drifting to the floor, and extracted a small photo of Patrick in his dress uniform. He held it up. Everyone peered to see. "This was my brother. My brother who died. Was killed. By Muslims. Jesus! Why is it so hard to do the right thing?"

"I'm sorry," a woman said. Sean looked at her. He couldn't have picked her face out of a lineup, but he knew the red scarf. He had seen, too many times, his hand reaching for it. It couldn't be an accident she was wearing it today.

"You only have one scarf?" he said.

"I'm sorry?"

"You're wearing the same scarf as that day. You think I'm a bull — that I'll see it and go nuts again?"

"I didn't realize —"

"Did you say you were sorry? Sorry for what? I'm the one who's supposed to be sorry, remember? Isn't that why I'm here? So you all can humiliate me, make me bow down, kiss your ring or whatever?"

"No one made you come," she said gently. Her face was pumpkin-round; her eyes, striking, hazel, long-lashed. "No one's making you stay." She was talking to him like he was the man on the ledge; it surprised him not to mind. He bent to stuff his possessions back in his bag, casting about for his next move as he did so. He was red-faced — he didn't need a mirror to know it.

"I want to talk to you in private," he said to Zahira. "Not so many people."

"That's not appropriate," Malik said.

"How so?"

"Our religion believes in modest interchange between the genders. And her humiliation was public, so the apology needs to be as well."

"In private," Sean repeated.

"Not possible —" Malik started to say.

"We'll go in there," Zahira said, pointing to Malik's office, "with the door open."

Over Malik's objections, Sean and Zahira rose, complicitly, to take possession of his office. A desk epic enough to protect her reputation dominated the room. Zahira seated herself behind it, folded her hands atop it. Sean took a chair on the other side. There were three TVs in the room. He tried not to watch.

"Before an apology, Sean, I'd like an explanation," she said. Ever since she first spoke he had been trying to pinpoint what struck him as odd in her speech, and now he had it. It was the lack of accent. She sounded as American as he did. "What made you pull my scarf? Had you planned it?"

"No!" he said. "Your sign made me mad." Aware how childish this sounded, he borrowed Debbie's words: "But also, we don't make women cover their hair in this country."

"No, we don't make women cover their hair." She put the stress on "we." It seemed to amuse her. "But women are free to choose to, as I did. No one's making me do anything. My own father is against me covering. It's my choice," she repeated. "No one else's."

Sean's eye wandered to one of the televisions, on which his passage through the bawdy gauntlet outside was being replayed. He looked tense, even fearful. Less brave than he had felt. He had imagined that moment of deciding to plow ahead as his version of Patrick's charging into a burning building. Now he saw how foolish that idea was. Patrick was dead.

Zahira was watching the television sets, too: Sean's arrival, the screaming SAFIs. After a few moments she picked up the three remote controls, one by one, to switch off the screens. Then she turned to Sean with a new gentleness and said, "So other than protecting women from themselves,

Sean, what do you do with yourself? Where do you live — never mind, you said you're homeless. Not forever, I hope. What kind of work do you do?"

He thought about his days hanging pictures and caulking tile. About the itchy suit — bought for Patrick's funeral, repurposed for his speeches — that he was wearing. "I'm in transition," he said. "You?"

A Columbia University student double majoring in literature and economics. The sting of "Bigot=Idiot" returned.

"You called us names," he said. "Is that what they teach up at Columbia?"

"No, I thought that up myself. Maybe it was a poor choice. But I do think bigots are idiots. I'm not saying you're bigoted if you're against this memorial design. But I'd like to hear why you are against it."

"It's an Islamic garden!" he said. He struggled for words, again pilfered Debbie's. "It's a paradise for murderers. A way to take us over, to colonize us."

"Really?" Zahira said. "I thought it was just a garden. Honestly, Sean, even if it has elements in common with traditional Islamic gardens, that doesn't mean it's a paradise. And if he were consciously trying to invoke the afterlife, how do you know he's trying to encourage terrorists? For all

352

you know he's reminding Muslims that we'll never reach paradise if we do what they did. Why is my theory any more far-fetched than yours?"

Sean had no answer. She went on: "But for me, no architect can create paradise. Only God can. When Muslims think about paradise, the hope we feel about getting there, the exhilaration at the possibility — it's not about trees, or silks, or jewels, or beautiful women or boys or whatever you've been led to believe. It's about God. God. The description of paradise in the Quran is just a way to convey to our limited imaginations the ecstasy we will feel in God's presence. That's what should inspire us to live correctly."

Sean retraced her words as if he were walking a path trying to find something he had lost. He said the only thing he could think to say, which was, "I'm sorry. Really sorry."

"You mean it?" she asked warily, suddenly small behind the desk. They were like two children pretending to be adults in their father's office, although Frank, a firefighter, had never had an office. Zahira's must have: she was at Columbia.

"I mean it. I'm sorry I pulled your scarf."

She measured him with pretty, distrusting

eyes, then said, "You should say it publicly, then, to send a message to all the people copying you."

"That's what Issam Malik wants," Sean said. She flushed and said quietly, "It's what I want."

He chewed his bottom lip for a bit, nodded his assent, then pushed up out of his chair. In their absence, Malik had packed the conference room with reporters, and Sean tried not to be annoyed. He stepped, with Zahira, to a spot ringed with microphones. She smelled of bubble gum, or maybe that was a scent relic of the Dawson girls. Malik planted himself on Sean's other side.

Sean put his gym bag at his feet and cleared his throat. "I am really sorry I pulled Zahira Hussain's headscarf, and I told her so," he said, giving the reporters time to take down his words. "What I did was wrong. If anyone else does it, it's wrong. My brother, Patrick, he would have been ashamed of me, and I wish I could apologize to him, too." He had said his brother's name hundreds, maybe thousands of times since Patrick's death — "You talk about him more now that he's gone than you talked *to* him when he was alive," his mother once accused — but saying it this time seemed to lift, finally, the weight of that last drunken night.

But almost immediately, a new weight landed. Maybe it was Patrick's name that spirited Sean to his parents' living room, where, lacking a home of his own, he would soon return. Seeing himself framed in their television, sandwiched by Muslims, he tried to reconstruct how he had wandered here, to the other side, and he tried to scramble back. "But Patrick also died trying to save people from Islamic terrorists," he said, "and we will never apologize for not wanting anything Islamic connected to this memorial — not a person, not a design. It's not personal, not prejudice. Just fact."

Delight flared in the reporters' eyes. Outrage fluttered from Malik's lips. The room convulsed with the rearranging of bodies, furniture, air. Sean heard shouts, then felt rough, unforgiving hands propel him out the door, as if he'd been discovered with a bomb after all. The gym bag came after him. Through it all he kept his mind with his parents. Only at home with them later, watching the replay on television, did he see Zahira Hussain's anguished face.

16

At 3:00 a.m., Mo woke and reached in the dark for the roast beef sandwich next to his bed. He chewed dutifully, then glugged water and tried to get back to sleep. After a few fitful hours he woke again and dressed for work. Only twelve or so hours until he could eat or drink again.

For five days now, he had been fasting. He was a grain of sand, just one of hundreds of millions of Muslims observing Ramadan — no food, no liquid, no sex from dawn to dusk each day for a month. He made of the period a building, paced from crescent moon to crescent moon; made of each day a room, measured from sunrise to sunset. The predawn meal was a threshold, and for the abstaining hours the mouth a sealed door. But these were an architect's conceits. The truth was he didn't know why he was doing it, why his first act each day now was abstention, and this uncertainty harbored so many others, even as it was born from them: uncertainty about whether he was right to pursue his memorial, whatever the cost, or right to refuse to explain it. He bore no responsibility for the headscarf pullings. His position was an immovable object that moved everything around him. He wondered how the God he didn't believe in would judge him.

Never had he been shakier. That rally, the hatred there, gave off a heat as intense as if he had been standing next to the man igniting his face. Mo had tired of the bellicose, lachrymose religion the attack had birthed, was sickened by the fundamentalists who defended it by declaring the day sacred, the place sacred, the victims sacred, the feelings of their survivors sacred — so much sacredness, no limit to the profanity justified to preserve it. But he also wondered if not practicing the religion made him an unsuitable architect for its temple. For the memorial.

He was angry that Paul Rubin wouldn't give up trying to make him give up; angry at the governor's impugning of the jury; angry at the jury's certain cowardice. But mostly he was bone-achingly sad. After fighting with Laila, he packed his suitcase, left her keys on the table, and went to a hotel. Soon after a colleague offered use of her newly vacated, and completely vacant, apartment in Chelsea. It was the baldest possible refuge. Mo's life had compressed to suitcase, laptop, air mattress, the trinity less of a man hunted than of one being slowly erased.

At work, food, not buildings, was all anyone around him seemed to be discussing: what they'd had for dinner ("Have you ever tried a raw bay scallop? The small ones? Like fucking candy"), where they would go for lunch. It was like discovering sex as an adolescent, his horny mind finding it in every smell and swell, every conversation. He had not realized the degree to which food — planning for it, obtaining it, preparing it, eating it, talking about it, wasting it, fetishizing it, creating it, selling it — made the twenty-first-century American. Before he began the fast, it had seemed magical, even noble, to willfully shun all of that. His rhythm was ever contrapuntal, and he knew fasting would suit him less well in a Muslim country, where it meant conforming, not defying. But it was harder than he expected to be among people who not only weren't sharing his sacrifice but took no consideration of it.

Throughout the morning his body yowled, his irritability rising as his blood sugar plunged. His piss was the chemical yellow of a traffic signal, so concentrated it almost looked solid. Fearful that his breath stank, he kept covering his mouth with his hand to check it, avoided getting too close to anyone. He could brush his teeth, if he didn't swallow, but the fasting sent a smell up from his stomach — the acids working on nothing — or from his tongue that brought to mind a dead animal trapped beneath a house.

Thomas stopped by his desk. A group was heading out for sushi. Did Mo want to come?

"No, I've got to meet someone," he said, only to see Thomas's eyes flicker with doubt: Mo keeping secrets, again. "Laila," Mo added, a lie to defuse the mistrust. Saying her name out loud was like cutting himself, but he said it again. "Laila." Pleasure rimmed the pain. His "assistant" listened, as if he didn't trust Mo, either.

The day's headache set in soon after, a squatting brute as disinclined to move as Mo's listless tongue was from the roof of his parched mouth. He went for a walk. Students took exams, soldiers fought wars, presidents ran countries during Ramadan — surely he could handle a walk. He canvassed food trucks as if they were targets, the halal food trucks the worst. It was unthinkable that the proprietors would likely be fasting, too. The smell of grilling meat and spices, the savory smoke pummeled up his nose, as if furious that his mouth was barred. But more than food, he wanted drink — water, a sugary orange soda, anything to lubricate his dry and papery mouth, which felt as if it had been vacuumed out at the dentist. More than a drink, it was coffee he craved, to free his head from its vise. He talked to himself: he was weak. No, he wasn't. Feeling weak meant he was strong, meant he was persisting.

Late in the afternoon, Mo took a cab to the studios of WARU, where a young man of jaundiced affect led him into an anteroom and asked if he wanted tea, coffee, or a soda.

"Nothing, thanks," he said.

"Water? It helps if you have a bit of nerves."

"Why would I have" — nerves, Mo started to protest, then, embarrassed at the rasp of his voice, the taffy quality of his speech — "No thanks. Really, I'm fine."

"Well, well, well, *are* you well?" It was Lou Sarge, and without preparation he guided

Mo into the studio. They sat in facing chairs. The microphone hung between them like a reverse periscope, an eye tunneling down in search of something. The studio was dark, a paling salon: a place that sucked out the color.

Agreeing to the interview was not Mo's idea but Paul's, yet another demand masquerading as a request. "You've got to go into the heart of the opposition," Paul insisted. "Show them you're nothing to fear. Get Sarge on your side and you neutralize a lot of the craziness out there." He offered no tips on how Mo was supposed to get a man who routinely described Muslims as "raging ragheads" on his side.

Sarge put on earphones so he would know when the commercial break was over and seemed to sink so deep within himself that he forgot Mo was there. In the soundproof studio, a hostile womb, Mo heard only his own breath.

"So, Mohammad — may I call you Mohammad?" Sarge asked at last.

"I prefer Mo. That's what everyone calls me."

"So, Mo, here's how it's going to work. Come a little closer — I don't bite. We're going to chat for a few minutes, and then we'll take some calls. You won't be able to hear the calls — we find it's too confusing to guests to be trying to track what's going on outside the studio — so I'll relay the questions. Just talk into the mic, but no need to tongue it. That's it. We're glad you came on. Did they offer you anything to drink?"

Mo, not having expected Sarge to be so charming, so friendly, was disarmed. They had a few minutes while the commercials ran, and Sarge began talking about his background, how he'd briefly dabbled in architecture — "Buckminster Fuller–type stuff" — before becoming a radio host. "My designs were straight out of the future," he said, "but that's a hard sell in the present. It's hard to be an architect on your own — you must know what I mean. You can't just sit in your room and draw, it's like trying to make children through masturbation. You need someone who wants to build the things, which really just means they believe in them. I couldn't get people to believe. I know what you're thinking: I'm pretty good at getting people to believe now. But that's just it — I was selling the wrong thing. People didn't want my designs, they wanted my voice. They wanted my courage. I'm not scared, and everyone else is — scared to speak because they'll be called anti or phobic or racist or whatever. You have to attune yourself to the historical moment, sense the current of time, where it is" — he held his hands up as if he were parceling the air — "and then adapt to it. Spoon with it."

"I'll bear that in mind," Mo said, tired of the monologue, wanting to conserve his energy for the show.

"All right, time to suck up to the sponsors. Three new ones today alone. We put the word out you were coming on and everyone wanted in."

Having sucked up, Sarge addressed his listeners. "We've heard a fair bit about Mohammad Khan on this show, if you know what I mean, and today I'm pleased to tell you we have the man himself. We can talk to him instead of about him, get answers straight from his mouth. He's an architect and, well, we all know his religious background, and he's a New Yorker — born and raised?"

"Uh, Virginia originally. But a longtime New Yorker."

"So what did you feel, really feel, the day of the attack?"

"I felt devastated, like all of us. Like a hole had been blasted in me."

"That sounds pretty bad," Sarge said. "It

must have been like finding out your brother is the Unabomber."

"No, that's not what I meant."

"And so you came up with this memorial, which has attracted a fair bit of controversy. Tell me, where'd you get the idea?"

Mo was still stuck on the Unabomber comment, wondering if he should try again to rebut it. Too late. "From my imagination," he said. "I thought a garden would be symbolically resonant as a memorial, given its interplay of life and death and —"

"Got it. So is it, actually, an Islamic garden?"

"It's just a garden."

"A martyrs' paradise?"

"It's a garden."

"A jihadi playground?"

"It's a garden."

"A joke on the American people?"

"Excuse me? The American people include me."

"I mean, if I were a Muslim — it hasn't been an easy couple of years for you, I'm guessing, you know, maybe you're a little bit peeved, maybe you're thinking, let's just slip this in under the radar."

Mo was so furious at the assertion, and at the kernel of truth it contained, that he couldn't speak for a moment.

"Mohammad? Oh Mo-ham-mad, are you in there?" Sarge had lowered his voice and leaned in close, as if the two of them were alone in this dark universe, their only audience distant stars. His tone had a soft sympathy, more powerful for being unexpected, and Mo felt strong emotions pressing for expression. What a gift this man had to spin the cotton candy of trust from the sugar of his voice. And yet Mohammad, not Mo — the full name a way for Sarge to remind his listeners that Mo-ham-mad was everything they feared.

"I wanted to do something for my country," Mo said. The words came thick, slow, as if they marched in tar. "It's as simple as that."

At the commercial break, Sarge downed a Red Bull. Mo turned away. "The honest truth," Sarge told him, "is that I barely felt a thing the day of the attack, not a fucking thing, although you wouldn't have known it to listen to the show. You know when you sit too long and your foot goes to sleep? It was like my soul had gone to sleep. I felt like the walking dead, the walking fucking dead. You know what I mean, Mo?" He tilted his head back to stare at the ceiling. "Maybe you should design a memorial to me."

The show resumed for the callers' questions, all of them politely parried by a battered Mo, who only later would comprehend the distrust they conveyed.

Mildred in Manhasset: "If you testify in court, will you swear an oath on the Quran?"

"I will do what any American does in court."

Warren in Basking Ridge, New Jersey: "Do Muslims pray to the same God as we do?"

"Muslims, Jews, Christians, they all pray to one God."

Ricky in Staten Island: "I just don't get why you won't withdraw when it's clear so many families want you to."

"The process should be allowed to work as it was meant to."

"I was just thinking, Mo," Sarge said when the show was over. They were alone in the studio. The sun, Mo was sure, had set, but the assistant who had brought Sarge an odd fizzy, creamy orange drink had offered nothing to Mo, who was too proud, too wary of this strange chameleon, to ask for anything. "Isn't it possible," Sarge continued, "that your subconscious did something with this design that you didn't intend for it to do? It happens to me all the time. Half the stuff I say on this show shocks me — it comes out and I think, 'Well, Lou, that's kind of appalling.' But I don't disown it, do I?"

"Which half?" Mo asked, but Sarge, deep into another soliloquy, didn't answer.

Claire's fortieth birthday began with hot chocolate and croissants, brought into the room by William and Penelope after being carried upstairs by Margarita, who hovered in the hall. The children climbed into the bed, snuggled up to her, jabbed her with their small bony limbs. They had made her cards; William's showed her with a birthday hat like a traffic cone on her head. And there were, for the first time since the Circle Line cruise, drawings of the Garden. Claire had hoped the attachment might fade.

"Are those lollipops?" she asked, pointing to a mass of red dots on green lines.

"Tulips," he said, giggling. "Red tulips."

"Are you sure you don't want a bed of lollipops?" She tickled him. "A candy garden?"

"Daddy didn't like candy," he said, and something flipped inside her. William's reminding her of this reinforced the sense that Cal's absence was alive today. Alive and painful. He had always promised to soften the blow of her fortieth birthday — he was three years younger — and it had become a running joke in the months before his death. His plans had grown epically, comically, more elaborate — scuba diving in the Maldives discarded for a trip to Galápagos, which ceded to a month on a yacht in the Mediterranean, which was deemed insufficient, too, until Cal settled on a round-the-world trip (children, and presumably nanny, in tow) that would have taken Claire all the way to her forty-first birthday, thus making her nostalgic for her fortieth.

Instead the day would unfold drearily in Chappaqua. There would be calls — her mother from California, her sister from Wisconsin, a few friends, Cal's parents. There would be random, computer-generated e-mails from the spas and clothing boutiques that always "remembered" her special day. At dinner the children would surprise her with the cake they had baked with Margarita; sing to her, probably more than once; and go to bed, after which she would nurse a glass of wine and hurry the night to its end. And always in the background now, today, every day, the insistent whine of the memorial controversy. The encounter with Alyssa Spier was just a few days past, and for all Claire's resistance, Spier's insinuations about Khan had slithered inside to coil around Claire's own

doubts. This repulsive, reptilian distrust —
it never left her now.

The morning was spent receiving a massage and giving the complaisant gardener
imperious commands on the fall planting,
for which she had succumbed, once again,
to the tyranny of mums. When the delivery
van arrived at noon bearing an oversize
flower box, Claire's gratitude for the surprise alone almost overwhelmed her. She
held the small envelope containing the card
and thought, with almost childlike wishing,
please don't let it be from some smitten fogy
(Paul Rubin; the family financial adviser).
Let it be from — she didn't even know the
word she was looking for, only the longing
inside her, the sudden, acute despair at her
isolation. Her ossification.

"Some dates, like some people, are hard
to forget," the card read. "I hope the day
brings more pleasures. With fondness, Jack."

Wish granted — it almost defied believing. Jack Worth, two years ahead of her at
Dartmouth, had been her boyfriend, on and
off, until she met Cal. Jack had accused her
of throwing him over for Cal's wealth, a
misconception that saved her from saying
she preferred Cal's temperament. They
hadn't spoken for years after the breakup,
until they ran into each other, with spouses,

and enacted an awkward truce. After Cal's death Jack had sent a note: "I know it's hard to see yourself as lucky now, but it sounds like you found that rare thing that has eluded most of us — an enduring love." That was the last she had heard from him, until now.

The gift, less venturesome than the card, was a miniature garden of sorts, herbs and buffalo grass and clover nestled in a beautiful aged-wood planter. Smart, she thought, not to send something overtly romantic when he didn't know if she was single. Still, he must have softened with age. In college they had argued, more than once, over his disdain for the niceties — he forgot her birthday, the date they met, even her sister's name. The only flowers he ever gave were in a bouquet picked near his parents' place in Maine.

The card included his phone number. She called to thank him. He invited her for a birthday dinner, saying her partner was welcome if she had one.

"No, but if you do . . ."

"No, good, just the two of us."

The corset of marriage, her mourner's garb, burst open all at once, leaving her naked with desire. Sex with Jack had been so intense that she would barely be dressed

before she was imagining the next time —
where, when, how, as if the life between was
merely filler. Giving that up had been the
hardest thing about leaving him. Lovemak-
ing with Cal had been less consuming; she
had convinced herself this made it deeper.

The mayor had decided, as he put it, "to
stand with my Muslim friends," telling
anyone who would listen that he could afford to, since he was being term-limited out.
"So if he were running again, would you no
longer be his friend?" Thomas, who had
become Mo's sole source of levity, asked
wryly.

Mo was invited, along with various Muslim leaders, notables, and activists, to an Iftar at Gracie Mansion — a dinner to break
the day's Ramadan fast. He invited his
parents to come up from Virginia, figuring
it might mean more to them than to him,
and also hoping that they would buffer him
against the MACC members, who were sure
to be there. Mo hadn't seen any of them
since he'd pulled out of the ad campaign,
which had gone ahead with taxi drivers,
teachers, and a stand-up comic in his place.

His parents knew he was not living at
home; he had arranged a hotel room for
them. Now he wished they had planned to

meet there. Their footfalls echoed in the empty space. Their faces were full of horror.

"My goodness, Mo," his mother said. "This is . . ." She walked into the bedroom and back, then perched on the edge of Mo's suitcase, which was in a corner. "Can't you stay with a friend? With Thomas?" She loved Thomas, Alice, and their children, not least because they reassured her that an architect could have a family, too.

"He has three kids, remember? Besides, they were caught a little off guard by this whole thing."

"You didn't tell him you were entering?"

"Can we talk about something else?" Mo didn't bother to hide his irritation. "I like living on my own — it's what I'm used to." This was what his mother feared. He pivoted to avoid her expression.

"Maybe too used to it," Salman said. Eager for sunset and food, he had opened Mo's refrigerator and spotled the telltale white cartons: the Chinese, Indian, and Thai food with which Mo had been ending his fast each day. "Breaking the fast is meant to be communal," his father said. "Not a man at home alone with his takeout."

Mo stiffened, disliking this image of himself. "Then it's good we're going to the mayor's," he said curtly.

"Mo, you know we are proud of you, but we are even more worried." Salman had made many similar comments by phone, but the vehemence in his face spoke much louder. "The costs of pursuing this — they are too high."

Mo wasn't entirely surprised. His father had made brave moves: coming to America for his engineering degree; marrying the woman of his choice — an artist, no less — rather than that of his parents; choosing modernity over tradition. But then, as Mo saw it, he had settled into conventionality. Mo's deciding on architecture as a career choice had worried Salman. For an Indian son, the preferred professions were business, academia, medicine, not necessarily in that order. Or engineering. Architecture was a low-paying field in which success, unless extravagant, was hard to measure. As Mo's talent became evident, as buildings he worked on came to be, Salman's skepticism morphed to pride. He praised his son's work to everyone. But Mo hadn't forgotten his initial doubt.

"The costs of not pursuing it are high, too. I can't just give in."

"You are drawing attention to yourself, to us — all of us, all Muslims in America — in a way that could be dangerous," Salman said. He was pacing with his hands behind his back. "My mosque has hired a security guard because of the threats it has been getting, and I almost feel like I should pay for it. Think of the community."

Salman's newfound attachment to his mosque was a sore point with Mo. Sometime after the attack, Salman, indifferent if not antagonistic to religion his whole adult life, had begun to pray, first alone, then at the mosque. "Curiosity," he said when Mo asked why, "or maybe solidarity." When he asked again a few months later, Salman said, "Because I believe." Mo hadn't known what to say to that.

"Which community, Baba? My community is people like me. People who are rational."

"But even some of your supposedly rational friends are questioning whether you should do this," Salman said. "Even some of those people are admitting they don't entirely trust us. That is the most dangerous thing." Salman sat next to Shireen on the suitcase, which sagged beneath their weight. They looked like they were waiting to be packed up and shipped into exile. A moment later, Salman stood, clumsily, and began to pace again.

"Your mother and I were talking about your name the other day," he said. "Why Mohammad, of all names? The most obviously Muslim name you could have. It was your grandfather's name, of course, and he embodied what we wanted you to be: people talked about his piousness, but he was simply good. But also your name was a statement of faith in this country. We could have given you some solid American name. But as much as we turned our backs on religion, we never shied from being Muslim. We believed so strongly in America that we never thought for a moment that your name would hold you back in any way. And now —" He stopped, bent his head, and pressed his hands to his eyes. "You are not responsible for the reaction, Mo. And yet it is my own son who has brought about this doubt — my doubt for the first time about whether this country has a place for us."

"Baba, please," Mo spoke softly. "Of course it does. But sometimes America has to be pushed — it has to be reminded of what it is."

"Mo, look at what your life has become." Salman's extended arms and upturned palms beseeched the vacant space.

The buffet tables were piled high with kebab

meats and pita, dates and fried feta. Mo stuck close to his parents, nodding at familiar faces, disappointed that Laila's was not among them. He couldn't know whether he or the council had kept her at bay. Without mentioning Mo or the memorial, the mayor made brief remarks about the need to not compound the tragedy of the attack by inflicting new traumas on Muslims.

An older man who looked familiar approached. He had a gray beard and no mustache. Mo put out a hand. It wasn't taken.

"I hope you are satisfied," the man said gravely. He had been at the first MACC meeting, Mo remembered. Tariq.

"With . . ."

"With what you've unleashed, with the position you've put us in. Before you came along, it would have been shocking, unacceptable to refer to us as the enemy. Now it's no big deal."

"That's not my fault," Mo said. He wished his father weren't listening.

"You've made your point. You won. You can withdraw now."

"No, no. We need to counter the backlash, not give in to it." Issam Malik, who had been expertly monopolizing the mayor, magically appeared at Mo's elbow.

"Counter, or capitalize on?" Tariq said.

"What's that supposed to mean?" Issam asked.

"Just that we seem to be sending out a lot of e-mails soliciting donations on the backs of this controversy. A lot of e-mails noting how many times MACC — you — are in the press. All well and good, but in the meantime, we've got people yanking head-scarves off our women, and our young people being radicalized in return, and who can blame them? This is going to end in a bad place." He turned to Mo. "You're *lead-ing* us to a bad place. It's you, not the ter-rorists, who've hijacked our religion. At least the terrorists believe. What's your excuse?"

"I'm sorry, but you cannot accuse him of such things." Everyone looked at Salman; who was he?

"My father," Mo mumbled.

"He is just exercising his rights, his rights as an American," Salman continued. "You cannot hold him responsible for how people react to that."

"He has the right, we all agree on that, and it is the message non-Muslims should hear." Jamilah, MACC's vice president, had joined them. She sounded more imposing tonight than she had at the MACC meeting. "But among us I'll say" — she turned to Mo — "that if you step aside, you show we are more interested in healing than confrontation."

"Why is it always up to us to show that?" asked another woman. Her headscarf, canary yellow, was covered with intricate swirling lines that suggested both calligraphy and fallen leaves. Mo's eye kept returning to it.

"Exactly," Malik said. "The real extremism is among those opposing him. And if they succeed in forcing Mohammad to stand down, they're likely to inspire attacks from so-called Islamic extremists."

"It sounds like you're making a threat," Mo said. All of their hands were full with plates and glasses, and their inability to gesture imposed an awkward and inauthentic politesse.

Mo hadn't seen Malik since the day they had presented the ad campaign. The loathing from that day returned now, accompanied by blame, no doubt unfair, but visceral anyway, for the sundering between him and Laila.

"But it's true," the woman in the yellow scarf interjected. "We need to warn everyone that the extremism of the opposition is fueling Islamist extremism. If we don't, they'll

378

hold us responsible if something happens."

"If something happens, from any quarter, *he'll* be responsible," Tariq said, pointing a judging finger at Mo. "You'll have blood on your hands."

"That's outrageous," said the woman in the canary-yellow scarf.

Suddenly everyone was yelling and interrupting one another so that their words seemed to be layered like the complicated, somewhat mystifying Middle Eastern dip the Gracie Mansion chef had put out on the buffet table. They also were still jamming food in their mouths because they had a whole day of fasting to make up for and the next day's fast to prepare for, so the food was going in as fast as the words were coming out — jabbering then gobbling, jabbering then gobbling. The very eating seemed angry.

The mayor, seeing a group around Mo, had wandered over to join the conversation, then, hearing the clamor, retreated to the safety of his aides. He looked baffled that his moderate Muslims could be so hot-tempered.

"I guess I changed your mind," Mo said to his father when he and his parents were free of the mansion. The cockiness in his voice was bravado. The argument had left

379

him aghast at his own turbulent wake, suggesting that he was bound to disturb every space he entered.

"You changed nothing," Salman said in answer. He sounded morose, even bitter. "I still think you're making a terrible mistake. I think even if you win, you will lose. We all will. But you are my son; I had no choice but to defend you in there."

17

"In any garden, more is happening than you know, than you see," Mohammad Khan said. "Something is always changing, being changed, outside our grasp."

His meaning evaded her. She reached toward him in an effort to understand. His hands settled on her head, jolting her inside, and he guided her sight to fibers rotting, leaves curling, aphids sucking sap, Japanese beetles gnawing petals, spider mites scorching leaves, oaks wilting . . . With microscopic vision, she saw it all.

"Death, it's all death," she said. "And no reason for it."

"There is a reason."

Wanting comfort, she leaned toward him, those green eyes, that soft mouth . . .

His beard pricked her awake, except that she came to alone in her bed, shaky with shame and confusion. Her subconscious, dispatched to ascertain his true nature, had instead ferreted out her own buried attraction.

He had not explained the reason for all the death. Cal's death. The revelation had been so close. She wanted to erase the kiss and continue the conversation. But she couldn't, for all her trying, will herself back to sleep.

It was 5:30 a.m. She tiptoed downstairs and out the back door. The sky was a vast canvas, pale, almost milky gray, the trees primitive black slashes against it. With all the concentration she could muster, she watched the rising sun shepherd tree branches and bark knots and leaf veins, every delicate particular, into being.

The white marble counter's dark veins read like a map of country roads. As she waited at the bar, Claire traced the faint lines with a finger. The restaurant, Greek, painted in rich royal blue and white, recalled the summer when she took the bar exam, after which she and Cal spent two weeks in Greece, island-hopping. As in a film, she saw them on mopeds on Samos, its vineyards green ribbons, the sea a sapphire blur. A bandanna held back her hair; her filmy cotton shirt billowed out with the wind. Cal wore a tank top, a sartorial choice so unlike him that she couldn't stop laughing at it. Their skin had browned through a day of riding and hiking and picnicking, and all these years later she could still see the white outline of the tank-top straps against his dark skin when they made love that night.

Their picnic lunch had included a bottle of Greek wine and when they resumed riding Cal nearly collided with a stone wall. They had doubled over in laughter, possessed of the reckless freedom, the false sense of immortality that came from being young and childless.

When Jack's hand touched her elbow, Claire felt a jolt even before she looked at him. When she did she saw silver at his temples, interesting lines on his face, the rich dark brown of his eyes, that well-cut mouth. He kissed her with it now, lightly, electrically, on the lips, and took a seat.

Regret seized her as soon as thcy began to talk. Making conversation with him, given their intimacy and subsequent estrangement, was almost harder than talking to a stranger. They stuck to facts: her summary of life since Cal, her children. He had, as she assumed, divorced; he had one-third custody of his eleven-year-old son. Most of his time now went to the social activism:

financing progressive documentaries; attending Netroots camps; brainstorming with the young Turks of the Democratic Party. A political sugar daddy, Claire thought — one with enough money not to have to work.

After a glass of wine they moved to a table and groped their way to old familiarities.

"Do you remember all the nights in the shanties?" he asked. Pieced together from discarded wood, meant to point up the inhumanity of supporting South Africa's racist regime, Dartmouth's antiapartheid shanties were defiantly ugly on that green, pristine campus. Both her relationship with Jack and her political education had taken shape within their flimsy walls. They often spent nights in one of the shanties, often made love there on a carpet of cardboard boxes over hard cement. The shanty had no locks, and to take such a risk, so unlike her, was arousing. The air sneaking through the cracks onto her bare skin, the cricket-quiet of the night in the campus's brief dormant hours. She remembered all of it and saw, in his invoking this memory, an erotic portent of the evening ahead.

They were barely through the first course when Jack said, "So what's going on with the memorial?"

She told him how guilty she felt about

defying the families opposed to Khan, even if she believed that opposition wrong. How unsure she was what to make of Khan himself. As she unburdened herself, the weight of the choice lightened for the first time in weeks.

"Sometimes I feel like I've got one leg in New York and one in America," she said.

"New York is America."

"You know what I mean — we think so differently, so atypically, here. We're such a minority in our own country. Liberals, I mean."

"Which doesn't mean we're wrong."

"Doesn't mean they are, either."

"So everyone's right? How's that supposed to work?"

"I just meant there are two sides to everything, including this. Probably more than two sides. I mean, the protest was ugly, but I'm supposed to represent the families. I'm one of them, we've shared this searing experience. Their presence at that rally was their way of telling me, 'You let us down, betrayed us.' I have an obligation to understand their point of view."

"Some things don't deserve to be understood. Apartheid didn't deserve to be understood, even if the whites who benefited from it didn't see it that way."

This second reference to their shared history grated, and it cast his earlier evocation of the shanties in a new light, one neither erotic nor accidental. By the time he said "The memorial is the reason I got back in touch," she didn't need him to tell her, but the words wrecked her nonetheless. He was here to remind her of their common values and summon them forth. Except that she saw now that they were his values. At twenty she had subscribed to them so strongly because he did, because she wanted to win his approval, which, in retrospect, made her poor soil for the plant of principle. For the first time she wondered if that night at Gracie Mansion it had been Jack's principles as well as Cal's that she had been defending. This disconcerted her, to not know where one man's ideals ended and another's began, to not know which were her own.

He spoke with earnestness, even desperation.

"Your support needs to be unconditional. There's more, much more, at stake here than a memorial — don't you see that? I know you've had so much of your own pain to deal with, maybe it's been hard to follow what's been happening in this country. The attack made everyone afraid of appearing unpatriotic, of questioning government, leaders. Fear has justified war, torture, secrecy, all kinds of violations of rights and liberties. Don't let it justify taking the memorial away from Khan. Everything these past couple of years has been about abdications. Don't succumb to the fear; don't mistake the absolutism of Khan's opponents for morality . . ."

Somehow he managed to say all this and more while polishing off his lamb, a feat of ingestion given that he did not talk with his mouth full and Claire had said barely a word. Her grilled fish, in contrast, sat almost untouched on her plate, its taste lost to disappointment. Here was what she had wanted — someone reaching out to her, offering reinforcement for her stand — but it did not have the desired effect. How foolish she felt, and how crestfallen, to have dressed for a date and gotten a lecture instead.

Wanting the last word, or the last something, she suggested a nightcap back at the house, saying she had promised to be home by eleven to relieve the babysitter, hoping this would imply that she had anticipated nothing beyond a cordial catching up. He followed her home, his headlights bobbing in the dark, the beams signaling lighthouse comfort one moment and ominous chase the next, like a dream that blurred rescue and pursuit. As her car crested the top of the driveway, the automatic lights around the house came on, bleaching the front yard.

"Nice house," Jack said, coming up behind her as she opened the glass front door. Madison was curled up with a book on the sofa. As they watched, she stretched with feline indifference, her rising T-shirt revealing a band of tanned stomach and a navel piercing. "You're home early," she said. Claire hurried her out and poured two cognacs. They sat in the living room, a polite distance between them on the couch. Claire could hear, within herself, fury's low thrum.

"Let me try to explain about the Garden," she said. Her doubts, she told him, were not about Khan but about what the design symbolized.

"That's bullshit, Claire. It's all a question of trust. Do you take what he says at face value? Or do you look for something hidden and duplicitous because he's Muslim?"

"That's not it at all."

"Then what?"

"You don't think it's a problem if Cal's memorial is a paradise for Islamic martyrs?"

"That's the same mistrust," he said. "The same fear. A garden's just a garden until *you* decide to plant suspicion there. Has he said it's a paradise garden?"

"That's just it — he won't say —"

"Why should he?"

"It's not the same as mistrusting him," she said. "It's not."

They sat in silence.

"There are things you don't know," she told him. She considered telling him about Alyssa's information but knew he would be even more skeptical than she had been. "That *Post* column — that I'm sleeping with the enemy? Some of the other family members came to my house to protest. I got threatening, hateful calls. I had to unlist our phone. All those lights outside — they're new."

"I'm sure that must have been terrifying," he said, with a reasonable approximation of sympathy. "But isn't that more of a reason, not less, to defend Khan? I was cheering you on when I read that column."

But he had only bothered to get in touch once she publicly wavered. Claire couldn't stand it. His concern was greater for Khan, a man he'd never met, a face in the news, than for her, the woman whom he once wanted to spend his life with. There was a kind of abandonment, a betrayal in this. "You should write editorials!" she burst out shrilly. "You have all the arguments.

389

Always did."

"No one's interested in my point of view," he said. "Like a lot of Americans, I've felt really helpless the past few years, powerless to stop the change in this country's direction, and bolstering you is a way to do something. Look, I'm not saying it's easy, I know there are all kinds of pressures, but this really matters. You need to be strong. There's no evidence our Muslim population is a threat; why should we make them one?"

"Still fighting for the underdog, I see," she said, and although she didn't mean it as a compliment, he took it as one.

"Whom else would I fight for?"

"The victims? The families?"

"Oh, I don't think there's any shortage of recruits for their army," he said.

"There are a billion Muslims in the world!" Her laugh faked lightness. "You think they're short of recruits?"

"In this country, I do. Khan's the underdog. He won, fair and square, and you want to take it away from him."

His inability to grasp the complications was making her, for the first time, judge him to be stupid. "I don't want to take anything away, I just want to know what he's given us —"

He interrupted: "Promise me you won't renege on Khan."

"Renege? It's not a *contract,* Jack. You're as bad as the people who want me to promise to stop him. It's my decision, and I'll make it, thank you. Let me ask you a question. You, with your liberal causes, how do you reconcile your support for Islam with your support for gay rights, for feminism, when you look at how women, or gays, or minorities get treated in so many Muslim countries?"

"That's not the kind of Muslim Khan is."

"But then it's your own litmus test — the 'acceptable' Muslims are the ones who agree with you."

He downed his drink, seemed peeved. To her surprise, she was enjoying flustering him as much as she once had enjoyed pleasing him.

"You've changed," he said.

"I'm sure I have," she said, refilling his glass and her own, even though the cognac's warmth was already leadening her muscles and her tongue. "I can't imagine that anyone who lost someone that day didn't." What she wanted to say was that maybe it wasn't a change but a becoming — a coming into herself. But she could sense his judgment. "Try to understand, Jack. It's been — there aren't words for how painful it has been to lose Cal this way."

She looked at the tableau she had constructed on the ottoman, an artful display of family pictures and branched coral and stacked art books, its maintenance in the face of childish sabotage a constant struggle. Her glance caught on the picture of Cal, grinning, then his arm was around her, or so she imagined until she looked up to see that it was Jack moving closer, encircling her, pulling her to him, saying, "Hey, hey, I'm sorry, I'm sorry." He cradled her head against his chest, as if she were his daughter, and stroked her hair with his hand, undoing its coil, stroked, stroked, until she relaxed, tingled. "I'm sorry," he said again. "I'm sorry." He turned her face up and leaned down to put his mouth on hers and they were twenty again, panting, nervous, the charge between them now almost stronger for their friction. His other hand began deftly pulling open her blouse and rubbing her breast in little circles that made every dormant part of her surge to life. Then he gave her nipple a hard twist as if to say "I know you, I know what you are."

The idea of luring him to her house only to spurn him had come to her on the drive home from the restaurant. Yet here she was leaning up so he could pull off her shirt and unhook her bra, here she was letting him pull up her skirt and slide his hand into her underwear, inside her, so that she gasped, almost shouted, at the shot of pleasure and pain.

"Easy," he said, laughing. "You'll wake the children."

"Their rooms are too far away," she said, irritated that he had invoked them at this moment. Yet she still couldn't bring herself to remove his hand, until memories of their dinner conversation intruded and her desire clicked off. She twisted away from him and tried to look bored. "I'm just — not ready," she said. He seemed unperturbed, as if he didn't care how far they went. She pulled her shirt on and her skirt down, and saw him out, turning her cheek to him when he bent to kiss her.

"Be strong, Claire, and don't forget to put on the alarm." A half sob nearly escaped her. It was the first protective gesture from him, from anyone.

The motion sensors did their work, making him cross a field of light as he walked to his car. He disappeared down the driveway. She had been shaped, was being shaped, not only by those she met on her journey but also by how she lost them.

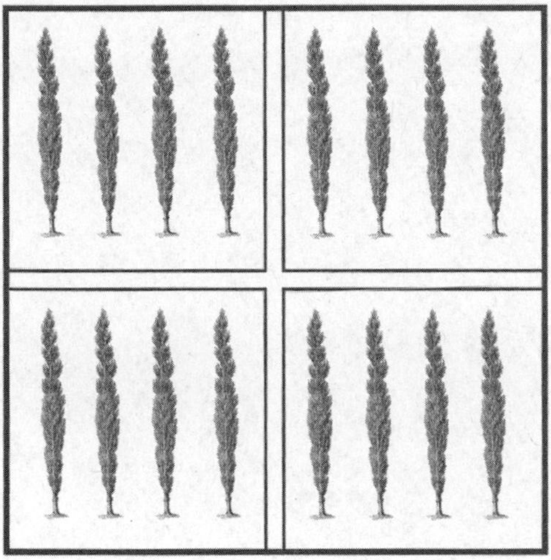

18

Fourteen headscarf pullings across the country; twenty-five Muslim self-defense squads patrolling in response. Eleven mosque desecrations in eight states, not counting a protest pig roast organized outside a mosque in Tennessee, but including the dog feces left at the door of a mosque in Massachusetts. Twenty-two Muslim countries expressing concern about America's treatment of Muslims and its media's portrayal of Islam. Six serious threats to American interests abroad by Islamic extremists vowing retaliation for the persecution of Khan. And, most worrying for a country previously free of indigenous jihadist terrorism, three thwarted plots at home.

These bulletins, these confounding facts, came to Paul at all hours, from all quarters. So did the opinions they fostered. The FBI and NYPD, in rare harmony, suggested that

397

Paul cancel, or at least postpone, the public hearing because it might inflame passions further. A member of the president's National Security Council argued the opposite — canceling the hearing "would not play well in Peshawar." State Department officials agreed that the hearing might help the global campaign for Muslim "hearts and minds," unless the hearing's ugly tenor damaged it. The governor insisted that the public needed the catharsis of tension that a hearing could provide. "Some conflicts have to be fought out, rather than papered over," she said, which prompted New York's mayor to accuse her of sanctioning violence. The president, who had once owned a baseball team, suggested trading Khan ("He withdraws, then we make him a goodwill ambassador to the Muslim world") or sending him to the minor leagues ("His memorial gets built, just in some other town or city").

Paul's trusted yellow legal pad was proving useless against these competing claims. Both canceling and proceeding with the hearing were perilous, unpredictably so. Stress, having already diminished his appetite, now stole his sleep, shortened his fuse, and prompted Edith and the household staff to speak in uncharacteristic hushed tones. His home took on the quality of a deathbed watch, an ominous ambience for a man newly feeling his age.

In his study at midnight, Paul flipped through his files on the memorial and came across the paper that had first revealed Khan's name. Ever since he had pulled it from the envelope, he had been unsuccessfully trying, in one form or another, to stuff it back in. His efforts at containment had bred only more chaos. Maybe the answer, he thought now, was to let chaos, let chance, be history's architect. He was, by profession, a gambler, albeit one who operated with society's respect. The young love of risk, which had drawn him to his banking life — it was resurgent now. He took a quarter from his pocket, assigned heads and tails, and flipped. George Washington gazed into the distance, as if to see how the nation he founded would manage this pass. To start, by allowing the public to vent its spleen.

The strain on Mo, which had built by the week, then the day, now seemed to intensify by the hour. As the hearing approached, rumors pulsed in malevolent syncopation: the United Arab Emirates had "bought" rights to the memorial; Islamic extremists were going to sabotage the attack site; Mo's opponents were going to blow it up and blame it on Muslims; Mo was going to pretend to accept Jesus Christ as his personal savior to get his paradise built.

In truth he was looking for salvation only from his new lawyer, but this, too, fed new rumors. Scott Reiss was confident, droll, professional, and expensive. As soon as word of his retention leaked — was leaked by Scott's firm, which believed all publicity good — the *Post* ran a nasty story questioning how Mo was paying for such a high-powered firm and insinuating that the Saudis were underwriting him. The article noted how low architects' salaries were in New York, even quoted anonymous sources at ROI. Mo's take was slightly higher than their estimate, but the paper was right: not high enough to finance a five-hundred-dollar-an-hour lawyer-cum-PR firm. The truth was that Mo's father had tapped into his retirement account, four decades of savings dripping like an IV into Reiss's Armani-suited arm. This could have been publicly documented with a single 401(k) statement, but Mo wanted to shelter his parents. Even more, he refused to prove his innocence. He knew this position was right, but it was like keeping his arms in stocks with no padlock. His muscles ached.

Reiss's first plan was for a public relations offensive.

"We need you holding up pictures of your children," he said, and, when Mo reminded him he had none, "Borrow some. We've got to humanize you. No, Americanize you. We want your family albums. Your Boy Scout medals. We want to run ads in advance of the public hearing. You have a lot of supporters out there willing to pay for commercials."

Mo was ashamed to imagine Laila watching an ad campaign after he had said no to MACC's. But also he didn't want to hawk himself; he wouldn't reassure his own compatriots that he wasn't to be feared.

"No ads," he told Reiss, who rolled his eyes.

Ramadan stretched on. Mo still fasted from dawn to dusk each day, still ate alone most nights, despite his father's admonition. The memory of the mayor's Iftar seared, left him sure that he would upset any gathering of Muslims he entered. But the solitude wore at him, especially as the hearing approached. Four nights before it, he went to Brooklyn to dine with five Protestants: Thomas, Alice, and their children.

Alice still dolloped out anger for Mo's

having, as she regularly put it, "screwed over Thomas and endangered our family," but mostly she doled out new conditions for forgiveness. The latest was the construction of a Lego Seattle Space Needle for Petey. Once dinner was finished and the children tucked in, Mo worked on the living-room floor, happy to lose himself in the relative mindlessness of miniature construction. Alice was stretched out on the sofa, her feet in Thomas's lap, and Mo tried to block out the memory of Laila arching her dainty feet like cats' backs and settling them in his.

Channel surfing, Alice paused on Mo's face. Mo automatically shifted, as he always did now when watching himself, from the first person to the third. Issam Malik and Lou Sarge were debating the memorial, and seeing them jolted Mo back to that night with Yuki less than a year ago. These two men had been strangers, cartoons to him then, and he non existent to them. Now they were all characters, cast members in some sinister opera, unable to leave its stage or, in the case of Malik and Sarge, its TV screen.

Some of their exchanges were so perfectly turned Mo wondered if they practiced off camera.

"You, with this rhetoric, you're putting up

walls of suspicion," Malik said.

"No," Sarge said. "Mohammad Khan is putting up suspicious walls."

Malik smiled involuntarily, and Thomas, Alice, and Mo looked, as one, at the Space Needle. Sarge continued: "He's created the perfect bind. If we build it, it's a martyrs' paradise, which will only embolden the enemy. If we don't, the enemy comes after us for discriminating against a Muslim."

"It's you who's created the bind, Lou. If Khan fights for his rights he's an aggressive, angry Muslim waging stealth jihad. If he gives in, he's conceding they weren't his rights to begin with." Mo harbored the secret hope that Malik continued to take his side because of Laila's influence. More likely, he knew, was that Malik still saw maximum capital in Mo's cause.

"That's ridiculous!" Sarge roared. "They're his rights — we all agree. But he can have the decency to choose not to exercise them."

Mo wasn't sure why hearing this in the presence of Thomas and Alice made him uncomfortable. Thomas, from friendship, from intrinsic loyalty, would never admit even to himself that he thought Mo should withdraw. Alice was a different case.

"Do you think he's right, Alice?" Mo asked.

"Honestly?" Alice said.

"From you I'd expect no less."

"If I were talking about anyone but you — any other Muslim, let's say — yes, I do think he's right. I also think he's an asshole who wouldn't know decency if it pissed on him, but that's irrelevant. I know you want your design to heal, and I respect that. But it's not healing, at least right now."

"Alice," Thomas said.

"He asked!"

"I did," Mo said. "And if I were any other Muslim I might agree with her."

The exchange twanged dissonantly in the air even after the talk turned elsewhere. Half an hour later Mo stood, his legs cramped, the Space Needle unfinished, and said he needed to get home. The word burned his mouth.

"Good luck at the hearing," Alice said, hugging him before he got in the elevator. "And I meant what I said: my opinion only holds for any other Muslim, which you're not. You're ours."

"Alice!" Thomas exclaimed.

She rolled her eyes at him. "Mo knows what I mean. He doesn't need you to protect him from me."

Mo had been desperate to escape his solitude; now he wanted only to reclaim it. He gave an exhausted half wave and let the doors close. Avoiding the subway, as had become his habit — he didn't want to be recognized, applauded, or confronted in its close quarters — he had called a livery cab.

"Mohammad Khan," the driver, one Faisal Rahman, said without emotion when Mo climbed in the car.

"That's me," said Mo, grimly resigned to a long, interrogatory ride home.

But Faisal was quiet most of the way. Only when they swung onto the Brooklyn Bridge and saw the Empire State Building lit up red and white, like a parfait, did he speak. "The first two years I lived here," Faisal said, "whenever I saw green lighting on the Empire State Building, I thought it was for Islam. I told everybody back home; half of Matlab still thinks it's true. Then I found out it was for the Jets!" He started laughing, and despite his mood, Mo did, too. "But for those two years, I couldn't believe how much this country loved Islam."

When they reached Mo's destination, Faisal refused to accept payment. "I wish you luck and blessings from Allah," the driver said. "You will need them."

■ ■ ■ ■

Three nights before the hearing, Mo dreamed of drought, the dry ground hard. He dreamed of floods, his garden turned to swamp. He dreamed of locusts devouring plants and swarming him, and from this dream he rose, twitching, groped to the kitchen, took the orange juice carton from the refrigerator, and drank, drank with the same sickening weakness he suspected a relapsing addict must feel, but also the same sordid relief: this is who I am, now I can stop pretending otherwise. Orange juice first thing, an American routine, but with it he had ended his Ramadan fast. He didn't even know why, only that he had woken with the sudden, abrupt sense that strength wouldn't come from this kind of sacrifice, that his abstention would never be anything but hollow. If he couldn't say he believed in the paradise fasting was meant to obtain, how could he believe in the fast? This Ramadan would test him even without it.

Once, about a year earlier, Mo, curious about his father's newfound piety, accompanied him to Friday prayers. From the moment they pulled into the parking lot, Mo began critiquing the mosque's architecture. The cartoon dome and minaret, the gaudy, chilly interior spaces: "No one's going to find God in there," he said when they left.

"I know buildings are your religion," Salman had answered, with something like bemusement. "But they shouldn't keep you from God, and they can't bring you to Him."

The barbershop was tiny and nondescript, just four chairs and a newspaper rack, one barber to do the fourteen-dollar cuts and sweep up, an old-school place, an unbrilliantined patch of Manhattan. Mo stood outside for a moment, then ducked in and approached the white-shirted proprietor, face hidden behind his newspaper. The man folded his paper, revealing chalk-white hair and matching mustache, then folded his arms.

"Cut it short," Mo said. "Neat."

The barber directed him to a chair and necklaced him with the black bib. He lined up his tools with a surgeon's precision and began to work. Dark locks sank to the floor. The barber whistled. Mo registered every clip as a concession. The hearing was two days off. He was cutting his hair — grown shoulder-length in the wake of his Afghanistan trip — at his mother's behest, or so he told himself. His image, she had argued, was diverting attention from his design; perhaps a more conservative look would sap some of the opposition, allay fears. His answer had been that he shouldn't tailor himself to prejudice. Yet here he was, tailoring.

"Shave?" the barber asked, hesitating before he removed the bib.

Mo shook his head.

The morning of the hearing, Mo woke early, his boxers sweaty, despite the cool fall air, and his sheets tangled. He palmed his face, its softness and bristle, showered, wiped a hole in the mirror fog, and leaned over the sink. His image, with its short hair, caught him off guard, as if someone else had slipped into the medicine cabinet. He locked eyes with himself and began the next argument. Doing this was practical. No, it was cowardly. It would grow back. It wouldn't be the same. He was in control; he was caving. To do this was smart; no, shameful. "Next you'll shave for them." Laila's words echoed.

He had grown the beard to play with perceptions and misconceptions, to argue against the attempt to define him. If he shaved, would he be losing the argument or ending it? Was he betraying his religion? No, but it would look that way. Was he betraying himself? That question shook the hand holding the razor.

In a bold swoop, he began clear-cutting, watching strips of paler skin emerge beneath the hair. When he finished, his countenance looked younger, wan, weak, just as his shorn head looked smaller, boyish. He was humbling himself, maybe only to rob others of the chance to do so. He opened his suitcase, took out his old, plainer titanium glasses, and folded up his tinted ones. He felt like he was putting himself away in the case.

The deodorant went on double, beneath his best-cut dark gray suit, a white shirt, a silk tie striped diagonally with dark gray and subtle silver. Not bad, he thought, studying his image, sedate and foreign, in the mirror. But this wasn't a beauty contest.

The sky was an expressionless face. Mo took a cab to the city council chambers where the hearing was to be held. The police were setting up barricades in anticipation of the crowds. Bomb-sniffing dogs patrolled City Hall Park.

Mo entered through a side door, as Paul Rubin had instructed. A police officer checked his name, "Khan, Mohammad," off a list, then instructed him to empty his pockets and pass through the metal detector blocking his path. He shoveled his coins, keys, and phone into the small plastic bin, slipped off his shoes, walked through, and heard a loud series of beeps.

"Belt," the cop said, looking at Mo's waist.

Mo removed the belt. He had been eating little, even apart from the fast, and the pounds had dropped off his already thin frame. That morning he had cinched his belt an extra hole. Now the suit pants gaped at the waist.

"Again," the cop said, nodding toward the metal detector. Mo passed through again; again the alarm sounded. The cop eyed him with suspicion.

"Glasses?" Mo said, wondering if the titanium frames could be the problem. The officer snorted and mumbled something into his radio, remembered to turn it on, repeated the mumble, held it to his ear for the reply, then said gruffly to Mo: "Arms out, legs spread." At Mo's panicked expression, he added, in a milder tone, "Search."

Dizzy, Mo felt the beginnings of shock at this indignity on this day. His body, against his will, began to tremble, and he worried this would suggest a guilty conscience. The guard strafed Mo's outstretched arms and, with almost tender intimacy, slipped his fingers inside Mo's sleeves and beneath the back of his jacket. Just then Paul appeared, a bit breathless, from inside the building, accompanied by an officer who had unholstered his authority.

"Captain," Mo's man greeted him.

"Oh," Paul said, when he saw Mo. "Oh." Then, to Mo's officer: "It's okay — let him through."

The officer looked uncertain, began to shake his head.

"Please," Paul said with impatience, turning to the captain. "I take full responsibility. He's the, he's the —"

Everyone waited politely, as if he were a stutterer, while Paul grasped for the correct term.

"Guest of honor!" he finally trumpeted, as if they had gathered for Mo's surprise party.

The captain nodded. After a moment's more hesitation, like a dog unwilling to release a bird, the officer lifted his hand from Mo's back, where it had come to rest without Mo realizing it. Mo gave the detector a wary berth, feeling like a child allowed back into the classroom or a prisoner randomly granted clemency. He was embarrassed at having to be rescued. His feet went into his shoes, his miscellany in his pockets, and he began to walk, eager to move on, only to realize that Paul Rubin was not beside him. Hearing a polite cough, he turned back.

"Your belt," Paul said, averting his eyes.

A model of the Garden sat onstage beneath a spotlight and a field-size American flag. The model had been on display for two weeks now, along with Mo's drawings, for the public to view. "That has to be the most heavily guarded architectural model in history," Thomas reported back after a visit. "The Hope Diamond of architectural models."

Mo had made half a dozen visits to the model shop while the miniature garden was under construction, but still — seeing it displayed made him swell with pride. Its white wall, with the date of the attack imprinted on the exterior, glowed like exposed bone beneath the light. A tiny battery-powered pump pushed water through the canals. For tact's sake, the names on the inside of the wall were random amalgamations of letters meant to stand for the dead, but their patterning did evoke, to Mo's satisfaction, the exterior of the destroyed buildings. Steel trees twisted from tin and green trees made of wire and paper towered over the walls.

The audience, invisible to him from backstage, gave off a hornet buzz. At the last possible moment he descended to the front row and took his seat. The buzz deafened now. Breathe, breathe, he told himself. He glanced down his row to the right and saw Robert Wilner, the governor's man, looking at him and idly stroking his chin. A few seats to the left he saw Claire Burwell staring. Her gaze darted away when he caught her eye, and this unnerved him. He had seen the *Post* story about her wavering but assumed that, like most of what that paper reported, it was exaggerated or untrue. Her support had been so effusive, seemed so solid, with her talk of her son. He hadn't thought to doubt it.

A high-school student stepped up to sing "The Star-Spangled Banner," its strained, fragile last note hanging in the air like a teetering vase. Paul Rubin ambled onto the stage, took his seat, tapped his mic, thanked everyone for coming, and asked for a moment of silence for the victims of the attack. Mo remembered to bow his head just in time, kicking himself for the near-mistake; he could imagine the pictures, the reprobation if he alone had continued staring into space. The cameras clicked like emptied guns.

"To the families," Rubin said, "I just want to say, what we're doing here is about your lost loved ones. You've really been the conscience of this process, and I want to thank you for that." Then, like a man used to running meetings, he briskly explained how things would work. Mohammad Khan would make a statement first. Then a sampling of the public would speak, with priority given to family members. He asked for civility. "This is the beauty of our democracy," he said, "that we give everyone a chance to speak, to be heard. The jury's decision was only guidance, only one step in this process. We want as democratic a process as possible, and so it is you, the people, who will have the final word." It took Mo half a minute to grasp that Rubin was stripping his own jury of its power and putting the decision in the public's hands. His eyes itched; he looked down to regain himself.

"Mr. Khan?" Paul said. "Mr. Khan."

Despite giving up fasting, Mo had forgotten, with all his attention on shaving, to eat that morning. He stood and walked, foal-wobbly, to his left. He looked down at Claire, who looked down at her notebook,

414

leaving visible only her coiled blond chignon and long slender legs. Ariana at least gave an encouraging nod — compassion from an unexpected quarter, the small humanity of a window opening in a skyscraper.

From the stage, the audience passed in and out of focus, one minute a pale, undifferentiated blur, the next every scowl and squint registering in high definition. He had told his parents not to come, even though he knew they would watch on television. His father's doubts rattled his certainty; his mother he wanted to spare the visceral atmosphere in the room. But now he wished they were here. He scanned for Laila but did not see her. No reason he should. Reiss he spotted punching away on his BlackBerry.

The room finally quieted. Mo set his text, its words in an eighteen-point font, on the table and leaned into the microphone. He took in the faces before him and imagined all the others who would watch. With the hearing to be broadcast globally, it was the largest audience he would ever have for a discussion of his work. And he was reduced to explaining why a religion he barely practiced hadn't contaminated it. Seated at the small speakers' table onstage, he felt like a foolish hand puppet behind which

415

gargantuan shadows wrestled. He tried to remember his life's most trying experiences — the charettes and crits of architecture school; the difficult meetings with clients and Roi. His best preparation for this moment had been the interrogation after the attack.

"I'd like to thank you for having me here today," he began, his voice confident, steady. "I was honored to have my design selected for the memorial. I want nothing more than to do justice to all the lives that were taken on that terrible day." Never mind justice for me or my design, he thought petulantly, before a seep of regret at his own anger, its polluting, distorting force, began. He took a breath.

"I'd like to talk about the design a little. To me, the wall framing the garden, the wall with the names, is an allegory for the way grief frames the aftermath of this tragedy. Life goes on, the spirit rejuvenates — this is what the garden represents. But whereas the garden grows, and evolves, and changes with the seasons, the wall around it changes not at all. It is as eternal, as unalterable, as our mourning —"

He heard a series of low hisses, slow leaks of poisonous air. For a moment it seemed as if the glare of the crowd's hostility was

416

blinding him. It was the spotlight on him, which had been turned up. He squinted. A dull pain, from the light or the hunger or the strain, roosted in the right side of his head. He shifted in his seat, sat up straighter, skipped ahead in his text. "The design's influences are many, from Japanese gardens, which use structures, like the pavilion in this design, as anchors through the seasons —"

"No one's blowing themselves up to get into a Japanese garden!" a man yelled from the audience.

"They don't have seventy-two virgins spreading their legs!" another voice shouted.

Paul Rubin stirred and moved to turn on his microphone with all the haste he would bring to a mildly contentious board meeting. "We will not have such interruptions," he said. "We will let the speaker finish. Anyone unable to control himself — or herself — will be removed."

Rubin's lack of urgency puzzled Mo; he seemed to have no interest in controlling the situation. As the spectators settled themselves, Mo scanned his statement. He had not so much lost his place as forgotten it for a moment: he couldn't remember what he had just said. The large type loomed up like a foreign alphabet. He extemporized.

"— from Japanese gardens, to modern artists and architects like Mondrian and Mies van der Rohe, to the gardens we now call Islamic —"

The stunned silence in the room translated to a roar in Mo's ears. He had intended to emphasize all the non-Islamic influences on the Garden, to show that if critics were evaluating the same design by anyone not named Mohammad, they would have seen its ranging roots. But the heckling suckled his rage, and he decided, in that moment, that to downplay any Islamic influence was to concede the stigma attached to it.

Boos reverberated, chants of "Save America from Islam!" and "No Muslim memorial!"

"Quiet!" Rubin rapped the hecklers in vain. "Quiet!"

Mo kept on. "The gardens we now call Islamic," he repeated, "although they predate Islam by at least a millennium, because agriculture, not religion, shaped their structure —"

"Taqiya!" one woman shouted.

"He's lying about everything! Taqiya!" shrieked another.

"Order!" Rubin bellowed, finally alive. He had gone pale; sweat gleamed from the halfmoon of his pate, which he was dabbing

418

furiously with a handkerchief. "Order!" Rubin boomed again. "Or we will end the hearing. Order!"

Mo stopped trying to speak, and after a few minutes, the room went quiet. "If you — the public — can't conduct yourself with decency," Rubin said sternly, "you don't deserve to have your viewpoint weighed."

"We're not the public, we're the families," a voice called out. "You can't say we don't count." Righteous applause rippled.

Rubin, perspiring still, but composed, held up a hand. "Of course the families count. But the families also have respect for this process, so I'm confident that they're not doing the interrupting. The families deserve dignity as they seek the right memorial, so anyone disrupting these proceedings clearly has no respect for them."

The logic, however convoluted, seemed to work; the audience calmed. Paul nodded at Mo to continue. Double deodorant or not, he was perspiring, too. He tried to pick up where he had left off. "The gardens predate Islam, so perhaps the gardens we read about in the Quran were based on what existed at the time, maybe the gardens Mohammad saw when he traveled to Damascus. Maybe man wrote the Quran in response to his context: compared to the desert, gardens

419

seemed heavenly, and so that's the heaven they created. That became their model for paradise."

The worry that he had said something unwise licked at him, but like a football player who has fumbled, he could only keep after the ball. "My point" — what was his point? — "my point, my point is that the Garden, with all of these influences — this mix of influences is what makes it American." With the light shining he could see only Rubin's face, and Rubin looked confused. He should wrap up.

The virgins, the seventy-two virgins, should he address that . . . seventy-two versions of the truth. No, it would only make things worse. The flaw, the setup, in the process — he saw it now: he wouldn't have a chance to answer the speakers who came after him. How to personalize it, make them see what they were doing to him. They wouldn't care, he couldn't count on that. Make them see what they were doing to themselves. But hurry: the sweat staging on his forehead soon would sting his eyes.

"What history do you want to write with this memorial?" he asked, then, still unable to recover his prepared remarks, unable to remember what, after his influences, he planned to discuss, he could think of nothing more to say, so his speech ended abruptly, like a sentence without a period, and because no one realized that he was done, or because he had no support, or because this restive crowd was suddenly heedful of Paul's admonition against outbursts, there was no applause.

A firm named U.S.PEAK had been hired to run the public-response portion of the hearing. Alyssa, penned in the press section, perused their glossy brochure, which had been included in her media packet, and guffawed. The company described its mission as "fulfilling the Jeffersonian ideal for every American to have his or her fifteen minutes" and offering a voice to time-pressed "citizen-generalists," who were contrasted with "specialists" like politicians and lobbyists. Their slogan was "Even Democracies Need a Little Viagra Now and Then." If the response to Mohammad Khan's remarks was any indication, a lack of testosterone was not the problem of this audience, the SAFI women least of all.

U.S.PEAK's emcee was a woman named Winnie whose smile looked like it had been surgically fixed. She was explaining that she would call speakers from the list of ninety names she held in her hand. Other than to

421

say that family members of the dead had been given precedence, Winnie gave no indication of how the list had been assembled, and Alyssa wondered who — U.S.PEAK, Paul Rubin, the governor? — had composed it and with what criteria. It irked her a little, as if the story had been edited before she got to write it.

The speakers began.

"Alan Bolton. I lost my son, Jason. I don't find the prospect of a Muslim designing this memorial, or even that it has Islamic elements, insulting. I find it insensitive, which is different." Alyssa looked at Rubin, wondering if he would rule references to Khan's religion out of bounds. He didn't. "We, who have carried the weight of loss, are now being asked to carry the weight of proving America's tolerance, and it . . . well, it's a lot to ask. Back when the Carmelite nuns wanted to put a convent at Auschwitz, the pope decided to respect the sensitivities of Jews and move it. He wasn't saying the nuns had no right to be there; he wasn't saying they were in any way responsible for what happened to the Jews. He was saying: rights do not make right, that feelings matter, too. I have nothing against Mr. Khan. But if even one member of his religion is out there gloating over his selection, or what this

422

design might represent, that would be incredibly painful to me."

As Bolton left the stage, Alyssa looked at her notes. "Insensitive," she had written. "Families prove tolerance=unfair. Pope to nuns: move convent b/c Jews mad. Rights ≠ right. Feelings. Muslims gloat." It evoked Bolton's testimony as much as a bloodless specimen afloat in formaldehyde did a working liver. After checking that her tape recorder was on, she created a quick shorthand to track the comments: FQ meant "For Khan and Quotable," FB "For Khan but Boring"; the same with against: AQ, AB. N for "Neutral," R for "Random," CR for "Comic Relief." Now she could just listen.

"Arthur Chang." The dean of the Yale School of Art and Architecture, and Mo's former professor. He was Chinese American, a refined, silver-haired man in his late sixties. He praised the cleanness and elegance of the design, its tension between form and freedom, between the natural and inorganic.

"If I may speak to another matter: I have known Mr. Khan for fifteen years. His character is as strong as his talent. And he is as American as I am."

"Debbie Dawson." Under the glare, in full makeup, she looked like the Joker. As if aware of how she would translate on television, she asked for the lights to be turned down, then waited, nodding to familiar faces, while the technicians fiddled for her comfort.

"The Prophet Mohammad took slaves, raided caravans, and married a six-year-old, although it was not consummated until the ripe age of nine," she began. "Is that the name we want connected to this memorial?"

Cheers and a new chant — "No Mohammad memorial!" — erupted from the audience.

Winnie tapped her microphone and said, "Please, let Ms. Dawson finish," although Ms. Dawson seemed to be savoring the interruption.

The chants went on.

Rubin gave his bow tie a sharp tug and said, "Be aware, Ms. Dawson, that your supporters' contributions are being counted against your time."

"She can have my time — I'm on the list," someone yelled out.

"Time cannot be donated, or sold, or otherwise disposed of," Rubin said. "If there are speakers who do not want to use their time, we will conclude earlier."

Dawson waved a merry hand in the air, as if conducting a fanfare to its end, then returned to her remarks. "When the ring-leader of this massacre told the others 'We'll meet in paradise,' I bet even he didn't imagine it would be right in the heart of Manhattan. People who say this is benign probably also believe jihad means merely 'inner struggle,' and if they believe that, I've got a bridge to sell them in Brooklyn. American Muslims need to be condemning the actions of their brethren, not encouraging them. And —"

Suddenly Mohammad Khan stood, pushed out of his row, strode up the aisle and out the door. As he passed, Alyssa glimpsed the squall in his face. A man in a suit, his lawyer, hurried after him. Dawson paused with a smile. "I assume this interruption won't be counted against my time, Mr. Chairman," she said. Rubin ignored her.

Alyssa stood, thinking to go after Khan, but, as if they were handcuffed together, the other reporters in her section instantly stood, too. Fuming, she sat. They did, too. Khan didn't return until another speaker had taken the stage.

"Arlo Eisenmann." Lost his wife. "I happen to think the design is very beautiful. Very powerful. My concern is not with the shape of the garden, not with what it may

425

or may not resemble, but with the idea of a garden itself — its impermanence. Its nature, if you will. It's inherently a fragile form — a risk, and I'm not sure we want to take a risk here. Gardens require a tremendous commitment of resources, of attention, through generations. Put up a stone or granite memorial and you can neglect it all you want. But what if we run out of money for maintenance, or climate change gets so bad that everything planted goes awry? The symbolism of a garden destroyed, returned to nature, by man's heedlessness or neglect would be devastating."

Alyssa had a sudden, uncharacteristic vision of an untamed garden taking over the middle of Manhattan, with trees poking from buildings, roots rampaging beneath sidewalks. It made her shiver, this imagining, partly in delight.

"Florence Garvey. My brother-in-law died that day, but I'm also a historian of early America." She listed, at tedious length, her credentials, then said, "I don't mind a garden, but I don't understand why it's a walled garden. Walled gardens are un-American or — I dislike that phrase — perhaps 'not American' would be better. We have no tradition of them. It privileges some spaces over others. The Puritans called nature 'God's second book,' and to select, as a memorial, a walled garden is to tear off a single page. This memorial is like importing an exotic species, when today we understand the beauty of native plants. Don't we want a more indigenous symbol?"

An hour passed. Alyssa, desperate for nourishment, discreetly slipped some gummy bears into her mouth.

"David Albon." A professor of Middle Eastern studies, complete with professorial beard. "Islam is an expansionist religion, and where Islam has gone, gardens have often followed, which is why we see them in India and Spain and Morocco and elsewhere, and now we'll see one in New York. As the saying goes, if it looks like a duck, walks like a duck, quacks like a duck, it's going to taste like a duck, too. So here we have, right in Manhattan, an Islamic paradise, and achieving that paradise through martyrdom — murder, suicide — has become the obsession of Islamic extremists, the ultimate submission to God. We toy with that idée fixe at our peril."

Winnie called a fifteen-minute recess. Alyssa, ruing her morning coffee consumption, spent the entire time in line for the bathroom.

"Maxwell Franklin." Ex-CIA, now a

consultant tracking the jihadist threat. An Arabic speaker. "Other than the president of Iran, who knows how to rile us, I haven't found evidence that Islamist extremists are out there rubbing their hands in glee about this garden. They're tracking the *reaction* to the Garden, the treatment of Mohammad Khan, and all of that is proof to them of the West's hostility to Islam. We're handing them a great way to rally their base. But the Garden itself? It's barely merited a mention."

"Betsy Stanton." The frail, white-haired author of a book on Islamic gardens who happened to also be the widow of a late United States senator. "Since when did we become so afraid of learning from other cultures?" she began. "Islam and the West have always influenced each other — in gardens, in architecture. Those buildings so mourned by us all: some say they had Islamic elements. Their architect — not a Muslim, I might add — spent time in the Islamic world, designed buildings there." She held up photographs, small for the in-house audience, but perfect for television, and said, "The arches at the bases of the buildings are clearly influenced by Islam, and so is the geometric filigree that covered them" — the same filigree, Alyssa realized, perking up, with which Khan had patterned the names in the Garden. "Some scholars believe the entire façade amounted to a mashrabiya, the latticed screens and windows used in mosques and other urban structures."

The word "mosques" set off a round of booing. Rubin leaned into his microphone, but Stanton got to hers first. Her controlled tone managed to penetrate, then deflate, the raucousness. "You're not listening. My point is that the buildings we all mourn so deeply contained these possibly Islamicate elements. Are the towers less missed because of it? If you rebuilt them, as so many people want to do, would you purge these aspects? You might as well pull the crescent moon from the night sky while you're at it."

Alyssa surveyed the room. Some people were nodding; others looked confused. Even Alyssa wasn't sure what to make of Stanton's comments: she was saying that this element of Khan's design was Islamic — but only if the buildings were Islamic, too. Way too complicated for Chaz.

Another hour gone. Alyssa tucked her leg beneath her to relieve her aching butt. Her foot went numb.

"Jody Iacocca." Lost her husband. "I'm not an intellectual. My husband wasn't in the Senate — he was just an entry-level accountant, an ordinary Joe. I don't have an Ivy League degree; I didn't teach at Yale. But I can read — thank a good, solid American public education for that — and I've gone through all of Mr. Khan's public statements, including what he said here today, and nowhere has he denounced the attack, denounced terrorism." Was this true? Alyssa made a note to check, and jabbed her thigh with her pen, less to stave off fatigue than to punish herself. To be scooped by an ordinary (if intrepid) Jody! It pained her.

"Jim and Erica Marbury." Lost their daughter. Jim spoke. "We represent the organization Families for Reconciliation. We find the design poetic, healing. It's become almost real to us. That gardens need care and maintenance is exactly the point. The Garden represents a covenant between us and future generations. It's a beautiful metaphor for tending the memory of this tragedy. But the design is not getting a fair hearing here, and so we want to say that any reference to Mohammad Khan's religious background or heritage is a disgrace, an insult to what this country is. Our daughter would have wanted better from us. And if this garden contains Islamic elements — well, we *should* be looking for ways to unite our cultures."

"James Pogue III, but everyone calls me the Master-Servant." He declined the chair the other speakers had used. With his daddy-longlegs frame and worn black suit, he looked like a gaunt usher to the afterlife. Alyssa could see Paul Rubin consulting his list in puzzlement. "My brother perished that day, and I fear for his soul." There were horrified gasps and a few boos. He made obeisance but didn't look sorry. "I am here to bring the word of my Lord so your souls will be safe on Judgment Day," he said, and read from Ecclesiastes in a voice so stupefying the entire audience looked as if it had been cornered by a party bore. Then he held a pamphlet aloft: "I have developed a formula for meaning, and will be distributing it outside. And a CD" — also held up — "which will be for sale."

"This isn't QVC," Paul said. "And time."

"R," Alyssa wrote. "CR."

"Sean and Frank Gallagher." Alyssa, flagging now, revived. Sean had proved to be full of surprises — apologizing for pulling the woman's headscarf, then undercutting his own apology by telling a roomful of Muslims that he still didn't want a Muslim memorial . . . and now came another one.

He leaned into the microphone, said "I'm going to let my father speak for both of us," touched a startled Frank on the shoulder, and walked off the stage. Alyssa had no code for this. She starred their names.

The spotlight made a halo of Frank's white hair. His blue eyes were undiluted by age, his bearing pugnacious. He watched his son make his way down the stairs, then put on his glasses and began to read from a prepared text: "This garden is insufficiently" — he stumbled a bit — "heroic to commemorate the lives lost. We would like a more powerful memorial, one that does not suggest America lay down like lambs in the clover, instead of fighting back. We want, we want —"

He lowered his reading glasses and looked at the audience. "I have nothing against anyone personally," Frank Gallagher said. Then his face crumpled, and Alyssa thought, against her will, of the buildings falling in on themselves. He paused. "But . . . all I want to say is . . . I lost my son. I lost my son."

Alyssa heard sniffles, saw people weeping. The audience seemed to retract from Khan as if he conducted an electric current.

"Murderer!" The voice rent the air.

"It looks like there are no more speakers,"

Rubin said blandly, as if he hadn't heard that shout. But he had to have heard: everyone did. The governor wanted catharsis; Rubin was carrying her water without spilling a drop.

"We will continue accepting input in the form of written statements for another week, and I promise they will be read. Otherwise, we're finished."

"Unless there are family members who haven't spoken but were supposed to," Winnie reprimanded gently. "Any family members who should have been on my list? Last chance."

A murmur rolled through the spectators and grew so pronounced that Alyssa turned to see the cause. At the back of the room she saw a brown-skinned woman in a headscarf raising her hand, then the older man next to her tugging it down. The arm shot back up, was tugged down, up, down, up, down — heated whispering passed between them, until the woman twisted herself free, stood, and said in a voice strong enough for the whole chamber to hear, "Me."

19

Asma had awoken that morning, as she often did, around the time Inam used to say goodbye. Her body, of its own will, had put a marker there. For many months, in the quiet she would think, in her first moment of wakefulness, that he was still alive. Now she knew better.

No one had called to invite her to the public hearing. If any invitation had been mailed, she couldn't read it. She didn't know what would happen at the hearing — would there be a vote? — but she wanted to be there. She was a family member as much as the white women she saw on the news. She had the fatherless child and empty bed to prove it.

She prayed, and at seven-fifteen, knowing he would be awake, wanting to catch him before he began his work for the day, she called Nasruddin.

■ ■ ■ ■

Tiny sequins sparkling from yellow flowers on a hot-pink background: this had been Inam's favorite among her salwar kameez, which was why today she chose it. She begged Mrs. Mahmoud to watch Abdul for the day, offering, to her landlady's obvious apoplexy, no explanation, and walked over to Nasruddin's house. His van, trapped in his small driveway by a low gate with frilly metalwork, looked like an oversize animal in a cage. Nasruddin looked a little like a trapped animal himself. When she told him she wanted to attend the hearing, he balked. If she did anything to draw attention to herself, she could jeopardize Abdul's future here. And for what?

"Are you saying I don't belong there?" she snapped, and was instantly sorry: without Nasruddin's help these two years, she would have drowned. Softer: "Let's just go listen."

She felt like skipping, realized it was because this was the first time she had been out of the neighborhood since the headscarf pullings began. Free! But Nasruddin wasn't enjoying the outing nearly as much; as they descended into the subway, he released a torrent of talk. It seemed to meander, but a

435

purposeful current ran beneath. He told her about coming to America when he was only nineteen, younger than her. Kensington wasn't full of Bangladeshis then. He was lonely. His English was poor. He wondered why he was here. But little by little, he saw. What Nasruddin revered about America was its systems — its predictability. You could trust the government, even perfect strangers, not just your family or fellow villagers, as was the case back home. There, outcomes too often depended on the capricious — or rather covetous — whims of individuals. Almost nothing happened without a bribe to grease the way. Here, he rounded up donations from the community for the local politicians and for the policemen's union. He knew this would help obtain a hearing, solicit their attention, but the donations were not demanded, not coerced. Every time he visited Bangladesh, he would return to Brooklyn with renewed appreciation for the emergency room doctor who treated his cut hand without insisting he schedule a follow-up at the same doctor's private practice. What was expected by most Americans, to him seemed heroic. When he went to the construction-permit office they gave him the right forms and accepted his applications without demanding

more money than the form specified. Nasruddin never stopped missing his own
country, but he loved this one.

They were on the subway now. Asma
watched a woman apply gloss to her doughy
bottom lip. She relished the way private lives
were conducted in these public cars, as if
they were just extra rooms in a house.
Women put on their makeup and took off
their heels, ate their lunches and cooled
their coffee. They had no shyness about
sharing the lines of their underwear or the
color of their bras, the veins in their calves
or the moles on their arms. They chewed,
read, spoke, sang, and prayed, as she, but
privately, did now.

Nasruddin was still talking. There had
been too many problems after the attack.
She had not dealt with them: he had. The
detentions, worst of all; the deportations;
the decision whether to submit to voluntary
registration; the agonizing choice of whether
to go see family in Bangladesh and risk not
being let back in the country. Normalcy was
returning. She shouldn't draw unneeded attention to their vulnerable community.
There were always new groups arriving; this
was the nature of New York. The brownstone
work did not belong to Bangladeshis alone.
Lately he had found flyers left in entryways

by Polish construction workers, offering good work for cheap. They included group pictures of themselves — white men in white overalls, clustered like bouquets of white carnations. What was this about, he asked Asma, not waiting for her answer, other than to draw attention to their skin color? He spoke of his daughters. He wondered often if he should have raised them in Bangladesh. He wanted to create a cocoon for them here, but it was impossible. Like little chicks they pecked their way out of their eggshells. They saw the world around them and wanted to explore it. He talked so much she wondered if he ever talked to his wife. Two decades of strain flowed onto her. She felt so honored to hear his troubles that she almost forgot that she was adding to them.

They exited the subway in lower Manhattan and found their way through the crowds outside, the rows of police officers, to the packed hearing room. She had never been to city hall, but they were late and she had no time to study it. The room was already full. Asma, newly nervous, knitted her fingers together. A police officer managing the spectators who were trying to squeeze inside looked them up and down and said, "All full up. At this point seats for family members of the deceased only."

Remembering Laila's admonition to avoid contact with the police, Asma's mouth went dry. But Nasruddin showed no nervousness. "We are family members," he huffed, producing Asma's documents from the Red Cross. "I am her interpreter."

"Right," said the officer. He surveyed the rows and motioned to two spectators to give up their seats. The thrill of being, for once, at the center of things, came over Asma. She saw all the cameras, remembered watching the Circle Line cruise on television. Now she was in the circle, inside the television, acknowledged as a family member. She blinked back tears.

The proceedings began, the speakers traipsing one by one to the stage, reminding Asma of occasions in her town when, as a high-school student, she had had to sit, passing notes to friends, legs bobbing in impatience, through the endless felicitations of some visiting government official.

Nasruddin translated for her as best he could, dropping whole chunks of speeches. She knew this; the talk was too quick for him to do anything else. People turned around to shush them, and she shot dark looks back, telling them with her eyes that she had as much right to understand as they did. Go on, go on: she prodded Nasruddin.

Mohammad Khan looked stiff, wooden, when he took the stage. He scowled against the bright light. She wished for him to soften himself. But she liked what he said, at least as Nasruddin translated it, liked less when audience members interrupted to shout things Nasruddin claimed he could not hear. Khan looked nervous to her.

"Ssss," Nasruddin said at one point, making a disapproving noise. "What is he saying? That the Quran was written by man? Is he mad?" She didn't know what he was speaking of.

Then came a parade of speakers — a brown-haired man with glasses, a blond lady dressed elegantly, a white-haired lady, a father and son, and so on. For two hours Asma listened. She had not felt so angry since the conspiracy to deny her husband's existence. Those who spoke in defense of the design were outnumbered by those against it. Some of them said anything associated with Islam was "painful" to them, that the Garden was a paradise for the killers, that the name Mohammad was connected to a religion of violence, of the sword. The chairman allowed all of these comments, as if Muslims were second-class

440

citizens — or worse, as if they deserved no respect.

Fury rocked her. For the name of the Prophet, peace be upon him, to be taken so. For Mohammad Khan to be so abused.

"I want to speak," she whispered to Nasruddin, and raised her hand.

He pulled her arm down. "You cannot."

"I must." Arm back up.

Arm down. "Think about Abdul."

"What kind of country is this for him?" Arm up.

Down. "You'll get yourself deported!"

"Let me speak," she hissed at him. "Help me speak."

People had turned to watch their tussle. Heat rose to her face; her bones seemed emptied by her Ramadan fast. Never before had she addressed a crowd. If she didn't move now, she would be paralyzed. Scraps of a poem by Kazi Nazrul Islam that she had memorized in school came to her — "I am the burning volcano in the bosom of the earth, / I am the wild fire of the woods, / I am Hell's mad terrific sea of wrath! . . . I am the rebel eternal, / I raise my head beyond this world, / High, ever erect and alone!" — and even before she had finished running the lines in her head she had wrenched her arm free, whispered "I'm begging you," stood, and shouted "Me!" Face aflame, she walked down the aisle toward the stage, willing Nasruddin to follow so he could translate. She berated herself for being too lazy to learn better English, despite watching so many hours of American television.

Hundreds of eyes bored into her, each pair seeming to claim a tiny piece of her. On she marched, fighting her physical weakness, the fear, all of it with a prayer: God, help me, for You are the best of helpers, and the best of protectors, and the best of forgivers, the most merciful. And she did not need to spell out to Him why she needed forgiveness.

Even without direct orders, her legs moved where she needed them to go: to the right of the stage, up the stairs, one by one, into the chair. A few moments later Nasruddin sat next to her.

"Please give your name," the woman running the hearing chirped.

"Asma, wife of Inam Haque. His job was to sweep the floors and clean the bathrooms."

Nasruddin translated, but left out the bathroom cleaning.

She plunged on: "My husband was from Bangladesh. I am from Bangladesh. My son" — she beamed — "he is two years old, born three weeks after the attack. He is one hundred percent American. My husband worked. He paid taxes. He sent money to his family in Bangladesh — eleven relatives — and to mine. Do you know how little that left for us to live on? But we managed. Inam was not an uneducated man. He finished high school in Bangladesh, then got his university degree. But there were no good jobs there unless you bought one. He preferred to start at the bottom here because he believed it was possible to work your way up. There you were stuck. The politics, the corruption. Here there was none of that. People helped you. Even the Jewish people."

Nasruddin shot her a look. She knew enough English to grasp he was editing her. But there was no stopping. Her voice shook because she kept forgetting to breathe, but she also had the strange sensation of wanting to giggle, as if she were twelve again, with her father, riding a bicycle rickshaw through Dhaka's packed streets for the first time, barely holding on, laughing from fear and exhilaration.

"My husband was a man of peace because he was a Muslim. That is our tradition. That is what our Prophet, peace be upon him, taught. You care for widows and orphans, as

443

Mr. Nasruddin has done for me and my child. You have mixed up these bad Muslims, these bad people, and Islam. Millions of people all over the world have done good things because Islam tells them to. There are so many more Muslims who would never think of taking a life. You talk about paradise as a place for bad people. But that is not what we believe. That is not who the garden is for. The gardens of paradise are for men like my husband, who never hurt anyone." She took a breath. "We do not tell you what it means to be Christian, or what the rules of *your* Heaven are." This went untranslated by Nasruddin.

"I think a garden is right," she continued, "because that is what America is — all the people Muslim and non-Muslim, who have come and grown together. How can you pretend we and our traditions are not part of this place? Does my husband matter less than all of your relatives?"

The faces in the audience were melting into one another, which was a comfort.

"You don't like this architect because he is Muslim," she continued. "An American designed our parliament in Dhaka. He was also named Kahn. Louis Kahn. He designed our parliament."

Her father had taken her there when she

was twelve years old, showed her the massive, stoic building rising from the water, taken her inside to see the light slanting in, walked her across the vast, sedate lawns, which were a respite from a frantic city. He had told her about the American who had designed it, and how Bangladeshis had come to see it as the most powerful symbol of their new democracy. That democracy's defects were partly why Nasruddin and Inam, and also Asma, had ended up in New York; what Kahn designed her father pronounced too good for the politicians. And yet the complex's beauty, its strength, endured, as if it were ignorant of all the broken promises, or believed they might still be fulfilled.

"We were grateful for that building," she continued. "We are grateful. We have all tried to give back to America. But also, I want to know, my son — he is Muslim, but he is also American. Or isn't he? You tell me: What should I tell my son?"

Outrage, strong as acid, was filling her, threatening to spill over and burn everyone in the room.

"You should be ashamed!" she finished, heaving out the words, but Nasruddin did not translate that.

20

As the Bangladeshi woman made her way toward the exit, people seated alongside the aisle leaned out to whisper words of encouragement or condolence, to grab her hand or, failing that, her interpreter's. The two of them reminded Sean of a couple leaving the church at the end of their wedding ceremony. They approached the exit, where he had been hovering since leaving his father onstage. His own unexpected impulse to reach toward them he stanched by opening the door.

"Thank you," the translator said, looking right through him.

Watching the woman onstage in her headscarf, Sean had thought of Zahira Hussain. Up close they didn't look much alike at all. This woman was smaller, darker. Excitement, nervousness, gleamed from her face, but beneath lived qualities less transient. A determination, a stubbornness, that brought his mother to mind. With some primal kind of certainty, both women claimed this memorial for their sons.

But their claims weren't equal; he had to remember that. Patrick, trying valiantly to make too-small, too-distractible Sean into a high-school football player, had taught him to marry public sportsmanship with the essential psychological tool of the private gloat. Pitying the other team, Patrick instructed, would erode Sean's will to crush them, would worm deep within him, even into his hands, so that he would start giving away plays without meaning to. Sean had to stamp out these glimmerings of sympathy. To lend his heart to the other side would weaken his own.

After watching the Bangladeshis hurry off, Sean made his way outside. It was almost evening — they'd been inside practically the whole day — and the sky, brewing a storm, had gone asphalt-gray. His departure from the stage would need explaining to his family, and he canvassed possibilities. The truth was that he hadn't thought before he acted. As always, he learned what he felt by what he did. Some strange scramble of images had beset him up there: Debbie serving him eggs at home, then hurling insults outside MACC; Zahira warming behind that desk, then aghast; Eileen, cold fierceness one minute, childlike grief the next. All these doubles. He couldn't get a fix on anyone, least of all himself, the brother left behind and the striving son, the shabby handyman and the suited man on the make, the guy pulling the headscarf and the one apologizing and somehow meaning both. His empathy kept settling in new, unstable places. It — he — couldn't be trusted.

Any more than Claire Burwell could be. There she was now, fighting her way out of city hall, surrounded by agitated family members. Already taller than most of them, she was straining, with the regal annoyance of a woman who believes herself better than her circumstances, to hold her head even higher. The cluster moved down the steps with her, so that she appeared to be shepherding the relatives even as she tried to shake them off. They pressed close to hear the questions she wasn't answering.

"Claire!" he shouted. "Claire Burwell!" He climbed the stairs, shoved into the knot, and pulled her roughly by the arm to extract her. Down they went, into City Hall Park, where she wrested free.

"You hurt me," she said angrily, rubbing the spot where his fingers had been.

"I was trying to help you."

"Sure you were. You're a really helpful guy, Sean. I'm sure you were trying to help me when you brought your gang to my house, too."

He was embarrassed that she had been watching, even though he had wanted her to be. Stewing that day over how to make her repudiate Khan, he had also been imagining her naked upstairs, eager for him, Sean. The fantasy of drilling himself into her was so arousing, given her proximity, that he could have hurled that rock just for release. It wasn't news to him that anger and sex lived inside each other, but he'd never felt them pair with such force.

"And at your rally," she continued, "when your people were waving those posters of me with a question mark, that was you helping me, too, right?" In her voice, unvarnished loathing.

Needing to neutralize her beauty, he trained his gaze on the faint smudges, like erased pencil marks, beneath her eyes, on the fray of lines around their edges. "I was trying to say we were confused by you, Claire. We still are. You won't hear us. My father up there, how can he not affect you? You choose Khan over him — Khan who got up there today and shoved all our faces in his Islamic garden, didn't even have the decency to pretend it was anything else. What did they do to you, Claire, people like my parents, that you'll do anything not to see their pain?"

"I do see their pain. That's what makes this so hard." The edges of her mouth quivered. The question mark in her face, his dubious creative stroke for the rally, hadn't been wrong. Fury at her transparency seized him, a desire to crush the weakness, the equivocation, he saw in her face. For others, surely, could see the same thing in his.

She stood statue-still while he paced and turned and once even circled her. "You don't know what you want," he said, halting in front of her, peeved by the difference in their height. "You know what you're supposed to want, but not what you really want. Step aside, Claire. Let people who know their own minds fight this out."

"No, people like me, who can see both sides, are needed. It's called empathy." Her tone had turned patronizing, superior.

"Cowardice is what it's called! You can see all the sides you want, but you can only be on one. One! You have to choose, Claire. Choose!" He was yelling now. That familiar, dreaded tightening, the build of frustration, had begun. Down at his sides, his fists balled and unballed, balled and unballed.

"Sean! Sean Gallagher!" he heard his father call. Behind Claire he saw Frank barreling, to the extent a sixty-three-year-old man could, toward them. If he was trying to save Sean from himself, it worked.

Sean pushed his arms at Claire like he was throwing a basketball at her, so that she jerked back, flailing a bit to keep her balance. But he didn't touch her, he hadn't touched her.

It was dark and beginning to rain by the time Claire made her way to the jury's meeting place, the office suite on the twentieth floor. The glow from the site below, which was lit, as always, for night, seemed to hover outside the windows like an aurora borealis. Claire couldn't stop staring at it.

Her arm hurt from where Sean had gripped it; her head clattered with his accusatory words. "Maybe it's different losing a husband," his mother had said to her. Maybe she was right. Maybe the problem wasn't the Gallaghers' passion but Claire's lack of it, her reasonableness, her rationality revealing something — to others as much as, or more than, to herself — about her marriage. To have loved Cal: she no longer knew what that obligated.

Her head echoed, too, with the heckles

and taunts Khan had endured. To question him, she feared, would ally herself with his tormentors, yet questions were all she had. If the Garden was Islamic, did that mean it was a paradise, and did that make it a martyrs' paradise, and so on. Each question contained another, like those nesting matryoshka dolls that Cal had commissioned as a playful family portrait.

His original idea for the dolls, presented to the one-time art restorer from Moscow he had found to do the work, was for little Penelope to sit within William, who would sit within Claire, who would sit within Cal. But when William asked why Daddy got to be the biggest doll, Cal ordered three more sets in which each of them got to be the biggest once. Claire now could create a matryoshka of just herself — Claire within Claire within Claire within Claire. During the hearing, all these different Claires, who just happened to look alike, seemed to rest inside her, so that every argument, no matter how contradictory, found sympathy. Each time she thought she had reached the last Claire, the true and solid one, she was proved wrong. She couldn't find her own core.

"We wasted months just to offer *guidance?*" she heard Elliott, the critic, say.

"And 'not even the most meaningful' at that?"

"It's like letting the public decide on tenure," Leo, stalwart of academia, sniffed, as if his imagination encompassed no greater affront.

In the span of her reverie, the room had filled with jurors. Unhappy jurors, snapping at Paul for giving the public the final word.

"The man who lives to quote Edmund Burke turns out to be from the Thomas Paine school of how to run a public hearing," said Ian, the historian.

Paul looked queasy. "I was trying to protect you," he said. "You saw the tenor of that hearing. To have this decision rest on the thirteen individuals in this room — we, you, will be too easily targeted. Blamed for consequences you can't predict. Better to let the voices we heard today — the loudest ones, the saddest, whatever you want — count for something, too."

"The saddest, you said?" Ariana asked. "The most compelling speaker today was the Bangladeshi woman." There were nods. "Let her decide."

"Asma Anwar," the mayor's aide, Violet, said, consulting her notes.

"An authentic voice," said Maria, the public art maven, huskily.

453

"What makes her voice more authentic than Frank Gallagher's?" Claire broke in, prodded by the ache in her arm. The young woman's speech, admittedly inspiring, had stung Claire with implicit rebuke, as if Jack Worth was lecturing her on Khan's behalf all over again.

"Nothing, except that we've heard a lot from the Gallaghers and families like them. We never hear from people like this woman."

"To have her up there in a headscarf, after these barbaric headscarf pullings — it was like some brilliant piece of performance art." Elliott, the critic, gave a small, ecstatic sigh.

"Performance, maybe, but not art," Claire said, then regretted the words. "Look, we need to figure out how to weigh all of the families' competing views."

"Competing views? You make it sound like there's no right and wrong, Claire, just different feelings," Ariana said. Her glance was vivisecting. "You were our conscience. I guess now Asma Anwar is. I move that we should affirm our support for Khan tonight."

Claire had scaled to a longed-for view, only to find it vertiginous. Their backing of Khan, which she had sought so vigorously,

454

now dizzied her. With a fierce gaze she urged Paul to remind the group that they weren't meant to vote tonight, but rather to discuss the hearing and how to survey the public comments. But Paul, looking less like a chairman than like a barman sociably eavesdropping on an interesting conversation, said nothing.

"You didn't even like the Garden," Claire reminded Ariana.

"It's not about like, it's about the fate of art in a democracy," Ariana said. "We all watched — well, not literally, because they did it in the dead of night — Serra's *Tilted Arc* being carved up and carted away from Federal Plaza because 'the public' inveighed against it. Now they don't like Khan's religion or what his design might or might not mean. Empower the public in this way, and anything ugly or challenging or difficult or produced by a member of an out-of-favor group will be fair game."

"So anything the public opposes is worth protecting?" Claire asked. No one answered, as if the question was beneath consideration. "This isn't a work of art. It's a memorial. It's wrong to vote now. If we do, we lose all leverage to get Khan to explain or change the Garden."

"Khan's not obligated to explain anything.

455

And I won't ask him to change anything because of our speculations."

"It's not speculation — he said today it was Islamic."

"No, he said it has Islamic influences."

"Pre-Islamic, I think he was trying to say?" Maria interjected.

"Is that like pre-Columbian?" asked the critic.

Claire, in exasperation, turned to Maria. "You remember when I told you that with the Void, families wouldn't want to go there?" Claire asked. "Now they're saying that to me about the Garden. What am I supposed to do?"

"Tell them to get over it," Maria said. Her crudeness shocked Claire. Her fingers, fidgeting with an unlit cigarette, sent tiny drifts of tobacco onto the table. "To be blunt, I'm tired of hearing about the families. You wouldn't know from the way we talk that an entire nation was devastated by this attack." Nervous half-smiles eeled across jurors' faces. The words had broken some taboo, robbed Claire of some talismanic enrobement. In a comic book, power would be leaking from her like a liquid.

"The families aren't the only ones who want to know what this design is," she said, carefully. "Americans, many of them, are afraid."

Ariana fixed her obsidian eyes on Paul, but it was Claire she spoke of. "Before we had to weigh her stance more because she stood for all the families. Now she stands for all of America. Now she wants us to accommodate her ambivalence, her pivots. Enough!"

"But Claire has a point." Paul bestirred himself to speak. "It wouldn't be wise to shove this down everyone's throats. We need to effect consensus among the public, among all the constituencies. That's the right thing to do."

"No, that's the cautious thing," Ariana said. "The right thing is not to give in to the pressure to abandon Khan." Her small frame seemed newly dense, so that she looked, in her trademark gray, like an iron ingot. "The Garden," she said defiantly. "As is."

"The Garden, as is." Juror by juror, the phrase was taken up, until Paul said, in the unconvincing manner of a father having to discipline his children after a long day at the office, "We're not voting."

"And if we are I'm voting no," said the governor's man, to which Maria, then Leo, then Violet, dithering, fretful Violet, said,

"The Garden, as is."

Only Claire, waiting fruitlessly for Paul to stop the vote, hadn't spoken. The whole table was watching her. Her thinking bullet-trained around turns and through tunnels and underground at breathtaking speed, so that in the fraction of time between opening her mouth and the words coming out she moved from voting for Khan, if only to avoid the embarrassment of admitting her internal disarray, to saying, "I abstain. I abstain."

Her body had fought doubt like a virus and lost. Up and up ticked her fever at the thought of Alyssa Spier's questions and Sean Gallagher's condemnations and Jack Worth's principled manipulations and Khan himself, elusive. Her mind returned to the Russian dolls, not as a stand-in for Khan's mysteries or her own, but the actual dolls of the Burwell family, and how they taught her the un-mystery of Cal. Dreaming them up had been one of his last acts; this, not a twenty-year-old resignation from a country club, revealed him. The giving of pleasure was, for him, a creative act, which meant he would have rebuked her less for her uncertainty than for the seriousness she brought to it. In inflating his relatively low-stakes political principles, she had forgotten his highest value, which was to relish life. This understanding — Cal wouldn't have cared about Khan anywhere near as much as she had pretended — was levitating, freeing. She could decide for herself, could abandon a position she wasn't sure was hers, could accept that her innermost doll was an uncertain one.

"I abstain because I don't know," she said. The silence that followed felt like a pinhole in history. The other jurors, she realized, hadn't been on the train in her head, hadn't even seen it go by. Before she could begin to re-create the steps that had taken her to so confidently abandoning her once-firm position, Ariana said, "We have ten votes even without you."

Claire flinched at the statement, at the lack of respect in its delivery. Then Wilner, the governor's man, nodded at her support-ively. The gesture enfolded her, to her dismay, in his camp. They were gathered like a family around the huge round table, and the intimacy was awful. The adenoidal breathing of the historian next to her could be too clearly discerned. Desperate for air, for space, Claire stood and turned to the window, only to be blasted by the light from the empty, expectant site below. She re-turned, shattered, to her seat.

"You don't have any votes yet," Paul, severe at last, told Ariana. They needed to wait a decent interval — three weeks, he insisted — so they would at least appear to be considering the comments flowing in. No public discussion of their deliberations tonight, he warned; no assertion of any decision. And it would be better for all concerned to find common ground with the sole relative on the jury.

"Claire needs time to sort through her confusion," he said.

Heat filled her face at the word, but she didn't disown it.

Mo slept for eleven dreamless hours, then woke disoriented and famished. Only after he scavenged a breakfast of three-day-old Chinese beef-and-broccoli from the fridge did he feel strong enough to turn on his phone. Both mail and text boxes were full. "Call me," Reiss had messaged, too many times. "Where the fk r u. Call. Call."

"Good news, bad news," Reiss spit without greeting. Mo waited, strangely calm.

"Good news: your Bangladeshi cheerleader" — an unlikely image of the woman in short skirt and pom-poms came into Mo's mind — "dominated the news cycle last night, and that's created a surge of support for you. The quick polls — keep in mind the small sample size and the large margin of error — show your support has doubled from pre-hearing levels."

"And the bad news?"

"Apparently you blasphemed at the hearing."

Blasphemed? The word had a virgin, untested sound.

"I don't know if you meant to, but you suggested that a man wrote the Quran, not God. It's spreading over the Internet, and imams from the Netherlands to Nigeria are lining up to denounce you, even though I'm sure most of them have no idea what you actually said."

"And what did I say?"

"The money line — maybe 'bankruptcy line' would be the better phrase here — was: 'So perhaps the gardens we read about in the Quran were based on what existed at the time, maybe the gardens Mohammad saw when he traveled to Damascus. Maybe man wrote the Quran in response to his context.' You outed yourself as a nonbeliever. Some asshole in Iran has already issued a fatwa against you. You're a blasphemer, a godless blasphemer," Reiss reiterated with a little too much enthusiasm. "Even worse, a beardless one." Mo put his hand to his face and began to laugh as if it were the most natural response to being in the crosshairs of nations, religions. He laughed until tears streamed down his cheeks; he laughed as if he were stoned. "Maybe I should have shaved half my face," he gasped.

"I'm missing the humor here."

"I can't win, in such a ridiculous way that it's funny. I'm like a child in a custody battle, or, or, the Falkland Islands or something. Whichever way I turn, I'll have my back to somebody, and so they'll be offended. People read my face like a text, but the text I wrote, I couldn't even read." He was laughing so hard he could barely speak. "I'm laughing because I'm stressed and I'm pissed off and I'm probably on the edge of a fucking nervous breakdown. Is that good enough for you?"

"The Falkland Islands?"

"Never mind, Scott," Mo sighed. "What do we do?"

The Internet was full of references to him in languages he couldn't read: Arabic, Urdu, Farsi. What he could read told him that he deserved the death penalty. CNN showed snippets of indignant clerics, marching children, and in Pakistan, a mob burning

462

him in effigy. It wasn't even a flattering picture.

The crazies he was supposed to keep watch for had broadened beyond Muslim-haters to Muslims who hated him for not being Muslim enough. His mother, on the phone, made no effort to keep the worry from her voice. She wished, she said, that Mo had never entered the competition. "I worked so hard to convince you of your specialness," she said. "It would have been better to let you think you were ordinary."

Laila understood Islamist politics, but he hesitated to reach out to her; they hadn't spoken since the argument at her studio. From pride, from failure to see past the abiding difference between them, he had been unable to apologize. Yet he wanted nothing more than the reassurance of her voice, which would return him, even briefly, to her clear, totalizing presence.

But that voice was behind a scrim now. A mashrabiya. Laila spoke intently, politely, as if he were a client.

"How can I help?" she asked.

"The death penalty?"

"I wouldn't worry about that. It sounds dramatic and gets them tons of press, but only a state would have the power to carry it out, and you don't live under Sharia. The

463

big beards make hay from what they can. Besides, you didn't do it on purpose, did you?"

"I didn't even know I'd said it. You saw what I was dealing with up there." Fishing for sympathy, or simply proof that she had watched, he got neither.

"Of course it's always possible some crazy gets the wrong idea, so be careful." The words were kind enough; the withholding of true tenderness killing.

"How do I make it all go away?"

"You issue a statement saying you did not mean to imply that the Quran was not the word of God."

He kept silent.

"I thought so," Laila said at last, and the simple words drew on such deep intimacy that she couldn't help but let some affection creep into her voice. "Then you're just going to have to wait for it to die down."

He wanted to keep her on the phone. "You okay?" he asked.

"Let's keep things professional, Mo," she finally said, not sounding professional at all.

21

"And who is Oprah?"

Nasruddin could not tell if Asma meant to be imperious or just sounded that way because she looked, in posture and attitude, like Bangladesh's female prime minister receiving supplicants. Ladies, so many ladies-in-waiting, surrounded her, since seemingly every wife and a good many daughters of the neighborhood had crowded into Mrs. Mahmoud's apartment. Trills and squawks flew back and forth across the room, which steamed tropical from all the bodies crammed inside.

Nasruddin squeezed in, pushing away the glass of water and sweets thrust at him. It was still Ramadan. Why were they offering food? "Oprah Winfrey called," he had told Asma in Bengali. "Or she didn't but a lady working for her. She wants you on her show."

"Oprah!" squealed his daughter, Tasleen,

after Asma asked who she was. "She's the black lady. Very famous, very famous. She gives away cars. I will drive you. I am learning to drive . . ."

She was? This was news to Nasruddin.

"Did you say something about Oprah Winfrey? Does she want Asma on her show?" Amid the chatter and colors and chaos he had not noticed the white woman, pen poised above her notebook, curled at Asma's feet, since Mrs. Mahmoud and Mrs. Ahmed had filled the rest of the couch. A journalist, he thought, a guest, which explained the sweets, but how was she conducting an interview with a woman who spoke almost no English?

"I'm translating, Baba," Tasleen brightly volunteered before he could ask. "And yes" — turning to the white woman, switching seamlessly from Bengali to English — "he said Oprah Winfrey called."

They had left the hearing quickly, Nasruddin dragging Asma past staring family members and clamoring reporters and the police officer, who tipped his cap. The clattering smelly crowded subway was, for once, a reprieve, and they sat without speaking all the way home. Too many thoughts turned in his head for words. She had spoken, and he was proud of her and maybe ashamed of himself. Having always believed leadership should be quiet, today he wondered if this approach suggested a lack of courage. What better served his people: his devotion to bureaucratic details and cultivated relationships, or Asma's demand to be heard?

He dropped her at home with an awkward bow and a compliment: "Now I know what Inam meant."

Asma looked puzzled.

"Once he told me: 'Asma cannot speak English, but she has a very good mind.'"

However impressed he was, Nasruddin had no idea of the impact of her words, of how many times, over the succeeding hours and days, they would be rebroadcast. America thirsted for heroes, the commentators said. Here was one.

A few hours after he left her at home came a frantic call: some white people (and a black man, she whispered) were at her door, Mrs. Mahmoud was out, and Asma didn't understand what they wanted. Some had cameras. He raced over to find a small press pack calling out "We just want to have a few words with you." A few words — "Mrs. Anwar said everything she had to say at the hearing" — were all Nasruddin gave them. But ever since, everyone from local news channels to now Oprah had been clamoring for interviews with Asma. The Muslim American Coordinating Council wanted to put her in an ad campaign. Feminists — Muslim and non-Muslim alike — claimed her as their own, casting Nasruddin as the villain for trying to shut her up. "A typical Muslim male," they said; one of them compared him to genital mutilators in Africa. T-shirts were printed showing a raised hand and the words "Let her speak," as if Asma now stood for Muslim women across the globe.

Nasruddin rued damaging the image of Islam. His own image had been damaged in turn. His brazen grabbing of Asma's arm, repeatedly, in public, had started rumors, or perhaps confirmed them: a married man so casually handling a widow, especially one he had spent much time helping since her husband's death, did not go unnoticed by his neighbors, or his wife. Every time he entered his house the temperature seemed to drop forty degrees.

But soon these troubles were forgotten. Letters were finding their way to Asma, even though she had no listed address. Unable to read the English, she passed them to Nasruddin, who alone saw the words: "we'll burn you," so wounding, given how Inam had died; "terrorist bitch"; "fucking cunt."

Nasruddin did not know the English language could be so vile, did not even know some of the words himself, and faced the embarrassment of having to ask his daughter, who knew them all.

Nasruddin wanted to go to the police, but he feared exposing Asma to deportation. He spoke informally to Ralph Pasquale, a beat cop he considered a friend. "Nobody forced her to get up there and speak," Ralph said. His eyes were unsympathetic. "What do you want us to do? Park someone outside her door? You know how short we are on bodies. You're always complaining we don't do enough foot patrols. Don't think it will sit well if an officer's off the street full-time because the lady sounded off. File a report if you want." It was the first time in years Nasruddin, so polite, so respected, had been dismissed like that. To be described as "complaining," when he thought his requests gentle, was painful.

He felt a new kind of exposure. The day after the hearing, he went to pick up a set of keys from the landlord he worked for. The landlord, whom Nasruddin called Senior because he and his son shared a name, was also a butcher. Nasruddin found him in white cap and bloody apron, disemboweling a lamb.

As usual, no greeting, but instead of the usual barked orders or complaints — "Leak at 28 Baltic Street"; "Mrs. Whiting said your boys didn't sweep up all the paint chips from the floor" — he got this: "The missus says I should fire you."

Nasruddin had met the missus a number of times through the years. She was a full-breasted, red-faced woman who seemed to bear him no animus. "But why, sir?" he asked, although he knew.

"She saw you on TV defending that Muslim and thinks you're on their side," Senior said.

The butcher's son, Junior, was young and good-looking and not so bright, by Nasruddin's assessment. He was interested in Tibetan Buddhism and yoga: he would disappear from the butcher shop for a month at a time "chasing his girlfriend's pussy to India," as Senior put it. Junior assumed that Nasruddin's brown skin signaled an encyclopedic knowledge of all things Eastern and spiritual, even though Nasruddin had set him straight several times, putting on a goofy grin to soften the corrections: He had never done yoga. He knew nothing about Tibet or Buddhism. And as a Muslim, he had no problem with the bloody cuts of meat in the butcher shop, as Junior had assumed he would. But no, he then had to explain, he did not want to buy choice cuts at a discount, or be given the less choice ones, since he only bought halal meat. Then he had to explain what that meant — "Like kosher, but for Muslims," he said — thinking to himself is it really possible that a butcher couldn't know about halal meat? And then thinking, in this neighborhood of Irish, Italians, and prosperous, pitiable atheists: Yes.

But on this day the son showed surprising wisdom. "Mom's crazy," he said to his father. "You can't fire him. Besides, everything they say about Muslims they once said about Catholics — they didn't trust us, either."

Nasruddin looked at him with gratitude. Perhaps he had been wrong about the young man.

"It's only the ones with the big beards you have to worry about," Junior went on. Perhaps not. Nasruddin left the store to the sound of a knife tearing flesh.

He had tried to silence Asma once and been wrong. How could he make her listen now?

"For whom do you write?" he asked the white woman, who had given neither her name nor publication. "There have already been many stories. I think it is enough."

"The *Post*," the white woman said. "Just trying to get a sense of the woman behind the story, her life story, you know, all that."

"How long has she been here?" he asked his daughter in Bengali.

"Forty-five minutes."

"What has she asked?"

"Oh, lots, she's very nice, where Asma is from and about Inam and why they came to America and how they got here and all of that." Tasleen kept switching back and forth between Bengali and English, as she did at home.

"Use your Bengali," he muttered in Bengali. He didn't want the journalist to glean clues from his questions.

"But Baba, you're always telling me to use my English," his daughter said, in English. This was true, indeed was the core of an ongoing argument between him and his wife. She worried that Tasleen would lose her Bengali, making it harder for her to find a good Bangladeshi husband. He worried that Tasleen's poor grades in English would make it harder for her to get into a good college. But her tone, her deliberate missing of his meaning — when had his obedient little girl turned into an impertinent teenager with this American attitude? And when

472

had she started wearing lipstick? Time flew and left bird droppings. He would have to talk to his wife.

He dared not ask his daughter whether Asma had said anything about her immigration status, but this was his worry — that she would draw the government's attention to her illegality.

"Do you have a card?" he asked the woman.

He glanced at the name, Alyssa Spier, and pocketed the card. He was jumpy the rest of the day and all through the night. He said a prayer and tried but failed to sleep. When his wife woke him, unsmiling, for the predawn Ramadan meal he brushed her off, backed the van out of the driveway, and hurried it through the still-dark streets to his friend Hari Patel's newsstand. The papers had not arrived yet, and neither had Hari. At last he came, and they waited together, Nasruddin pacing back and forth, almost as nervous as he had been at Tasleen's delivery. Then came the truck. Its driver hoisted and tossed a stack of *Post*s that thumped down a few feet away. Hari rushed to cut the binding, but Nasruddin didn't need him to finish to see, on the cover, a photograph of Asma — laughing, head reared back and teeth exposed, as if

473

she found hilarious the word written in huge capital letters across her face.

ILLEGAL

Once again, Paul found himself in the governor's pied-à-terre at an ungodly hour. This time he had company: Kyle, Bitman's chief of staff; Harold Dybek, the attorney general; and, from an oversize oil painting above them, the governor's late husband and his late, aloof Afghan hound.

"Good morning, all." The governor bustled in with what Paul knew to be her post-workout glow, today set off by a navy-blue suit. "Let's look a little more alive — it's not that early."

She then subjected Kyle to a detailed inquisition about the public comments, which now numbered in the thousands. He, along with Lanny, had been tallying opinions and extracting representative samplings for the governor and jurors to read. They were running six-to-one against Khan, Kyle told her. A type-A asshole with a sailor's mouth, he seemed unusually docile today.

"The hearing does seem to have influenced opinions in Khan's favor," Paul ventured. "His discussion of his design seems to have softened the opposition a bit." He knew from Lanny that the shift was due less to Khan's rocky presentation than to the Bangladeshi woman speaking with such passion. Americans, it seemed, could still be shamed; she had woken some dormant noble impulse.

"Khan had nothing to do with it," the governor said. "You're referring to what Kyle so nicely framed as the Bangladeshi bounce" — Kyle shifted as if he itched — "and I think that's been taken care of." Her smile was breezy.

Paul stared at her. A career in investment banking inured even the most sensitive soul, which he was not, to ruthlessness. But his mouth was agape. Had Geraldine leaked Asma Anwar's immigration status to Alyssa Spier? The young woman now faced deportation. The president himself had apologetically explained that immigration officials couldn't turn a blind eye to her status, however tragic her story. Her exit was far from certain: her lawyer was vowing to fight her removal, which could take years, and her defenders within Congress and out were demanding "mercy citizenship." But her life had been upended and the damage compounded by the subsequent leak of her $1 million in government compensation. Had Geraldine put that out there, too, the better to sap more sympathy? The governor's ambition kept outflanking Paul's imagination. And in this case, it offended his sense of decency, too. The Bangladeshi bounce had worked on him.

"Earth to Paul," Geraldine said impatiently. She wanted his thoughts on how long she should wait after the jury announced its decision to announce hers, and whether to then convene a new jury. "That's my thinking," she said. "One with more family members."

"I'm not sure things are going to wrap up so neatly, Geraldine" — she stiffened — "Governor. Assuming the jury backs Khan, which is where they're leaning, they won't be complacent about your vetoing their choice."

"Perhaps they need to reread the bylaws. They have no recourse."

"But they'll keep looking for one," Paul said. "They don't want this decided on public sentiment alone. You'll remember that's why we had a jury in the first place — to yield a more considered judgment than the public has the capacity — the time, I should say — to provide."

"And the jury did a brilliant job," Bitman said, with a lift of her eyebrows. "But the process was always meant to allow the

476

people to weigh in, and they have, quite clearly. They don't want it."

The looks Kyle and Harold exchanged suggested, to Paul, two brothers arguing over which one would tell their mother her Spode teapot had shattered.

"Thetroubleissortingoutwhytheydontwantit," Kyle said, too fast. He excelled at bringing the governor's bad news to others but was unpracticed in delivering such news to her. Her brow furrowed. "The trouble is sorting out why they don't want it," he said more slowly. "If they don't want him simply because he's a Muslim — the bottom line is that you can't rely on public opinion if it's only about his religion."

"Then Paul, you should have called all of that crap out of bounds."

"You said the people needed to vent," Paul said, pleased that he had managed to tie her hands while appearing to do her bidding. "They vented."

Her pupils went bullet-hard. "They vented about the design: that, not his religion, is the problem here. He created an Islamic paradise!" she snapped. "If nothing else, we should deny him for being an idiot. Did he really think that would fly?"

"The problem," Harold said, with another look at Kyle, "is that he hasn't acknowledged it's a paradise, in fact he said explicitly in the hearing that Islamic gardens were only one possible influence, and that, structurally, the features we point to as Islamic actually predate the religion. Which means we're only deducing it's a martyrs' garden, what you will, because he's Muslim. That places the Constitution on his side, not ours. If a Catholic designed that same garden no one would care. And even if he were to admit it was —"

"Which he won't," Paul interjected.

"That might not be sufficient to bar him, either, since — I've done some research — this iconography is cultural as well as religious. It's hard to separate."

"If it will ease your worries, I'll find it unsuitable without saying why. I'm the governor," she added. "I'm allowed to pronounce."

"Queens pronounce," Paul said. "Governors explain."

A black look came at him. "Fine. The plants will die, and that will be depressing. Is that reason enough for you?"

"The reasoning has to be defensible in court," Harold said. He held his polished glasses up to the light to scrutinize them for scratches. This allowed him to avoid Bitman's eyes. "The state and city will be

478

responsible for maintaining the memorial, so if the plants die, it will be our fault, not the design's —"

Her smile chilled him into silence. She examined the faces around the room, then, as if disappointed, stared at her outstretched hands. She looked up with a glance that seemed to swallow all of them at once. "So it's a lawsuit we're worried about, correct? Being sued by Khan?"

"Absolutely," said Harold. "If we deny him his memorial and he sues —"

"I will have to testify about why I vetoed his design —"

"Yes, and —"

"Remind me why that's so terrible?" She winked at Paul, and he could see her imagining herself on the stand, in a trial covered by every news outlet in the country, defending her defense of the memorial site, of America itself, from the Islamist threat. Even if the state lost, she would win. Every time she had gone on the offensive against Khan she had risen in the polls. He was her oxygen.

22

Asma awoke before the sun. The darkness flowed around her like water, filling every hole and crevice of her body: her nostrils, the indent between her lips, the dip between her breasts, the concavity of her belly, the gap between her legs, the cracks between her toes. Her mind flew to Bangladesh, as if to prepare. With dawn the call to prayer would vibrate through her. Inam's mother would rise to make tea for his father, or more likely Asma would be making the tea for both of them, listening for the roosters and the rickshaws, and in monsoon season, the pounding of the rain, dancing feet on the roof.

Here she heard only an occasional car and her own breath: in out in out. She focused on it until she became only breath, felt that she could just float away. Her bones alone held her down, pinned her in place. They and the boy next to her. His breath —

softer, shallower — sounded, too. For a few seconds she held her own breath, silencing the dirge of her life to hear the song of his.

She was almost packed. She had only to place Abdul's clothes and toys in the carry-on bag. Her suitcases and boxes were lined up by the door. Her expensive new pots and pans. Her television and DVD player and video camera. She had tried to fit a whole country, the idea of a country, in her luggage: Nike shoes; T-shirts with Disneyland and the White House and all the places she had never been; glossy magazines and American flags; history books; tourist brochures. MetroCards she would never use, children's books she could not read. DVDs of American movies and television shows, even though the pirated versions in Bangladesh would be cheaper. As Bangladeshis had created a Little Bangladesh here, she would create for herself and Abdul a Little America back home.

It was her choice to go, and yet not. In the days since her exposure as an alien, politicians had whipped the public into a frenzy of fear over the thousands of untracked Bangladeshi Muslims in New York, starting with Asma's own dead husband. "I'll ask it, even if no one else will," Lou Sarge proclaimed on his show. "What was her husband doing in those buildings, anyway?" The governor invoked the attack: "I feel for Asma Anwar, but she represents a serious problem. When we don't watch who's coming through our open door, thousands of Americans die. I won't let that happen again while I'm leading this state." She demanded that the federal government comb the Bangladeshi community for illegals and for terrorist links.

"Next door, upstairs, there are illegals everywhere," Nasruddin said. "The whole building could go. Half the neighborhood." Her neighbors were gossiping about her. Blaming her. Saying that Asma put herself before everyone else. The community would starve to feed her pride. Because of her, Bangladeshis were being lumped with Pakistanis as a threat. Asma had a good lawyer in Laila Fathi and public sympathy: she would probably win her case. Not so the others who might be rounded up because of her. Perhaps, she had begun to think, her leaving might ease the pressure.

But it was the revelation, in the *Post,* that she had received $1 million in compensation from the government that made her decision. The Mahmouds were furious that she had taken advantage of their generosity by paying only $50 a month for her room.

Asma knew that for Mrs. Mahmoud it was less about the money than the embarrassment of missing such sensational news right in her own apartment. Hadn't she noticed Abdul's new toys or Asma's swollen pride, people chided, as if pride were a physical change. Mrs. Mahmoud's powers of observation were called into question. Mr. Mahmoud announced that Asma would need to find a new place to live. But who in Kensington, or even Jackson Heights or any other Bangladeshi neighborhood, would have her? Everyone was angry at her; or fearful that her illegal status would somehow call attention to theirs; or greedy for a ransom in rent, since, with her million, she could afford it. The world beyond Kensington — the white people's neighborhoods with their sprinklers — seemed less alluring when she was being forced into it. Where to go, then, speaking so little English? Nowhere but home, Bangladesh, however reluctantly. As soon as she told her landlady her decision, Mrs. Mahmoud forgave her, perhaps because Asma confided in her first.

Her exile was ending. She was, after all, returning to her own country. Yet it was exile she felt herself entering. Of the boat trip with Inam — the impudent wind, the gulls dropping their cries like loose feathers,

483

stilled Manhattan — flat, mute photos were all that remained. She feared that the ever-thinning cord that still bound her to her husband would snap once she left New York. She was breaking her vow to raise his son in America, and she was abandoning him. Inam's remains swam in the city's rivers, hung in its air.

She was abandoning, as well, her own hopes of being something more than mother, widow, daughter-in-law. She and Inam had lived with his parents for a few weeks after they were married while they waited for their tourist visas to come through. Her mother-in-law was always correcting her — the way she served tea or cooked or washed clothes — as if in those first weeks Asma's wifely character would be formed and she, Inam's mother, could risk no leniency. She was always telling Asma what Inam wanted, as if he could not speak for himself. Now she would go to live with them, be less their guest than their servant, always dependent on their kindness. They would blame her for Inam's death, she suspected, and they would not be wholly wrong. The money would color everything. She discussed this with Nasruddin. One condition of her receiving the funds from the American government was that she agree in writing to abide by America's inheritance laws and those of no other country, including Bangladesh, where widows inherit only small portions of their husbands' estates. Neither her parents nor Inam's would be able to take control of the money; if they did, the American government would take it back. She had tried to look chastened when she learned this, but felt a small glee. In this respect, America had given her power.

But she had met the limits of that power. She thought her freedom here was limitless but in truth it was bounded — by a larger circle than at home, but a circle nonetheless. When she spoke out, pushed at it, crossed over it, she offended. It was entirely different than at home, and yet the same. Maybe her speaking out would help bring Mohammad Khan's memorial for Inam into being. But neither she nor Abdul would be here to visit it.

Sorrow at this flooded her, not once but in waves. Loss piled on loss. Into sleep she slipped, into a place where someone was laying huge, flat, heavy stones on her body to see how much weight she could take. She could not breathe, could not bear it, then saw her little boy trying to lift stones three times his weight from her body and she struggled upward from sleep, only to find nothing had changed: she was in her bed, he by her side, and they were being cast out.

Except maybe God, the greatest of all plotters, meant for her to return home. She had her money and her American experience, which told her that hard work made any enterprise possible, even if Bangladesh's corruption and chaos would test that. She would found a girls' school there. Maybe they couldn't change a country of 140 million people now, but if each girl founded a school, and each of those students founded a school . . .

The power was God's. This was what the imam had been trying to tell her about Inam's death, that she had no right to anything in life, not a place, not a position, not a person. Even her own child, born from her womb, was His creation and could be safeguarded only with His blessing. He could take away all He had given. Only He could not be taken. He would not abandon her if she did not abandon Him: she trusted in this. The garden in New York, all that she was being wrenched from, would be nothing next to what awaited her.

Tugging her chunni, the parrot-green one, away from her perspiring neck, Asma marched down the stairs from the Mahmouds' apartment. She carried Abdul, and behind her Nasruddin and Mr. Mahmoud came laden with her bags and boxes; and behind them Laila Fathi, holding Asma's travel documents; and behind her Mrs. Mahmoud and Mrs. Ahmed, crying and holding each other.

As soon as Asma came out of her building a crowd surrounded her, women reaching out to touch her in a way that reminded Nasruddin of pilgrims at the graves of saints. What they hoped to take from the touch he couldn't say: her luck wasn't something to covet — losing her husband, losing her place — and yet he understood. It seemed every Bangladeshi in Kensington and many from beyond had come to witness Asma's departure, to commiserate or gloat or simply gawk at this woman, one of them, who had become a celebrity. They filled the sidewalks and the street, hung from windows, clung to fire escapes, peered from roofs. Without hearing them, Nasruddin knew what they were saying. They'd been saying it ever since the effort to deport Asma had begun. *Bhabiakoriokaj, koriabhabiona* — "Think before acting, don't act before thinking."

To her face they were all kindness, all

sympathy. Her efforts to pack had been complicated by the endless stream of visitors, all of them picked over like a pile of burro bananas by Mrs. Mahmoud. She determined who got access to the inner sanctum (Asma's room), who to the apartment at large, who had to wait in the hall. They brought sweets and small gifts, toys for Abdul, but mostly they came to take news of her purchases and packing back to the street.

Intermingled among the Bangladeshis today there were also police, who had come to keep order, and reporters and news crews, the satellites atop their vans like giant ears cocked to the sky. The *Post,* not satisfied with exposing Asma's status, had also somehow obtained her itinerary. In full gloat at its success in pushing Asma from the country, that morning's paper had informed the whole world when she would leave.

At Asma's appearance the press pushed forward, shoving through the Bangladeshis to get close to her. Already peeved at the reporters' sense of entitlement and his neighbors' deference toward them, Nasruddin was furious when he saw Alyssa Spier in their ranks, notebook ready to chronicle the humiliation she had engineered. He tried to order her away, but his hands were full with Asma's boxes. The reporters circled Asma, shouting questions at her, pressing in on her with their microphones and cameras, swallowing her up.

Nasruddin lost sight of her, and his attention wandered to the crowd, which had a relaxed air, as if it were celebrating a minor holiday. In honor of little Abdul's departure, Abdullah's Sweet Shop was distributing his favorite snack, yogurts, free to children too young to fast. The imam, whom Nasruddin had helped bring from Bangladesh, was encouraging people to come to mosque for the day's Iftar and not to forget the poor during Ramadan. Someone was playing Hindi music from a window — Nasruddin, a lover of movies, his sole escape, tried but failed to place the soundtrack — and beneath it were layered car horns and the giddy laughter of children and —

The woman's scream pierced the air so violently that Nasruddin's hair tried to leap from his scalp in fright. It had come from Asma's direction, but he couldn't tell who it was — nothing in a woman's speaking voice could predict her scream, and the sound was met quickly by its own echo, wave after wave of echo, coming at Nasruddin from all directions. Not an echo, he realized, but other women screaming in response, in fear.

"She is hurt!" someone shouted in Bengali. "Find a doctor!"

Nasruddin pushed his boxes into the arms of the man next to him and shoved his way through. The crowd parted to reveal Asma, her skin a sickly gray-brown. She saw him and opened her mouth as if she had something important to tell him, but no words came out, at least none that he could hear. Her body bent to one side, then slowly she began to fold like a shirt being put in a box. So thick was the humanity around her that she did not topple, as she otherwise would have; instead she slumped, half upright, against a wall of shifting, juddering flesh. But her eyes had closed and her head was lolling unnaturally and her grip on Abdul had begun to slip. He was bawling now. Laila tried to grab the boy and one of Asma's arms even as she shrieked, "Help me, she's fainting! Hold her up!"

"No, lay her down!" someone shouted in Bengali.

"Keep her up!"

"Lay her down!"

The words raced back and forth through the crowd.

"Get a doctor!"

"The boy!"

"A doctor!"

"Air!"

And then someone, a woman, screamed, in Bengali, "Blood! She is bleeding! Blood!" and the crowd grew panicked and fearful and began to move in a hundred different directions at once so that it went nowhere, constrained by its oppositions yet full of movement, like water beneath which a crocodile is devouring its prey. Screams, more screams, some very close, some far away, ricocheted in air, seemed to collide with one another.

"Lay her down!" Nasruddin commanded, even as the crowd jostled in front of him and he again lost sight of her. "Gently! Gently! And find Dr. Chowdhury!"

"Dr. Chowdhury!" the call went back through the crowd. "Dr. Chowdhury!"

Nasruddin didn't care where he laid his hands, whom he peeled back to push through. Bangladeshis wheeled in annoyance then, recognizing him, murmured apology before turning back to stare. Useless men crowded around Asma like balky, mooning cows. Nasruddin whipped them with his voice: "Move aside! You think this is a test match? If you are not a doctor, move back. If you can't help, move away."

491

"She was stabbed!" came a shout. Still he couldn't reach her. "Stabbed!" Panicked men and women tried to run and banged into one another, not knowing whether their movements took them farther from danger or brought them closer to it. Nasruddin was slicing time as finely as his wife cut ginger, trying to remember, freeze, anything he had seen — had a white man in a black coat been standing behind Asma before Nasruddin lost sight of her? — while still seeing what was in front of him: a white woman putting her black coat over Asma to shelter her from shock. He was living in the past and present at once: the white man, he was tall, but everyone seemed tall next to Asma; or was his coat blue; or was there even a white man at all, or was that just Nasruddin's vision of who might be capable of this? He strove to remember that last moment he had seen Asma, but the truth was he had lost sight of her just before the stabbing; he was of no use; then he was in the future, now, too — whoever had done this was still among them, no one was safe, how could he protect his people without alarming them more? There were so many unfamiliar faces mixed in with the ones he knew; but he had to suspect the ones he knew, too. "Take care," he called out in Bengali. "Whoever did this is still here among us. Look around you. We must find them."

So much pressure in his head, on his heart. He should have officially reported the threats against her; he should have stopped her from speaking that day. Now he was guilt-sick along with his worry.

"What happened?" he could hear reporters asking each other and any Bangladeshi they could collar. "What are they saying? What's wrong with her?"

He reached her at last. She was on her back, her eyes were closed. In the dark streamers that spread from beneath her, Nasruddin saw the blood that flowed in the streets back home on Eid al-Adha, when hundreds of goats and cows and sheep were slaughtered for the festival. Dr. Chowdhury was there, too. He lifted off the coat and the shawls, then lifted Asma, gently, tearing the salwar kameez, cardinal with blood, to reveal a flash of blood-mottled bare brown skin before he applied pressure to the wound and covered her again. Nasruddin took in her closed eyes, the horrible pallor of her face. Asma would want to know if she had been exposed. She would want the whole scene described: Was everybody looking at me? Was I brave? And who took Abdul? Were the aunties fighting over him, or did you take him? And what was Mrs. Mahmoud doing? Screaming, I bet. Did the paramedics have to treat her, too?

Did you take him? This imagined question prodded Nasruddin from his shock. Where was Abdul? Nasruddin scanned the crowd. Maybe the police had him? With relief he saw Laila gripping Abdul, who sobbed still. A siren's mechanical wail grew louder, slower, as the ambulance nosed through the crowd. Two paramedics pushed through to the clearing the police had created around Asma and busied themselves over her. They gave no clue as to her condition, but Nasruddin knew and began to weep even as the ambulance pulled away, and at the sight of a man who had steadied his community for two decades so unsteadied himself, the crowd seemed to melt, women crying, men kneeling, everyone rocking, rocking.

Abdul: he needed to be removed from the scene.

"Mrs. Mahmoud! Take Abdul upstairs!" he ordered, then saw Mrs. Mahmoud puddle to the ground. She would have to collect herself to help wash Asma's body; so would Mrs. Ahmed, who now had found her way to the ground, too. Nasruddin grabbed Mr. Mahmoud and pointed to

494

Laila Fathi and Abdul and said, "Take them upstairs now! Now!" and Mr. Mahmoud, red-eyed himself, led them away, with a police officer clearing the crowd ahead of them. This was only the beginning of getting the boy home, Nasruddin realized — Nasruddin would have to fly Abdul, along with the body, home to Bangladesh. He felt helpless just thinking about it, him alone on a plane with a two-year-old orphan.

"The press! The press! They killed her!" someone called out. The reporters were scattered through the crowd, refuse on a deltaic river. Men in the crowd had grabbed some of them by the arms and were holding them; other journalists had formed a small defenseless knot by a building, the brick at their back. "Press!" they were shouting. "We are journalists!" Some had fake smiles to go with the terror in their eyes.

Bangladeshis, furious now, surged toward them, and Nasruddin saw a few of the bigger cameramen move to the front of the group and a few of the women frantically punching their cell phones and still others waving for the police, who moved toward them, shouting at the crowd, "Get back! Stay back!"

The crowd pushed forward. The reporters pressed themselves against the building, the women among them holding hands. "You killed her!" his neighbors were shouting in fury. Nasruddin didn't know if they meant this literally — had a reporter stabbed her? — or that the journalists had endangered her with their stories. He was being rocked so hard he could barely keep his footing but even so he saw the police officers' hands going to their gun holsters and he cried out, in Bengali and in English, "Back away, leave them to the police, back away!"

It was then that he saw Alyssa Spier being whirled around by the angry mob. There was fear on her face and he hated himself for the pleasure this gave him. He elbowed through to her. "Come, come now," he said roughly, grabbing her arm. She resisted, thinking him just another angry member of the crowd. "We met, you know me, I will help you," he spat through his teeth, and she yielded to him. He dragged her until he saw a police officer, then almost threw her at the cop. It was right she be safeguarded, whatever she had done, but inside he raged no less than the mob.

"Protect her," he said. "She is responsible."

23

In the midst of the mob, Alyssa had craved, for the first time in her reporting life, anonymity. Surrounded by wild eyes, livid mouths, shoving hands, stomping feet, sweaty stink, and foreign cries, her great terror had been that she would be recognized as the person who had exposed Asma Anwar to danger — exposed her first as illegal, then as rich, then, almost down to the hour, as entering exile (OUTTA HERE! the *Post* had headlined that morning). If she was identified, she would be torn apart. Instead, the sole person who recognized her had saved her, allowing the police to shove her into the safety of their mobile station. For all her fear, the minute she was out of the crowd, she wanted to be back in it. The news, for the first time in her experience, had been a completely physical phenomenon, one that absorbed and churned her, as if she were inside someone's bloodstream.

It was the closest she had come to covering a war.

Alyssa told the police everything she had seen, which wasn't much, since she had been in the outer ring of reporters around Asma Anwar. To make matters worse, she lost an hour of reporting time because of her rescuer's parting comment: "She is responsible." Three different detectives made her walk through, article by article, what he could have meant by it. By the time she finished, the crowd and any interview-worthy witnesses had dispersed, and she was reduced to interviewing her fellow reporters.

She had no clue who had killed Asma. No one did — so many people had been crowded around her that even news footage had so far proved useless. But that didn't stop the speculation. Debbie Dawson of SAFI was sure it was a Wahhabi offended by a woman playing a public role. "See what they do to each other!" she kept saying on television. Chaz was sure, with no basis in evidence, that it was a Bangladeshi jealous of Asma's money. Issam Malik of the Muslim American Coordinating Council insisted that Asma had been slain by an Islamophobe. No, a xenophobe, insisted immigration reform activists. Random groups —

Muslim, anti-Muslim — called news organizations to take credit. But as in psychological warfare, there was no knowing if the calls were legitimate or attempts to pin the killing on opponents.

To Alyssa's chagrin none of these calls came to her, which left her scrambling for an angle. Her own nagging feelings of guilt had been largely expiated by her fear in the crowd and her questioning by the police. Both seemed to her sufficient cosmic retribution. Besides, she had only reported on what Khan had started. If anyone was responsible, it was he.

"Unless he's the Tin Man, he's got to feel guilty," Chaz said approvingly when she mentioned this as a possible angle. "Find him and ask if he feels guilty. Ask him if he's going to withdraw. Think of the cover when he gives up: SAYAN-ALLAH!" He started laughing. "Get him to drop out just so we can use that. And find out if they're going to bury her in his garden: She's a martyr, right?"

Alyssa staked out Khan's Chinatown loft. He never turned up. But his type was her own: he couldn't stay away from work. She parked herself near ROI and waited him out. As the day ended, the architects, all disdainful glances and rectangular glasses, glided by. No Khan. But a hunch told her to hang tight and for hours she did. At eleven, he emerged, looking around warily. She stepped from her hiding place. He flinched.

"It's just me," she said softly, as if they'd known each other forever. In fact, she realized, for all her quarrying of him, they'd never met. "Alyssa Spier, *New York Post*." For a moment he looked blank, as if he didn't recognize her name. She felt crushed, even though she knew most readers didn't check bylines. Then anger dawned in his face.

"Leave me the fuck alone," he said.

"What are you going to do? Are you going to withdraw?"

Khan ignored her, walking off in long, measured strides, and she scurried to keep up with him, feeling like a cartoon mouse. "Do you feel responsible?" she asked. "For Asma Anwar's death?"

He heeled on her so abruptly it gave her a sharp fright. After what she'd written about Islam and violence, it would be almost funny, she thought, for a Muslim — especially this one — to go postal on her.

"You, of all people, are asking me that?" he said. "You're the one who pushed her out into that street. You were probably there, transcribing every bloody detail. You and your paper have done everything you could to make it open season on Muslims."

"No, you did, by entering the competition, by insisting on your right to win, even though it offended so many Americans, hurt so many of the families' feelings. So are you going to withdraw?"

"Offended so many Americans? Was that what you said?" Khan said. He was moving toward her. They were only a couple of feet apart, giving her no choice but to walk backward. "I am an American, too," he said, continuing to advance on her. "Put that in your paper. I, Mohammad Khan, am an American, and I have the same rights as every other American." She peddled backward; he moved toward her. "I am an American. That's the only quote I'm going to give you. I am an American." She glanced over her shoulder — a few more feet and he would have waltzed her right into Hudson Street, but she couldn't say that was his intent, that he had any awareness at all of their location, only that he kept moving toward her and she kept moving back.

"I am an American. I am an American." One more step and she was off the curb. "I am —"

"Wait a minute!" she said, coming to a

stop so suddenly that he nearly bumped into her. She narrowed her eyes. "You should be grateful to me. If I hadn't broken this story, they would have buried your memorial — you would never have known that you won."

"Bullshit," he said. He was breathing hard, as if he had been running. "It would have come out regardless."

"But I'm the one who brought it out. You should be grateful."

Khan put his hands on his hips and looked up. Alyssa took a step back and saw that he was smiling. She looked up, too, to see a crescent moon so slight it was as if a fingernail had scratched the sky.

NY1 kept replaying the same story on Asma Anwar's death, but Sean watched it each time as if it were new. Kensington wasn't far from his parents' house in Ditmas Park — less than half a mile — but the footage made it look like India. Hundreds of Bangladeshis milled in the street in anticipation of her exodus, then cried and shouted at the news of her death and the terror of a killer among them. He knew Bangladeshis lived nearby — brown-skinned women in headscarves sometimes trailed overstuffed handcarts down his parents' block — but he'd never known there were so many of them. He kept returning to when Asma Anwar went past him leaving the hearing. He'd said nothing to her. He wished he had told her she was brave. He wished he had apologized to her for pulling Zahira Hussain's headscarf, for his fear was that his own destructive impulses had unleashed, given license to, more murderous ones. Debbie was sure a Muslim had killed her, but Debbie's facts coincided miraculously with her opinions. He wondered who would raise Asma Anwar's son.

He wandered downstairs. His mother was alone in the living room, working a needlepoint. In the white light of the sole lamp, the frozen set of her features made her look more marble than flesh.

"Sit with me a bit," she said, and he did. He heard the clock's listless tick. The rattle of ice being born in the kitchen freezer. His mother's concentrating breath. He would remember it.

"I don't want to fight Khan anymore," he said abruptly. He hadn't known he was going to say that until the words came out.

Eileen jerked back, as if she'd been dozing with her eyes open, and looked at him. Deep lines marred the skin around her mouth. "It's terrible about that woman," she said. "Terrible. To leave a little boy. But it has

503

nothing to do with fighting Khan. Do you think they would want a cross erected at the spot where she died? Don't you think they would find it disrespectful?"

She resumed her needlepoint, stitching a relentless peace.

He churched his hands, balanced his nose on the steeple. "I feel like I started this," he said.

"Mohammad Khan started this," she said matter-of-factly.

"I guess I don't want to be the one to finish it. That's all I'm saying. I don't want the Garden, but I don't want to be the one to fight against it."

"And who's supposed to finish what you can't be bothered with, Sean? Nothing in life gets dropped without someone else having to pick it up."

"I think Claire Burwell is turning against Khan," he said. "I helped turn her." He felt like a fraud, to detest Claire for her weakness, then offer her up to hide his own.

"So why stop now, Sean, if you feel like it's close to being over? You're about to accomplish something, something important. Why stop now, why let them say we don't know what we want?"

"Getting in the way of this memorial — I'm blocking something. But I'm not accomplishing anything. They're not going to turn around and ask me to design the memorial instead," he said. "I need to find some other way to be. Some other reason to be."

"Other than God, there's no higher reason than family, especially given what happened to us." Her eyes gleamed watery in the low light, from sadness or age he didn't know. He cracked his knuckles and saw her flinch at the noise.

She returned to her needlepoint, and he tugged at loose threads on his sleeve, the two of them making and unmaking each other.

"I've never asked much of you, Sean," she said. Her ears shifted back slightly. "I would say we've asked very little of you. But I asked you for this, begged you to stop this memorial. And now you want to walk away before the job is done, just like you've walked away from almost everything in your life, left it half done or half broken. I shouldn't be surprised, I suppose. But I can be angry." Her voice sharpened on the words.

"I don't want to let you down, Ma. It's the last thing I want. But my heart's not in it, not anymore. And that means I'll be lousy at fighting for it."

"You think my heart was in everything I've had to do in this life? Where did you get the idea that you decide how to live based on how you feel when you wake up each morning? Not from me. You know, when you were born, I had a very hard time." He looked up; this was news to him. "Five children already, a sixth seemed too much. Now the doctors probably have some special name for it, but all I knew was that I was tired and I wanted something for myself. I wanted myself back, is more like it. Truth be told, I hated your father for bringing you about. And so I went away for a few weeks after you were born." She was looking at him, steady, unapologetic. "Maybe only Patrick was old enough to remember. Maybe it's why Frank has always had a tender spot for you, troubles and all. I just left. Took the housekeeping money I'd saved for emergencies — your father was never good at planning for emergencies, so I had to be — and went up and down the eastern seaboard. Rehoboth. Rhode Island. It was winter. I just walked on the beach. Hadn't spent so much time alone in years. Hadn't spent any time alone in years. Then I came back and did my duty. Came back because it was my duty. Never asked your father a single question about how he managed in that time I was gone. Alone with six children, including a newborn!" Her laugh burst forth, breaking up her face like jackhammered cement. It was as if the mere contemplation of Frank shouldering her burdens for a few weeks had helped her bear them for years.

"I came back because I was nothing outside this family," she said. "And you will be nothing."

"Maybe nothing is what I'm meant to be," he shot back.

"I lost one son," she said. "I don't want to lose another." She paused, resumed stitching. Small fingers, steady hand. This, too, he would remember.

"Why would you lose me?"

"You can't be half in a family. You're in, or you're out. You want to go on living here like some pacifist suddenly too good to fight, but still eating our food, warming your feet, while the rest of us go get bloody in the war. It doesn't work that way, Sean."

"Let me sleep on it, Ma," he said abruptly. "We'll talk in the morning." He held his hand out to her, and she looked at him with suspicion, then let him help her from the chair. He switched off the lamp, and they moved together through the dark.

507

24

Manila walls, worn corporate carpet, no window — the room might once have been a supply closet. Claire wondered whether Paul Rubin had deliberately procured the smallest possible space at his old bank in which to cage her with Mohammad Khan. She and he were seated, in uncomfortable proximity, across a narrow metal table, the walls too near their backs.

"Take your time," Rubin commanded from the doorway. Here was the forceful man who once ran this bank, Claire thought. Too often of late he had vanished, had withdrawn from the messy process of leading. But Asma Anwar's death had resurrected the natural chairman. The morning after the murder he had called and, sounding both shaken and brusque, ordered her to meet with Khan to hash out her ambivalence. He had indulged it long enough, he said, just as he had indulged Khan's stubbornness. She needed to get to a place of certainty; Khan, one of flexibility. When Paul shut the door, Claire wouldn't have been surprised to hear it lock.

Khan's comfort with his physical self, long and lean, struck her forcibly in this small space. When she had last seen him, at the end of the public hearing, he had looked exhausted, depleted. His confidence had been restored, and somehow this unnerved her. They were so close they had no choice but to look directly into each other's eyes, as they had in her dream of him. Except in the dream his face held warmth, the desire to explain. Here it simply withheld. His affect was dispassionate, as if the news of this contretemps had reached everyone but the man who prompted it.

"I'm so sorry about Asma Anwar," she began.

"I am, too," he said, his look intent.

"Had you met her?" Claire asked. "After the hearing, I mean. Did you speak to her at all?" She didn't like herself for feeling competitive with a dead woman, but she couldn't help it: she wanted to know if Khan had thanked Asma for her support, as he never had Claire.

"I didn't," he said. "I didn't call her." Claire glimpsed regret, maybe even embarrassment, in his face, which consoled her, until she thought to be ashamed herself: she hadn't reached out to Asma, a fellow widow, one facing deportation, either. Those last images of Asma — her green salwar kameez like a blade of grass — came to her now.

"To have terror touch this process, of all things: it's very hard," she said. The words sounded forced, static: they didn't begin to capture how the killing had shaken her. The threats she had received surged back to life, even though she knew that, in her privilege and isolation, she was well defended. At night, her heart thudding, she thought about that little boy, an orphan; the noun perched like a vulture over her own children, already halfway there. Her self-pity at being a widowed mother evaporated at the prospect of not being able to mother at all. Perhaps Khan was afraid, too. But he had no children.

"We don't know who killed her, so we can't say what it means," Khan said. The statement, perfectly rational, peeved her for its very rationality. The who almost didn't matter when the what — his memorial, everything that happened in response — was so clear.

"To be honest, it makes me uncomfortable about posing questions to you," she said. "I want to — to honor her defense of you. But I can't go on backing the Garden without knowing more. So I'm asking out of respect for her."

"Respect for her precludes invoking her as a reason for asking or not asking anything, Mrs. Burwell. Ask because you need — or want — to know."

"But it's not just me," Claire protested, fighting her own chagrin. "I have a lot of families to answer to."

"Then we'd better get to your questions," he said.

"Let's start with the hearing, what Betsy Stanton said, about the buildings using Islamic visual language. Does that mean your garden — at least the motif for the names — does, too?"

"The names were patterned on the exterior of the buildings themselves, just as I said in my submission essay. But I was as surprised as you, as everyone, to learn there might have been Islamic antecedents to those buildings. Intrigued, but surprised. It does seem fairly speculative."

"But the architect who designed the towers had spent time in Islamic countries, right?"

"I believe so, but I don't know his career well."

"And have you?"

"Have I what?" One side of his mouth smiled, as if he sensed her trying to trap him.

"Spent time in Islamic countries."

"Only briefly," he said.

"Which ones?"

"Afghanistan. Dubai, if five hours in the airport counts as spending time."

"What were you doing in Afghanistan?"

He shifted his chair back from the table so he could cross his leg and, perhaps, get a better look at her. "Representing my firm in the competition to design a new American embassy in Kabul," he said, "although I'm not sure what bearing that has on the memorial. We didn't win."

Her brain was idling; she wasn't sure where to go next.

"Where did your idea come from — for the Garden?" she asked.

"From my imagination." The line was a wall: she couldn't see around it.

"Of course," she said after a beat. "Of course. But you must have to feed your imagination."

"Constantly," he said evenly. She couldn't tell if he was joking.

"So at the hearing, you mentioned — before you were interrupted, and I want to say I'm sorry about that, too. It was very disturbing to watch; I can't imagine what it was like to experience."

He didn't respond, so she plunged ahead. "You said you fed it, your imagination, in the case of your design, with Islamic gardens. That's what you said at the hearing."

"I said the gardens we now call Islamic were one influence. Architects — at least the good ones — don't plagiarize. They quote."

"So what were you quoting? Gardens you saw in Afghanistan?"

"I did see a garden there, yes."

"And what was it for — what's its purpose? I mean — Afghanistan must be full of martyrs." Clumsy, but she had to know.

"So that's why we're here," he said. He looked strangely sad.

"You've never answered that question," she said, "about whether it's a martyrs' paradise, or a paradise at all. Since the question was raised by the *Times*. You've never said."

"The question, as I recall, of it being a 'martyrs' paradise' " — he mimed quotes around the phrase — "was first raised by Fox."

The same embarrassment came over her as when Wilner, the governor's man, now the Garden's only opponent, affirmed her in the jury room.

"Whoever raised it," she said, "it's now been raised. And left hanging out there."

"Where it will hang forever," he said.

"What?"

"Why should I be responsible for assuaging fears I didn't create?"

"But Paul said you would answer my questions," she said, baffled. "Because of Asma Anwar."

"I told him I would answer whatever questions I could," Khan said. "He chose not to hear me. It's exactly because of Asma Anwar that I won't answer questions like the one you just asked me. Didn't you listen to her speech? She was saying terrorists shouldn't count more than people like her husband. But your questions — the suspicions they contain — make them count more. You assume we all must think like them unless we prove otherwise."

"I'm not assuming anything. A question doesn't make me a bigot. How can I support a memorial when I don't know what it is?"

"You seemed very comfortable with what it was when you first laid eyes on it," he said softly. "Even when we first met. You seemed to love the Garden. It was very moving to me, what you said about your son."

"My son, like any child, forms and forgets attachments very easily," she said. At Khan's surprised look, she tried to backpedal. "I just need to know what it is — even for William, when he's older. Can't you understand —"

"Maybe this will help," he said, extracting a narrow white pad and a pen from the inside of his jacket pocket. He drew two intersecting lines and asked, "What's this?"

Claire studied it. "A cross?"

He turned it diagonally. "And this?"

"An X."

He drew a square around the cross and turned it back to her. "And now?"

"Not sure — a window maybe?"

More lines. "A checkerboard?" she said. "Or maybe Manhattan — it looks like a grid."

"It's all of those things, or maybe none of them. It's lines on a plane, just like the Garden," he continued. "Lines on a plane. Geometry doesn't belong to a single culture. The grid is the quintessential modernist form, as I'm sure that *Times* critic grasps. It barely appeared in art before the twentieth century, then suddenly it's everywhere. Mondrian wasn't a Muslim. Mies, Agnes Martin, LeWitt, Ad Reinhardt — none of

515

them were. I can't help the associations you bring because I am."

"The problem isn't just the associations I bring but those your fellow Muslims might bring. They'll read it a certain way —"

"Is that what all your Muslim friends tell you?"

Claire swallowed. "I think it would be helpful if you just came out and said that it's not meant for martyrs, or whatever the worst-case scenario is. Or make some change to the Garden to calm the fears. Take out the canals, so your opponents won't be able to say it's the paradise in the Quran. 'Gardens beneath which rivers flow,' or whatever the line is."

"You want me to change the Garden," he said slowly.

"Just some symbolic change, as much to show you are eager to find common ground, that you're flexible, as for any substantive reason."

"You want me to take out the canals because it reminds you of a line in the Quran," he said, as if he hadn't understood.

"It's just an idea."

"Asma Anwar got up there and talked about how the paradise of the Quran was for people like her husband — and now, we can only hope, for her. You can't say you

516

want to honor her memory, then insist on erasing anything that reminds you of the paradise she spoke of."

"So it is meant to evoke that paradise."

"I didn't say that," Khan said. His jaw was clenched. "I said it's insulting to her to want to purge the Garden of anything that you've decided evokes that paradise."

"These distinctions are too fine for this country, given what's happened. Can't you see that it's natural for people to be afraid?"

"As natural as a garden," Khan said. The line was too perfect: she wanted to tear at it.

"I'm not going to apologize for wanting to be comfortable with the design for my husband's memorial," Claire said with exasperation. "Your design becomes more threatening if you won't change it: it tells me there's something there, something hidden, you want to preserve. Followers of your religion have caused enormous pain. Caused me enormous pain. And for all of us, it's very difficult to sort out what Islam actually means or encourages. What Muslims believe. A lot of Muslims who would never commit terrorism still support it, for political reasons if not religious ones. Or they pretend it wasn't Muslims at all who did this. So it's not unreasonable for me to ask

517

where on that continuum you sit. To learn at the hearing that you've never denounced the attack — I'll be honest, that was upsetting. Why haven't you?"

"I guess no one ever asked me to." No flippancy in the voice, but there in the words.

"And if I ask you now?"

"Same principle, Mrs. Burwell." His use of her married name grated. She was barely older than him.

"Which is what?" she flared up. "What is the principle behind refusing to say a terrorist attack was wrong, or that you don't believe in the theology that spawned it?"

"And what is the principle behind demanding that I say it, when your six-year-old son can tell you it's wrong?" He tried to run his hands through his hair, only to realize it was too short. He clenched his fists on both sides of his head and looked down at the table.

"What William tells me has no bearing here. I'm interested in what you believe."

There was an uncomfortably long silence. "Wouldn't you assume that any non-Muslim who entered this competition thinks the attack was wrong? Why are you treating me differently? Why are you asking more of me?"

"Because you're asking more of us!" she said. "You want us to trust you even though you won't answer questions about your design — what it means, where it came from."

"But you're only asking those questions because you don't trust me."

"And I don't trust you because you won't answer, so we're stuck." She smiled, and to her surprise so did he. If they could recognize, even laugh at, this bind, she thought, her antagonism easing, they could escape it.

"It's just that — it's hard for me to have you design the memorial if I don't know what you think."

"It's a question of faith, isn't it."

This silenced her. She reached her arm back, wanting the wall's solidity. Khan had turned his chair slightly to the side, seeking still more room for his legs, so they were no longer looking directly at each other. She studied him from a three-quarter angle. The historian on the jury, ever the pedant, once commented on how the Germans, even those who hadn't been born when Hitler died, kept finding new ways to apologize to the Jews, to atone. Individuals innocent of a crime could still feel or bear collective responsibility for it. It was for some sign of accepting this responsibility that she searched Khan's face.

"Can't you see you're only hurting yourself?" she said. "If you want me to fight for you — you wouldn't know this, but I was the only juror who didn't waver when we learned your name — I need to know more. I need you to, if not denounce, distance yourself from some of these ideas, or just make some accommodation in your design. This isn't about you. It's about the religion."

Even in profile she could see the jerk of shock. He turned his chair to face her, its legs catching in the frayed carpet, and asked:

"How would you feel if I justified what happened to your husband by saying it wasn't about him but about his country and its policies — damn shame he got caught up in it, that's all — but you know, he got what he deserved because he paid taxes to the American government. I get what I deserve because I happen to share a religion with a few crazies?"

Claire went taut. "Damn shame." "What he deserved." The words seemed to strike the fragile bones of her ear, even as she wasn't exactly sure what he had said: she had been thinking and listening at the same time, which made it hard to hear. But this, at last, had to be what he really thought. It pained her, sickened her, to think that perhaps vile Alyssa Spier was right, that Khan did see Cal as mere collateral damage in a war America had brought on itself, that he believed Cal, generous, good-natured Cal, bore responsibility, guilt, simply because he was American. She jerked to her feet like a mishandled marionette, grabbed her purse, and in one unbroken gesture reached the door, flung it open, stepped through, and slammed it behind her. In the hall, unable to find the elevator, she wandered down corridors and scurried past occupied offices until she spotted an exit sign — the stairs, that would do — and bore toward it as if to head-butt her way out. She opened the door to a dank stairwell and began the bleak mechanics of descent.

Down the stairs, back in time, until she came upon herself and Cal standing in front of Picasso's *Weeping Woman* at the Tate in London. Claire could still visualize the portrait today — the blue in her hair, the red in her hat, that ghastly, skull-like area around the mouth — more clearly, in fact, than she could see the husband who had stood next to her.

"Kind of ruins it that Picasso was so horrible, doesn't it," Claire had said. "He probably made Dora Maar cry, then painted her crying."

"So great art requires a morally pure artist?" Cal asked. "You look at the creation, not the creator."

"So you ignore that he tormented poor Dora."

"No, you judge the paintings as works of art, and Picasso as a man. There's no inconsistency in loving one and reviling the other. And thankfully the converse is true as well: you love me even though I made some pretty lousy art. Maybe arrogance is necessary for greatness."

A ground-floor exit expelled her into midtown. An inexplicable series of police barricades diverted her to a Times Square packed with tourist-naïfs. Her breath sped up in time with the intemperate digital collage — videos, commercials, neon, news tickers — that flickered at the edges of her eyelids. She cut through slow-moving knots, indifferent to indignant looks, until she made her way onto a less packed eastbound street. It was one of those miserable humid days when the pressure squeezes in like walls, the whole surly city waiting on edge for it to break. By the time Claire reached Bryant Park, she was damp.

Along the sides of the lawn, trees with twisting trunks lined up in perfect allées. The public library stretched before her. On the park's other three sides, glassy sky scrapers rose, their surfaces trapping greenery and clouds. It was a walled garden. She sank into its grass.

Even here, in this attenuated form, Khan's vision beguiled as much as his contempt burned. Perhaps they were inseparable, as Cal had argued — the arrogance firing the creation — but she wanted the Garden pure again, free of associations, free of Khan. The Garden as she first had seen it. But she couldn't take it from him, because it was his as much as, more than, hers. He had created it.

She bent her head to her hands and cried.

Seeking solitude and air, Paul took to Central Park. Other than being driven through by Vladimir, which didn't count, Paul hadn't set foot there in months. In fact, he realized, he had been so busy shuttling from home to jury meetings, offices, and politicians' lairs, that he had barely been outside. Khan's garden — the reality, as opposed to the controversy — had vanished from his thoughts. Now, strolling the Sheep Meadow's studied informality, the barely veiled evidence of Frederick Law Olmsted's designing hand, he realized that the Garden would be, would have been — he no longer knew what tense to use — the first public garden in Manhattan since Central Park's creation a century and a half before. He imagined a spot of green flashing on the subway map, then vanishing, flashing, then vanishing. A pulse.

Perhaps it was the breeze and birdsong, or maybe the young people streaking by on Rollerblades and bikes, but Paul felt content as he hadn't in a long time. His brief foray into inaction, into letting chaos reign — it had been a mistake. Far better that he forced Claire and Khan to confront their differences and work past them. Geraldine Bitman would persist in her demagoguery, but if Claire, as the most prominent family member, insisted that Khan could be trusted — that she trusted him — especially after her very public doubts, there would at least be a showdown between the two women, and Paul thrilled to imagine it. It amused him that this was what his once-racy fantasies of Claire Burwell had come to.

Edith called, atypically breathless. "Paul, there's a press conference — Claire Burwell. I'm sending Vladimir."

"I can walk," he started to say, falsely invigorated by the young people taking flight all around, then, faltering: "Yes, Vladimir."

Back home he settled into the couch with Edith to watch. Claire was seated at a long table, with members of the Muslim American Coordinating Council on either side of her. Her energy radiated through the screen as she began to read their joint statement.

"We, the undersigned" — she gestured to the right and left of her — "are asking Mohammad Khan to withdraw his memorial design so that the country can unite around a different memorial. We do not want to take anything from Mr. Khan. His effort to help this country heal is appreciated. We simply think a memorial other than the Garden, at this point, would be better for the families of the dead, for American Muslims, for the country. We are not telling him what to do. We are asking him to use his compassion and his judgment."

"Asma Anwar's death was devastating," she added, looking up from her pages. "Even without knowing who is responsible, it shocked us into realizing that this is a time for unity, for flexibility, not for rigidity."

She had seduced the jury into backing the Garden, insisted it support Khan, then turned on both design and designer. Without her, the jury's support of Khan would look like a bunch of artists defending one of their own — the governor's dream scenario. Paul took umbrage not just at Claire's betrayal of her fellow jurors, their months of work, their willingness to argue through their differences, but at her lack of humility — her sense that she alone could decide when was the time to fight, when to stand down. She didn't understand her own country, he thought: it would take more than a new memorial to unite it.

Yet he, perhaps, had sown this idea. When he had called Claire to insist on the Khan meeting, he had said, almost as an aside, that the best thing would still be Khan's withdrawing. She had done him one better: she grasped that her request would carry both more force and less risk if she joined with Muslims to make it.

"I wish this had gone differently," Claire was saying. "If Mr. Khan had shown more willingness to explain his design, so it wouldn't be subject to misinterpretation, or even to modify it, I would have continued to push for the Garden and many of the families would have done the same."

So Paul had misread not just Claire but Khan. Why had he thought that the architect, after such consistent resistance, would yield to her demands? Khan would fight on, but the fight would get even muddier now, more drawn out. Geraldine Bitman would ride the irresolution and its attendant anxieties as far as she could, no matter the wreckage in her wake. Paul couldn't imagine the Garden ever coming to be any more than he could imagine Khan giving in. Suddenly he craved a retirement filled not with chairmanships and prestige and continued relevance, but with him and Edith watching the musicals of the 1930s from the couch.

"She doesn't know her own mind," he said of Claire.

"Really?" said Edith. "It looks to me like she knows it quite well."

25

Mo almost laughed as he watched the press conference, the orchid-white WASP framed by Arab, South Asian, African American Muslims. He had wanted to unite East and West, and he had — against himself. She sat at the center of a long table, members of MACC on either side: Issam Malik to her left, Jamilah to her right, Laila thankfully nowhere in sight. "Safeguard us and we'll safeguard you": he should have listened.

He watched Claire and the MACC members fall over one another to display their mutual respect. See? she seemed to be saying, I don't have a problem with all Muslims, with Muslims at all, only with Mohammad Khan! This edifice of unexceptional beauty, as he had categorized her, now flaunted newly intriguing angles, as if false ceilings and partitions and scaffoldings, all the conventional interventions, had been cleared to reveal her true and startling bones. To unite with Muslims as opposed to other victims' families — it was a creative stroke. Even as her principles collapsed, even as she conformed, she had found a way to set herself apart. Mo had dismissed her as a type: the well-off woman who married for money, was married for beauty, and lived on a barren plateau of motherhood, philanthropy, and irrelevance. Now he saw, for the first time, her singularity.

It was more than odd to be casing Claire at this moment, he knew. But it was the least painful place he could dwell. He had wanted to undo their encounter the moment she walked out the door. He couldn't say what she wanted him to say; she couldn't see why he wouldn't say it. If they couldn't find common ground, what hope was there?

"Our jihad — and I use the word mindfully," Malik was saying primly, "is to show that it is possible to be both good Muslims and loyal Americans, to worship God and care for your country. God will be the judge, of this as of all things. All we can do is look at the facts before us — this young woman, a mother taken by terror; the ugly passions on all sides — and say that pushing for this memorial serves neither Islam nor America. Even one death — Muslim, non-Muslim, it doesn't matter — from this controversy is too many. To add another name to those on the wall, all for a fight about what those walls might symbolize, makes no sense. Mr. Khan's principles, or should I say his ambitions, are not worth any more lives."

That last sentence reverberated in Mo, for even he no longer knew where the line between his ambitions and principles lay. It was that line Laila had been searching for, and her fear that she had mistaken one for the other that ruined them.

Still floating from place to place, he had landed, for a few days, in a hotel room. He switched off its television, his choice clear: to fight for his garden as it was or withdraw. There was no middle ground. It wouldn't be hard to change the design — take down the walls, perhaps; set the canals loose to meander. A garden was just a garden. And yet he knew he would refuse to change a thing, even if that refusal doomed his submission. They would have to take the Garden as they had first seen it or not take it at all.

His lawyer had read the hearing transcripts, the interviews, the bylaws of the competition jury. "No one's showed you're in any way 'unsuitable,' and no one has brought forth a single legitimate ground for killing the design," Reiss told Mo. "If they try, a lawsuit would be very viable with all the Islamophobic talk Rubin permitted at the hearing. People get millions for tripping on a pothole. You've had your reputation tarnished, your design denied —"

"This isn't about money," Mo said.

"Just remember the law is your friend," Reiss said. "If you decide to stick it out, and they try to move ahead with any other design, you can sue for injunctive relief and block them from going forward with anything else. Maybe one day passions will settle enough for your memorial to be built."

So he could use his country's own laws against it, judo his way to victory, force his vision onto a people who seemed more foreign to him by the day. He could live, indefinitely, this waiting life, from which love, home, even work had been stripped away. Emmanuel Roi, concerned that the controversy was interfering with "the practice of architecture," had put Mo in a quarantine from which he was to deal with neither clients nor contractors. Thomas talked, too often, of their own practice — "We'll have more business than we know what to do with once the Garden is being built" — but the words sounded tinny, forced.

He called Laila for advice.

"Don't listen to Malik," she said. "You can't blame yourself for Asma's death." It was more accurate to say he couldn't blame himself alone, he thought. Historical events, as much as skylines, were collaborations.

"Don't give up." There was pleading in her voice. "If you give up it's like Asma died for nothing."

The footage of her last hour replayed as often in his mind as it did on every TV channel, Asma's small frame the axle of a pinwheeling crowd whose dangerous democracy confirmed Mo in his solitariness. Laila clutching Asma's son, the sun in her face eclipsed. It was shock Mo had felt at first, but fear that stalked him now: the sense that if it could happen to Asma, it could happen to him, no matter how many precautions he took. Should he chance his own death to make hers worthwhile, sacrifice himself for a memorial his country might never embrace? Or preserve himself for the work, his best work, ahead?

"I just have one thing to add," he heard Claire Burwell say. "Mr. Khan says he shouldn't have to say what the Garden is, or where it came from, and he's right." She looked directly at the cameras. "But I want him to."

■ ■ ■ ■

On his second morning in Kabul, Mo had called his embassy to say he was too sick to make the day's meetings and set off to brave the city on his own. He had in hand a thirty-year-old guidebook from the hotel gift shop, but of the gleaming cosmopolitan capital it promised he saw only bedraggled remnants — bullet-pocked façades, shuttered restaurants, dead architecture. The Kabul River had been reduced to a fetid trickle where Kabulis laundered clothes, and there was no trace of the gardens Mogul emperors had laid along it. Kabul blossomed with sewage and trash.

Batting away hunger and thirst, he crossed a bridge and began to climb a steep, dusty path. The air dried and thinned. Below, the city spread like a grand carpet of indecipherable pattern, every house, every life a knot. In the distance the mountains crested over a low-hanging haze.

He was in some kind of slum. The hills of Kabul had been left to the poor. Garbage clotted the gutters that ran alongside the unpaved pathways, which rain would churn to mud. Children lugged canisters and plastic jugs full of water back to their homes; the air rioted with cooking smoke. The earthen houses, well-fortified rectangular structures with walls and high windows that made it impossible to see inside, turned their backs to him, made a canyon of the path. Hide everything, show nothing. Women in burkas hurried past, their voices gurgling brooks beneath the cloaking fabric. Men stared, or smiled, or greeted him in soft streams of words that he couldn't understand. A few boys trailed behind him. "Amerkan?" one asked, giggling when Mo nodded. Their faces were dirty and scabrous, their hair matted, their clothes dustfilmed, their eyes rich with curiosity and mirth.

Still hungry, even thirstier — and then without warning his stomach turned to liquid, made thunder, began to cramp and roil and clutch in pain. He revisited his meals — maybe the rare steak at the French restaurant — but the problem was not what he had ingested but where to excrete it. He saw an elderly man working his prayer beads in the shade of his house, his white skullcap above his white beard like the clouds over the snow-covered mountains. Mo's approach sparked light in his glaucous eyes. His smile was riddled with stumps and holes, as if it had been mined.

"Asalamu alaikum," the man said.

"Alaikum asalam," Mo replied.

He waited, as his stomach squeezed in agony, for the soft murmur of the rest of the man's greeting.

"Toilet?" he asked.

The man shook his head, uncomprehending.

"WC?" Again the man shook his head, and Mo tried to think if there was a universal gesture for bathroom. He clutched his stomach. The man pointed to his mouth, thinking Mo hungry, perhaps offering food. Desperate, Mo squatted, patted his rear end, again rubbed his stomach, turned up his hands, and scrunched his face in a question, looking searchingly around him. Chuckling now, the man nodded and motioned for Mo to follow him down a narrow opening between two houses. The foul smell grew stronger as they moved along the alley; then there was the small outhouse. Inside Mo shut the door and squatted over the hole, gagging before he remembered to hold his breath, trying to keep his balance without touching the walls. His bowels emptied in furious stinking squirts; he became pure animal. Standing up, rocking to get his balance, he looked down into a sea with islands of shit.

As he turned to urinate, a tiny side window revealed the flat roofs of the homes spilling down to the city below, and then, like a sunspot on his vision, a patch of green. When he left the outhouse, stepping over the waste trickling into a gutter nearby, he located the clearing again, seeing it now as a vast green square with the glint of water, cradled by walls all around. Fresh air, clean breath: he pointed to it, and his rescuer gestured toward a path that led down the hill. Mo put his hand on his heart in thanks.

"Chai?" the man offered.

Mo shook his head; he thirsted more for that green. The man called out and clapped his hands and two little boys appeared, impish in their salwar kameez, trying to hide behind each other even as they peered at Mo. The old man said something to them and motioned for Mo to follow. Mo again put his hand on his heart and began to trail the boys, breathing the spumes of dust their plastic sandals sent up. The sun drilled into his head. After about ten minutes they emerged from the hillside slum onto a paved road that sloped downward. The boys, after indicating that Mo should keep walking, vanished back up the hill from where they had come. Soon a smooth mud wall inscribed with pointed arches, too high for him to see over, loomed up on his right. He continued downward, shoulder to the wall, until the ground flattened and he reached a corner. Turning right, he at last found an enormous open wooden gate. He walked through the gap and left the city behind.

Before him a vast garden rose up to meet the slope of the mountain he had just descended. From his new vantage, the hillside slum's cantilevered houses looked like an Escher drawing, one that could be smeared — by an earthquake, a mudslide — as easily as wet ink on paper. The jumble on the hill broke abruptly at the garden's rear wall, which demarcated an entirely different landscape, one marked by symmetry, order, geometry. Straight paths climbed the garden's stepped terraces, a straight canal flowed down toward Mo. Trees — almond and cherry, walnut and pomegranate — marched off to the sides in neat orchard-like rows.

A Ministry of Tourism signboard told him where he was: Bagh-e-Babur, Babur's garden, designed around 1526 by the first Mogul emperor, who was now buried in it. After serving as a front line in Afghanistan's civil war, the garden was being restored. It came closer than almost anything he had seen in Kabul to matching the description he now found in his book.

Mo began scaling the terraces, then wandered off to the side, into the intimate shade of the tree canopies, the grassy turf sinking slightly beneath his feet. Pink blossoms frothed against the green foliage; tulips, tiny cups of color, were scattered offhandedly around the bases of the trunks. Near the garden's perimeter wall, densely planted mulberry, almond, and fig trees created a deeper shade. He smelled damp earth, spring air, trodden grass, and a faint, floral sweetness.

The garden's flaws didn't escape him: he hadn't left his critical mind back at the hotel. Bagh-e-Babur lacked crispness. There was no natural or guided progression for a visitor, no journey. Uncoordinated interventions through the centuries — a tomb, a mosque, a pavilion, a swimming pool — had given the garden the random aspect of a poorly developed city.

The tomb belonged to Babur, an emperor Mo's book described as warrior and aesthete. His resting place was encased in white marble, contravening Babur's wish that nothing cover his grave "so that the rain and the sun could beat upon it and perhaps encourage a wildflower to grow." Instead,

Judas trees nearby flaunted scarlet flowers.

On a lower terrace sat a delicate white marble mosque, beneath whose portico three women heated a lunch of rice and meat. The white of the mosque was offset by the dark, well-groomed vestments of the Mediterranean cypress trees on either side. Their shape reminded Mo of tall bottle brushes or calligraphy quills. Of that "Design Against Terrorism" seminar: cypresses as a line of defense, blasted but erect.

Descending to yet another terrace, he found his way to the veranda of an elegant small pavilion and sat. Before him the canal stretched like a long runner reflecting the sky. From under the almond trees sprang a joyous cry: the boys who guided him to the garden had rematerialized to play a hybrid of croquet and cricket and horse shoes, each aiming at the other's tossed rock. The faint thwack of a hit called forth a whoop, a soft thud in the grass, a groan of despair. At a water tap a young man groomed himself in a small, handheld mirror, twisting his face this way and that as if searching for flaws. A group of women raised their burkas atop their heads like nuns' wimples and turned toward the sun. The walls muffled but didn't erase the city's sounds.

Memories drifted in. Mo recalled a childhood trip to India, to Kashmir, that had included visits to baghs. He remembered his feet in a rectangular pool next to a waterfall and wanting to swim; giant dahlias, purple flowers shaped like bells, terraces like those here; and at the back of the gardens a mountain rising, furred dark green. Clear, cool air. A pavilion — black marble? — where they had sat for a few moments. Fountains spurting up water. Across the road a giant lake, smooth as a mirror, gleamed silver.

He dawdled in memory until dusk, when the light in Babur's garden turned murky, soft, and the muezzin's wail poured over him. From all corners men moved toward the exit and the city beyond as inexorably as the canal flowing down the terraces. Mo felt a pull, more passive than volition, to follow them, as if he were a drop being absorbed by a body of water whose size he had no way to measure. And yet he held back, until he saw one man kneel to pray, alone, on a stone border at a terrace's edge. He went to join him, pausing first at a tap to splash water on his face and hands in a gesture toward ablution.

Mo had last prayed maybe a year ago, visiting the Virginia mosque with his father. It was perhaps the first time he had prayed as an adult, and with the steps of the salat foreign to him, he watched his father. It was a lesson of odd intimacy. Salman was past sixty, and his age told in the creak of his knees, the pause of his body in a question mark on the way to the floor, the gathering of breath before he bent to his forehead, the slight stiffness of the rise.

Mo, even as he moved himself, had been nearly paralyzed by self-consciousness. To see young professionals like him, Black-Berrys blinking from their belts, with their rears hoisted in the air and their socked soles exposed, had made him wince for their dignity and for his own, had made him think that men weren't meant to be spectators of the prayers of others.

But today, the Afghan, deep in his prostrations, did not acknowledge Mo, even as together they formed a line, a wall, a mosque; he cared not at all for Mo's judgment. He had forgotten himself, and this was the truest submission.

Mo pressed his hands to the window. The Arabian Sea unrolled to the horizon like a bolt of tussar silk. Behind him stretched Mumbai, its blurry edge embroidered farther every time he looked. The megacity, always expanding: new arrivals in the birth wards and bus stations each day, the dying and departing unable to keep pace. Mumbai spread, Mumbai rose. Mo watched from forty stories above the sea.

He meditated on the water, trying to collect himself. He had spent the past hour in an argument with a Kuwaiti prince for whom he had designed a modest palace, clean-lined and energy-efficient. The commission had gone well until this morning, when the prince announced that he wanted a lawn, a vast, American-style lawn, with sprinklers embedded and mowers at the ready, a lawn on which balls could be bowled, horses cantered, picnics spread, tea parties laid, soccer wars waged. The prince didn't care that even England and America had turned away from swards of green. With the profits from oil, he could buy water. He wanted a lawn.

He couldn't have one, not with Mo as his architect. "The landscaping isn't an accessory, it's part of the design, so you take all of it or none of it," Mo had snapped, irritable even by his own standards. It had been a mistake to work this morning: he should have taken the time to subdue his memories, discipline his feelings. He was on edge, a man near sixty anxious about meeting a couple of American kids less than half his age.

They were here, the doorman messaged; he was sending them up. Mo surveyed his immaculate space, then opened his door to a young woman, pretty enough, with crinkle-edged brown eyes, a salting of freckles, a wide smile. She wore a vintage wrap dress, but he suspected, from its awkward draping, that she preferred pants. Behind her stood a cameraman with tousled hair and a tentative smile. Mo politely asked that they remove their shoes.

Molly had pestered him for months, outlining the documentary she hoped to make for the twentieth anniversary of the memorial competition, which she called a "seminal moment" in American cultural history. She was exploring the "politics of memorial," "America in argument with itself," "the plight of Muslims after the attack." Her guiding idea, borrowed from one of her professors, was that the process of creating a memorial was itself part of the memorial.

"But this memorial was never created," Mo wrote back. "The process doesn't matter."

She wouldn't give up. Family members, jurors, journalists, activists, all had talked to her. Mo was the missing piece, and the most important. At last, to end her siege, he agreed. He planned to offer some generic remarks about the past being ancient history, then send her off into Mumbai to explore how memorializing had metastasized. As India continued to Westernize, it had become obsessed with naming its dead just as America did. The plaques were everywhere: at the train station, listing those who had fallen from overcrowded cars; at the airport, remembering those felled by ongoing terror attacks; in the slums, whose handwritten signs recorded those lost to sewage-born infections or police brutality.

He told himself he admired — recognized

— her persistence, but this elided the truth. For nearly two decades now, he had been a global citizen, American only in name. K/K Architects had a New York office, but Thomas Kroll ran it. Mo could pretend only so much of the time that he wanted it this way.

Two years earlier, the Museum of New Architecture, in New York, had mounted a retrospective of his career. *Mohammad Khan, American Architect* was a tribute to his blaze of work, most of it in the Middle East, India, or China, over the past twenty years. It was unusual for an architect to complete so many projects so quickly, although Mo knew this was as much about his clients — rich patrons; undemocratic governments; Gatsby nations in a hurry to buy identities with their newfound wealth — as his own talents. But the exhibit also examined his influence. His style, widely copied, married a remarkable simplicity of form with geometric patterns of dazzling complexity. Indeed, he was known as much for what he had convinced his clients not to build — gaudy, gargantuan palaces and mosques — as for what he had built for them. Critics and historians credited him with helping to shift the aesthetic of the Middle East. "Even in a mosque you should feel yourself in a garden," he had told one interviewer. "Nothing between you and God."

Planning to attend the opening, Mo instead canceled at the last minute. It took him some time to puzzle out that the memorial was to blame. The Garden's drawings and model were displayed in the "Unbuilt" section of the exhibit, along with a half dozen projects either in development or already abandoned. The caption read: "Khan's design represented his first foray into melding modern minimalism with elements of Islamic design. He withdrew his submission in the face of heated political opposition, but the controversy brought his talent to the international stage." It was a quintessentially American story — that you could profit even by losing — but not the accounting Mo was looking for.

The country had moved on, self-corrected, as it always did, that feverish time mostly forgotten. Only Mo was stuck in the past. He wanted acknowledgment of the wrong done to him, awaited credit for his refusal to agree that the attack justified America's suspicion of its Muslims any more than it justified the state's overreaching. Today most Americans thought as he had, but at the time his stand had been lonely. Hard.

More than his ego was at stake. American

Muslims were now, if not embraced, accepted. Trusted. Their rights unquestioned. Mo wanted to embody this rapprochement through architecture, considered it incomplete otherwise. There wasn't a single Mohammad Khan building in the United States, but it was his style as much as his name that he longed to imprint. He wanted to design structures that borrowed as freely from Islamic architecture as others borrowed from the Greeks or from medieval cathedrals. Yet his own stubbornness spited him, kept him from the thing he most desired.

At the time of the opening in New York, he was seized by a regret so powerful it curled him in his bed in Mumbai. Ever since, he had been seeking another way back in. He had never spoken publicly of the memorial controversy, barely spoke of it privately. Perhaps opening up about it now could elicit the conversation, the apology, he wanted. Here he was, playing another game with his country, imposing another test. He couldn't help himself.

Molly plunged in. "Can we look around the apartment and see if there are any shots we'd want to get, and where we want to set you up?"

"You should be able to get what you need out here," he said, gesturing at the living room. "The light's best on that side —"

"I'll figure it out, thanks," said the cameraman, whose name Mo had already forgotten.

"This is some place," Molly said. Mo didn't say he had designed it, designed the whole building, in fact, taking the top floor for himself. His apartment was simple, spare, naturally cooled by shade and currents of air. A balcony embraced the entire apartment; its overhang shielded the art and artifacts inside from the afternoon sun. Filigreed screens on windows dappled intricate carpets of light and shadow onto the floor. Where they stood, the actual rug beneath their bare feet was so soft it begged stroking. Its pattern had faded with age — great, expensive age — but could still be seen: a tree of life, cypresses, flowers. A garden.

"Be careful!" Mo said. The cameraman, like an overexcited Labrador, had nearly knocked over a folio of Persian miniatures displayed on a stand. The cavalier clumsiness of the gesture made Mo homesick as much as irritable. The young man had the peculiarly half-formed quality of his age, class, country. He seemed nervous. This began to make Mo nervous, too.

Over tea, Molly updated him on everyone they had interviewed, or tried to. Vice President Bitman had not responded to repeated interview requests. Lou Sarge had died of a prescription drug overdose before they could speak with him. Sean Gallagher — "the headscarf-puller" — they had yet to find. He surfaced from time to time to check on his family, according to his tight-lipped mother, then disappeared.

Paul Rubin had died some years back, of a heart attack, but they had interviewed his wife. Did Mo want to see? Molly asked. They had brought some footage.

Mo logged her into his wireless system. The image of a white-haired, sharp-eyed woman bloomed on the wall screen. Well past eighty, she was impeccably coiffed, with a string of pearls at her throat, a pale mint suit, discreet lipstick, and a fierce expression that would make Death himself nervous to approach. Edith Rubin.

She began by quoting, from pained memory, Rubin's obituary: " 'Despite a distinguished career in finance, he will be remembered mostly for his failed stewardship of the memorial process, which some argued set back America's long

552

convalescence.' "

"I spent years arguing with the obituary writers over that," she said in a tart tone. "It's wrong. It's not fair to Paul. No one could have handled the process better than he did. It was an impossible situation. Impossible, especially with the way Geraldine Bitman behaved, and I hope you'll put that in your film. He always thought the best thing for the country, even for the Muslims, was for Mohammad Khan to withdraw, and that is what happened."

"But I didn't give in — withdraw — because he asked me to," Mo protested over Edith's speech. "Rubin pressuring me only made me fight harder."

Molly checked some notes and fastforwarded a little. "What Paul told me of his interactions with Khan — it reminded me so much of the way he related to our sons," Edith continued, as if in conversation with Mo. "He always wanted the boys to be something other, something more, than they were. They resisted, and Khan, in his own way, resisted even more zealously. Poor Paul. And Claire Burwell: Paul was so surprised when she united with that Muslim group to ask Khan to withdraw. I think he tried to be like a father to her, too. But she had ambitions.

"So many things evaded Paul's grasp in that period," she went on. "It was a strain for him, and for me, having to watch. But in the end, what he believed needed to happen did. That wasn't an accident, not entirely. He deserves credit."

"It's an awfully convenient way of looking at things," Mo said. "Everything he did was right, even the things that were wrong, because it all turned out well in the end. For everyone but me, that is."

The tinge of embarrassment in Molly's face made Mo regret his self-pity.

"She loves him," the cameraman said. "Loved him, I guess." Both Mo and Molly looked at him in surprise. "Sorry," he said, halting now. Red. "It's just — that would color her view of what he did."

Molly gave herself over to a radiant smile, briefly forgetting Mo, then turned back to him: "She's right that it did turn out well for others. Issam Malik's in Congress, you know."

Mo did, because Malik had the gall to solicit him, regularly, unsuccessfully, for campaign contributions. Before entering the House, he and Debbie Dawson — who had become his sparring partner when Sarge became unreliable — had taken their gladiator act on the road, feeding the global appetite for debates over whether Islam was a threat. Dawson, having written three international bestsellers about the threat of Islam, was especially popular with India's Hindu nationalists. Mo still loathed Malik — for turning on him, for implying that he had brought on Asma Anwar's death. But everyone then had claimed to be honoring the dead woman's memory, Mo included.

As if following his thoughts, Molly turned to Asma next. Laila Fathi had tried to keep Abdul in the United States, so she could raise him herself, Molly told Mo. But she had no legal rights, and no support in the Bangladeshi community. He had returned home to be raised by his grandparents. Mo, trying to absorb this information, remembered Laila holding the wailing boy at the scene of the murder. She had said nothing, when Mo called to tell her he was withdrawing from the competition, braced for her disappointment, about trying to keep Abdul. Did she know then she wanted to? At the time he had been preoccupied with his own decisions, never thinking she might be making one of her own. Now he remembered her silence on the phone when he said he was leaving the country and wondered if he had blown up the bridge behind him.

Once she had asked Mo if he wanted

children.

"Later," was his reply, which was the truth. Later had never come. Work had been his child, his partner. And yet the more buildings he added to his name, the more hollow a frame they seemed for his life. Every real relationship over the years had sputtered out, his stretches alone lengthened to something like permanence. What he had with Laila, the briefest, most indelible of his entanglements, had been both created and destroyed by his memorial.

"Laila," he said. The name caught in his throat. He coughed. "Laila Fathi. Did you speak with her?"

"Yes," Molly said, "we can show you —" Her magic fingers went to work, summoning ghosts. In a few seconds Laila would be on his wall. This mirage of a memory — it might dissolve if he came too close.

"No," he said, abrupt. "No. Let's move on, I can't give this my whole day."

On the way to seeing Mo in India, Molly had gone to interview Abdul in Dhaka. This footage Mo agreed to watch. The young man's face was warm-hued, thick-browed, and sorrowful. Mo couldn't remember what Asma looked like. He had never seen an image of the father. A fund had been set up

556

for Abdul after Asma's death, even though, with her compensation money, he needed little. But Americans horrified by her murder — after watching her speech, they felt as though someone they knew had been killed — gave anyway, and Mo was among them. Then, consumed with his own departure, he forgot the boy.

"I don't remember New York," Abdul began. "I was two when I left. I came home with my mother's body. And all this." The camera panned across a meticulously organized array of children's books and trucks and Nike shoes and DVDs and clothes. Pristine, none of it played with or worn. These objects had been studied.

"My parents idealized America. I know this from my relatives. I grew up hearing, over and over, how my mother had refused to come home after my father's death. If she had, she would still be alive — I heard this all the time."

The image changed. Now Abdul was watching, with intense concentration, his mother's speech defending Mo at the public hearing. Mo could see Abdul's lips moving ever so faintly, matching both his mother's Bengali and the English translation provided by the man sitting next to her. Abdul had memorized the words. Mo didn't want to think about how many times over the years he must have listened to them.

Abdul had applied to and been accepted at colleges in the United States, but under pressure from his relatives decided to stay in Bangladesh. America tempted him and scared him. Both of his parents had died there. This was reason to go, reason not to. Mo remembered how his own decision not to go home had curled him in bed. How many nights had Abdul spent in the same position?

"I sometimes feel each place is the wrong place," the young man on the screen said softly.

The image on the screen cut to a gray-haired man — the same one who had sat at Asma's side during the hearing — polishing a brass memorial plaque. Affixed to the side of the Brooklyn building where she had lived, it bore her name in English and Bengali, and her image. The man worked till it gleamed, placed a small bouquet of pink plastic flowers in a holder on the plaque, and put his hand over his heart.

Mo looked suspiciously at the camera, which had been removed from its case. So far it had brought only grief. And there was more: Molly had tracked down all the jurors and reported gently that most of them — Ariana Montagu, most of all — still felt betrayed by Mo's abdication. Mo knew this but had worked to bury the knowledge. After deciding to give up, he had packed in haste and fled the country like a fugitive, leaving Paul Rubin to issue a brief statement saying that he had withdrawn. Reading some of the coverage from abroad, Mo had been flabbergasted by Ariana's assertion that the jury was going to back him. The artist's condescension toward his design, the scraps he had overheard from other jurors, Claire's contention that only she had resolutely defended him — all had combined to convince him that the jury would never support the Garden. His face, as he read the interview with Ariana, had burned, as it did even now, at the prospect that he had misread his country as much as he had accused it of misreading him. From then on he shut out all coverage of the Garden. He didn't want to learn facts that would make him regret his choices. In part, he was ashamed before Asma Anwar, before Laila, too: he had justified his decision to withdraw — to save himself — by saying his memorial would never be built. What if he had been wrong?

■ ■ ■ ■

The camera was on, Mo seated near a monumental two-handled water jar carved from marble. Molly didn't waste time with warm-up questions. "Why did you leave America?" she asked.

Mo hesitated, then began: "The memorial experience opened the world to me. I began to learn about Islamic architecture, and it became what would seem to be a lifelong interest. And there were so many opportunities abroad — India, China, Qatar, elsewhere in the Arab world. Architecturally it was more exciting to be abroad. The center of gravity had shifted, even if Americans didn't recognize it back then. I guess they do now. And I figured I might as well work somewhere where the name Mohammad wouldn't be a liability." He forced a smile.

"Your instincts were right — you've done well."

"Well enough," Mo said with false modesty. He was better-known internationally than he had ever dreamed, and wealthy, too. And yet his gloss — that he had been pulled abroad by opportunity — was a false one. He had been pushed. America had offered his immigrant parents the freedom to reinvent themselves. Mo had found himself reinvented by others, so distorted he couldn't recognize himself. His imagination was made suspect. And so he had traced his parents' journey in reverse: back to India, which seemed a more promising land. When he called his parents to tell them he was withdrawing from the memorial competition, he felt ashamed, even though this was what they wanted. "Don't feel bad, Mo," his mother said, and, as if she had been practicing the line: "Eden, paradise — all the best gardens are imaginary."

His submission, which had seemed so monumental at the time, had turned out to be only a small fragment of the mosaic of his life. From catastrophe — from failure — had come his true path, his life calling, as if all was meant to happen this way. Even as he was still unsure about God's existence, he counted this God's will. Or perhaps this was how he made uneasy peace with what had happened.

He looked away from the camera, resting his eyes on a sixteenth-century ceramic bowl from Iznik. The artistry of exquisite objects like these — and his apartment was full of them — had come to express his faith more than any ritual or text, including *the* text of Islam. He had stumbled into sacrilege all those years ago and found he belonged there. He barely prayed. Months could pass without the urge. His uncertainty had abided all these years and most days barred the way to faith. Only rarely did it seem like faith itself.

Yet these objects were reflections of faith, meant to express divine principles visibly, and so suggest the invisible. Sometimes, studying them, or the complex geometry he spun from computer algorithms, he would sense himself on the edge of something vast, awesome, infinite. Then the feeling would be gone. He didn't know whether the makers of these objects were merely executing their patrons' wishes, or had found their way to God, or were looking with their hands, their minds. He wondered the same about himself. If he was ever to find his way to belief, it would not be through fasting, or even through prayer, but through his craft. In the meantime his creations served the belief of others.

"Looking back now, is there anything you would have done differently?" Molly asked.

He kept his eyes on the bowl, its lustrous green glaze. His chest tightened. Over the years he had revisited this question hundreds of times in his head, never arriving at a satisfactory answer.

"I would not have entered," he said to the camera now. "That was the original mistake — the original sin, perhaps."

He sounded bitter despite himself. I am bitter, he thought, and, sensing that the words were on the verge of escaping his lips, pressed them shut.

"Everyone's full of regrets," Molly said elliptically. Then, as if reading his mind: "Who do you blame?"

"It's not as if I've been tending some enemies list all these years," Mo said. In fact he had. There were the obvious candidates — Debbie Dawson and Lou Sarge; Governor Bitman; the headscarf puller; that reporter, now a Web doyenne, who from time to time messaged Mo — "Just checking in! Anything new? Alyssa Spier" — as if they were old friends or collaborators.

But more painful were those who should have been on his side, or who began there. Malik and MACC. Rubin. Claire Burwell. All these years later, she was still disappointing and provoking and mystifying to him. Her turn against him had a kind of logic; he could trace the steps, including his own, that had led her there. He had taken her support for granted; he had pushed her too hard. Her turn against the Garden, when absolutely nothing in the design she loved had changed, still defied belief.

"Claire Burwell," he said, surprised they hadn't brought her up. "What became of her?"

Her head was covered with a silk scarf the color of one of the sea's blues, and for half a second Mo saw her as a Muslim. Then he registered her gray skin, the face devastated like the ruins of Kabul. She was sick.

Claire's voice filled the room. "What did I think of him? I thought he was sanctimonious. Rigid. I guess that made it harder — he wasn't the easiest to deal with, you know. And talented — let's not forget that. I did think he was very talented. I just couldn't handle all the vagueness, the elusiveness about what the Garden was because — and I'm trying to be as honest as I can — it made me wonder what he was. You know, he wouldn't make things clear and simple. He wouldn't come out and say he didn't believe in the theology that inspired the attack, wouldn't even say he thought the attack was wrong. I was under so much pressure. The families. The press — that woman from the *Post*. It wasn't all my fault. *The New Yorker* didn't trust him! What was *I* supposed to do? I had thought myself so sophisticated. I was naïve. I do regret . . . I regret so much."

"Do you go to the memorial?"

"Never. I went to the dedication, then never returned. A Garden of Flags? Hideous. As ugly as the whole process. And with all the in-fighting, picking a whole new jury, soliciting new designs — by the time it got built I'm not sure anyone cared. I was so sick of the whole thing, and it was my husband's memorial! And so many more Americans ended up dying in the wars the attack prompted than in the attack itself that by the time they finished this memorial it seemed wrong to have expended so much effort and money. But it's almost like we fight over what we can't settle in real life through these symbols. They're our nation's afterlife."

"Have you ever told Mohammad Khan how you feel?"

"No, no, I haven't. It was just too, too —"

He leaned forward in his seat, awaiting her next words, then realized he was still being filmed. "Please, turn that off," he told the cameraman, who started in surprise, as if he had imagined himself invisible.

"Why not?" Molly was asking Claire. "Why did you never contact him?"

"Oh, I don't know. His design would have been so much better than what we ended up with, and I did come to believe that we were in the grip of some frenzy, possessed almost, at that time. I felt like little by little I was pushed — by him among others — until I found myself on the other side of a line I hadn't wanted to cross. But then he went abroad and began working for whichever Muslim ruler would pay him, and again — I didn't know what he was about. So even though I wanted to apologize, I must have felt conflicted because whenever I would start to write to him, I could never find the right words."

"How about 'I'm sorry'?"

Mo laughed aloud at Molly's assertiveness. On-screen, Claire laughed, too. "Yes, you're right. Sometimes simpler is better, right? I'm sorry. Not sure why I felt I needed more than that. Except for never being entirely sure I was sorry. There were times, I'll admit it, when I still thought he should apologize to me, to all the families for asking them to operate on trust when he refused to give us any reason to trust him. It was the hardest part of all for me, really discerning what I felt. So many people — the dead, the living — were telling me what to do. I thought — I thought I finally knew myself, that I was casting off what I was supposed to be. I guess I haven't lost all of that confusion." She looked off into the distance, at what he couldn't see. The screen went to black.

They sat in silence for a few moments. Molly asked if they could turn the camera back on, finish the interview. He nodded, although he wasn't in the mood for much more.

"Do you still think about the Garden? Did you keep the design in your head?"

Mo smiled. "You could say I never stopped thinking about it."

"We have something to show you," Molly told Claire.

Mohammad Khan ghosted on the giant screen on her living room wall. Gray threaded his hair; the high white wall he was approaching dwarfed him. He passed through a towering steel door cut with elaborate fretwork, then bent to pick a stray leaf off the path. Before him spread a garden, governed by strict geometry.

Claire had seen it only on paper, only in miniature. Yet she had no doubt about what was before her.

"I don't understand," she said to Molly. "The Garden. But how? I don't understand."

"It's the private pleasure garden of some

567

rich Muslim — a sultan or emir or something," Molly said. "He commissioned it after Khan withdrew from the memorial competition. Khan took us there after we interviewed him. He wanted you to see it."

"Before I died?" Claire's laugh was brittle, but she turned back toward the screen.

Two canals bisected the garden, forming four squares. Khan walked, narrating. The camera's focus was tight as he ticked off trees — cherry, almond, pear, apricot, walnut. Rows of Mediterranean cypresses, proud, self-contained. Plane trees of great girth. Steel trees, glinting and upside down, with roots like a distraught woman's tangled hair in place of branches and leaves.

The pavilion sat, slightly elevated, at the center of the garden, a giant sculpture floating above land and water. Its design was simple, elegant: a flat roof, unadorned gray marble columns, sharp right angles. Inside, grilles of white marble cast elaborate geometric shadows, creating a series of contemplative spaces with benches. The canals flowed from beneath the pavilion, fed by a reservoir revealed, as if it were the source of all life, by an open circle within the floor.

Claire closed her eyes and heard the water rippling, Khan's footsteps crunching, birds singing, chattering, telling their stories, maybe hers. She wished she could move into the scene before her. Cal felt closer than he had in twenty years. Seeing the Garden alive was a gift and a rebuke. She had, at first glimpse, made it an allegory for Cal's perpetual optimism. In walking away from it, she had walked away from him. The real act of will was not in the creating of a garden but in the sustaining, the continuous stand against wildness. She had let herself be overtaken.

With shame in her face she turned to the cameraman. "Did you tell him?"

His own look was sheepish. "I wanted to, planned to," he said. "But once he mentioned the garden, I thought . . . I was afraid . . . I thought he might not show it to me."

Claire saw William, at that moment, not as a broad-shouldered young man but as the little boy to whom she had described, again and again, the magic of the Garden. He had traced its lines so many times with his hand. How strange it must have been to finally walk them. Garden, then no garden — too much, she grasped now, like father, then no father. He had been a troubled teenager, his poor grades and errant behavior so at odds with her own regimented adolescence that she didn't know how to help him; she was never sure whether his problems owed to misfortune or an excess of fortune or both. She tried to talk to him about her own father's death, how it had driven her to excel. He didn't want to hear it. At last he pulled himself together enough to get into art school.

When he came to her and told her that he and his girlfriend, Molly, wanted to make a documentary about the memorial competition, she tried to dissuade him. But not as hard as she might have.

The camera strips the eye of its freedom, holds viewers hostage to its choices. The focus in the footage Claire saw was narrow at first, staying on Khan, on the garden's details. But now the camera shifted away from him and panned the inside walls, and as it did, Claire heard an odd, primal sound. It took her a moment to realize she had made it. Across the walls, where the names should have been, flowed Arabic calligraphy.

"The names," she whispered. "Where are they? What is that?"

"It's the Quran," William said.

The room wavered around Claire. This wasn't a gift but a taunt. Doubt was all Khan deserved.

"I told you this film was a mistake," she said.

"It's a commission," William pointed out. "I don't think he had a choice."

"We don't know whose idea it was," Molly reminded him. "His or the emir's."

"He must at least have agreed to it," Claire said. "He was too independent — too unbending — to allow it otherwise. From what I saw of him, he wouldn't do something he didn't believe in for a patron any more than he would for the families."

The footage paused, they sat in silence.

"We don't know what it says," Molly said abruptly. "Being in there — it was like being under a spell. I didn't think to ask anything. I didn't want to ruin it. He said it was the Quran, and I was like, okay. But which verses? What's the message? We'll have to get someone to translate it."

The screen unfroze. A few moments later — or much longer — Molly's voice floated over the scene. "What would you say to Claire Burwell about the garden? It's obviously the same, but different. I mean, the names." Not just the names, Claire thought — the steel trees upside down. The emir couldn't have wanted that. These were messages.

Khan was walking back toward the garden's entrance now, not looking at the camera. When he spoke, she couldn't see his face.

"Use your imagination," he said. Claire heard his words, closed her eyes, tried to see her husband's name. But the Arabic script ensnared her like concertina wire.

Use your imagination.

She had, and with it assumed the worst. When she opened her eyes, Khan was gone. Only the garden, empty, remained. The camera, or the hand holding it — her son's hand — trembled. How else to explain why the image before her pulsed with life?

"Mom," she heard William say. "Mom — are you still with us? I want you to see one more thing."

The screen showed, in close-up, a few small rocks stacked in a corner of the garden.

"It was the best I could do," said William. "There wasn't much time."

He was waiting for her reaction. A paltry heap of pebbles: she didn't see what he wanted her to see.

"The cairns, Mom. You remember."

That day flooded back, the shade of every stone, the shape of every mound they left for Cal to find his way, even as she lost hers.

In Khan's garden, her son had laid his

hand. With a pile of stones, he had written a name.

ACKNOWLEDGMENTS

Thank you:

Bill Clegg and Courtney Hodell

The American Academy in Berlin, Ledig House International Writers Residency, the Radcliffe Institute for Advanced Study, the Frederick Lewis Allen Memorial Room at the New York Public Library

Lorraine Adams, Katherine Boo, Chloe Breyer, Rodrigo Corral, Kimberly Cutter, Shaun Dolan, Jonathan Galassi, Scott Glass, Eliza Griswold, Juliette Kayyem, Mark Krotov, Mark Laird, Siddhartha Mukherjee, Ratish Nanda, Philip Nobel, Rachel Nolan, Asad Raza, Sarah Sayeed, Jeff Seroy, Mohammad Shaheer, Lisa Silverman, Brenda Star, Sarah Sze, Sarita Varma, Abdul Waheed Wafa, Don Waldman, Marilyn Waldman

Oliver and Theodora, and Alex most of all

ABOUT THE AUTHOR

Amy Waldman was co-chief of the South Asia bureau of *The New York Times* and a national correspondent for *The Atlantic.* Her fiction has appeared in *The Atlantic* and the *Boston Review* and is anthologized in *The Best American Nonrequired Reading 2010.* She lives in Brooklyn.

For sources of information and inspiration for *The Submission,* please see www .thesubmissionnovel.com.

The employees of Thorndike Press hope you have enjoyed this Large Print book. All our Thorndike, Wheeler, and Kennebec Large Print titles are designed for easy reading, and all our books are made to last. Other Thorndike Press Large Print books are available at your library, through selected bookstores, or directly from us.

For information about titles, please call:
  (800) 223-1244

or visit our Web site at:
  http://gale.cengage.com/thorndike

To share your comments, please write:
  Publisher
  Thorndike Press
  10 Water St., Suite 310
  Waterville, ME 04901